Praise for Linda Kavanagh

Praise for *Still Waters*

'Plot-driven with twists and turns that keep the reader on edge' *Irish Independent*

'A thrilling book – that will keep you up all night' *Irish Daily Mail*

'Strong characters and intriguing plot, chapters filled with suspense, increasing tension right through to the last page' *Evening Echo*

Praise for the NUMBER ONE BESTSELLER *Never Say Goodbye*

'Dark, gritty and addictive, this is definitely worth a read' *RTÉ Guide*

'If you are a fan of Jodi Picoult, this one's for you' *Irish Independent*

'It's a great story that will keep you up late at night in your pursuit to find out . . . what happened to Zoe Gray?' *Irish Farmers Journal*

Praise for *Time After Time*

'An imaginative and unusually plotted novel with a clever ending that brings all the threads together and solves the mysteries encountered on the way" *Books Ireland*

'Definitely a page-turner!' *RTÉ Guide*

Praise for *Hush Hush*

'*Hush Hush* will have you glued to its pages'
Irish Independent

'*Hush Hush* is a good combination of mystery, suspense and romance – I was gripped' *Irish Mail on Sunday*

Praise for *Love Child*

'A genuinely gripping read' *Irish Independent*

Praise for *Love Hurts*

'Totally unputdownable. Highly recommended' *Prudence*

LINDA KAVANAGH

Still Waters

POOLBEG

This novel is entirely a work of fiction. The names,
characters and incidents portrayed in it are the work of the
author's imagination. Any resemblance to actual persons,
living or dead, events or localities is entirely coincidental.

Published 2012
by Poolbeg Press Ltd
123 Grange Hill, Baldoyle
Dublin 13, Ireland
E-mail: poolbeg@poolbeg.com
www.poolbeg.com

© Linda Kavanagh 2012

Copyright for typesetting, layout, design
© Poolbeg Press Ltd

The moral right of the author has been asserted.

1

A catalogue record for this book is available from the British Library.

ISBN 978-1-84223-537-9

All rights reserved. No part of this publication may be reproduced or
transmitted in any form or by any means, electronic or mechanical, including
photography, recording, or any information storage or retrieval system,
without permission in writing from the publisher. The book is sold subject to
the condition that it shall not, by way of trade or otherwise, be lent, resold or
otherwise circulated without the publisher's prior consent in any form of
binding or cover other than that in which it is published and without a
similar condition, including this condition, being imposed on the subsequent
purchaser.

Typeset by Patricia Hope in Sabon
Printed by CPI Group (UK) Ltd

www.poolbeg.com

About the author

Linda Kavanagh is a former journalist who has worked for various Irish newspapers and magazines, and was a staff writer on the *RTÉ Guide* for fifteen years. She lives with her partner and dog in Dun Laoghaire, Co Dublin. Her previous novels, *Love Hurts, Love Child, Hush Hush, Time after Time* and *Never Say Goodbye* are also published by Poolbeg.

You can contact Linda at **www.lindakavanagh.com** and **linda@lindakavanagh.com**

Also by Linda Kavanagh

Acknowledgements

Sincere thanks, as always, to Paula Campbell and all the Poolbeg team, to editor Gaye Shortland whose expertise and eye for detail has turned this novel into a far more polished product than it would otherwise have been, to my wonderful agent Lorella Belli for her encouragement, support and belief in me, and to my son Robert Kavanagh for deciding who the "baddie" should be. Special thanks to my partner Mike Gold for being there during every crisis, with cups of tea, suggestions and support, and to Scruff, my ever-patient canine companion, who inspires by her very existence. I couldn't have done it without you all!

Finally a big thanks to all my loyal readers, who helped to make my last novel a Number 1 – I hope you'll enjoy this one too!

This book is dedicated to the indigenous people of South Africa who, despite past repression and present-day poverty, possess a warmth, dignity and pride that is truly awe-inspiring.

Chapter 1

A minute ago, everything had been fine in Ivy Heartley's life. Now her worst nightmare was coming true.

She'd been smiling happily as she'd opened the email from her sister-in-law, who was also a lifelong friend. She loved Peggy's newsy letters, filled with gossip about the village where they'd both grown up, and where Peggy still lived. Her emails had the ability to bring everything to life, and Ivy could almost see the events she described unfolding before her very eyes.

Ivy had been chuckling as she read what had happened the previous week in the Lincolnshire village of Willow Haven. Peggy told her about the fund-raising drive for a new roof for the church, the disastrous garden party at the vicarage, and the thief who'd raided the church's allotment. She'd been concerned to hear that Mrs Evans had just had a hip-replacement operation, and glad that her old school friend Clara Bellingham had got engaged to Bill Huggins from Allcott, a nearby town.

Ivy regularly visited Willow Haven. She and her husband – Peggy's brother – had left as soon as they'd finished school, and moved to London where Ivy studied at RADA. Now, almost twenty years later, they were both very successful in their respective careers, and Joseph, their son, was at university. She was a highly paid soap star, and Danny was founder and managing director of the Betterbuys supermarket chain. Their tiny rented flat in London was now a distant memory, and today they lived in a luxurious mansion in Sussex.

Ivy stretched, and decided to make herself a cup of tea before she continued reading Peggy's long email. While she boiled the kettle and placed a tea bag in a cup, she'd revel in the anticipation. She smiled as she thought of the garden party at the vicarage – those occasions were usually cringe-worthy, and she'd attended more of them than she cared to remember. As a celebrity, she was often called upon to open fêtes or lend a touch of glamour to community social events.

Returning to the computer, Ivy sat down again and scrolled through Peggy's email as she sipped her tea, reading about Peggy's husband Ned and family, and about her father-in-law Fred Heartley's high blood pressure. Peggy kept a close eye on him, for which Ivy was grateful, since she and Danny were hundreds of miles away.

Suddenly, Ivy's heart gave a lurch as she read Peggy's final words. *Since the village has been expanding so much lately, there are plans afoot for draining Harper's Lake. The space will be used for landfill, which means that eventually the land could be built on. Ned thinks it's a crazy idea, but the local council has voted in favour of it.*

Ivy's hands were now shaking, and she could no longer hold the cup. Putting it down, she covered her face with her hands. "Oh God," she whispered, "what am I going to do?" The past was finally catching up with her. The secret she'd kept hidden for most of her adult life was now about to destroy her. And not just her alone, but her entire family. Her career would be over, Danny would hate her for what she'd done. And Joseph – how would he react when he discovered his mother's heinous secret? Peggy, too, would want nothing to do with her. And all because she hadn't told the truth all those years ago.

Ivy found herself shaking from head to toe. If the Council's plan went ahead, the ripples from the lake would spread out and devastate many lives in the process. Just as they had on that fateful day when her own life had changed forever.

2

Chapter 2

Rosa Dalton was sitting at her desk in the classroom, busy writing in the front page of one of her schoolbooks, her fluffy blonde hair almost touching the desk as she leaned over it. Class hadn't yet begun, and she was deeply absorbed in what she was doing, which was writing her name as Rosa Heartley over and over again.

Everyone in the school knew that sixteen-year-old Rosa was crazy about Danny Heartley, and dreamed of marrying him and living happily ever after. He attended the local boys' school and was in the same class as Rosa and her friends. Every day she'd wait outside the girls' school in the hopes of engaging him in conversation when he passed by on his way home. But despite Danny's disinterest, Rosa refused to accept defeat. If Danny would only ask her out, she'd show him what a wonderful girlfriend – and later, wife – she could be. She just needed the opportunity!

As the teacher arrived, Clara Bellingham, who was sitting behind Rosa, gave her a warning dig in the back, and Rosa quickly hid the book she'd been writing in. Flashing Clara a grateful smile, she got out the correct book and turned to the page the teacher called out. It was Geometry today, and Rosa was bored before the class even began. All she could think of was Danny Heartley and his flashing eyes, and the shock of unruly blond hair that fell across his left eye.

"*This morning, we're going to look at isosceles and equilateral triangles – please turn to page 47 of your texts,*" Mrs Jones announced, but Rosa heard nothing. She didn't see the value of all this theory – after all, when she and Danny were married, they weren't going to be discussing geometry over the breakfast table, were they?

As the teacher droned on about the importance of understanding the concepts of angles, equal and unequal sides, Rosa had a dreamy look on her face. Geometry had no place in her world view, and she regarded it as just another torment thought up by adults to keep young people from enjoying themselves.

She was having a lovely daydream about being married to Danny when the teacher noticed her gazing out the window with a faraway look in her eyes.

"*Rosa Dalton, explain what I've just been talking about.*" Mrs Jones had a triumphant gleam in her eye. She'd caught Rosa out, and she intended to make the most of it.

At first Rosa didn't answer because she was too absorbed in her daydream, but the sudden silence and tittering at the back of the classroom gradually began to filter through to her consciousness and she glanced around, only to see Mrs Jones bearing down on her.

"*Oh . . .*"

"*Stand up and repeat what I've just been explaining to the class for the last fifteen minutes.*"

"*Oh er, I'm sorry, Mrs Jones,*" Rosa faltered, "*I – I'm –*"

"*She didn't recognise her name, Mrs Jones!*" shouted one of the girls at the back of the room. "*If you'd called her Rosa Heartley, she'd have answered straight away!*"

The classroom dissolved into laughter since everyone knew about Rosa's feelings for Danny Heartley. Angrily, Mrs Jones called for order as she returned to the podium.

"*Sit down, you silly girl,*" she said haughtily to an embarrassed Rosa. "*You'd better buck up and pay attention if you want to get decent exam results. There's more to life than boys, you know.*"

The other pupils began to snigger at the mention of boys, and Rosa turned puce.

Ivy Morton, who was sitting at the back of the class, felt sorry for her. Rosa was a daydreamer, but she had a bubbly personality and was fun to be with. Although they'd never been close friends, she and Rosa hung out with the same group of boys, and Rosa was usually the centre of attention because of her outrageous jokes and coquettish behaviour. It was impossible to dislike her, even though she always tried to outshine all the other girls and focus the boys' attention solely on her. She had a presence and a sense of her own importance and Ivy, who desperately wanted to be an actress when she left school, often wondered if Rosa wasn't more suited to the profession than she was.

Rosa heaved a sigh of relief as the teacher began the lesson again. She tried to look nonchalant and unaffected by the teacher's comments – she didn't want anyone thinking she cared about what Mrs Jones had to say. On the other hand, she was well aware that she needed to knuckle down and start studying. But it was difficult when Danny Heartley occupied so much of her thoughts . . .

Since childhood, Rosa had wanted to be a flight attendant, and she'd never tired of telling anyone who'd listen that she hoped to work for one of the big airlines. Everyone assured her that with her personality and looks she'd be a shoo-in, and in her dreams Danny was always waiting at the airport to welcome her home from the exotic locations she'd been visiting. He'd be so proud of his high-flying wife . . .

Rosa sighed. But first, she had to catch Danny, and convince him that she was the girl for him. She couldn't understand what he saw in shy, mousey Ivy Morton, who'd never amount to anything. Much to Rosa's annoyance, Danny was always trying to talk to Ivy, and she always ended up laughing at his antics as he tried to get her attention.

Rosa was relieved that Ivy didn't seem to return his feelings – or was the minx playing hard to get? Rosa's heart plummeted at the thought that Ivy might simply be pretending indifference in order to snare Danny. If Ivy started going out with him, Rosa knew she'd never live down the shame. Since everyone knew how much she fancied Danny, the other students would either feel sorry for her, or be delighted she'd got her comeuppance. Either way, she wouldn't be able to face them day after day in school. If only she'd kept her feelings for Danny to herself! But she'd confided in a supposedly trustworthy friend, who'd told her own circle of friends, and suddenly the whole school knew about it. Before long, everyone in the boys' school knew too. But ultimately, all the embarrassment would be worth it if she and Danny finally got together . . .

Suddenly the school bell rang, and Rosa was catapulted back to reality. She sighed with relief – another day of torment was over.

Clara nudged her. "Are we going to the lake?"

Rosa nodded. This was the most important part of the day, and a rite of passage for pupils in both the boys' and girls' senior school years.

"See you in five," she whispered, hurrying out of the classroom and down the corridor to the school toilets. She needed to check her hair, apply some discreet make-up and lip-gloss, and dab on some of the perfume she'd sneaked from her mother's dressing table. Hopefully, Danny Heartley would be at the lake too . . .

Chapter 3

"Hmmm, you smell gorgeous."

Danny Heartley, fresh from his shower, nuzzled the back of his wife's neck as she finished her make-up at the dressing table.

They were going to an important dinner and charity auction that evening, where the important people of the business world and minor nobility would be rubbing shoulders. Despite being a charity event, many lucrative business deals would also be concluded while the patrons were bidding ridiculously high sums of money for the ridiculously cheap items on offer, all in the name of flaunting their wealth.

"What are you wearing tonight?"

"I thought the long blue dress – what do you think?"

Danny grinned as he towelled himself dry. "I don't know why you bother asking me, my dear, because you take absolutely no heed of my opinion anyway!"

Ivy smiled back. He was right, but she still liked to ask his opinion, and she'd never wear anything he positively disliked.

Danny leaned forward and kissed her hair. "Whatever you wear, you'll look stunning," he whispered. "I'm so proud of my beautiful – and talented – wife."

Ivy smiled back at him, but he didn't notice the shadow of fear that had crossed her face as she wondered how long things might remain that way.

"Are you bidding on anything tonight?" she asked him, trying to sound cheerful.

"I suppose I'll have to – it's expected of me at this stage. I might bid on that awful painting by your friend Anton. If I'm unlucky enough to make the winning bid, I'll donate it to the children's hospital."

Ivy laughed. "I don't think Anton should give up the day job."

Danny nodded, looking amused. "You're right – I think he should stick to acting. Talking of which, did you say that Anton, Emily, Sarah and Dominic are coming for dinner on Saturday night?"

Ivy nodded. Normally, she'd be looking forward to an evening of shoptalk and gossip with her fellow actors. They were all cast members of *Bright Lights*, a hugely popular soap opera that aired five nights a week. Their schedule was gruelling, but it had made them all stars, paid them substantial salaries, and given them the adulation of millions of fans.

Luckily, Danny never felt out of place in their company, nor did he mind when they started talking about people he didn't know. But then Danny was a very successful businessman in his own right, and could hold his own in any company. He had nothing to prove to anyone, and he never felt remotely intimidated by the celebrities at his table.

As she brushed her hair, Ivy recalled their flight from Willow Haven all those years ago. While she'd trained at RADA, Danny had worked in a supermarket to pay for their accommodation and living costs. Since his flair and ideas were responsible for substantially increasing the company's turnover, he quickly climbed the ladder to senior management.

But Danny had always wanted to be his own boss. He hadn't wanted to run a small shop like his father's – his aim was to establish a chain of supermarkets offering something different from all the others. By the time Ivy was treading the boards in West End shows, they were able to afford a full-time nanny for young Joseph, and Danny was able to put down a deposit on a small supermarket that was going out of business. He'd had a hard time convincing the bank that despite his youth he could resurrect the failing venture but eventually he succeeded, and before long he'd acquired a second store. Then a third. Now, Betterbuys was the second largest supermarket chain in the UK, built up by offering the consumer organic and cruelty-free produce at reasonable prices, running regular lines of special offers, and paying his suppliers fairly, which ensured their cooperation and a constant supply of top-quality produce.

He'd also introduced special staff-training programmes that ensured customers were treated courteously, and that every member of staff was knowledgeable about all the lines they carried. Before long, working at Betterbuys became a status symbol among retail employees, and there were always many more applicants than there were jobs.

"Come on, love, get a move on! No time for daydreaming!"

"Oh, sorry," said Ivy, jumping up from her dressing table and slipping on her dress.

Danny stood behind her and zipped her up, taking the opportunity to kiss her bare shoulders as he did so.

"I love you, Mrs Heartley," he whispered, slipping his hand inside her bra. "Maybe we could . . ."

"I love you too, but there's no time for any of that," said Ivy, laughing. "We really need to get moving –"

Danny laughed. "You've a nerve – you were the one who was wasting time daydreaming a few minutes ago!" He slipped his arm around her. "You look wonderful! Every man at the dinner tonight will envy me. I'm the luckiest man in the world!"

Ivy smiled in acknowledgement, leaning forward to plant an affectionate kiss on his cheek, but she felt a cold stab of fear in her chest. How long would he love her if he learned the truth? Very soon, her whole life could come tumbling down around her.

Grabbing her sequinned evening bag, she hurried out the bedroom door and down the marble staircase after Danny. For tonight, at least, she'd act as though she'd nothing to lose.

Chapter 4

Outside the gates of the girls' school, pupils from the local boys' school had gathered to chat and flirt, and test out their attractiveness on the opposite sex. There was a lot of giggling, jostling and occasional touching. Rosa was centre-stage as usual, laughing and flicking her halo of blonde hair at the boys, although none of them took her flirting seriously, since they all knew that Danny Heartley was the only one she wanted.

As Rosa, Danny, Clara Bellingham and groups of other boys and girls walked in the direction of the lake, Ivy lagged behind, chatting quietly to Joe Heartley. Joe was a year older than his brother Danny and to Ivy he seemed much more mature. He was an interesting and intelligent boy, and Ivy liked the way his freckles were flecked across the bridge of his nose, and the way the sun glinted on the blond locks of hair that curled around his ears. Ivy knew that a senior like Joe would never regard her as girlfriend material, which meant she could behave in a friendly and natural way with him, without feeling the need to attract his attention by pushing out her chest, flicking her hair or repeatedly licking her lips, as most of the other girls did.

Amazingly, Joe seemed to enjoy her company too, and they often walked home from school together. While the other girls flaunted their newly developing womanly charms, Joe was more interested in discussing science, history and geography with Ivy. He was taking his final school exams that summer, and was hoping to study architecture at university. Unfortunately, his father had other plans for him – he wanted Joe to study retail technology and eventually take over Heartley's Stores.

"No way am I going to spend my life in this village," Joe told Ivy vehemently. "I'm sick of fighting with Dad – it just seems to be one argument after another." Angrily he swung his schoolbag over his shoulder. "I'm not going to be stuck in Willow Haven forever! I want to be an architect, not run a grocery store – that may have been fine for Dad, but it's not what I want to do!"

Ivy nodded. She understood how Joe felt. She intended applying to RADA the following year, and she was lucky in having her parents' full support.

"What are you going to do?" she asked. "I mean, if your dad won't let you study architecture?"

"Then I'll leave home," said Joe determinedly. "There's a big world out there, Ivy – and I intend to see some of it!"

"Hey, you two – get a move on!" Clara called back, as the main group began walking up the steep incline in the road that ran beside Harper's Lake on the outskirts of the village. Further on, where the road sloped downwards again, there was an entrance to the lake that led along a well-worn pathway to a secluded area. It was quite a distance from the main road, and out of reach of prying adult eyes. All the senior school students in the area congregated there during the spring and summer months and, although it was now only February, the weather was already unseasonably warm. Which was a signal for all of them to head for the lake, where they enjoyed sitting in groups at the water's edge, chatting and flirting, as relationships began and ended amid the tranquil surroundings.

Signs warned of the danger of swimming, because there was a sheer drop into the water, which was close to thirty-five feet deep. But this element of danger made it all the more attractive to local teenagers. It was where they all liked to swim unbeknown to their parents. Splashing about in the water and doing dangerous acrobatics guaranteed attention, and increased the swimmer's chances of scoring with the opposite sex.

Today, however, the water was still far too cold to consider swimming, so everyone sat along the bank, chatting in groups. Many of them had brought drinks or sweets, and banter flowed between the groups.

"Hey, Smithy – we saw you looking up the English teacher's skirt this morning!"

"Don't be daft – she's about a hundred!"

"Didn't look that way to me – maybe you fancy older women?"

Everyone laughed as the embarrassed boy turned a deep shade of red. They all found comfort in disconcerting someone else – it made them feel a little more powerful and a little less vulnerable themselves.

Ivy felt sorry for the boy who'd been embarrassed. She longed to be one of the crowd, but found it impossible to draw attention to herself by being nasty or embarrassing others, yet that seemed to be the preferred method of getting yourself noticed.

Ivy and Joe sat on the periphery of the groups, beneath one of the trees, a little further back from the shore. It was darker there, and Ivy felt comfortable leaning her back against the large sycamore, largely out of sight of the others.

Joe turned towards her. "Danny likes you, you know."

Ivy's cheeks flamed. "Don't be daft – he's just fooling around, to make Rosa jealous."

"No, he really likes you – he told me so. He's not interested in Rosa." Joe paused. "Do you like Danny, Ivy?"

Ivy shook her head vehemently. "No, not in that way. I mean, I like him as a friend, but I don't fancy him."

Joe nodded, and Ivy thought she saw him smile.

"Ivy –"

"Yes?"

Joe's cheeks turned the colour of beetroot and his voice came out as a croak. "I really like you."

"I like you too, Joe."

"No, I mean, I really like you, Ivy."

Ivy waited, holding her breath, hoping but not believing that Joe might be interested in her.

In the darkness of the trees, Joe took her hand. "Would you go out with me?"

She could hardly speak with excitement. "Yes, I'd like that."

The silence between them lengthened, and Ivy began to wonder if she'd said the wrong thing, or sounded too eager.

"There's just one problem, Ivy."

Her heart sank. She might have guessed that things weren't going to be plain sailing.

"Dad would have a fit if he knew I was seeing anyone. He thinks that when I'm not studying, I should be working in the shop."

Ivy said nothing.

"And Danny would be furious if he knew I'd asked you out. All that flirting with Rosa is only a distraction. He told me he was going to ask you out soon – I didn't know what to say to him, because I wanted to ask you out myself."

Ivy knew that Danny fancied her but, in deference to Rosa, she'd always been quick to dismiss his advances. She wasn't remotely interested in him, even though he was extremely good-looking, and lots of the other girls found him very attractive. She was also determined Danny wouldn't use her to hurt Rosa's feelings.

"Well, I suppose it's flattering to be so popular," she said with a shy smile. "So you don't want Danny to know?"

"Would you mind keeping it a secret for a while?" Joe whispered, slipping his arm around her. "If Danny found out, he'd be livid with me, and he'd tell Dad – then I'd be grounded and we'd never get to see each other."

"Of course," said Ivy, disappointed she couldn't trumpet their new relationship from the top of a mountain. On the other hand, she didn't want Joe getting into trouble.

Checking to make sure that no one was watching, Joe quickly kissed her. As their lips met, Ivy felt a surge of joy. Joe was the nicest boy in the village, and he wanted to be with her! Besides, there was something quite exciting about keeping their relationship a secret. One day, when they were able to go public on their relationship, Ivy would watch the incredulous faces of her friends as she revealed how long they'd actually been a couple.

"You're beautiful, Ivy," he whispered. "I can't wait to make you mine!"

Ivy found herself experiencing sensations she'd never known before and she shivered with excitement. It was wonderful to have a boyfriend of her very own, and especially a gorgeous one like Joe Heartley!

No one seemed to have noticed them kissing, since all attention was focused on Rosa and Danny. Rosa, as usual, was making herself the centre of attention by dancing around Danny and stopping at intervals to press up against him. Everyone was laughing at Danny's good-natured embarrassment, and cheering at Rosa's bravado.

As the groups disbanded, and everyone began heading home for dinner, Joe surreptitiously grabbed Ivy's hand.

"See you after school tomorrow?" he whispered, and Ivy nodded happily.

* * *

As she reached home and let herself into the house, she found her mother baking in the kitchen. The atmosphere was warm and cosy, and Ivy could smell apple-pies already cooking in the oven.

"Have a good day, pet?" her mother asked, rolling out pastry for an additional batch of pies. "You look a bit flushed – you're not catching something, are you?"

Ivy laughed. She supposed her feelings for Joe Heartley were a bit like a disease – she certainly felt as though she was suffering from a serious case of something or other. And it felt wonderful.

"No, Mum – I'm fine."

Up in her room, Ivy changed out of her school uniform and, as she stood in her underwear, she surveyed herself in the mirror. Joe had said she was beautiful, but she certainly couldn't see it. She was reasonably well proportioned, with a pale, slightly freckled face and long straight blonde hair. What was beautiful about that? Yet inside, she could feel an inner glow that filled her with joy and made her want to smile all the time – maybe being Joe's girlfriend was what made her beautiful.

Ivy longed to tell her mother and father about her new boyfriend, but she had to respect Joe's wishes. Still smiling to herself as she dressed in jeans and a sweater and went downstairs, she hugged her secret to her like a warm cosy blanket.

In the kitchen, her mother surveyed her daughter's flushed smiling face again.

"Are you sure you're all right, Ivy?" she asked, looking worried.

Much to her mother's surprise, Ivy threw her arms around her and hugged her.

"Mum, I'm fine – in fact, I've never felt better."

Her mother sighed, recognising that faraway look on her daughter's face. Could Ivy be in the throes of first love? She could only hope her daughter would come through it unscathed. First love could be so painful, and she hoped the object of Ivy's affections would treat her kindly.

Eleanor grimaced. It was probably time to remind Ivy about contraception – on the other hand, would it seem that she was condoning teenage sex if she did? Maybe it would be better to say nothing – after all, Ivy had received sex education in school, and mother and daughter had had several rather embarrassing discussions about condoms and the pill. As a result, she felt confident that Ivy was too sensible to ruin her chances of an acting career by getting pregnant . . .

Chapter 5

Ivy was shivering as they returned by taxi from the dinner and auction. She'd had far too much to drink, and knew she'd have a monumental hangover in the morning. Somewhere in the deep recesses of her brain she knew she'd deliberately drunk too much to take the edge off the worries that seemed to be taking over her mind.

She'd laughed and joked her way through the evening, and had cheered wildly when Danny became the final bidder for Anton's painting. He'd bid a ridiculously high amount of money, but it was all in aid of the children's hospital, so that was all that mattered.

Carrying the painting into the house, Danny grinned at Ivy. "It's dreadful, isn't it?" he said. "If I saw it in a charity shop, I wouldn't even pay a tenner for it."

Ivy looked at the childish squiggles and splashes of colour with obvious distaste. "On the other hand, if he can make all that money for the hospital, maybe I should try my hand at painting myself?" she said, smiling as she turned to her husband. "I certainly couldn't do any worse than this!"

Danny grinned, nodding in agreement.

Taking the painting from him, Ivy carried it into the drawing room. "Hmmm – be a love, will you, Danny? Take down the Canaletto and hang Anton's painting there. He'll be thrilled to see it there on Saturday night."

"I think he should be appalled!" said Danny, laughing as he gave a mock shudder. "If I was him, I'd be too embarrassed to put my name to something as ghastly as that!"

Unlocking the safe in the drawing room, Danny placed the Canaletto inside, then hung Anton's painting in its place.

He turned to his wife. "I'll ring the hospital tomorrow and tell them it's theirs – hopefully, they might be able to raise some more money from it – or perhaps they could hang it in the foyer."

"And make the patients even more ill?"

Danny laughed. "Anyway, they can't have it until after your dinner party – I want to see everyone's reaction – I bet they'll all be gob-smacked in the worst possible way!"

Tenderly, Ivy returned her husband's smile. Her love for Danny had developed over time, helped by Danny's own devotion to her, and his desire to please her in every possible way. As she looked at his golden hair, now flecked with grey at the temples, she thought of how much she loved him. And how much he looked like someone else she'd once loved . . .

Right from the start, Danny had professed his love for her. It had taken her longer to feel the same way, but she'd needed him, and gradually that need had turned into love. How could she not respond to a man who clearly adored her? Over time, she'd learned to revel in his kindness and attentiveness, the way his eyes lit up every time she entered a room, the way they could communicate across a crowded room with simply the lift of an eyebrow or a wink, the way they both knew exactly what the other was thinking. Then there were the thoughtful gifts he always chose for her while he was away on business trips. Danny was almost too good to be true, and she liked it that way!

Ivy smiled to herself. Even when they were together at parties and public functions, other women often made a play for him, and she would watch, amused, as Danny charmingly and tactfully disengaged himself, never leaving any of these women feeling angry or embarrassed by his rejection. And she always felt a surge of pride and overwhelming love for him when he hurried back to her side after such encounters. He'd raise his eyes to heaven and smile, saying:

"Well, it's nice to be wanted, but the only woman *I* want is you," and she'd feel like a million dollars as he slipped his arm around her.

Seeing the way she looked at him now, Danny's expression softened. "Come on, my love – let's go to bed. I want to hold you in my arms, but I don't know if I'm capable of anything else after all the wine I drank . . ."

Arm in arm, they stumbled up the stairs. As she climbed each step, Ivy recalled all the happy years they'd had together. And she thought of Joseph, who was the centre of their world, and of the career successes they'd both enjoyed. They'd led a charmed life together, and neither of them wanted for anything financially. In addition to the Canaletto, they had a house full of beautiful antiques, several top-of-the-range cars garaged at the back of their large country mansion, twenty acres of pasture and woodland, and a 40-foot motor yacht in the marina at Brighton.

Each time she looked at Danny's handsome face, his hazel eyes flecked with gold, his blond hair falling over his left eye, Ivy realised how lucky she'd been. Life could have dealt with her more harshly, but instead she and Danny had survived many ups and downs together, and come through it all still loving each other.

Yet now, it was likely to end. For twenty years, she'd hoped and prayed that this day would never come, and all that time her secret had lain hidden in the cold and murky depths of Harper's Lake.

Well, I'm not going to go down without a fight, Ivy vowed as she cleaned her teeth in the ensuite bathroom. In the bedroom, Danny was already asleep, his legs sprawled diagonally across the bed, and snoring heavily. Ivy gazed down at him and felt a surge of love and affection. Leaning down, she tenderly kissed his cheek, feeling the stubble that was already forming. She had so much to lose. They all had so much to lose.

As she climbed into bed, Danny reached for her in his sleep, pulling her body close to him and wrapping his arms around her. She returned his sleepy embrace, clinging to him tightly, wanting never to let him go. That was when Ivy made a decision. She had no other choice but to confront her demons head-on. Which meant there was only one thing she could do. She'd have to go back to Harper's Lake.

Chapter 6

It was Danny Heartley's birthday, and after school the usual crowd of senior school students gathered at the lakeside, where Danny was showing off his new camcorder.

"Dad spoils him – he buys him anything he wants," Joe said angrily as he and Ivy watched from beneath the sycamore tree. "Do you know what I got for my last birthday, Ivy? An annual subscription to a retail magazine! If Dad thinks that kind of present is going to get me interested in running the shop, he must be off his head!"

Ivy squeezed his hand. "You can't blame Danny for that – anyway, he's always been interested in photography. He got his first camera when he was twelve, remember? You probably didn't tell your dad what you'd like – knowing Danny, he was probably dropping hints for months before his birthday!"

At a distance, Danny was now sitting under a tree, his eye to the viewfinder, trying out the camcorder's various features while his friends watched him eagerly. Everyone was keen to be in Danny's first home movie.

"Come on, don't take it so much to heart," Ivy urged her boyfriend. "It's not long till your own birthday – why don't you start dropping hints yourself?"

But Joe refused to be mollified. "I'll be eighteen, so I'll be an *adult at last. But that won't make any difference to my father – he'll still keep treating me like a child! He gets on fine with Danny and Peggy, but every time Dad and I are in the same room, he picks a fight with me."*

Rosa was posing provocatively in front of Danny.

"Come on, Danny – you know you want to film me!" she said, pouting and strutting exaggeratedly along an imaginary catwalk.

"Go away, Rosa!" Danny muttered, turning away from her and deliberately focusing the camera on a group of his friends who were playing cards by the water's edge.

Rosa looked around her at the faces of the other students, all of whom were grinning and urging her to entertain them with her antics. Everyone enjoyed Rosa's attempts to get Danny's attention, and they actively encouraged her to provoke him. This encouragement was balm to Rosa's soul, because even if she didn't get Danny's attention, at least she was the centre of everyone else's.

"Come on, Danny, you know you want to take my picture," she said seductively, sashaying past him again. She was enjoying herself, and thinking that if she didn't become a flight attendant, she might become a famous model. Already she could see herself as the new face of Chanel or Dior . . .

As she paraded up and down, she decided she'd ask Danny to take some photographs of her, which she could then submit to modelling agencies and airlines. And maybe, if he took the photos in his own room, one thing might lead to another . . .

Danny was still focusing his camcorder on a group of his friends, who were now hamming it up for the camera. He was adamant he wasn't having Rosa in his film, and she was equally adamant that he was. Their stand-off was a source of amusement to the others, and eventually even the card-players gave up their game in favour of watching the goings-on.

As Danny wandered off into the nearby woodland, Rosa began doing the can-can for the other boys' benefit, lifting her school skirt high and displaying her panties for all to see. Everyone began cheering, encouraging Rosa to adopt even more risqué poses. The attention soothed her ego after Danny's very public rejection, so she *threw caution to the wind and whipped off her school blouse, dancing around in her bra with her skirt lifted high in the air. As her breasts jiggled, the boys cheered, and Rosa's fury began to abate. At least the other boys seemed to appreciate her womanly charms . . .*

After a while, it dawned on her that while the others were still egging her on, they weren't looking in her direction any more. She spun round to discover that Danny was hiding behind a nearby tree, his camcorder pointed in her direction.

"That's not fair, Danny!" Rosa shrieked, grabbing her school blouse and hurriedly pulling it on again while everyone else laughed.

Rosa was furious. Clearly the others had seen that Danny was filming her, and had let her carry on regardless. Oh, they were all so mean!

Danny grinned. Rosa wanted everything on her terms, but he wasn't going to pander to her.

"I thought you said you wanted to be on camera?" he said insolently. "You can't have everything your own way!"

"Well then, I hope you'll give me a private showing!" Rosa retorted, trying to regain some semblance of power.

Danny shrugged his shoulders. "Sorry, Rosa – you'll have to watch it in the church hall next week, like everyone else. I presume you know about the art competition being held there? Well, your performance was so impressive that I've decided to enter it in the film section of the competition. The whole village will be able to watch you on the big screen."

As Danny turned on his camcorder again, this news rendered Rosa almost hysterical.

"Danny, no! Mamma's going to kill me if she sees it!" she groaned. "You're way out of line, Danny –"

Danny ignored her, continuing to film her as Rosa became more distressed.

"Hello, hello, Danny – are you listening to me?" she wheedled. "Come on, it's me, Rosa – you wouldn't want me to get into trouble, would you? Why are you being so mean?"

Everyone else was highly amused, enjoying the spectacle of Rosa being wrong-footed.

LINDA KAVANAGH

"Tell you what – if I win, I'll split the prize money with you," Danny told her. "That would only be fair since you're the star. It might even launch your career –"

"You're a bad bastard, Danny Heartley!"

Danny laughed, his camcorder still filming her. Rosa was becoming more and more agitated, because Danny had the upper hand and she didn't like it.

"Oh damn, how am I going to –"

Danny's face finally broke into a good-natured grin. "It's okay, Rosa – I was only teasing you – I didn't take any shots of your bra or knickers, so you can rest easy!"

"But you said – I mean, what about the competition?"

Grinning, Danny shook his head. "I was only winding you up – I doubt if there's even a film section in it!"

By now Danny had stopped the camcorder and was putting it back in its case. Rosa was suffused with relief, but annoyed with herself for so blatantly displaying her fear. She quickly reverted to being her usual ebullient self.

"Oh well, you can see my knickers any time, Danny!" she said in a loud stage whisper. "Or not, if you prefer!"

Everyone laughed at Rosa's innuendo, but it was clear to them all that Danny had won this round. Most of them hoped that Rosa and Danny would never get together, because there was too much fun to be had watching Rosa's attempts to snare him, and Danny's efforts to avoid being snared.

It was time to go home, and everyone began moving off, satisfied that they'd had a good afternoon's entertainment. There would always be fun and drama when Rosa Dalton was around.

As the students separated into groups and headed out towards the road, Joe grabbed Ivy and kissed her passionately behind the sycamore tree. "You're wonderful!" he whispered. "I'm sorry I was grumpy this afternoon – it's just that Danny gets away with so much. I shouldn't let it bother me – after all, I have you in my life, and he doesn't."

Ivy smiled. It pained her to see Joe so upset, but soon it would be his turn to have a birthday, and she felt sure his parents would *mark the occasion in some special way. How marvellous to be eighteen! She'd have to wait for another year and a half before reaching that age. Nevertheless she felt very grown-up because she had a boyfriend who'd soon be regarded as an adult.*

"What would you like for your birthday, Joe?" she asked shyly. "I haven't much money, but I'd like to get you something you'd really like –"

Joe smiled for the first time that afternoon and, as Ivy gazed at his handsome face and glorious blond hair, she saw once again the person she'd fallen in love with.

He squeezed her hand gently, and she could see that his eyes were filled with love for her. "Don't worry, Ivy – as long as I have you, I have everything I need. You're the only birthday present I really want."

Ivy felt as though her heart was about to burst with joy. And suddenly she knew what she was going to give Joe for his birthday.

Chapter 7

The following Saturday morning, Ivy began preparations for the dinner party that evening, grateful for the distraction. When the caterers arrived with the food, she was pleased with its beautiful presentation. She wasn't remotely interested in cooking herself, but she appreciated the skill and effort that went into such preparation. The day before, their regular team of cleaners had overhauled the living areas of the house, and everything was neat and pristine.

As she laid the table in the dining room, she felt terribly alone and isolated. The secret she'd carried inside her since her teens had affected everything she'd done since then, and tempered her behaviour with family and friends. In fact, she didn't really have any close friends, because her secret prevented her from becoming close to anyone. Friendship meant sharing your feelings and confiding in others, and that was something she could never do.

She'd made many friends on the set of *Bright Lights*, but all these friendships were based on the Ivy Heartley her colleagues thought they knew – the actress, the wife, the great party-giver, the shoulder to cry on. But she didn't dare cry on anyone's shoulder herself, because none of them knew the real Ivy Heartley. *That* Ivy Heartley was a woman with deception at the very core of her being.

Ivy sighed. She always needed to be on her guard, and especially at parties, because she couldn't risk giving in to a drunken urge to confess.

She'd seen what happened to people who'd chosen unwise confidants while in the throes of drunken bonhomie. Besides, her secret was so juicy that few would resist passing it on. And her celebrity would make it worth a lot of money to any tabloid newspaper.

Ivy shivered. What she'd done was so heinous that few would want to be friends with her if they knew. And unless she managed to take evasive action, life as she knew it would soon be over.

* * *

"That was delicious, Ivy!" said Anton, patting his stomach as he finished his main course. "Food for the gods – you're a wonderful cook!"

Ivy smiled, not bothering to tell him that she'd used caterers. If he didn't remember how much she hated cooking, she wasn't going to remind him yet again! The vast amount of wine he'd already consumed had probably addled his brain anyway.

"Yes, the food is absolutely yummy!" said Sarah. "I doubt if I'll have room for pudding – but what is it, anyway?"

Danny smiled. "It's Ivy's sherry trifle – and you know you love it, Sarah!"

Ivy smiled back. This was one dish she *had* made. And the main ingredient was sherry.

Sarah smiled impishly. "Okay – you're on."

Ivy turned to her guests. "Sherry trifles all round, then – or would you prefer the cheese board, Anton?"

"I don't see why I can't have both!"

Everyone laughed. Earlier, they'd all been highly amused to see Anton's painting hanging on the Heartleys' drawing-room wall.

"We much prefer this to the Canaletto!" Danny had told them with a straight face, and Anton had almost believed him.

"I'll get the grub, love," Danny said, getting up from the table. "You stay and chat to your friends."

Ivy nodded gratefully. "The cheeses are in the pantry, Danny – and don't forget to serve the ice wine with the trifle!"

"Your wish is my command!" Danny said, leaning over and kissing the top of her head before leaving the room.

"You're so lucky, Ivy!" Sarah said, watching enviously as Danny departed for the kitchen. "I'd kill for a wonderful man like that! None of my three husbands were ever as attentive. What's your secret, darling?"

Ivy smiled. "Just good luck, I suppose. We've known each other since we were teenagers, so I suppose that helps."

Sarah gave her a wry look. "Clever you – you snapped him up before anyone else got a chance!"

Dominic leaned across the table, grinning conspiratorially. "Aha! Does that mean you never had time to accumulate any dark secrets, Ivy? Not for you the intrigues of other lovers and nefarious deeds – or have you simply managed to hide them well?"

Ivy blanched. She knew that Dominic simply intended his comments to be amusing. But a feeling of terror swept over her as she considered the enormity of what she had to do when she next visited Willow Haven. She felt as though she was suffocating, and couldn't stay in the room for a minute longer.

"Excuse me –" she managed to say before hurrying from the room.

In the downstairs bathroom, Ivy splashed cold water on her face, not caring if her make-up streaked. She wasn't wearing much anyway – away from the *Bright Lights* set, she tried to wear as little as possible.

She heard someone outside, followed by a tentative knock on the door.

"Ivy, are you okay?"

She opened the bathroom door, to find Emily standing outside, a concerned look on her face.

"Are you sure you're okay, Ivy? You looked upset when Dominic said –"

"I'm fine," she replied gaily. "I just felt a bit hot all of a sudden." She laughed. "I hope I'm far too young for the menopause!"

But Emily didn't look convinced.

"Are you sure you're okay? I mean, if you want to talk –"

Ivy smiled. "What on earth would I want to talk about?"

"I don't know – you just seemed a bit, well, preoccupied all evening. You didn't seem aware of half the topics being discussed. Every time I looked at you, you had a faraway look on your face. Is there something worrying you?"

Ivy was thinking fast.

"To tell you the truth, I'm exhausted, Ems," she said, leaning forward conspiratorially. "I need a break – and I'm relieved that you and Dominic are going to be centre-stage for a while. Your storyline means that I get some time off, so I can assure you I'm going to put my feet up."

"You poor love," Emily said, giving her a hug, relieved to learn that nothing more than tiredness was bothering her friend and colleague. "I know the money is great, but we really do work long hours, don't we? I'm going to take a break myself when this new storyline is over."

"The next few weeks will put you back on the map, Ems," Ivy said kindly. "Your character Marina has been in the background for too long – it's time she was given a storyline that puts her in the limelight again. Aren't the scriptwriters planning for her to have an affair with her tennis coach? "

Emily pulled a face. "Yes, but I'm dreading that bit, because I'll have to kiss Tony – his breath is always terrible, so I'll have to try and get it right first time!"

Ivy laughed. "The hazards of the job, eh?"

Together, the two women walked back to the living room, to find that Danny had already carried in a fully laden cheese board, and was now dishing out bowls of sherry trifle while Anton poured the ice wine into fresh glasses.

"Did you know that the grapes in ice wine are allowed to rot before they're harvested?" Anton announced. "That's what makes it so sweet – and so expensive!"

"Only the best for our guests!" Ivy told him, smiling as she took her place at the table once again.

Now well inebriated, Sarah tugged at Ivy's sleeve. "Danny really is a treasure," she slurred. "If you ever decide to get rid of him, please send him *my* way!"

Ivy smiled benevolently at her old friend. "Don't hold your

breath, Sarah – I intend hanging on to him – at least for as long as he's useful at dinner parties!"

But even though she was smiling, Ivy's insides were in turmoil as she reached for her wineglass and gulped down its contents without even tasting the wine. Sarah mightn't have to wait long before Danny was single again. If he ever found out what she'd done, he'd be the one leaving their marriage.

Chapter 8

At the lake after school, no one seemed to have noticed Ivy and Joe casting meaningful glances at each other, because all eyes were once again on Rosa and Danny, who were fooling around on the riverbank.

Rosa was intent on getting revenge for the previous day's humiliation, and she'd grabbed one of Danny's schoolbooks and was threatening to throw it into the water. The others watched, amused, as Rosa used the opportunity to get Danny to grab her round the waist, then she swung around and threw her arms around him, accidentally letting the book slip from her hand. There was a splash, then a horrified silence, and suddenly everyone was talking at once. They all rushed to the water's edge as the book floated briefly, then slipped below the waters and gradually sank into the depths of the lake. Danny was furious.

"Oh God, Danny, I'm sorry – I never meant that to happen!" Rosa was deeply contrite, her face pale with shock.

Danny ignored her. "Look, I'll dive in and find it," he muttered, as several of his friends tried to dissuade him.

"The water's too cold, man – you'll freeze to death!"

"It's only a maths book, for Christ's sake – it's not worth risking your life!"

"It'll be all wet by now anyway – forget it, mate!"

"No, no –" Rosa grabbed his school pullover. "Look, Danny – I'll give you my own maths book as a replacement – it's only fair."

The group briefly considered Rosa's offer, then there was a collective nod. It seemed like a reasonable solution, since the incident was clearly Rosa's fault.

Suddenly Rosa looked stricken. This was the book in which she'd been practising her new signature as Rosa Heartley! Oh God, she'd die if Danny saw it!

But it was too late. Already, a helpful boy in Danny's class had gone to her schoolbag, rummaged inside and taken it out. He laughed as he saw the pages obliterated by Rosa's swirling handwriting. Soon, all the boys were studying the book, grinning and turning their pimply faces towards her. Oh, how she hated them all!

Everyone's attention was now completely focused on Rosa and Danny.

"Go on, Danny – ask her out!" yelled one of the boys.

"Yeah, go on – she fancies you big-time!" shouted one of the girls.

"She's gagging for it!" sniggered another boy.

Rosa's cheeks were now bright red, and Ivy, watching from beneath the sycamore, felt deeply sorry for her. It was one thing to fancy someone, but another altogether to have your feelings publicly paraded in front of all your peers.

Danny glanced across to where Ivy was sitting and gave her a regretful smile. He felt cornered by Rosa's passion for him. It was Ivy he wanted, but she never showed any interest in him, no matter how often he tried to get her attention. She was always deep in conversation with dull old Joe, and seemed positively animated by boring homework!

Danny dug his hands into his pockets. Joe had sworn he wasn't interested in Ivy, so at least he didn't have to worry about that. Maybe he should go out with Rosa for a while, and hope it made Ivy jealous. He'd play a long game if necessary. He was going to have Ivy one day, so he could afford to bide his time for the present.

"Rosa and I have already arranged to go to the cinema on Friday night," he told the group nonchalantly. "So we don't need your help. We arranged it ages ago, didn't we, Rosa?"

Astonished, and grateful for the lifeline she was being offered, Rosa nodded vigorously. She guessed that Danny was simply salvaging his own position. Nevertheless, she was overwhelmed with gratitude.

"Yes, we're going to see that new thriller," she confirmed, gathering up her coat and schoolbag, and linking her arm through Danny's.

With a backward glance at Ivy, Danny turned to Rosa and gave her a winning smile. He wasn't letting the others think they could tease him into going out with Rosa, but he'd give her a good time until Ivy was ready for him.

As if by tacit agreement, all the other students began gathering up their possessions as well. There was no longer any fun to be gained from teasing Rosa, and it was time to go home for their evening meal and to do their homework for the following day. In twos and threes they began walking through the trees and out onto the road that led back into the village.

Ivy and Joe were the last to follow. As they gathered up their schoolbags, both were still basking in the glow of their new relationship, and kept darting glances at each other. Before they stepped out onto the road, Joe pulled Ivy into the bushes and kissed her passionately.

"Careful, Joe – someone will see us!"

Joe smiled between kisses. "They've all gone on ahead. Besides, none of them think of us that way – they just think we're a pair of swots!"

Ivy bridled. "What you mean is, they don't think you'd ever fancy me!"

Joe gazed adoringly at her. "You daft thing, they'd never expect you to fancy me! You're amazing, Ivy – all I want to do is kiss you."

"Come on," said Ivy, disentangling herself from Joe's embrace. "We'd better catch up with the others, or someone will figure out there's something going on."

Reluctantly, Joe nodded. "I guess you're right. Danny watches me like a hawk – he'd be furious if he knew about us!"

"Well, now that he's going out with Rosa, he's hardly in a

position to tell us how to live our lives, is he, Joe?" She looked directly at him. *"You can't let your younger brother rule your life, you know."*

Joe grimaced. *"It's not that – I couldn't care less what Danny thinks. But if he found out about us, he'd tell Dad – then Dad would say that if I've time to spare for a girlfriend, I should be helping him in the shop instead. Then I'd never get to see you!"*

"Well, I suppose your dad needs your help sometimes. Besides, Danny helps in the shop too, doesn't he?"

Joe grimaced. *"The difference is, Danny actually enjoys it. He doesn't see it as a chore, whereas I hate it! He should be the eldest son, then the shop could be his when Dad retires."*

At the corner of the lane, Ivy and Joe waved goodbye to each other as casually as they could manage.

"See you tomorrow," Joe whispered, and Ivy nodded.

Then waving a general goodbye to the others, she set off home too. She was smiling as she walked along. She still couldn't believe that Joe Heartley was her boyfriend!

Ivy was also pleased that everything was working out for Rosa, and relieved that Danny would now be fully occupied, and wouldn't waste any more time trying to attract her attention.

Chapter 9

Ivy thought long and hard about what she was going to do. As a well-known actor, she couldn't hope to go creeping around the lake without being spotted. It was one of the disadvantages of being famous. The paparazzi were forever following her and her colleagues, in the hopes of finding them in a compromising situation, or discovering a juicy bit of gossip that could be turned into a big story. Since Ivy led an exemplary life, the photographers got nothing. But all that could change now, she thought fearfully. It would be quite a scoop if they discovered her lurking around Harper's Lake!

She had a tight schedule for the next week, but then she was due a week off, when the soap storyline was concentrating on the infidelity of Emily's character. That was when she'd drive to Willow Haven. Even though the Council had approved the draining of the lake, Ivy was reasonably confident that it wouldn't happen immediately, and that she'd have time to carry out her mission.

Since her mother and father still lived there, as did Peggy and her family and Danny's father Fred, Ivy was looking forward to seeing them all. They'd be surprised that she wasn't accompanied by Danny, but that couldn't be helped. And if she was spotted by the lake, she'd claim that she'd suddenly decided to visit one of the places she remembered from her childhood. None of the locals could consider anything unusual about that, could they?

At breakfast, Ivy made her announcement.

"Darling, I think I'll drive down to Willow Haven during my week off," she told Danny, hoping against hope that he wouldn't suggest coming with her. That would be an unmitigated disaster!

"Hmm, that's a good idea. I'm sure everyone would love to see you."

"I presume you're not free to come with me?" asked Ivy, holding her breath.

"Sorry, love – too many meetings on the agenda next week."

"What a pity," she said, trying not to look relieved. But this was a journey she needed to make alone.

* * *

A week later, Ivy set off for Willow Haven.

"Give my love to everyone, and tell Dad to go easy on the coffee," Danny said, indirectly referring to his father's high blood pressure, and kissing her as she set off.

"Will do," said Ivy, kissing him back. Then she clung to him tightly, suddenly filled with an urge never to let him go. If she achieved her goal, next time she saw him she'd have no further worries. But if things didn't go according to plan . . . Ivy shivered. Things *had* to go to plan. She'd just have to play things by ear, and hope she got the opportunity she needed.

Danny stood on the doorstep. "Bye, darling – and safe journey. Love you so much!"

"And I love you, too," she told him, smiling as she crossed the driveway to her sleek black BMW, but inside she wanted to cry. If Danny only knew what she had to go through before she saw him again! "See you next week – hopefully, I'll be rested and raring to go again!" she said brightly.

Now that she was actually setting off on this venture, she was filled with terror. The advance planning had enabled her to forget what she actually had to do when she got to Harper's Lake. But now the reality was hitting home, and what she was planning to do was outrageous.

Blowing kisses to Danny as he waved her off, Ivy smiled at his enthusiasm for her, even twenty years after they'd married. Not many women of her age could claim such devotion. Of course, to Joseph she was just 'Mum', and that suited her perfectly. She just hoped he'd never have occasion to discover that his mother wasn't the woman he thought her to be.

Glancing into the back of the car, Ivy quickly checked to see that her travel bag was there. Among her clothes and toiletries were several items that were essential for her trip to the lake. But they certainly weren't items a woman would normally bring on a break to visit her family.

Ivy was aware that she wouldn't be able to rest when she got there – she'd need to study the movements of the locals around Harper's Lake, in order to ascertain the best time for her own secret visit there. She'd need the area to be quiet, but not too dark or she'd be unable to see anything in the already murky waters. Ivy took a deep breath. She had no choice but to dive into the depths of the lake.

Briefly, she'd considered bringing a wet suit to keep in body heat, but she dismissed that notion just as quickly. If anyone spotted her, it would be impossible to claim she'd just decided on a spur-of-the-moment dip.

Ivy decided that in order to look casual and unprepared, she'd just wear her bra and panties when she jumped in. Then she could claim she hadn't been able to resist the lure of the lake because swimming was part of her daily keep-fit routine. In truth, Ivy rarely had time to swim these days, but since receiving Peggy's last email she'd started going during her lunch break to a local swimming pool near the studios in London to get in some practice. Obviously, there was a huge difference between a heated indoor pool and a cold lake, but it was Ivy's only chance of honing her swimming skills. The dive to the bottom of the lake had been difficult enough as a teenager. Today, she was twenty years older and far less fit.

When she reached her parents' house in Willow Haven, her mother and father rushed out to greet her.

"Hello, love, it's great to see you!" said her father, crushing her in a bear's hug.

"You look the picture of health!" said her mother approvingly.

Eleanor and Peter Morton were justifiably proud of their daughter who had reached the dizzy heights of wealth and fame, and their son-in-law, who ran one of the country's largest supermarket chains. In fact, the whole village was proud of its two successful protégés – their fame had put the Lincolnshire village on the map, and Ivy and Danny regularly ploughed some of their wealth back into the village. They'd paid for the building of a community centre, provided financial support to young start-up businesses in the locality and paid for staffing and veterinary care at the local animal rescue centre.

Ivy loved being with her family. It was like slipping back into her childhood and being a normal human being again, rather than a TV star who was expected to look perfect all the time. At her parents' home, she could slum around in her old jeans and not wear any make-up. Or relax in the conservatory she and Danny had had built for her parents, or watch TV on the wall-mounted large-screen television set that Danny had given them the previous Christmas.

"We had a phone call from Owen yesterday," Ivy's mother said. "He seems very happy in South Africa. I just wish he wasn't so far away . . ."

"Why don't you and Dad go and visit him, Mum? Now that Dad's retired, there's no reason why you can't. I'll pay your fares."

Ivy's older brother Owen was a vet in South Africa's Eastern Cape, where he and a colleague ran a nature reserve, wildlife-breeding programme and centre for injured animals. He'd been there for five years now, and was constantly urging his family to visit.

"Thanks, love – maybe we will," said her mother, and Ivy knew Eleanor had no intention of making the eleven-hour plane journey. Eleanor was a home bird, and travelling abroad would take her too far out of her comfort zone.

Neither had Ivy been to South Africa, mainly because of her gruelling schedule, but now she made a silent vow to visit her brother soon. Maybe she, Danny and Joseph could make the trip together . . .

Upstairs in her old room again, surrounded by the books and trinkets she'd left behind a lifetime ago, Ivy expected to feel comforted. But this time, it only served to bring back frightening memories of that fateful day during her teens, and heighten her fear and uncertainty about what she was proposing to do. Memories seemed all the more vivid in this room. She could almost feel the power of the lake as she unpacked, and she jumped when she thought she saw a shadow beside the window . . .

Later that night, she dreamt of the man she'd once loved, watching horrified and helpless as his golden hair turned to grey and he called out to her, begging her to help him . . .

Screaming, she awoke to find her mother and father rushing into her room to comfort her, just as they'd done back when she was a teenager.

"Are you okay, love?" said her mother.

"My God, you look like you've seen a ghost," her father added.

"I'm fine – it was just a nightmare," said Ivy, looking into their earnest, worried faces.

"Are you sure you're okay? Would you like a cup of tea?" Eleanor asked anxiously. "You had terrible nightmares in this very same room when you were sixteen . . ."

"I'm okay now, Mum," Ivy assured her, feeling guilty for waking them up.

"Well, if you're sure . . ."

After hugging her and assuring her of their devotion, her parents reluctantly left the room, and Ivy settled down in her bed again.

Alone in her room, she shivered. It was all this unfinished business that had her so stressed out. The sooner she did what she'd come to do, the better it would be for all of them.

Chapter 10

As the girls packed away their schoolbooks after Friday afternoon classes, everyone was looking forward to the weekend. Rosa Dalton was, as usual, the centre of attention. The other girls liked hanging around with her after school, because even though she was now dating Danny, she still drew the boys towards her, and she always had something outrageous to say. As they left the school together, she was already waxing eloquent on the subject of sex.

"Are you doing it with Danny?" Clara asked her, and the other girls waited eagerly for Rosa's reply.

"Of course!" said Rosa, smiling impishly. "I'm on the pill now, although I wasn't when we did it the first time – but luckily I didn't get pregnant."

Ivy, who was silently listening, was relieved to hear that Danny and Rosa were 'doing it', which meant that Danny was now fully occupied with Rosa, so she didn't need to worry about his attentions any longer.

She could also feel the excitement bubbling up inside her as she thought of doing it with Joe. They hadn't gone the whole way yet, but that was about to change. They were careful to go to places where no one would see them, and the barn at Johnson's farm had become their favourite spot. There they could lie together in the hay and go as far as they dared. But they both longed to consummate their relationship.

Ivy closed her eyes, vividly remembering every second of her last encounter with Joe.

"Oh God, Ivy – I can't wait to make you mine!" Joe panted, as they both lay semi-naked in the barn as she caressed him, thrilled to think that she could make him feel this way. He, in turn, teased and tantalised her body as they lay in each other's arms. How wonderful it would be when they could consummate their love!

Ivy had decided that losing her virginity to Joe would be his birthday present – she intended surprising him by making love to him uninhibitedly in the barn that very afternoon. Since Rosa hadn't become pregnant the first time, Ivy felt it augured well for her own first experience. She'd been so lucky in love that surely nothing could go wrong? Anyway, she couldn't possibly go to the local pharmacy since the owner was a friend of her mother's and would undoubtedly feel obliged to let her know what her daughter was buying . . .

The girls' laughter brought Ivy back to reality. Rosa had said something amusing, and they were all guffawing and poking each other in the ribs as they walked along. But Ivy didn't mind missing the joke. She smiled to herself, hugging her own secret close. How she wished she could tell the others that she had a boyfriend of her own, and a senior to boot! They'd look at her differently; they'd see that Rosa wasn't the only one who could snare a man.

The usual group of boys and girls were heading out of the village towards the lake, but this time, Ivy didn't follow. Pleading a headache, she turned towards home, but as soon as her school friends were gone, she made her way up the hill to Johnson's barn, where Joe was already waiting for her.

In an instant, they were in each other's arms. "God, I can't keep my hands off you!" Joe whispered, urgently opening her blouse as Ivy unbuttoned his shirt. Then they pulled off the rest of each other's clothes, eager to press their naked bodies together. The atmosphere of the barn was warm and sweet smelling, and Ivy sighed with joy as she felt Joe caress her. Her whole body was on fire with desire for him, and she didn't want to wait any longer.

"Come inside me, Joe – this is my birthday present to you," she whispered. "*I want my first time to be with you, and every other time for the rest of my life!*"

Joe groaned as he tried to contain his longing for her. "*It'll be my first time too, but let's wait – I'll buy condoms tomorrow,*" he said, reluctantly pulling Ivy's hand away.

"*Stop worrying, Joe,*" said Ivy, her voice now husky with desire. "*I want you, too – I want us to make love now!*"

"*No, Ivy – no, we can't take the chance –*"

But Ivy pulled him down into the hay again and lowered her body onto his. She gasped as he pushed into her, and she felt a dart of pain as her hymen broke. But the pain was quickly over, and Ivy felt like a real woman at last. She was filled with joy as she felt Joe climax inside her for the first time, and she finally knew the meaning of two people becoming one. His thrusting then brought Ivy to a shuddering release, and as they lay together in the afterglow, they whispered words of endearment to each other.

"*I love you, Ivy,*" Joe told her.

Ivy nodded, warm and sleepy in his embrace. "*I love you too, Joe,*" she replied. "*Happy birthday – this is just the start of our lives together.*"

But now Joe was beginning to feel guilty, aware that he'd let his desires run away with his common sense. "*Oh God, Ivy, I hope nothing happened –*"

But Ivy wasn't concerned. She smiled as she wrapped her arms around Joe's neck. "*I'm sure there's no need to worry – but you'll have to get condoms for the next time.*"

Joe kissed her, already thrilled at the thought of a repeat performance. "*I'll get as many as I can from the dispensing machine in the cinema toilets tomorrow!*"

Ivy nodded. But his mention of the cinema reminded her once again of the unfairness of their situation. They still couldn't even go to a movie together for fear of being spotted.

Joe seemed to read her mind. "*I'll be eighteen in a few days' time, and after that, Dad can't treat me like a kid any more. Then we'll tell everyone we're a couple.*"

Ivy nodded happily. She couldn't wait to tell her classmates that she was dating the most gorgeous boy in Willow Haven.

The following day, Joe bought several packets of condoms, and he and Ivy had great amusement trying to put one on as they lay together in Johnson's barn on Sunday afternoon. Ivy felt so grown up and responsible. How lucky she'd been to meet the man of her dreams so early! She knew from the magazines her mother read that many women searched for years for their soul mates but never found them. Yet she and Joe already had their future mapped out, and they were going to be together forever. She'd be a famous actor, and Joe would fulfil his dream of becoming an architect.

Ivy sighed happily. She just knew that life with Joe was going to be wonderful.

Chapter 11

It was close to midday when Ivy came downstairs, to find her parents still at the kitchen table.

"At least you got a decent sleep after that nightmare of yours," her mother said approvingly as she got up to put bread in the toaster.

"Thanks, Mum, but I'll go for a jog first," Ivy said, refusing the offer of toast. "It's a nice day, and I need the exercise."

"Maybe your father could go with you, Ivy," said her mother, darting a disapproving look at her husband. "The doctor says he needs to take more exercise."

Ivy caught her father's eye, and was relieved to detect an almost imperceptible shake of his head.

"Well, he'll need to dig out his old tracksuit and trainers," she said firmly. "We'll go for a jog another day, Dad, okay?"

Her father looked relieved, and winked conspiratorially at his daughter. "Suits me, pet – I'm not the one who's keen on exercising – that's your mother's idea!"

"But, Ivy, you'll need someone to show you where the new factory is!" said her mother anxiously.

The locals were very proud of the area's new state-of-the-art canning factory, which had created employment for many in the local community.

"Don't worry, Mum, I know where it is. I'll go past it on my way back. See you both later – bye!"

Leaving the house, Ivy started jogging briskly. She'd no intention of spending time looking at the new factory. Instead, she'd be using her time to skirt Harper's Lake, to calculate the volume of traffic going past it, and to see if any people went by on foot. As far as Ivy was concerned, the less human activity there the better. She'd need time at the lake alone, and she needed to select the time of day when she was least likely to be spotted.

As Ivy jogged along the road past the railway station, she spotted her old neighbour Hannah Dalton coming out of the station, dragging a suitcase behind her. Ivy immediately stopped to help.

"Thanks, Ivy," Hannah puffed, surrendering her suitcase gratefully. "I'm just back from London – I've been to visit Rosa."

"How is she?"

"Great – we had a lovely few days together in a very plush hotel. How the other half live, eh? Now she's gone off on her travels again!"

"Rosa has a wonderful life, hasn't she? She gets to see so many interesting places!" Ivy said, knowing how proud Hannah was of Rosa's career. But Ivy was also acutely aware that, because of her and Danny, Rosa never came back to Willow Haven. Instead, Hannah was the one who travelled to visit her daughter when Rosa had time off from her travels.

As Ivy deposited the suitcase in Hannah's porch, the older woman opened her front door and stepped inside.

"Would you like to come in for a cuppa, Ivy?" Hannah asked eagerly.

With a rueful expression, Ivy declined. "Got to get my daily exercise," she told the older woman, "but I'll drop in another day, before I leave the village."

Hannah nodded, happy at the prospect of Ivy's visit. "Then I'll be able to show you the latest cards Rosa's sent me from her travels," she said, delighted at the opportunity to keep Ivy *au fait* with what her daughter was doing.

Ivy felt a pang of guilt. Technically, she'd been the victor, winning Danny from Rosa all those years ago. She and Rosa hadn't seen each other since then. Of course they'd be civil to each other if they ever met, but there would never be any love lost between them.

Waving to Hannah, Ivy set off on her jog once again. But when she reached the vicinity of the lake, her worst suspicions were confirmed. The volume of traffic and the number of passers-by had increased dramatically. Progress had brought lots of activity to the village, all of which could put her plans in jeopardy.

Even more galling was the fact that word of her arrival had spread – no doubt her mother had been boasting again – and lots of local people made a point of stopping and chatting to her. They were all keen to know about *Bright Lights*, and whether Isabella would have an affair with the man who'd just married another of the soap's characters. As always, Ivy pretended she'd no idea where the script was leading, and politely excused herself. But all this recognition meant her privacy was seriously compromised, and while it wouldn't normally matter, this time it was critical.

* * *

At her mother's insistence, her father accompanied Ivy on her jog the following morning. Grumbling, he'd acquiesced to his wife's entreaties, and squeezed into his ancient tracksuit and trainers, but in reality he was pleased since it gave father and daughter the chance to connect again.

Ivy made a point of walking rather than jogging so that her father could keep up, and selected a route that took them well away from Harper's Lake.

"You're very tense, Ivy," her father said. "Is everything alright?"

"Yes, of course!" said Ivy brightly, but she didn't fool her father. He'd known her too long for that.

"Is everything okay between you and Danny?" he asked, darting a concerned a glance at her.

"Yes, Dad, everything is fine," said Ivy happily, pleased to be able to tell him the truth on that score.

"You've seemed preoccupied since you arrived," her father persisted, "and you had that nightmare the other night . . . if there's something bothering you, just remember your old dad is here."

"Thanks, Dad, I'm fine," said Ivy, linking his arm, a lump in her throat. Her father would be thoroughly shocked and disappointed if he knew the secret his daughter had been hiding all these years. "To tell you the truth, Dad, when I'm not on the set, I do get very tense." She knew she was telling him a load of waffle, but he seemed to accept it.

She longed to be able to confide in him, but of course it was out of the question. He was so proud of his famous daughter, and she couldn't bear to disillusion him.

* * *

The following morning, Ivy was relieved that her father didn't want to accompany her on her daily jog. He came down to breakfast complaining about aches and pains in his legs from the previous day's efforts, even though he and Ivy had walked at only a moderate pace.

"You're right not to overdo it, Dad," Ivy told him. "Maybe you'll feel like another jog tomorrow?"

Nodding, her father sat down at the breakfast table, rubbing his shins and looking to his wife for sympathy that wasn't forthcoming.

"See how out of condition you are?" Eleanor told him tartly.

Smiling, Ivy left the house for her jog. But as soon as she was out in the street, a pall of despair seemed to descend over her like a cloud. As she jogged along, she kept meeting neighbours anxious to chat, and on the main road out towards the lake, the constant din of traffic was deafening.

Eventually, Ivy conceded that there was only one time of day when she could safely go to the lake – and that was just after sunrise. She needed daylight because of what she had to do, and she could only hope that at such an early hour few people would be about. Willow Haven's elderly population rarely stirred before nine or ten, but she'd discovered that employees at the new factory clocked in at eight. Therefore, she'd have to make a very early start.

Ivy sighed as she turned back towards her parents' home. She decided to slip out of the house early the following morning, leaving a note to say she couldn't sleep and had gone for a walk. Then she'd make her way to the lake, and do what she couldn't afford to put off any longer.

Chapter 12

As Ivy waited in Johnson's barn for Joe to arrive, she was looking forward to another bout of lovemaking. She couldn't wait to hold him, and smell his skin and feel his kisses all over her body …

But as she looked out across the fields and saw Joe striding towards her, it was obvious that he was far from happy. As he reached the barn, she could see that one side of his face was a deep crimson, his expression like thunder.

"What's wrong, Joe – are you alright?"

"No, I'm not alright, and my father's lucky I didn't kill him!"

"Oh God, what did he say? Did you have another fight?"

"Yes, we did, and I swear, Ivy – this was the last one!"

Joe sat down on a hay bale, his head in his hands. Ivy waited on tenterhooks, afraid to say anything. Tentatively, she reached out and touched his reddened cheek, and was relieved when he turned and took her in his arms. Ivy could see he'd been crying.

"Oh Joe, is there anything I can do? I hate to see you so sad!"

Joe shook his head vehemently.

"What happened?"

"I told Dad that since I was eighteen this week, he couldn't treat me like shit any more. I said I didn't want to work in his bloody shop for the rest of my life – I was going to study architecture, with or without his help!"

Ivy nodded. She knew what it was like to have a dream. It was like an itch that needed scratching, a gnawing in your stomach that wouldn't go away, and she could empathise wholeheartedly with Joe. When you had a dream, you couldn't let other people stand in your way.

"And what did he say?"

"He said I was too young to know my own mind, and that I'd thank him in years to come! Then he hit me across the face. Oh God, Ivy – I hate that man so much! Why does he want to destroy my life?"

Ivy didn't know what to say, since anything that came to mind sounded lame.

"Maybe he didn't mean it," she suggested.

"Oh, he meant it alright!" Joe said bitterly. "He thinks I'm as small-minded as he is. That shop is his life – but it isn't mine! I don't want to inherit it and spend the rest of my life serving the old dears of the village – Danny may be happy doing that, but I'm not!"

"So what are you going to do?"

Joe had a wild expression on his face. "I'm leaving, Ivy – I can't stay in this backwater any longer."

"B-but what about us?"

"Come with me!" Joe whispered urgently. "Let's go to London – we can achieve our dreams together!"

As she held him tightly, Ivy was turning over the idea in her head. Why not? She could sit her school exams in London. In fact, it would be easier to attend RADA if she was living close by. Joe could go to college and they'd both get part-time jobs to pay for food and a bedsit. Then someday in the future they'd come back to Willow Haven and show everyone how successful they'd become.

But as she thought of her parents and Owen, her heart sank. How could she leave the people she loved? They'd be so hurt and disappointed in her.

Joe seemed to read her mind.

"You're lucky to have a family that cares about you, Ivy – and I'd never want you to do anything you'd regret. If you don't want to come with me, I'll understand. We can still keep in touch."

At the thought of being without Joe, even for a day, Ivy's heart sank. And if he met someone else in London . . . she just couldn't bear it. She would die. She could feel panic welling up inside her – she and Joe were meant to be together forever! Her parents would understand that she had to go with the man she loved – they cared for each other, so they'd surely know how powerful love was.

As she looked at him, Ivy's eyes were glistening with tears. "Yes, Joe – I'll go with you! Oh, I love you so much!"

Joe was suddenly happy. "And I love you too, Ivy. We'll show them all that we're not to be trifled with."

"W-when are you – I mean, we – thinking of going?"

Joe's expression was grim. "Mum and Dad are planning a surprise party for me at the hotel for my eighteenth birthday next Friday night. They think I don't know about it, but Peggy let the details slip by accident. So we're going to leave that morning – I want them to realise that a party won't make up for the way Dad's been treating me."

Reluctantly, Ivy nodded. It seemed a particularly hurtful thing to do, but then Fred Heartley hadn't shown much concern for his eldest son's feelings, had he?

"Couldn't we wait until afterwards?" Ivy ventured. "I mean, if your dad's organising a party, he must care about you. Maybe everything will work out, and you won't have to go . . ."

"I'm going, Ivy – with or without you. Dad crossed the line when he hit me – I'll never give him the chance to do that again."

Ivy bit her lip. She could understand how Joe felt. She felt angry with Fred Heartley too, and not just on Joe's behalf. She herself was being forced to leave her family in order to support the man she loved. Maybe leaving just before the party would make Fred realise the harm he'd been doing to Joe.

"Okay, Joe," she said reluctantly. "What train will we take? I know there's one that goes to London in the afternoon –"

"No, Ivy – we're not going by train!" Joe said, smiling as he hugged her. "I'm going to take Dad's new car and when we get to London we'll sell it to a dealer. It'll give us enough money to live

comfortably for the first few months until we get ourselves sorted out."

Ivy felt a frisson of fear. It was one thing to run away, but quite another altogether to steal a car.

"But your dad loves that car – it wouldn't be fair to take it," she whispered.

"Well, he hasn't exactly been fair to me, has he?"

Nevertheless Joe could see how uncomfortable his suggestion was making her feel.

"Look, when we make enough money ourselves, we'll pay him back."

Ivy nodded, feeling a little better about this proposal. After all, Joe was simply being practical. They couldn't go to London empty-handed, and Ivy only had a few pounds in her savings box, certainly not enough to live on, even for a few days. She hadn't been thinking about the practicalities, but luckily Joe had.

"Okay," she said, sounding more cheerful than she felt. She was far from happy, but she couldn't let Joe down. Since they were going to spend their lives together, she had to be willing to take chances so that they could make a successful life for themselves in London. It would all be worth it in the end, and when they made lots of money, they'd buy Fred another new car. By then he'd be so proud of them that he wouldn't be mad at them any longer.

"We'll celebrate my birthday in London," Joe promised her. "We'll book into a smart restaurant and drink champagne."

"Really?" Ivy's eyes opened in awe. Right now, she believed that Joe could achieve anything if he put his mind to it.

Joe nodded. "Dad opened bank accounts for Danny, Peggy and me years ago, and I've got a few hundred pounds in my account. That'll keep us going until we can sell the car." He tweaked her nose affectionately. "We might even spend my birthday in a plush hotel – I want to make love to you in a real bed, Ivy. No more sneaking around Johnson's barn. It's only the best for us from now on!"

* * *

"Yippee! We're on our way, Ivy – at last, we're free!"

Ivy smiled as Joe raced his father's new red Ford saloon down the road, far faster than was safe, but today was a special day – their special day – and nothing could possibly go wrong.

"We're finally getting out of this hick village – we're going to make our fortunes in the big city!"

Ivy looked again at Joe's profile. How lucky she was to have such a handsome boyfriend! The sun was shining on his golden hair, and his rugged features always set her pulse racing. Now they wouldn't have to keep their relationship a secret any more, or worry about people telling them they were too young to be so much in love.

Nor would they have to worry about Danny any more. Ivy hoped he'd be happy with Rosa, who genuinely wanted to be with him. Ivy hadn't wanted to hurt Danny. She liked him a lot, just not the same way she liked his older brother.

Joe was enjoying the forbidden delight of driving his father's car – Fred had refused to let him drive the new red saloon even though he'd just passed his driving test – well, now he didn't need permission! Stealing his father's pride and joy had been the final payback for all the insults and tauntings he'd endured at his father's hands over the years. It was a pity they'd have to sell it as soon as they got to London, but they'd need to do it before his father could report the car stolen.

Slipping his arm around her as he drove, Joe nuzzled Ivy's cheek. "I can't wait to get to London, and have you all to myself!"

"Careful, Joe – please keep your eyes on the road!"

"Stop worrying, Ivy – everything's going to be okay. You're not sorry to be leaving Willow Haven and your family, are you?"

"No, of course not!" Ivy assured him. But she did feel guilty – terribly guilty. She was missing her parents and brother already, but she had to support Joe, who hadn't been as lucky with his parents as she had with hers. When they got to London, she intended phoning home to let her mum, dad and brother know that she was safe. She hoped they'd understand.

Joe had turned the radio on, and was singing along tunelessly.

*Just then, they reached the steep incline that ran beside Harper's
Lake. Hurtling along, lost in his own thoughts of the future, Joe
suddenly realised he'd miscalculated his speed. He slammed on the
brakes just as he reached the apex of the hill.*

"Watch out, Joe!"

*Ivy screamed as the car spun out of control, and Joe tried in vain
to apply the brakes again. The car shot forward into the air, and for
a few seconds they seemed to be flying. But their flight quickly
came to an end as the car plunged into the lake alongside the road.*

"Oh my God!"

"Jesus!"

*Following a gigantic splash, the car slowly sank to the bottom,
surrounded on all sides by murky water. The temperature
immediately dropped and they found themselves entombed in the
water's menacing depths.*

*"We've got to get out! Open your door!" Ivy screamed, releasing
her seat belt. The water was already crashing in through the open
passenger window and the car was quickly filling up.*

*"My foot – it's stuck behind the pedal –" Joe's voice was lost as
the water rose over his head.*

*Ivy was consumed by terror as the car was rocked violently by
the impact of the water. She became disoriented as she struggled to
escape through the window, all her thoughts narrowly focused on
survival. The dark waters seemed to claw at her, as though it didn't
want her to escape its clutches. Battling her way to the surface, Ivy
spluttered and gasped as her lungs finally filled with air. But
looking all around her, she couldn't see any sign of Joe. What was
keeping him so long? He was a competent swimmer, so he should
have surfaced by now.*

*Having reached safety, Ivy was scared to return to the murky
depths of the lake, but she'd no other choice. Taking a deep breath,
she plunged beneath the water again, her eyes stinging from the
debris and algae that seemed to be all around her, its tentacles
seeming to ensnare her. Already her lungs were bursting, and she
could barely make out the shape of the car. Joe was still in the
driver's seat with the door closed, and Ivy felt a momentary sense*

of bewilderment. Then she remembered something about his foot being caught . . . Trying to wrench open the driver's door proved impossible, and she had to fight her way back to the surface again.

Ivy took another lungful of air then plunged back into the water. Back in the murky depths, she swam in through the open passenger window this time and tugged in vain at Joe's foot, but she couldn't manage to pull it out from behind the pedal. She couldn't even get his shoe off, because his entire foot was wedged behind it. Then she looked at Joe and her blood ran cold. He wasn't moving. His head was bobbing about unnaturally, his mouth frozen in a scream, and when she touched his face and hands, there was no response. He was dead already. No, he couldn't be – they were going to be together forever!

Her lungs bursting, this time from shock as well as lack of oxygen, Ivy surfaced again, then immediately made another plunge into the depths. She'd get Joe out, no matter what it took! Filled with a burst of almost superhuman strength, Ivy pulled at Joe's trapped foot, but all to no avail. She felt tears of anguish forming, but she had to keep on trying. Although by now it was obvious that Joe couldn't have survived this long under water.

She touched his ice-cold face that now flopped from side to side, his hair weaving like snakes as the currents of water buffeted it about. It was an image she'd never forget. There was no doubt any longer – Joe was dead.

Her lungs bursting, Ivy surfaced. This time, there was no going back down again. It was pointless trying to save Joe any longer. Tears stung her eyes. Their dream of leaving the village was over. The love of her life was lying dead at the bottom of the lake, and she'd never love anyone ever again.

Big salty tears ran down her face as she clung to the grassy bank at the side of the lake. Nothing felt real any more. If only she could close her eyes, and will things back to the way they'd been before . . .

Eventually, she hoisted herself up onto the bank and sat shivering as she stared down into the water. How could she tell Joe's parents what had happened? His father, who was always angry, would be angrier than ever. He'd loved his new red car, and he'd accuse Ivy of encouraging Joe to steal it, and Joe's mother Julia would blame Ivy for the death of their son. Her own parents would be furious with her for trying to leave the village secretly, and they'd blame her for Joe's death too. Her family and the Heartleys would probably never speak to each other again. Everyone would point fingers at her, and she'd become the village pariah.

Looking out across the lake, Ivy found it almost impossible to believe what had just happened. The water was completely still, and there was absolutely no evidence of the tragedy that had unfolded a short time before. As she gazed around her at the view, she was shocked at the normality she saw all around her. Had the tragedy happened at all, or had she imagined it? She longed to wake up and find that she'd just had a bad dream, but her saturated clothing and broken fingernails told her that this was a real-life nightmare.

Nevertheless, the lake looked as it always did, glass-like and tranquil, surrounded by trees about to bloom, the sun shining down on the entire vista. How could the sun dare to shine while the boy she loved lay dead at the bottom of the lake? A boy who'd been so full of life less than an hour ago? It was so unfair! And although she'd done her utmost to rescue Joe, she knew she'd be blamed for what had happened.

Ivy wept as she sat on the bank of the lake. Although she was safe on dry land, her breath was coming in short painful gasps, as though she was slowly being suffocated by the sense of loss that threatened to overwhelm her. A knot of grief curled up inside her, and she wondered if she would ever feel at peace again. Her beloved Joe was gone – it had only taken an instant for their dreams to be overturned. Not long ago, she'd been filled with joy at the prospect of a future with the boy she loved. Now she was alone again, her hopes dashed and her dreams in tatters. She didn't even care that her handbag with her passport and school certificates and her weekend case filled with her best clothes were now at the bottom of the lake. Joe was dead and nothing else mattered any more.

For a long time, Ivy sat staring into space. She didn't want to go home. She didn't want to face all the accusations and recriminations *that would inevitably follow, nor did she want to foist heartbreak on the Heartleys. If she could spare them all the pain, she gladly would . . .*

Looking around her, Ivy suddenly thought the unthinkable. No one knew what had happened here, except her. No one knew that she and Joe had been leaving town that day. It had been their secret. Now, Joe wouldn't be telling anyone.

Trembling, Ivy stood up, and surveyed the lake once more. There wasn't even a hint of what lurked beneath its tranquil surface. The tears came again, but now she brushed them angrily aside. If she said nothing, no one would ever know what had happened. The car wasn't near the area of the lake where the local school children swam during the fine weather, so no one was likely to find it. Her beloved Joe was gone, and wasn't it better for Joe's family to believe he was off somewhere, making a better life for himself?

Leaving the lake, Ivy walked out onto the deserted road and surveyed the surface. She couldn't see any skid marks or any evidence they'd ever been there. She felt dizzy at the prospect of what she was planning to do, or maybe it was just the cumulative effect of all that had just happened to her.

As she walked along the road in a daze, Ivy made a bargain with herself. If anyone drove past or stopped to offer her a lift, she'd tell the truth. She looked completely bedraggled and wet, so it would be obvious that something awful had happened. But if no car appeared before she reached the outskirts of the village, she'd cross the fields behind her house, sneak in by the back door and tell no one what had happened.

No car appeared on the deserted road, and Ivy eventually let herself into the house and crept up the stairs to her bedroom. This was the room she'd left forever only an hour earlier. Now she was looking at the rickety old bedstead again, and the worn eiderdown covering it. Locking the door, she stripped off her wet clothes and crawled beneath the eiderdown, weeping hot tears that ran down her face and soaked into the sheets on her bed. She cried for the boy she'd loved, for the lost opportunities they'd both craved, and for the life of deception she was about to embark on. She could still *change her mind, but she wouldn't. At least Joe's family would be protected from sadness, and she'd be protecting herself as well. A small village could be cruel to people who broke its rules, and running away would be regarded as a cardinal sin by many village folk.*

Well, you've got me back again, Ivy whispered savagely into the darkness of her bed covers.

Chapter 13

As the alarm on her mobile phone went off at 5 a.m., Ivy awoke, quickly turned it off and sat shivering on the side of the bed. Today was D-day, meaning Dive-day, and she felt sick inside. She'd been so worried the previous night that she'd hardly slept at all, with the result that she now felt like someone with a hangover. Her head was pounding and her stomach was rebelling and she wanted to throw up. How on earth could she dive into the lake in this state? Perhaps she should call it off, and try again the following day. Then another part of her brain took over and urged her on – there was no point in wasting time since she wasn't likely to feel any better the following day and, besides, she'd have to be back on the set of *Bright Lights* soon.

In the dark of early morning, Ivy couldn't rid her mind of images of Joe Heartley as he lay trapped in the murky waters of the lake. As she dressed, she kept picturing him struggling to get out of the car, and she wondered if she could face seeing him again. But she desperately needed to remove her possessions from the car before the lake was drained and the car recovered. Otherwise, everyone would know she'd been in the car that fateful day, and they'd want to know why she'd hidden the truth for so long, and allowed the Heartley family to suffer so much.

The night before, she'd packed a sports bag with a towel,

goggles and a change of underwear. She'd put a hammer in too, which she'd bought several weeks earlier in a DIY store, although she'd no idea if it would be of any use under water. She'd purchased an assortment of other tools at the same time, so that later on, no one could ever single out the hammer as something that soap star Ivy Heartley had bought. The sports bag also contained a large plastic sack, into which Ivy hoped to put the incriminating evidence when she brought it up from the floor of the lake.

Shivering violently from a mixture of cold and fear, Ivy quickly put on her bra and panties, covered them with a T-shirt and tracksuit bottoms, grabbed her sports bag and tiptoed down the stairs, leaving her previously prepared note on the hall table. Closing the door as quietly as she could, she listened outside the house for a few moments, until it was clear that no one inside had heard her leave.

Glancing around her as she ran down the quiet street, it appeared that the whole village was still thankfully asleep. The sky was already bright and it promised to be a fine day, but Ivy knew the sun wouldn't have had time to warm the water of the lake, so it would be freezing in there.

As Ivy hurried along the country road leading out of the village and towards the lake, she felt confident that she looked like a typical jogger. Except for the sports bag, of course, but that couldn't be helped. If anyone she met commented on it, she could always claim it contained either special energy drinks for a long run, or weights to make her running more effective.

Suddenly, as she neared the lake, Ivy was overcome by fear. What in God's name was she doing? Was she totally out of her mind? She was about to risk her life!

Would the cold water prove too much of a shock to her system? Ivy had no wish to die of hypothermia, but there was no other option.

As she stood shivering on the bank of the lake, Ivy tried to envisage the hot coffee, and toast dripping with butter that would be waiting for her when she returned to her parents' house. But it was no good. All she could see was the bleak expanse of water.

Local youngsters had always been forbidden to swim there

because it was so deep. There had been a fatality many years ago, which had been used as an example to youngsters of what could happen if you disobeyed your parents. Ivy wondered if young people today still gathered at the secluded spot further down the shore to dabble in danger and risk their lives for prestige among their peers.

Bracing herself, Ivy stripped down to her undies and put on the goggles. She checked all around her, but as far as she could see, there was no one within miles. This is it, she thought, it's not going to get any easier so I might as well get in. Taking the hammer from her sports bag, she stuffed it down the front of her bra. Hopefully, when she'd recovered her possessions, she wouldn't need to bring the hammer back to the surface again.

When she jumped into the water, Ivy had to suppress a scream. It was colder than she could ever have imagined. How would she survive the even colder depths of the lake bottom? Her teeth were chattering as she swam around in circles, letting her body become acclimatised to the temperature.

In truth, she dreaded diving further down into the lake. She was filled with horror at the thought of seeing Joe again, or what was left of him. Twenty years earlier, she'd been horrified by the sight of his freshly dead body, with his blond hair weaving in the current, his mouth open in the rictus of a scream. After all this time, would there be any flesh left? Or would there be a skeleton sitting in the driver's seat? And would the skeleton still resemble a human, or would parts of it have begun to disintegrate? Ivy felt the urge to vomit, but there was no food in her stomach, so she was left with the taste of bile in her mouth.

There was nothing for it – she might as well get on with what she had to do. Taking a deep breath, Ivy dived beneath the ice-cold water and began to swim towards the bottom of the lake.

In the cold, dark water, Ivy felt panic. It was like being entombed in a watery grave from which there was no escape. There was algae and waterweed all around her, which seemed to be clawing at her as she swam through it. In order to stay calm, she had to keep reminding herself that there was daylight and sunshine up above.

At last, she could make out a large shape, and her heart gave a jolt as she recognised Fred Heartley's much-loved red Ford, although now it was covered in algae and mud. Quickly she surfaced, filled her lungs with air and dived down again.

Ivy hoped she'd be able to reach her possessions through the open front window through which she'd escaped all those years ago. The hammer was just a precaution in case her task wasn't as straightforward as she hoped. When she and Joe had set out on their journey, her handbag and weekend case had been stashed behind the front passenger seat, but her possessions might have been thrown around when the car plunged into the water. Brushing away several clumps of floating weed, she swam towards the vehicle, averting her eyes from the driver's seat. She didn't want to see Joe if she could possibly avoid it.

Ivy felt a vague sense of unease as she surveyed the closed front passenger window. Hadn't it been open, twenty years ago, when she'd got out through it and fought her way to the surface?

After trying unsuccessfully to open the back door, she turned her attention to the back window and tried to swing the hammer but, given the pull and weight of the water, smashing the window proved impossible. She felt as though she was swimming through treacle, and she had to surface several times between tries. By now she was exhausted and emotional, but finally the force of the hammer and the rust of the window frame helped to knock the glass out, and Ivy took a quick look inside. But there was no handbag or weekend case where she'd left them. In the semi-darkness, Ivy leant in and frantically ran her fingers along the back seat and the floor. Where on earth were they?

Abandoning the hammer, Ivy surfaced again, gasping as her lungs filled with fresh air. She longed to scramble out of the water and hightail it back to her parents' house, but she simply had to find her possessions. They had to be down there somewhere, because she'd checked them herself before she and Joe left Willow Haven.

Feeling the desire to cry with frustration, Ivy filled her lungs with air again and dived back down. Now she'd have to steel herself to look in the front of the car, in case they'd been moved by the impact of the crash or carried there by underwater currents. Ivy wasn't sure what effect water and time would have had on her possessions, but it was essential she found them.

On the periphery of her vision, Ivy could see the remains of Joe's body, unrecognisable now as the handsome boy he'd once been, lumps of a soft blubber-like substance still clinging in places to his bones. She'd hoped he'd look less human by this stage, but obviously the depth of the lake and the lack of sunlight had preserved his remains far longer than if they'd been in the sea. She wanted to cry out, but couldn't because she'd only ingest the murky water. Nevertheless, she felt overwhelmed by emotion for what might have been. She'd never allowed herself to grieve for Joe, because she'd needed to suppress her feelings in order to survive. But he'd always been there in the background and often, when playing sad roles, memories of Joe's untimely death had been the catalyst that enabled her to weep. It was ironic how those very occasions had elicited praise for her 'realistic' performances. But apart from those rare opportunities to express her pain, she'd always maintained tight control of her feelings.

Now, she felt the searing pain of loss pervade her whole body once again. Twenty years ago, this man had meant everything to her. Now, in the depths of the lake, the two of them were alone again. Oh Joe, she thought, I wish I could have saved you. And if I hadn't lied to save myself, you wouldn't be entombed here forever. Those who loved you could have mourned your loss. Instead, I let people believe you were a callous adventurer who abandoned your family without a backward glance . . .

Suddenly, Ivy froze. There was a second body in the front passenger seat of the car! Ivy was so shocked, she momentarily forgot she was underwater and opened her mouth, then nearly choked as the water rushed in. Coughing and spluttering, she rose to the surface again, vomiting up the bile in her stomach, leaving her throat raw and a bitter taste in her mouth.

The fresh air and daylight restored a sense of normality, and Ivy realised she'd been imagining things. It had simply been a trick of the light – after all, she herself had been Joe's front-seat passenger. It was impossible that there was another body there – she'd imagined it simply because she was spooked already. Or perhaps her handbag and weekend case were piled up on the front passenger seat, creating the shadowy configuration she'd thought was a body. Feeling relieved, Ivy filled her lungs with air and descended to the bottom of the lake again. This time, she intended grabbing her possessions and heading straight back to the surface. Then all her worries would be over.

In the gloom of the water, Ivy made her way to the car again. She'd have to try and reach her stuff through the broken back window . . .

Suddenly, her heart jumped in her chest – there was definitely a body in the front passenger seat! In horror, Ivy looked at it through the glass. It was in the same state as Joe's body, with bits of soft fatty flesh still clinging to the bones. Ivy wanted to vomit again as acid reflux burned her throat. Quickly she rose to the surface again.

Hauling herself up onto the bank, Ivy sat shivering, and momentarily in a daze. What on earth was going on? How could another body be sitting in the seat she'd originally occupied? And if there really was a body there, who on earth could it be?

Like an automaton, Ivy stripped off her wet bra and panties, and brushed off the plant debris still sticking to her skin. Taking out her towel, she quickly dried herself off, got into fresh underwear, T-shirt and tracksuit, wrapping her wet underwear in her towel and placing it with the goggles in her sports bag.

Still shocked by what she'd seen, Ivy found herself shaking from head to toe, even though she was now dressed. It couldn't really have been a body, could it? No, she was just imagining it. But despite her attempts to rationalise what she'd just seen, she still couldn't get the picture of the decaying figure out of her mind. It was as though its image had burned itself into her brain. Ivy felt a bizarre and dizzying sense of puzzlement. She didn't know of anyone from the locality who was missing.

Despite her intention never to return to the depths of the lake, Ivy knew she had no choice but to make another dive soon. Which meant facing whatever – or whoever – was in the front passenger seat of the car.

Tying her hair back to disguise its wetness, Ivy left the field beside the lake and made her way back onto the road. It felt as though she'd been in the water for an eternity, but her watch told her that she'd been less than an hour at the lake. She'd have to find out from Peggy when exactly the lake was being drained – hopefully it wouldn't be for a while, because she couldn't face another dive any time soon. Besides, she needed to get back to work later that week.

Deliberately putting all thoughts of the body aside, Ivy began to walk briskly. The area was still deserted and, if she was lucky, her parents wouldn't be up yet. As she approached the village, her sports bag over her shoulder, she began jogging. She needed to look the part. Locals would appreciate that soap stars had to exercise regularly to keep in shape. Luckily, no one in the village seemed to be up yet. So far, so good, Ivy thought. Even though she hadn't located her belongings, at least she'd managed to get in and out of the lake without being spotted.

As she let herself in the front door of her parents' house, her mother was just coming down the stairs.

"Good morning, Mum!" Ivy called cheerfully as she stepped inside.

Her mother looked at her in surprise. "Your hair is all wet!"

"That's just sweat!" Ivy lied, smiling as she hurried past her and headed quickly up the stairs to avoid further scrutiny. "I've just been on a really long run! Got to have a shower now, Mum – see you later!"

In her bedroom, she quickly hid her sports bag beneath her bed, grabbed her dressing gown and headed for the bathroom. Luckily, her father was still asleep and the bathroom was free. A long hot shower would help to warm up her body and soothe her aching limbs.

Ivy stepped into the shower and turned on the tap. But even as the cascading water warmed her, she felt her insides chill with fear. She couldn't hide from the truth any longer – there was definitely a second body in the car beneath the lake. Who on earth was it, and what was she going to do about it?

Chapter 14

The coloured bunting stretched across the hotel's conference room. Tables had been set up on either side of the room, and staff bustled in and out of the kitchen, putting out plates of assorted finger food. A large banner was being strung across the centre of the room, proclaiming 'Happy 18th Birthday, Joe', and Julia was fussing because she felt that it wasn't perfectly straight.

In the kitchen, a huge cake had been iced and a birthday greeting written across it. Julia had secretly made it in her own kitchen, and it was a work of art as well as a work of love.

A group of musicians were tuning their instruments, and Fred felt pleased that he'd been able to track down and employ one of Joe's favourite bands. Between the party and the band, the event was costing him an arm and a leg, but it would all be worth it when he saw the surprise on Joe's face. Then his eldest son would know that despite their differences, he was deeply loved. He'd immediately apologise for striking Joe – it had been a dreadful thing to do, and he was thoroughly ashamed of himself.

Fred envisaged himself and Joe in a warm backslapping embrace, all their differences forgotten, each of them promising the other that they'd be more understanding in future, and assuring each other that their problems were far from insurmountable.

As the guests began arriving, Fred hurried forward to greet

them. Many of them were his customers, and he felt that the party was also an ideal way of thanking them for their custom over the years. But there were also many young people arriving and before long the conference room was full, and Fred hoped he'd hired a big enough venue. What a tribute to Joe, and to the Heartleys, to see so many people here! Fred was beside himself with happiness.

"Peggy – it's time," he said to his daughter, an excited expression on his face. "Go and find Joe, and tell him his dad wants to buy him his first legal pint. That should get him here in a hurry!"

Peggy nodded. She hoped Joe would fall for the ploy, because she'd noticed how tetchy and uncooperative he'd been lately. In fact, she'd almost let slip about the party herself, but Joe had been so preoccupied he hadn't seemed to notice.

As Peggy let herself into the Heartley house, she found the silence unnerving. Usually their home was full of noise and people, but now it had an eerie quality to it. As she moved from room to room, calling her brother, it soon became evident that he wasn't there.

Opening the door into the shop downstairs, Peggy checked the aisles and the storage area, but there was no sign of Joe anywhere. Heartley's Stores was closed for the evening, but Fred had given his customers notice, so that everyone had a chance to stock up on groceries or fuel in advance. Of course, most of the villagers would be attending the party anyway, and Peggy and Danny had contacted all Joe's classmates as well.

Locking up the shop and the house again, Peggy began walking back to the hotel. By now she was worried in case the party turned out to be a disaster – surprise parties were all very well, but they didn't take account of the guest of honour's own plans. Maybe Joe had gone to visit friends? On the other hand, surely those friends would be attending the party anyway?

Back at the hotel, Peggy relayed the information to her father, who'd been waiting outside on the steps, ready to inform the guests inside that Joe was arriving. Everyone had been primed to keep quiet as Joe approached the hotel. Then, when Peggy steered him into the conference room, they'd all shout out: 'Happy Birthday, Joe!'

Fred was now becoming extremely agitated as he and his daughter entered the conference room again. Over in a corner, Peggy could see her mother chatting to Ivy's parents, Eleanor and Peter Morton, unaware that her eldest son couldn't be found. Peggy longed to ask the Mortons if they'd seen Joe, or if they knew where he might be, but she didn't want to make an issue of it, since everyone seemed oblivious to the fact that there was a problem, and anyway Joe might turn up at any minute.

Peggy noticed that Ivy wasn't present either – could Joe be over at her house? She'd noticed that Ivy and her eldest brother had become very friendly lately, and always seemed to have their heads stuck in some schoolbook or other. Maybe they were studying together? On the other hand, since Ivy, Owen and their parents knew all about the surprise party – and Owen was already on the dance floor with Mrs Evans – surely they'd have made certain that Joe got to the hotel?

Nevertheless, Peggy slipped out and made her way to the Mortons' house, only to find it in complete darkness. She knocked tentatively, but there was no answer, so she made her way back to the hotel.

As the band began playing an upbeat number, people started to drift onto the small dance floor, and before long all the young people were dancing. Rosa Dalton was showing off as usual, twirling around dramatically to draw attention to herself, and even some of the older villagers were shaking a leg too, and getting into party mood. Peggy decided that the only thing to do was to join in, so she stepped onto the dance floor. It wouldn't look good if the host family were all looking miserable!

As he stood on the sidelines, Fred's brow was furrowed. Where on earth could Joe be? They hadn't spoken to each other since their most recent spat, therefore he could hardly expect Joe to keep him apprised of his movements. But surely his eldest son would instinctively know that hostilities would be dispensed with while the family celebrated? After all, his eighteenth birthday was a special event for the family, and his parents would want to mark it in a special way. Now, all his family, friends and neighbours were gathered in the hotel to celebrate, yet the guest of honour was nowhere to be found. And where on earth was Danny?

Just then, his younger son appeared, and Fred quickly sidelined him. "Thank goodness you're here, I was beginning to wonder if any members of the family were going to turn up! I can't find Joe anywhere – have you any idea where he might be?"

Danny shrugged his shoulders. "I haven't a clue, Dad. Since you didn't tell him about the party, he could be anywhere."

Fred felt a strong urge to cuff his younger son for his insolence, but he knew that it would only damage his relationship with Danny as well. His violence had already caused enough problems with Joe. He was suddenly frightened. How could such a marvellous plan go so terribly wrong?

As Rosa rushed forward to claim him for a dance, Danny disappeared into the crowd, and Fred found himself alone again. Suddenly Hannah Dalton was at his side.

"Fred – are you okay?"

Fred quickly converted his frown into a smile.

"Oh, hello, Hannah, I hope you're enjoying the party?"

"Yes, thanks, Fred – it's wonderful. You and Julia have gone to a lot of trouble. But you look worried – is everything alright?"

Fred sighed. "It's just that Joe hasn't turned up yet."

"Oh, don't worry, I'm sure he'll be along soon," Hannah said, smiling. "He's probably having a few drinks at one of the pubs before he gets here. A first legal drink is a big milestone for young people!"

Fred smiled gratefully at Hannah. She was probably right – why hadn't he thought of that himself? He'd had a sentimental notion of buying his son his first pint himself, but maybe Joe had taken the matter into his own hands.

Feeling a lot more cheerful, Fred allowed himself a beer from the bar. Since he'd be making a brief speech later, congratulating Joe on reaching his majority, he wanted to stay reasonably sober. But right now a beer would take the edge off his nerves.

As the evening progressed, people seemed to forget the reason they were there, and were simply enjoying themselves. Food and drink were being consumed at an alarming rate, but Fred wasn't worried about the cost. Although still perturbed by Joe's absence, he was relieved that no one seemed to be missing the guest of honour so far. Hopefully, Joe would turn up in time to blow out the candles on his cake, which Julia had baked so lovingly.

Fred spent much of the evening chatting inanely to his neighbours, his eyes always turned towards the door. At intervals, he slipped outside the hotel to look for Joe, even walking into the village to check in the local pubs for his son. But there was no sign of Joe anywhere. One pub-goer suggested he might have gone into Allcott, several miles away, and Fred decided to drive there himself. But when he went to the garage to get his new red Ford saloon, it was no longer there.

Puzzled and angry, Fred returned to the party. Joe must have taken the car to Allcott without his permission! Fred felt there was little he could do right now, except suppress his anger and ensure that everyone enjoyed the rest of the party. Hopefully Joe would be mature enough to leave the car in Allcott and take a taxi home, although Fred intended giving him a piece of his mind the following day. But right now all Fred wanted was for his son to turn up, even if well inebriated. Everyone else at the party was merry by now, so it would hardly matter.

Hannah collared him as soon as he entered the conference room again, a querying expression on her face.

Fred shook his head, and told her about his missing car.

"Look, Joe won't be used to alcohol, so if he's had his first few pints, he's probably sleeping off his hangover in some friend's house," Hannah assured him.

Fred felt comforted by her suggestion. At least Joe would be safe. But he was still furious with his son for not turning up for his own party.

As the evening came to an end, the band announced that they were playing their final number, and suddenly guests realised that something was amiss.

"What about the cake?" someone asked plaintively. "Doesn't Joe still need to blow out his candles?"

Fred made his way up onto the platform where the band had been playing. There was immediate silence, since by now word had begun circulating that the guest of honour hadn't turned up, and everyone was anxious to find out what had happened.

"Good evening, everyone," Fred began falteringly. "Thank you all for coming to Joe's eighteenth birthday party. Unfortunately, we don't seem to have Joe here himself –" Fred gave a weak smile, "so I'll have to rely on the rest of you to tell him what a great party he missed!"

Everyone laughed loudly, but by now there was an undercurrent of unease among the guests. People were trying to remember when they'd last seen Joe, and his classmates were asking each other if any of them had been assigned the job of making sure he got to the hotel. Everyone was shaking their heads and looking mystified.

As Fred left the platform, Julia grabbed his arm. By now, she'd had more than a few vodkas, and was slurring her words as she clung to him.

"Where's my son? Why isn't he here – at his own party?" she sobbed, and Fred quickly summoned Peggy, who was talking to friends nearby.

"Better get your mother home," Fred whispered to his daughter, who instantly began steering Julia out the door of the conference room. Peggy felt almost hysterical herself – how on earth could Joe miss such a wonderful party? She knew their parents had spent a fortune on the event, and she felt angry with Joe on their behalf. When she next saw him, she'd tell him exactly what she thought of his behaviour!

By now, Julia was weeping copiously, and Peggy steered her down the road and into the Heartley home, where she helped her upstairs and finally got her into bed. When she eventually looked down at her mother's sleeping form, Peggy was filled with rage. How dare Joe ruin everything for their parents, and for her and Danny too! Despite all the money they'd spent, their parents had been publicly humiliated. How would her poor father feel as he opened up the shop tomorrow? The Heartleys would be the talk of the village, and she knew how seriously her father viewed his position in the community.

Peggy bit her lip. What on earth could have gone wrong? Maybe she should have told Joe about the party in advance, and then he wouldn't have gone off somewhere else. Maybe surprise parties weren't such a good idea after all.

Peggy headed down the corridor to her own bedroom. She wouldn't like to be in Joe's shoes when he eventually got home. Today had certainly been a day the Heartleys would never forget.

Chapter 15

During the next few days in Willow Haven, Ivy tried to relax. She was well aware that noses would be out of joint if she visited one set of friends and not another, so she undertook a round of visiting that occupied most of her time. She spent an evening with Fred Heartley, another with Hannah Dalton, and she took her parents for a meal at the local hotel. All this activity proved useful by keeping her mind occupied and away from thoughts of the second body in the lake.

By now, the initial shock had worn off and Ivy was left puzzled. How could the second body have got there? She and Joe had been the only passengers in the car. Even if someone fell into the lake, they'd never have ended up *inside* the car. Which could only mean that the body had been deliberately put there. It also meant that the person had been murdered – there was no other logical explanation. Which meant the murderer had to know that Joe and his father's car were at the bottom of the lake. Did that also mean someone knew Ivy had escaped from the car and kept Joe's death a secret? If so, there was someone out there who knew what she'd done. And could she now find herself implicated in this second person's death?

She racked her brain. Was anyone missing from the area? She couldn't think of anyone, and no one in the village had ever mentioned a disappearance to her. But of course, the body mightn't belong to a local person – assuming they'd been murdered, the body could have been transported hundreds of miles. For a few moments, that idea enabled her to feel a sense of relief. But then another thought struck her. How would a stranger to the area know about the car and the body already in the lake?

Ivy shook her head vehemently. No, it couldn't be true – she was simply imagining the second body. She'd been so spooked by what she was doing that her imagination had run riot. Anyway, all she'd really seen was a dark shape in the passenger seat. It could have been anything, maybe a clump of weed, or some kind of debris. Yes, that was it – her mind had gone into overdrive. In the dark and murky water, it would have been easy to imagine.

Yet deep in her heart, Ivy couldn't deny what she'd seen, its skin dissolving just like Joe's. Who was it and, worse still, was the murderer watching her? Was there someone out there who could overturn her life in an instant?

Ivy felt a desperate need to tell somebody. Otherwise she'd go mental from the stress. Besides, since the second body was undoubtedly there as a result of foul play, hadn't she a responsibility to do something for that person? After all, they might have family who were missing them. Tears filled her eyes. Hadn't she herself deprived the Heartley family of closure, simply because she was afraid of being blamed for Joe Heartley leaving the village and meeting his death? She was a hypocrite as well as everything else.

But who could she tell about the extra body? She couldn't talk to Danny – in fact, she couldn't talk to anyone, since they'd want to know what she'd been doing at the bottom of the lake. Maybe she could let the police know anonymously? No, she couldn't risk that either – not as long as her possessions were still in Fred's car.

Ivy bit her lip. She needed to think but, more importantly, she needed to work. She was due back on set of *Bright Lights* within days, and she still had lines to learn for the coming week's episodes. Since she was one of the main characters, she spent more time on the set than most other cast members, and she appeared in the majority of plotlines. Well, she thought bitterly, that's why I'm so highly paid. But sometimes money isn't everything. Right now, she needed more time off to return to Willow Haven. Despite being free at weekends, there was no point in visiting the lake then – people would be out walking their dogs beside the lake, and anyway, Danny would probably want to accompany her.

Well, if I don't do something quickly, she thought, my career will be over anyway, because it wouldn't survive the scandal that would occur when the lake was drained.

Maybe she could get the *Bright Lights* writers to leave her out of several episodes? She'd need to request another break soon, since the Council could start draining the lake at any time.

On her last evening in Willow Haven, Ivy dropped in to say goodbye to Peggy, to whom she was extremely close. Well, as close as she could ever allow herself to be to anyone. Her relationship with her sister-in-law was tempered by guilt at having deprived Peggy of closure over her eldest brother's death.

But Peggy noticed that Ivy wasn't herself.

"Is something wrong, Ivy?" she asked, looking concerned. "You seem a bit preoccupied – is everything okay?"

"Yes, fine," Ivy lied. "To be honest, I'm just a little worried about going back to *Bright Lights* – there's a complicated storyline coming up, and I hope I'm able to do it."

"You'll be terrific! You always are!" Peggy said warmly.

Ivy felt a total fraud. Peggy was always kind and supportive. How could she dare to call herself Peggy's friend when she'd already robbed her of so much? And was continuing to do so?

"By the way," Ivy said, as nonchalantly as she could manage, "you said in a recent email that the Council was planning to drain the lake . . ."

Peggy nodded. "Yes, they've decided to fill it in, with the aim of eventually building on it. The village is very divided on the issue – some people think the lake is part of our local heritage, and should be left alone. Others, like me, think it's probably a good idea."

Ivy tried to sound casual. "Have you any idea when they're going to start?"

"I heard from Mrs Evans that they've put the project out to

tender, so I suppose they'll get going when they've agreed a price with a contractor."

Ivy nodded, relieved that she'd gained at least a short reprieve. Hopefully the tendering process would be slow, and it might take weeks – maybe even months – before work could begin.

"Won't you miss the lake?" she asked her sister-in-law. "I mean, it's been part of our lives for so long."

Peggy nodded. "The village will feel very different, but perhaps it's for the best. Since Harper's Lake is such a sheer drop, I often worry that a child will fall in and drown – the kids still go there after school, despite all the warnings." She smiled at Ivy. "Remember how *we* used to hang out there when we were young?"

Ivy nodded again, then changed the subject. "How's your dad?" she asked. "I called to see him on Wednesday evening, but he didn't seem in the best of humour."

Peggy's face darkened. "He's never been the same since Joe disappeared. I think the shop gives him a reason to keep going – but I don't think he really cares whether he lives or dies."

Ivy nodded guiltily, knowing there was little she could say. Because of her lies, the Heartleys had been subjected to a life of torment.

And now the second body in the lake was complicating the situation even further. Ivy was terrified of going down into the murky depths again. But she didn't have any choice – she'd have to make another dive. There was just too much at stake.

Chapter 16

The following morning, Ivy woke to discover that nothing had changed overnight. Joe's tragic drowning the previous day was still fresh in her mind, and her head was throbbing and her stomach was heaving. Downstairs, her parents were discussing what had happened at the Heartleys' party.

"You're not going to believe this, Ivy –" her mother said, as Ivy entered the kitchen. "Joe Heartley never turned up for his own birthday party last night!"

Ivy tried to look surprised, but inside she felt sick and she wanted to cry. How was she going to keep on pretending for the rest of her life?

"Anyway, why weren't you there, love?" her father asked, as he buttered a piece of toast. "I thought you liked the Heartleys. And isn't Peggy a good friend?"

Ivy nodded. "I meant to go, but I had a terrible headache," she lied. "I climbed into bed, and I must have fallen asleep."

Her mother looked at her closely. "Hmm, you don't look well, Ivy – your eyes and your nose are all red. Maybe you're getting a cold – hang on, I'll get you something that will ease the symptoms."

Eleanor quickly prepared a concoction of honey and lemon in a glass and handed it to her daughter. "I've already had to supply your brother with paracetamol this morning," she added acerbically. "He's *still in bed, nursing a hangover from the party last night. I warned him to go easy on the beer, but did he listen to me? Of course not!"*

Ivy nodded her thanks as she took the glass, thinking that at least someone had enjoyed the events of the previous night. She doubted she'd enjoy anything ever again.

"Where were you earlier yesterday?" her mother asked, disapproval in her voice. "I called you for lunch, but you weren't in your room. And your bedroom door was locked when we were leaving for the party."

"Leave her alone, Eleanor, she's not well," her father intervened, enabling Ivy to avoid answering her mother's question.

Ivy threw him a grateful glance, wondering what he'd think if he knew she hadn't expected to be here in Willow Haven today, or any other day, ever again.

"I'm going back to bed, too," she said, hurrying out the door again. If she stayed in the kitchen any longer, she felt certain she'd break down and cry.

"Don't you want to hear what happened?" her mother called after her, disappointed that she'd lost her audience. She'd been bursting to tell Ivy all that had transpired the night before, but her daughter didn't seem interested. Maybe she was coming down with flu . . .

Upstairs in her room, Ivy climbed into bed again. All she wanted was to experience the oblivion of sleep. She'd freak out if she didn't get a break from all the thoughts that were swirling around in her brain. Yet sleep wouldn't come, nor could she escape from the horrific images of Joe trapped in the car, and the muddy water all around them. Ivy was beginning to understand why people resorted to alcohol or drugs to blot out terrible events in their lives. Right now, if she had whiskey or gin to hand, she'd drink the entire bottle.

* * *

Later that afternoon, Ivy felt she'd no option but to make her way downstairs again. She'd have to face her parents at some stage, and maybe a little food in her stomach would help to ease the queasiness she felt. She'd rejected the tray of food her mother had brought upstairs earlier, but now she was beginning to feel peckish. Of course, this made Ivy feel even guiltier – she was still alive and could feel hunger, but poor Joe would never be able to eat again.

In the kitchen, she made herself a tomato sandwich, relieved that Owen was still in bed, since she didn't want to talk to anyone. How could the world keep on turning when the boy she loved was dead? She was still in shock, and she didn't know how she could keep up the deception. But it was already too late to tell anyone.

While she chewed her sandwich mechanically, not really tasting any of it, Ivy listened to the drone of the television as her father watched a football match in the drawing room. Outside in the garden, she could see her mother pruning her beloved roses. To her parents, today was just like any other Saturday. Ivy closed her eyes and wished she could be transported back to the previous Saturday. Then, none of this would have happened. She'd insist on taking the train instead of stealing Fred Heartley's car, and they'd arrive in London safely. If only she'd been more persuasive, she and Joe could have had a glorious future together.

Ivy abandoned her half-eaten sandwich and left the house. She didn't want to go anywhere near the lake, but when she reached the crossroads and tried to take the opposite turn, her feet seemed to develop minds of their own and were pulling her inexorably towards it. Soon she found herself standing on the bank of the lake and staring into its deep waters.

She was relieved to find the lake deserted that Saturday afternoon. Normally, there would be lots of people about, but since most of the locals had been at the party the night before, they'd probably be nursing hangovers and staying close to home.

Gazing out across the water, she found it almost impossible to believe that any tragedy could have taken place here. Was she in some kind of dream, from which she'd soon awake and everything would be as it had been before? Then Joe would be waiting for her in Johnson's barn, and she'd feel the touch of his skin on hers as they made love among the sweet-smelling bales of hay . . .

Ivy stifled a sob as reality hit her again and she felt overwhelmed by grief. If she started crying she might never be able to stop, and the lake would overflow with her tears. The lake was glass-like, without a single ripple on its surface, and Ivy felt that she could almost walk across it. Its still waters were almost hypnotic, and she felt herself being pulled towards it. Maybe she was meant to join Joe and be with him for eternity . . .

Suddenly, she was woken from her reverie by a shout.

"Ivy – are you okay?"

Turning, she saw Danny Heartley waving as he made his way towards her. Ivy did her best to smile back at him, but the last person on earth she wanted to see right now was a member of the Heartley family.

"I'm fine," she said, as he reached her.

"I thought you were swaying a bit – I was afraid you were going to fall in!"

"It's just a headache," Ivy quickly explained. "I've been feeling weak and a bit off colour since yesterday."

Danny nodded. "Is that why you weren't at Joe's party last night?"

Ivy could feel her face turning scarlet, but she tried to sound relaxed as she answered him. After all, this was only the first of many acting roles she'd have to play over the years, and she might as well get used to it.

"Yes. I heard it was a great party – but is it true that Joe didn't turn up?"

Danny nodded. "He's also taken Dad's new car, so he's going to be in serious trouble when he gets home!" Suddenly, he looked sad. "I feel really sorry for my parents, because they went to so much trouble and expense. Mum's been crying non-stop, and Dad looks like thunder all the time. I wouldn't like to be in Joe's shoes when he gets back . . ."

Then he brightened. "But nevertheless, it was a great party! I just wish you'd been there, Ivy."

"How's Rosa – you know, your girlfriend?" Ivy asked him pointedly. "Did she enjoy the party?"

Danny shrugged his shoulders. "She's not my girlfriend – she's just someone I'm seeing at the moment."

77

Ivy gave him a knowing look. "Tell that to Rosa."

Danny smiled shyly. "Ivy, you must know by now that you're the one I want to be with. The minute you're ready to go out with me, Rosa is history. You only have to say the word – everyone in the village knows I fancy you."

Ivy tried to smile, but all she could think of was how close they were standing to where Joe's body lay. Soon, Joe's family would start to worry about his continued absence, and the police would eventually be notified. But no one would think of looking in the lake, and the Heartleys would spend the rest of their lives wondering what had happened to him . . .

When Ivy didn't reply, Danny touched her arm. "I'll win you eventually – just you wait and see!"

Ivy still said nothing.

"Come on – I'll walk you home," he said, looking down at her kindly. "It's not a good idea to stand at the edge of the lake when you're feeling weak or dizzy. You really don't look very well – maybe you need an early night." He grinned at her cheekily. "I need an early night myself, after all the booze I drank at the party – maybe we could spend our early nights together?"

Ivy gave him a dismissive look, and Danny grinned back mischievously. She couldn't help smiling back – Danny could be tiresome, but sometimes he could be very endearing. Which made her feel even worse.

As Danny walked on ahead, she glanced back at the still waters of the lake. Oh Joe, she thought to herself, I'll never forget you. I'll never love anyone the way I loved you – I'll probably never love anyone ever again! In a way, we're bound to each other forever . . .

"Come on!" Danny called impatiently.

She followed him through the bushes and out onto the road.

Chapter 17

Home again in Sussex, Ivy was relieved to be as far as possible from Harper's Lake. She needed time to think about what she was going to do next. If there really was another body in the car, she could hardly let someone get away with murder, could she? On the other hand, she couldn't do anything until she'd recovered her possessions from Fred's car.

Danny was delighted to have her back home, and hadn't seemed to notice how preoccupied she was. He'd wanted to hear all the news from Willow Haven, but his interest had only served to set her nerves on edge. Luckily, he didn't make any reference to the lake, because Ivy felt she'd go to pieces if it was mentioned by name.

Dutifully, she told him about her visits to his father, Hannah Dalton and her evening with Peggy. He was amused at Ivy's mother's attempts to get her father fit, and laughed out loud at the thought of burly Peter Morton in a tracksuit and trainers. Of course, Ivy avoided mentioning her own jogging trips past the lake. Or her explorations of the lake bottom, or the blurry shape in the front passenger seat of Fred Heartley's car.

On Sunday morning, Ivy declined Danny's invitation to go sailing. He was keen to take the boat out as it was a beautiful day, and Ivy urged him to go without her, feigning tiredness and yawning for effect. Reluctantly, Danny left in his Mercedes for the

LINDA KAVANAGH

marina down the coast at Brighton, but as soon as he'd gone, Ivy was on her feet and heading for the phone.

Her heart pounding, she rang the home number of Colin, her producer, and waited anxiously for him to answer. While the *Bright Lights* overall storyline was devised up to a year ahead of filming, individual characters' storylines were more flexible, and sometimes had to be adjusted to take account of the weather, illness or death of an individual actor. Ivy was hoping that Colin would agree to make immediate changes to Isabella's script.

After what seemed a lifetime, Colin answered and Ivy apologised for ringing him at the weekend, before begging for some time off, intimating, but not exactly saying, that she might need to visit a medical specialist. She hated lying to him and behaving unprofessionally, but right now she didn't feel she'd any other choice. She had to get back to the lake as soon as possible.

Colin reluctantly agreed to have a word with the writers and ask them to tinker with the script. "Hmmm – maybe we could have a fire at the nightclub, and put Isabella in hospital for a while," he said at last. "How long do you need? Is two weeks enough?"

"Yes – that would be great."

"I'll talk to the writing team tomorrow – if they can figure out a way to do it, you might be able to take a break by the end of the month. Is that okay?"

Thanking him, Ivy sighed with relief, assuring him that, if needed, she'd work extra hours when she returned.

Colin hesitated. "Are you okay, Ivy? I mean, if there's anything I can do –"

"I'm fine, thanks," Ivy assured him as she said goodbye, although she felt bad about causing him to worry.

Nor had she any intention of telling Danny that she'd asked Colin for time off. She'd simply tell him that Isabella was being briefly written out to accommodate another storyline, and she'd go to Willow Haven when Danny was too busy to accompany her.

* * *

When the sun continued to shine that afternoon, Ivy decided to sit

80

outside in the garden while she revised her lines for the following day's episode. The sky was a brilliant azure blue, and she turned her face up to the sun. Since autumn wasn't far away, she intended making the most of it.

As she began revising her script, Ivy was transported to the nightclub where her character Isabella had just spotted the man with whom she was about to embark on an affair. The actor taking on the role was a new recruit, and would therefore undoubtedly be nervous. Ivy hoped she'd be able to put him at his ease during their upcoming romantic scenes. A nervous actor meant time lost and re-shooting of scenes, and Ivy didn't want any delays that would keep her from getting back to Harper's Lake.

Although soaps steered clear of topical issues that would date the production and limit opportunities to sell it overseas, Ivy didn't crave meatier roles. She'd done theatre in the West End and played minor roles in two movies before finding her forte in the role of Isabella, which she'd been playing for many years. She enjoyed her character's antics in the bedroom, since playing her was the complete opposite of Ivy's own private life. Isabella was the kind of woman who played fast and free with the opposite sex, but didn't like her husband doing the same thing, which led to many on-screen spats between Ivy and Anton, who played her older screen husband. Off screen, Ivy and Anton often chuckled together at the carry-on of their characters. Invariably one or other of them was having a fling with someone else's spouse.

"I don't know where they get the energy, darling!" Anton was prone to say. "Just reading the script has me exhausted already!"

Ivy was getting to grips with the nightclub scene when she heard the landline ringing in the distance. Cursing, she ran inside, annoyed with herself for not having the foresight to bring the receiver outside. Normally, when she was learning lines, she'd ignore the ringing, but she knew Joseph was phoning home today, and she was anxious to find out how he was faring in his search for accommodation for his next year at university. She was breathless from the effort as she pressed the receiver to her ear.

"Hello?"

Suddenly, Ivy heard a hoarse whisper: "I know what you were doing at the lake – stay away or I'll tell everyone what you did!"

In shock, she dropped the receiver and it crashed to the floor. She felt as though the room was spinning around her, and she rushed to the nearest bathroom and threw up in the sink. Her mind was in turmoil – this couldn't be happening, could it? If ever she needed proof that there was a body in the lake, she had it now! Eventually she sat down on the bathroom floor to stop the room from going round and round.

Had the voice been a man's or a woman's? She'd been in such a state that she hadn't really noticed. The voice had been a whisper, so it could have been either.

Ivy bit her trembling lip. At last, her worst nightmare was coming true. Someone knew she'd recently visited the lake. And they knew what she'd done all those years ago. Carrying the weight of the secret alone had been bad enough – now it was ten times worse, because whoever it was could now destroy her life. Everything was starting to unravel around her and, worse still, she'd bring Danny and Joseph down with her.

As the dizziness passed, Ivy pulled herself up and sat trembling on the side of the bath. If this mystery person knew what had happened at the lake all those years ago, why hadn't they acted on the information before now? Clearly because now she might tell someone about the second body. Maybe they'd decide to murder her, too!

Suddenly, the fog in Ivy's brain cleared, and it dawned on her that if she dialled 1471, she might be able to find out who her mystery caller was. Her fingers shaking, she dialled the number and listened, her heart sinking as she heard the reply: Number Withheld.

Ivy covered her face with her hands. Naturally, the caller would be too clever to allow his or her number to be discovered. What on earth was she going to do? If only there was someone she could confide in. But the very reason she'd received the call was the reason she couldn't ask anyone for help. And the mystery caller knew that her secret kept her isolated from anyone who could help her. There was nothing she could do but wait, terrified, for whatever would happen next.

Chapter 18

During the days following the party, Fred Heartley was furious, assuming that Joe was too scared to come home. He was gearing up to administer a major telling-off. How dare Joe let down all those good people who'd turned up at the hotel to wish him well on his birthday! And how dare he take his father's new car! Fred figured that Joe had probably damaged the vehicle, and wasn't man enough to own up to what he'd done.

But by the second week of Joe's disappearance, Fred's anger had gradually turned to fear. The police hadn't found any trace of the car, and Joe hadn't made contact. Fred was also angry with himself – if he hadn't had that blow-up with Joe, maybe none of this would ever have happened. If Joe was staying away to scare his father, he was certainly achieving his aim.

By now, Julia was hysterical, and talking about "bad karma". She was convinced Joe would never return, and she blamed Fred for driving him away. In desperation, Fred was even considering returning to church, an institution he'd abandoned many years before. But nothing else seemed to be working, and maybe if he interceded with God, and promised to reform his life, the Almighty might see fit to send his son back to him.

* * *

As the weeks dragged by without any sign of Joe Heartley, an undercurrent of sadness began to develop in the village. People were beginning to realise that he mightn't be coming back.

There were few people in the village who hadn't liked the boy, and they knew all about the fights with his father. Although it was clear that he'd stolen his father's car, few begrudged him the opportunity of making a new life for himself. Most villagers accepted that Fred had been too strict with his son, and secretly hoped the police would never find him.

Since it was obvious by now that Joe wasn't sleeping off a hangover somewhere, Fred Heartley's mood swung from fear back to anger, and he was once again threatening all sorts of punishments should his eldest son ever dare to set foot in the village again.

* * *

As Peter Morton set off for Morton and Company Solicitors, he walked in the direction of Heartley's Stores to buy his morning newspaper. His thoughts were with the Heartley family, and he fervently hoped Joe would return soon, otherwise Fred might have a heart attack. The poor man hadn't looked well since the day Joe left.

In the shop, Fred and Julia were going about their individual chores, Fred changing the till roll and Julia wiping down the counters. As he picked up his morning paper and headed towards the till, Peter glanced at Julia, intending to offer her a cheerful greeting.

It was almost imperceptible, but Peter Morton caught the look of sheer hatred on Julia's face as she glanced at her husband. Dear God, he thought, she blames Fred for Joe's disappearance. Poor man – but poor Julia too.

The greeting froze on his lips as Julia walked off without a word, leaving an embarrassed Fred to cover up for her lack of manners.

"Julia's still upset – about Joe leaving," he said, his ruddy cheeks aflame.

"I'm not surprised," Peter said gently, "but I'm sure he'll be back soon."

Having paid for his newspaper, Peter left the shop and began walking in the direction of his office, which was situated beside the bank. He guessed there'd be no peace in the Heartley household that evening, or on any other evening either. The glue that had held Fred and Julia's marriage together was gradually being eroded by the departure of their eldest son.

Peter Morton sighed as he opened the outer door and began climbing the stairs to his office. As a parent himself, he knew how badly Fred and Julia must be hurting. If Owen or Ivy ever ran off like that, he didn't know what he'd do.

* * *

Every time Ivy heard people talking about Joe, she wanted to cry. On one hand, she was glad to know that people thought so highly of the boy she'd loved but, on the other, each kind comment was like a knife slicing through her insides.

At home, she avoided her parents and brother as much as possible, claiming variously that she was cleaning her room, washing her hair or reading. But when she claimed to be studying during the weekend, she'd taken a step too far.

"What's going on?" her mother asked, looking suspicious. "You've never made any effort to study at the weekend before. You haven't got a man up in your room, have you?"

"No, of course not!" said Ivy indignantly.

"Then why are you spending so much time up there? All you've been doing lately is moping around. And whatever happened to that lovely dress we bought you – the pink one with the white piping round the sleeves? And your new jeans – where on earth are they? Half your clothes seem to have disappeared!"

"Just leave me alone!" Ivy shouted, running out the front door, and into the street.

She was tired of being scrutinised by every member of her family. Even Owen had taken to watching her surreptitiously, and turning guiltily away when she caught his eye. Why couldn't they just leave her alone? In the privacy of her room, she could cry unashamedly, and at night she cried herself to sleep. Sometimes she wondered if she'd ever feel better. Even when her mood lifted a little, a picture of Joe's face would suddenly push its way into her mind, and she'd sink into a deep depression again.

As she walked along the street, head down and her thoughts miles away, she heard a familiar voice calling to her.

"Ivy, are you alright?" Danny Heartley asked, a look of concern on his face, and Ivy felt a total fraud.

"I'm fine thanks, Danny," she lied.

"You rushed out of your house looking so sad. Are you sure you're okay?"

"Yes, I'm fine – honestly. Just a bit of an argument with Mum, nothing serious."

Danny grinned. "Count yourself lucky you don't have the hassle that's going on in our house. Since Joe left, Mum and Dad are at each other's throats!"

Danny grinned again, as though the whole thing was a great laugh. "I wonder where my brother's got to?" he chuckled. "I can't believe he had the nerve to nick Dad's car. When he comes back, Dad will skin him alive!"

Ivy gulped. Keeping quiet was already taking its toll on her, but now it was far too late to tell the truth.

"I'm actually starting to miss him," Danny told her, kicking a pebble and suddenly looking glum. "I never thought I'd say this, but it's not much fun here without him. There's only me and Peggy at home now – and my little sister's far too studious for my liking."

"Hold on –" said Ivy, glad to find a focus for her anger, "– your sister got top marks in her class last term! You're the one who needs to study if you're going to get your final exams next year."

Danny grinned cheekily. "I'll make a deal with you, Ivy – I'll study really hard if you'll agree to go out with me!"

Ivy gave him a contemptuous look, and Danny held up his hands in supplication.

"Okay, okay, I won't hassle you, Ivy – but you are going to be my girlfriend someday, just you wait and see!"

In the silence that followed, Ivy knew they were both thinking of Joe, yet she didn't dare mention his name in case it proved to be her undoing.

"I'd better go."

Ivy had no idea where she was going but right now returning to face her mother's wrath was preferable to being with any of the Heartleys.

Danny nodded. "Okay – I hope you and your mum sort out your quarrel." He grimaced. "Just don't let it get out of hand like Joe and Dad did – right now, I'd give anything to have Joe come home." He brightened. "Anyway, I doubt if he'll stay away too long – I'll bet you the phone will start ringing soon, and Joe will be asking me what kind of mood Dad is in!"

Whistling, Danny walked off, leaving Ivy feeling sick.

Chapter 19

After several sleepless nights, Ivy decided that she couldn't allow herself to become a sitting duck, waiting for this mystery person to threaten her again. She'd have to do something about the situation, but she'd no idea what. The phone call had terrified her, and her heart jumped every time the landline rang at home. Even Danny had noticed how edgy she was, and had asked several times if she was okay.

She managed to hide her worries while on the set of *Bright Lights*, but, as soon as each scene was over, she felt herself consumed by fear yet again. It was also affecting how she reacted to her colleagues, because she couldn't help wondering if one of them could be the mystery caller. On the other hand, it being a work colleague made no sense. It had to be someone from Willow Haven – someone who had watched her dive into the lake that morning, and had as much – if not more – to lose as she had.

But who could have known she was there? Ivy had purposely gone to the lake when she'd assumed no one else was around, and she hadn't told anyone where she was going. Had someone been down there already, and watched her dive in? And had they been there by accident or design? Either way, someone definitely knew she'd been down to Fred's car and seen the two bodies.

Suddenly, Ivy remembered hearing from her mother that Hannah had been the victim of a mystery caller many years earlier.

At the time, she hadn't paid much attention, but now she wondered if there could be a connection? Extremely unlikely. All the same, she'd ask Hannah about it sometime . . .

Much to Ivy's relief, the writers agreed to adopt her producer's suggestion. Isabella and her new beau would be caught in a compromising situation when the nightclub caught fire. Isabella would end up in hospital, and Emily's character Marina would take centre-stage again for the two weeks while Ivy was away.

But since receiving the mystery phone call, Ivy's priorities had changed. She was now far too afraid to go back to the lake. The caller would probably be watching her every move in Willow Haven. And if she dived into the lake – well, they might follow her, pull her underwater and try to drown her. Ivy felt her throat constricting as she imagined someone's hands around her neck, choking the life out of her in the murky confines of the water . . .

Ivy shuddered. Right now, she felt she'd no choice but to get as far away as possible from the mystery caller. By putting distance between them, she'd be better able to clear her head and think logically about what she was going to do next. Since draining of the lake was still out to tender, it was unlikely that anything would happen during the two weeks she'd be away. She'd worry about diving in later.

* * *

Now that she had a two-week break ahead, Ivy decided she was going abroad somewhere – to a place where the mystery caller couldn't reach her. She hoped that Danny could come with her, but she suspected he'd be too busy since two new Betterbuys stores were being opened soon. Perhaps Joseph could spare the time?

On the other hand, she was aware that the start of the year at university wasn't the best time to start missing lectures . . . Well, even if she had to go alone, so be it. Right now, Ivy couldn't wait to finish the current *Bright Lights* storyline and get away as soon as possible.

Where would she go? She didn't want to sit by herself on a beach all day and dine alone each night. Nor did she want to wander through some strange city where she didn't understand the language. That would make her feel even worse than she did already.

Spending too much time in her own company would also make her paranoid – before long she'd be imagining that everyone she met was the mystery caller or someone hired by them to finish her off.

Suddenly, Ivy had a brilliant idea. She'd go to South Africa and visit her brother! Since he'd moved there five years earlier, he'd been asking them all to visit, and she'd intended going when she had enough free time. Now, the distance would also protect her. The mystery caller wouldn't know what country she was in or where she was staying, and they wouldn't have a phone number to contact her. No whispering voice could reach her if she was 6,000 miles away – could they?

Ivy shivered. She'd keep her trip to South Africa a secret, since she didn't know the capabilities of the mystery caller. And since she'd implied to Colin that she was attending a medical specialist, she'd need to ensure that none of her colleagues in *Bright Lights* found out either. She'd ask Danny not to tell Peggy or Fred – of course, it would be impossible not to tell her parents that she was going to visit their son, but she'd ask them to keep quiet about her trip. Hopefully they'd accept that she just wanted some privacy.

* * *

Danny was surprised when she told him of her plan to go to South Africa.

"But you're only just back from Willow Haven!"

"I know, but I'd like to see Owen. Are you free to come with me?"

Danny shook his head. "Couldn't you wait a few weeks?" he asked. "You know we've got two new branches opening, and I really need to be here. But after that, I could go. I've never been to South Africa either – it would be nice to see Owen again."

Ivy felt mean and selfish, but she couldn't let Danny know why she needed to get away.

"Sorry, love, there's a break in the storyline coming up, then I won't have another one for ages," she'd explained. "You and I can go to South Africa another time."

Her husband nodded ruefully. "I wish you'd told me you'd a break coming up. I could have organised things differently."

"Sorry, Danny, I thought you knew."

Ivy felt really bad. Poor Danny – her whole life seemed to involve deceiving the people she loved most in the world.

When she'd phoned Joseph in his new flat near the university, he'd been reluctant to turn down a free trip to such an exotic location.

"Love to go, Mum, but I need to get my lecture timetable sorted out first. I'm taking two new subjects this year, and I haven't even managed to get the books yet. Any chance you could wait a few weeks?"

Regretfully, Ivy gave him the same excuse she'd given Danny.

"Sorry – maybe you, Dad and I can go there together next year? Joseph sighed and Ivy felt terrible.

"You know that I love you, son, don't you?"

"Of course, Mum – and I love you too. Are you okay? You sound a bit on edge –"

"I'm fine," Ivy assured him, realising that she needed to keep her insecurities to herself. But it was difficult to hide the terror she felt when she thought of how her secret could ruin the lives of those she loved most. Every day was now critical since there was someone out there who could destroy them all.

* * *

There were no more mysterious phone calls before she left, and Ivy felt relieved as she sat in the back of the taxi taking her to the airport. She'd turned down Danny's offer of his company car and driver, reckoning that a taxi would be more anonymous. She'd also taken the precaution of wearing a short dark-haired wig, which Danny found highly amusing.

"Why on earth are you worried about anyone knowing where you're going?" he asked her. "I mean, the press know you've a brother in South Africa – what could be more reasonable than going to visit him?"

Ivy sighed. She could hardly tell him she was dodging a mystery caller who was possibly a blackmailer – or even worse, a murderer – and that she'd also lied to her *Bright Lights* producer. "I just like my privacy," she said firmly. "I'm in the public eye so much of the time, I just want to unwind without someone sticking a camera in my face."

Before she left, Ivy had primed Danny to tell any reporters who phoned that she was relaxing at a health spa. That would hopefully divert them from her real destination. Even if the gossip columns mentioned that she was at a spa, she'd covered herself with Colin too, since he'd know she'd never tell the newspapers that she was seeing a medical specialist.

In the taxi, Ivy finally began to relax, and fortunately the taxi driver wasn't particularly talkative. The taxi, too, had been ordered under a different name. Since taxi drivers and reporters were natural allies – taxi drivers often provided reporters with tip-offs about their celebrity passengers – she wasn't going to take any risks.

In the departure lounge, Ivy began to feel excited at last. The wig made her head feel very hot, but there was no way she was taking it off. She didn't bother using any of the executive lounges either – she'd always found them stuffy and overbearing. Instead, she was enjoying the rare anonymity of wandering around on her own, watching all the other travellers. No one was paying her the slightest attention.

At one of the shops in the departure lounge, she bought presents for Owen and his business partner Brian, whom she'd never met, but she assumed fudge and English cheeses would make an acceptable gift.

On the plane, Ivy settled herself in the comfortable business-class seat, and was relieved when no one took the seat beside her. She didn't want to have to make small talk for the entire journey. She intended reading, having a glass or two of wine with her evening meal, then sleeping for most of the eleven-and-a-half hour flight to Cape Town. On arrival, she'd take the one-hour flight to Port Elizabeth, where Owen would meet her and whisk her away to the lush grasslands of the Eastern Cape. And for the immediate future, she was going to put this anonymous person out of her mind altogether. As the plane took off, Ivy felt safe and cocooned from the mysterious caller at last.

Chapter 20

"Ivy, can I carry those for you?"

Ivy was returning from the local garden centre, weighed down by two large bags of compost that her mother had sent her to buy for her roses.

"Oh, hello Danny. Okay, thanks."

Handing the bags to Danny, who swung them over his shoulder effortlessly, Ivy fell into step beside him.

"How are you today?" Ivy asked.

"All the better for seeing you!" he said, laughing.

Suddenly, Ivy felt shy. When she'd been seeing Joe, she'd always regarded Danny as a pest. But now, she noted his muscular frame, and his golden hair just like Joe's. And, as she thought of Joe again, she felt crushed by guilt and sadness.

Immediately, Danny detected her change of mood. "Are you alright? You look sad all of a sudden. Come on – let's get a cup of coffee and you can tell me what's bothering you."

Steering her across the street to the local café, Danny deposited the bags of compost on the floor of one of the booths, and headed up to the counter. Looking back at Ivy, he called: "Black, no sugar, right?" and Ivy nodded. Danny really was attentive. He remembered even the tiniest detail about her, and right now, in her misery, any attention was balm to her soul.

As she sat in the booth, waiting for Danny's return, Ivy felt she should at least enquire about Joe, but she doubted she could get the words out. Anyway, that would make her an even worse hypocrite.

Returning with two coffees, Danny placed them on the table and sat down.

"Okay, tell me what's bothering you."

"Nothing – honestly."

"You missing Joe?"

Ivy's cheeks turned scarlet. "No – I mean, yes, I do miss him, like everyone else does –"

"Yeah, me too," said Danny. "In a way, I envy him. I'd give anything to get out of this village. When I finish school next year, I'm planning on going to London."

Ivy was surprised. "What about Rosa?" she asked. "Is she going with you?"

Danny shook his head vehemently. "You know Rosa means nothing to me. I mean, she's fun, but – you're the one I really want to be with."

"But –"

Danny looked at her earnestly. "Ivy, I love you – always have. We could leave town together when we've both finished school – I know you're planning on going to RADA. Just let me be the man in your life – please."

Ivy stumbled to her feet, almost overturning her untouched coffee. "Look, I like you a lot, but –"

Danny jumped to his feet too.

"Sorry – that was clumsy of me. I shouldn't keep hassling you."

Ivy bit her lip, sitting down again. "It's okay, it's just –"

"Maybe you think I'm too young, but I'm six months older than you – I'm seventeen now."

"No, it's not that –"

Ivy felt consumed by guilt. A few weeks earlier, she'd been running away with his older brother. Now the younger brother was offering her the same hope of escape.

Danny suddenly looked annoyed as he stared at her. "Maybe you'd rather wait for Joe? I'm sure he'll be back soon."

"No, of course not! I never fancied your brother!" she lied, hating the fact that she'd just denied her feelings for Joe while inadvertently giving Danny hope that she might change her mind. Everything she said lately seemed to trap her in more and more lies. "Look, Danny – let me think about all this. It's a lot to take in at once."

"Of course," said Danny, looking relieved since he hadn't been dismissed out of hand. "And as a token of how I feel about you, Ivy, I'm going to finish with Rosa anyway."

Ivy looked alarmed. "No, don't do that – I don't want to feel pressured into making some kind of decision. Besides, Rosa is mad about you – it's not fair to mess with people's feelings. Just leave things the way they are – please."

Danny shrugged his shoulders. "I'm not doing it to pressure you, honestly! But even if we never get together, I don't want to be with Rosa any more."

"But Rosa's much better suited to you than I am."

Danny grinned. "Let me be the judge of that!" Then his expression saddened. "I know Rosa will be upset, but it's not fair to keep on seeing her, since I could never love her the way I love you."

"Look, I –"

Her words tapered off, and Ivy felt embarrassed.

Danny looked disheartened. "Well, I'm not going to give up on you, and I think I can make you happy. Tell me what I can do to make you love me?"

Ivy felt terrible. Did she somehow owe Danny her love because she'd loved his brother, and hadn't been able to save him?

At last she found her voice again. "Look, I'm just not ready to go out with anyone right now. I need to work hard for my exams. Maybe later on . . ."

Danny nodded. There was still hope that Ivy might change her mind.

"Well, can we still see each other from time to time, for a coffee, maybe?"

"Of course!" said Ivy warmly. "I'd really like that."

Danny nodded. "Okay, I agree, but I'm not going to stop pursuing you."

Ivy said nothing. She felt bad about rejecting him, knowing that she was hurting yet another member of the Heartley family. But she couldn't manufacture feelings just to keep him happy. Anyway, if Danny did finish with Rosa, the poor girl would be feeling devastated, and it was insensitive of him to consider dating anyone else so soon.

Ivy bit her lip. On the other hand, she and Joe hadn't considered Danny's feelings – or her own parents' or the Heartleys' – when they'd planned their departure from Willow Haven, had they?

As they finished their coffees, Danny picked up the bags of compost and hoisted them over his shoulder again. Leaving the café, they walked in silence though the streets until they reached Ivy's door.

"Thanks," she said as she opened the front door, took the compost bags from him, and closed the door behind her.

"Who was that?" asked her mother suspiciously.

"Danny Heartley. He carried the compost home for me."

Her mother smiled. "That Danny Heartley is a nice boy," she said approvingly. "You could do a lot worse, you know."

Chapter 21

On arrival in Port Elizabeth airport, Ivy quickly headed for the toilets, relieved to be able to take off her wig at last. Her own hair was damp underneath, and she was longing for a shower. But she didn't dare risk washing it in the airport – anyway Owen would probably be waiting, and she didn't intend telling him why she'd felt the need to wear a wig.

She'd toyed with removing it in Cape Town airport while she queued in the heat to go through Passport Control, then waited for her flight to PE, but she'd still been fearful that someone on the same flight might notice the change in her. She knew she was being silly, but the mystery caller genuinely scared her.

As she exited the toilets, she saw her brother in the distance.

"Well, hello, kiddo!" said Owen, rushing towards her and sweeping her into a bear hug. "Why all the luggage? You'll need nothing but shorts and T-shirts while you're here!"

Ivy grinned. She'd been unsure of what to bring, so she'd brought the lot.

Looking at her brother, she could see that life here suited him well. His skin was deeply tanned, and he wore a khaki short-sleeved shirt, bearing the logo of the nature reserve, and shorts that showed off his equally tanned legs.

Ivy held a pale arm against his dark one. "Bit of a difference, eh?" she said, smiling.

"Don't worry – we'll soon get you nice and brown," he said, grinning as he carried her luggage out to his jeep.

"I'm not allowed to get tanned," said Ivy, laughing ruefully. "It would upset the storyline. I can't suddenly turn up with a tan when my character's been in hospital!"

Owen raised an eyebrow. "Can they really tell you what to do?"

Ivy laughed. "Yes, they can – I suppose that's why they pay me so much money!"

As Owen drove out of the small airport, Ivy sat back in her seat and enjoyed the sensation of the wind blowing through her hair. The weather was glorious, and she was determined to make the most of her time in South Africa. She knew that the country had once been cruelly divided by apartheid. Now that there was majority rule, she hoped things were improving for the previously impoverished population.

As she voiced her concerns, Owen gestured to one side of the road. At first Ivy thought she was looking at a rubbish dump, until she realised there were people living beneath the pieces of corrugated iron, wood and clothing that dotted the horizon for miles.

"That's a township," Owen explained. "Life hasn't improved for the majority of South Africans – millions of black and coloured folk still live like this, while the whites still control most of the wealth."

"Owen, surely the word 'coloured' is offensive?"

"Not here, it isn't," her brother explained, shaking his head sadly. "Everything in this country is still based on the colour of a person's skin." He laughed bitterly. "It's not called the Rainbow Nation for nothing!"

"But I thought that with self-government, things were getting better –"

Owen gave her a sarcastic look. "A new black political elite has developed, and many of them have got rich on the backs of their fellow countrymen and women. They've learnt well from their previous masters!"

Ivy was appalled at the conditions under which these people were living, yet she'd seen magnificent houses not half a mile away.

Seeing Ivy's worried expression, Owen smiled warmly at her. "Don't worry, sis – we'll visit some of the townships, so you can see everything for yourself – and the shebeens, too."

"Shebeens? Isn't that an Irish word?" Ivy asked, astonished.

Owen grinned. "Some Irishman must have set up the first illegal drinking house here a long time ago – it's what the pubs in townships are called. But I guarantee you'll have just as much fun there as in any Irish pub – and the prices are a lot cheaper!"

"But if we went to visit those poverty-stricken people, wouldn't it seem a bit like, well – like we were looking down on them?"

Owen smiled. "Not at all – people in the townships love to have visitors. Few white South Africans ever go there – they've convinced they'll be mugged or murdered if they do." Owen's face darkened and his hands gripped the steering wheel. "If *I'd* lived here during apartheid, I'd happily have bumped off many of the whites myself. But the people in the townships are unbelievably forgiving – I don't know how they can show such generosity of spirit to people who still treat them like shit."

"But there's equality now – isn't there?"

Owen shook his head vehemently. "Not while the whites and foreign investors still control most of the country's assets. You know, the die-hard whites still maintain that all non-whites are evil – I suppose they need to believe that, in order to justify what they did under apartheid."

Ivy shuddered. "It's such a soul-destroying viewpoint, isn't it?"

As they passed a beautiful church, Ivy turned her head to look at it.

Owen smiled. "That's a church for the whites – believe it or not, most of them are devout Christians."

Ivy looked astonished. "I didn't think Jesus was a supporter of apartheid!"

Owen chuckled. "Sometimes you have to see the funny side of it all, or you'd go mental. There are even racist dogs here – their white owners train them to bark only at blacks!"

By now, the city had given way to the countryside, and Ivy gazed in awe at the vast expanses of land on either side. The views were breathtaking and, despite her tiredness, she found herself savouring every moment of the journey.

Glancing at her, Owen asked if she was tired. Ivy nodded. She was longing to shower and change.

"We'll be at Siyak'atala in about an hour."

"Siyak – what does that name mean?"

"It means 'we do care' in the Xhosa language," Owen told her. "It seemed the perfect name to Brian and me, since we genuinely care about the people and animals here."

"Who are the Xhosa?"

"They're one of the many tribes that make up South Africa. The Xhosa people mainly inhabit the Eastern Cape, and their language is the one with all the clicks in it – I'm sure you've heard the famous click song, sung by the late Miriam Makeba?"

Ivy's eyes lit up. "Of course! Wow, I'm really looking forward to hearing the language in action."

Owen nodded. "There are eleven different official languages spoken here, but almost everyone speaks English as well."

They travelled the rest of the journey in silence, broken only by her brother pointing out the occasional giraffe, springbok or impala. Several times on the journey, kind-hearted Owen stopped the jeep and moved wandering tortoises from the centre of the road to safety.

At last the jeep turned off the main road, and Owen drove up a dirt road until they came to a clearing where the name 'Siyak'atala' was written above a large entrance gate. Just inside the gate were several buildings with an assortment of jeeps outside, and Owen explained that this was the starting point for their safari tours.

A little further on, they arrived at their destination – a magnificent sprawling African-style thatched-roof building.

"Let's get the hot water operating," Owen said, grinning. "I told Pumila, our housekeeper, you'd be ready for a soak as soon as you arrived!"

It suddenly dawned on Ivy that life so far from civilisation wouldn't have all modern conveniences on tap.

"How on earth do you provide power so far out in the wilderness?" she asked.

"Photovoltaic cells – we use the sun for all our energy."

"Well, you've certainly got plenty of that," said Ivy, smiling.

As she stepped down from the jeep, she felt a wonderful sense of liberation. Her old life was so far away and, although she was exhausted, she was filled with a sudden longing to dance, and absorb the rhythms of Africa.

At the entrance to the house, a smiling black man greeted her warmly, and Owen introduced him as Andile, the estate manager. Then Owen took her up the amazing expanse of wooden staircase, and showed her into her quarters.

"Brian and I have separate quarters in the house," he explained. "You'll meet him later, at dinner."

A small black woman emerged from Ivy's bathroom, where she'd been running her a bath. She explained how the plumbing worked then quickly made her exit.

Alone at last, Ivy stripped off and stepped into the bath, luxuriating in its relaxing warmth. When she eventually emerged, she felt restored to some semblance of humanity, and ready to enjoy the evening meal. Suddenly, she realised she was very hungry.

Downstairs, the sound of conversation directed her to the dining room, where she found Owen and another man sitting at the table. This was clearly her brother's business partner, and he instantly rose and grasped her hands in his. Ivy found herself gazing into a pair of startling blue eyes in a tanned, handsome face.

"Delighted to meet you, Ivy," he said warmly. "I'm Brian Davis. Owen's told me all about you."

Ivy was instantly struck by how attractive Brian was. He was at least six feet tall, and she liked the way his dark hair was lightly bleached by the sun. She suddenly felt shy in his presence, and overawed by his magnificently tanned arms and legs, which were clearly visible in his short-sleeved shirt and khaki shorts.

"We're honoured to have a TV star in our midst!" Brian added, but at the mention of her career, Ivy felt a sudden frisson of fear, since it reminded her of the mysterious caller. But she quickly dismissed it and returned Brian's greeting warmly. She was nothing if not a good actor!

Later, dinner was served by the cook, a friendly young black woman called Lumka. It was delicious, and Ivy ate everything on her plate. After Lumka said goodnight and went home, Brian, Owen and Ivy sat outside on the veranda, in the darkness except for an overhead lamp, and listened to the sounds of the countryside at night. As Ivy drank a post-prandial brandy, she was thrilled to see several bats swooping low, and Brian explained that the sounds in the distance were hyenas.

"Tomorrow, if you feel up to it, I'll take you on a game drive," Brian promised. He grinned at Owen. "Since your brother's on duty tomorrow, I'm the lucky one who gets to show you around."

Ivy nodded. The idea of spending time alone with Brian was a very pleasant one, and she hoped she'd have the energy to accompany him. But, right now, she was so tired she felt she'd sleep forever once her head hit the pillow.

Chapter 22

Ivy had been briefly tempted by Danny's declaration of love, because it would enable her to wallow in the comfort of someone's adoration. But it would be a one-sided relationship since she couldn't reciprocate Danny's feelings. Besides, Rosa Dalton was crazy about Danny, and Ivy knew that if she started going out with Danny, she'd make a formidable enemy in Rosa. Anyway, she was still grieving for his older brother, and it wouldn't be fair to Danny to embark on a relationship when her mind was still consumed with thoughts of Joe's body lying at the bottom of Harper's Lake.

She often had nightmares in which she tried in vain to pull him out of the car. She'd wake screaming for help, and her mother, father or brother would rush into her room and hold her while she shook violently from fear and sorrow. Other nights, she dreamt that she, too, was drowning in the lake, and she'd wake up gasping for air. Being unable to tell anyone why she was feeling so bad made her even more isolated, and that also made Danny's offer very tempting. Having someone to care for her was what Ivy craved right now.

One night, after a particularly vivid and frightening dream, Ivy's mother sat with her long after Owen and her father had returned to their bedrooms.

"Ivy, what's the matter?" her mother asked, as she cradled her

daughter in her arms. "Whatever it is, I'm sure I can help. There's nothing you can say that will shock me."

Ivy clung to her mother. There was no way she could ever tell her what the nightmares were about. In her wildest dreams, her mother couldn't imagine what was going on in her daughter's life.

"It's nothing, Mum – maybe something I ate?"

"You've eaten hardly anything lately," her mother retorted. "There's something bothering you, Ivy, and I wish you'd tell me what it is!"

Ivy gulped. "Well, to tell you the truth, Mum, I want to go to RADA so much and I'm afraid I mightn't get a place."

"Of course you will!" Ivy's mother said, relieved to think that this was all that was worrying her daughter. "You know you've got the talent – even your teachers at school are positive you'll get a place!"

Ivy felt bad about lying, but, if her mother believed her lie, it would ease her worries. Ivy didn't like causing her family problems, but there was nothing she could do about the nightmares. She longed for them to go away, but these nightmares were the price she had to pay for concealing Joe's death. She wondered if she should tell someone, even now, but at this stage her omission was all the more heinous.

Why had she ever decided to conceal Joe's death? Presumably the shock of what happened at the lake had momentarily atrophied her brain. If she'd been thinking straight, she'd have told the truth from the start. But she hadn't, and now her personal effects were in the car, and if it was ever pulled from the lake, she'd have some explaining to do. No, it was better to let sleeping dogs lie – in this case, it meant leaving poor Joe lying at the bottom of the lake.

Ivy sighed, snuggling into the warmth of her mother's embrace. "Do you really think I've got a chance?" she whispered.

"Yes, I do," said her mother firmly. "But you won't be able to act if you don't get a good night's sleep!"

Alone in the dark after her mother left, Ivy pondered on her future. Would she ever be able to get over what had happened? Or would it affect every performance she ever gave? When she stood on a stage or a film set, would she see Joe's face and forget her lines? Did she have a future as an actor at all? She envied her brother, who'd always known he wanted to be a vet. Owen was due to start at university that autumn, and he was already devouring every relevant book and watching every wildlife programme on TV.

Still unable to settle, Ivy climbed out of bed and tiptoed along the landing until she reached her brother's room. She tapped gently on the door so as not to re-awaken her parents and she heard him call: "Come in!"

Inside, she found Owen sitting in front of a pile of books on his desk.

"Don't you ever get tired of studying?" Ivy asked him, exasperated. "It's 3a.m.!"

"You're not the only one with a dream, kiddo – or in your case, a nightmare!" he said, grinning at his own unintentional wit.

Ivy smiled, curling up on her brother's bed. She liked it when he called her 'kiddo'.

"Why have you still got your head stuck in a book?" she persisted.

Owen cocked an eyebrow. "Didn't I hear you telling Mum you were studying all weekend?"

Ivy blushed as he stared at her.

"Of course, I don't believe for a minute that you're studying," her brother added. "I know you too well for that. These nightmares of yours, Ivy – is there anything wrong? If you've got a problem, you know you can talk to me – I won't tell the parents, if that's what you're worried about."

"There's nothing to tell," Ivy lied. "I am studying – I'm worried in case I don't get a place at RADA."

Owen was immediately contrite. "Poor old kiddo! But you've another whole year of school – you've plenty of time to prepare."

Ivy shrugged her shoulders, but her brother's kindness made her feel guilty. In fact, she felt guilty about everything lately, and she was tired of it.

Quickly changing the subject, Ivy hoped to distract her brother from any further scrutiny. "So why are you studying, Owen?

You've already got your place at university and you know you'll fly through your exams, so you don't need to worry."

Her brother's face lit up with enthusiasm. "I want to be a vet more than anything in the world, so I'm trying to read as much as I can about my subjects before I start. Yes, I'll sail through the A levels, but there's so much to learn about veterinary practice – I want to be ahead of the game if I possibly can."

Ivy nodded. It was clear that he was as passionate about his future as she was about hers.

"Are you going to look after people's pets when you graduate?"

Ivy's only experience of vets was at the local animal clinic, where they'd taken their beloved old cat to be put to sleep.

Owen shook his head. "I'm hoping to work with large animals."

"Do you mean cattle?"

"No, I want to work with lions, elephants, hippos and rhinos. Ideally, I want to work in a nature reserve, helping to protect endangered species."

Ivy nodded. It seemed a very ambitious dream, and while she hoped it would happen for him, she feared he'd end up compromising like most people had to do. Her own life had already been compromised . . .

She hopped off the bed and padded towards the door. "'Night, Owen."

"Night, kiddo – call me if you've any more nightmares. That's what big brothers are for, you know – to scare off the demons and the monsters."

Smiling, Ivy left and walked back to her own room. It felt good to have someone looking out for her. Even if she could never tell him the truth.

Chapter 23

The following morning, Ivy awoke to knocking at her door. When she called out, Pumila appeared with a breakfast tray, which she placed on Ivy's bedside table, and immediately began running her a bath.

"Stop – you'll have me totally spoilt!" Ivy told the woman, laughing. "It's so kind of you, but I really should be up by now."

Pumila smiled. "We've all been told to spoil you, miss."

"My name's Ivy – please, I hate formality."

"Okay, miss –" Pumila gave an infectious chuckle, "– I mean, Ivy."

When Pumila left, Ivy ate a leisurely breakfast before stepping into her bath. I could get used to this kind of life, she murmured. Then the thought struck her that this was how the whites had lived under apartheid, with servants to take care of their every need. Except that their staff wouldn't have been paid properly or treated like human beings. According to Owen, most non-white South Africans still worked for a pittance, assuming they were lucky enough to find a job.

Downstairs, Brian was waiting for her, and Ivy realised that it was almost noon.

"Oh, dear – have I kept you waiting?" she asked him anxiously.

"Not at all," he said, smiling. "You're on holiday, so you're entitled to stay in bed as long as you wish. For today, we'll just take a leisurely afternoon drive, but if you're prepared to get up early one morning – say five o'clock – then you'll see some really amazing wildlife."

Ivy nodded. She was very excited. She abhorred zoos and circuses that used animals, and was glad that her brother and his partner were instrumental in enabling so many creatures to live out their lives in their natural environment.

Down at the entrance gate, Brian selected one of the jeeps and they both climbed in. A group of German tourists were being taken out in another jeep, and Ivy also heard the sounds of Yorkshire accents as she and Brian were driving away. She was relieved to be leaving the base, since it had only just occurred to her that there could be tourists here who might recognise her. On the other hand, she was probably being paranoid – who'd expect to find her in South Africa? Anyway, her sun hat was covering her face, and right now she didn't look anything like the tempestuous Isabella.

As they drove across the vast grasslands, Ivy felt a wonderful sense of freedom. She was beginning to understand why her brother had chosen to come here.

"This view is breathtaking," she said. "I'm really looking forward to seeing the animals in their natural habitat."

Brian nodded. "It's the best way to appreciate them. Our safari tours help us to get the message across that wildlife is important to us all, and that we, as humans, have no right to exploit animals for our own vanity or financial gain."

He gestured out across the plains. "Of course, it would be better to leave the animals alone and undisturbed, but the tours make the money we need to maintain the land and the veterinary hospital, and it allows us to train and employ local people."

On their journey, Ivy saw giraffes, impalas, hartebeests, leopards, elephants, rhinos and warthogs. She also spotted several species of small monkeys, and was captivated by the magnificent plumage of the many birds she saw and the amazing diversity of wildlife all around.

To her surprise, a few hours later, Brian stopped the jeep,

climbed out and produced a picnic basket, a bottle of wine and two glasses from the boot.

Noting Ivy's surprised expression, he grinned as he helped her down from the jeep.

"This is a South African custom," he said, pouring her a glass of wine. "At this time of evening, we have 'sundowners'. Night comes quickly here – in half an hour it'll be completely dark."

What a lovely idea, Ivy thought, happily sipping her wine and eating the cheese, biscuits and *biltong*, a type of dried meat, that Brian had brought. Together they rested against the jeep and watched the sun slip beneath the horizon and the landscape gradually grow darker.

"It's like being the only people in the world out here," she said, gazing around her as the light began to fade. She felt totally at peace. "It must feel wonderful to know that you're responsible for successfully maintaining all this."

Brian nodded. "Owen and I see it as a duty," he said. "Animals are essential for humans' own future, so we're actually helping humanity by looking after them. The planet won't survive without diversity. Animals and humans need each other." He sipped his wine. "Neither Owen nor I approve of private ownership of vast tracts of land, but currently it's the only way we can ensure that the wildlife here is protected."

Ivy looked surprised. "Who are you protecting it from?"

Brian shrugged his shoulders. "From governments and individuals who want to offer canned hunting holidays, to people who'll kill animals for their skins, ivory and rhino horn. It all comes down to money in the end."

"But isn't there legislation that prevents trade in endangered species?"

Brian gave her a sarcastic look. "There's always a market for this stuff if you're unscrupulous enough."

"What's canned hunting?" Ivy asked.

Brian grimaced. "It's hunting where the animal is reared to be killed, and has no chance of escape, usually because they've been drugged – so that brain-dead idiots can think they're heroes by shooting a poor defenceless animal."

Ivy shivered. "My god – how could anyone do that?"

Brian shrugged his shoulders again. Her rhetorical question needed no answer.

As they continued to sit in companionable silence, Ivy followed his gaze across the vast horizon, as darkness rapidly descended. Even in the dark, Ivy could see that Brian looked sad.

"There's so much poverty, corruption and incompetence here, there's a danger that what really matters could be lost," he said. "Successive generations of whites from other countries have exploited Africa's gold, titanium and animals so that people in the so-called developed world can have the latest fashionable luxuries. People here see what's available in the western world and, not surprisingly, they want the same for themselves."

Ivy nodded, appalled at the thoughtlessness and greed of her world, and guilty for her own part in it. At least she didn't wear fur, leather or silk, and didn't eat veal, fois gras or buy products tested on animals. But she was well aware that there were many products still using animal ingredients, and medicines that involved testing on animals too. It was difficult for the ordinary person to be vigilant about everything they bought.

"There are lots of ways to benefit from animals without killing them," Brian went on. "Indigenous peoples all over the world have always lived this way, treasuring what they had, using it selectively and never destroying it all for the sake of a quick, short-lived return – like what's in danger of happening now." He gestured out across the vast plains. "These animals can actually support local communities. As long as we have them, people will want to visit, and they'll want to take home souvenirs of their trip. Owen and I have helped to set up several local souvenir-making cooperatives, which bring in money for impoverished communities." He looked at her earnestly. "Some day, Owen and I want to see this land returned to its indigenous people. But that will only happen when we can ensure its status as a nature reserve for future generations. In the meantime, Owen and I accept that we're just caretakers – in fact, we're all caretakers of this planet, and we have a duty to pass it on in as good a condition as we can."

Collecting the wineglasses, he smiled whimsically at her. "Lecture over," he said as he placed them in the back of the jeep. "Come on, it's time to head back."

As they climbed back into the jeep, their hands accidentally touched and Ivy glanced shyly at him. He really was incredibly attractive, especially when all fired up with enthusiasm for South Africa, its wildlife and its indigenous people. His passion was infectious, and Ivy found herself liking him more and more.

"Now that it's dark, different kinds of animals will appear," he said, "and you'll notice different sounds. Look, there's a rock monitor –"

Ivy gazed in astonishment at the giant lizard-like creature that was now visible in the jeep's headlights, as Brian turned on the engine.

"My God, it's nearly as big as a crocodile!" she said. "Do they bite?"

Brian shook his head. "No, they defend themselves by swishing their tails. You wouldn't want to get a whack – it can be very painful!"

"What a magnificent creature," Ivy said, as the monitor waddled away out of the jeep's headlights and disappeared into the undergrowth.

As they drove along, Ivy listened in awe to the sounds of assorted insects as they chirped and twittered in the darkness, and she gasped in joyful astonishment as a group of fireflies passed in front of the jeep.

As she continued to enjoy Brian's company, Ivy began to wonder if he was more than Owen's business partner. The two men seemed warm and affectionate towards each other, and Ivy wondered if they could be a couple. Thinking back, she'd never consciously remembered Owen being involved with a woman. Even at school, he'd always had his head stuck in a book.

Ivy darted a surreptitious glance at Brian. If he was gay, what a waste of a gorgeous man, she thought, then smiled, thinking that another gay man wouldn't be thinking that way!

Back at the house, Brian helped Ivy down from the jeep, and

thanking him she returned to her room. There she found a note from Pumila, saying that there was hot water if she needed another bath. Delighted, Ivy filled the bath and sank down into its soothing depths. She was also looking forward to dinner – exploring the vast lands of the Eastern Cape had given her quite an appetite!

Chapter 24

Rosa Dalton sat in her bedroom, staring at the walls but seeing nothing. She couldn't believe it. No, it couldn't be true! Danny, her beloved Danny, had just dumped her!

Tears ran down her cheeks, but she did nothing to wipe them away. Nothing mattered any more. Maybe she could cry herself to death, then Danny would be sorry for what he'd done. His life would be ruined and he'd spend the rest of his days mourning for her. Already, she could picture him alone in the cemetery, weeping over her grave, and regretting the ill-fated moment when he'd made his mistake. He'd beg her forgiveness, but of course by then it would be far too late . . .

Oh, how she hated Ivy Morton! The horrible minx had put a spell on Danny, and he couldn't see that he and Rosa were meant to be together.

What about all the times she and Danny had spent by the lakeside, making love? She'd done everything she could to make Danny happy – she'd made a career out of satisfying him, but it obviously wasn't enough. What did that Morton girl have, that made Danny want her more? She couldn't bear the thought of sitting in the same classroom as Ivy, and knowing that when school was over, she'd be the one Danny was waiting for. Everyone would know she'd been dumped, and they'd be feeling sorry for her. Oh, the humiliation! She simply couldn't bear it.

Rosa stood up and opened her wardrobe. She intended packing her rucksack and leaving the village immediately. She wasn't going to stay in Willow Haven a minute longer, and she'd never set foot in it again.

Throwing her clothes onto the floor, Rosa stuffed a random selection into her rucksack. She didn't really care what she was taking, because she was never going to be happy again.

As though picking at a scab, Rosa kept going over what had happened with Danny. He'd arrived, as arranged, at their special spot down by the lake after school, but he hadn't taken her in his arms as he usually did. Instead, he stood in front of her, looking ill at ease.

"Look, Rosa – I'm sorry, but I – look, there's no easy way to say this, but I don't want to go out with you any more."

"What?" Rosa shrieked. "But I thought you cared about me! After all we've shared!"

Danny looked embarrassed. "Look, I'm fond of you, but it was only a bit of fun between you and me. It's not as though we were serious –"

"But I was serious!" Rosa screamed. "You mean everything to me! I thought we were going to be together forever!"

Danny looked sad and awkward, but said nothing.

Rosa suddenly froze. "It's that Ivy Morton, isn't it?"

Danny bit his lip, then slowly nodded.

"You bastard!"

Rosa beat on his chest with her fists until Danny grabbed her wrists.

"Please, we've no control over who we love –"

"But I love you! I've no control over that, have I?"

"Honestly – you'll meet someone else before long," Danny pleaded. "Half the boys in the school would give anything to go out with you."

"But I don't want anyone else!" Rosa shouted, tears running down her face. "I hate you, Danny Heartley, I hate you!"

Running all the way home, she had rushed into the house and straight upstairs to her room. A shocked Hannah had seen her daughter's tear-stained face, and had begged her to explain what was wrong.

"Everything!" was all Rosa would say, before slamming her bedroom door behind her.

Hannah went upstairs and knocked on Rosa's bedroom door. "What's wrong, love?" she asked gently. "How about a nice cup of tea?"

She could hear Rosa sobbing inside. "Come on, pet – nothing could be that bad. Come and tell me what's the matter," Hannah coaxed. "Maybe I can help."

"No one can help me!" Rosa shouted. "Go away!"

Hannah retreated downstairs, puzzled. Rosa was usually such a sunny, good-natured girl. Maybe teenage hormones were making her behaviour unpredictable. Young people had a tendency to make mountains out of molehills, so hopefully what was bothering Rosa would soon blow over.

A little while later, a red-eyed Rosa came downstairs, carrying her rucksack. Hannah thought she looked a lot calmer now, and there was a determined jut to her chin.

"I'm leaving Willow Haven, Mamma," she said. "For good."

Hannah's jaw dropped open. She was so shocked that she was unable to say anything.

"Rosa – don't be ridiculous!" she said at last. "Whatever's happened, we can sort it out. Just come and sit down for a minute."

Rosa shook her head. "Danny's dumped me, Mamma, and I'll never be happy again," she said, starting to cry again.

Hannah didn't dare embrace her, because she knew Rosa would angrily resist any attempt to comfort her. Instead, she said "I'm sorry, love, I know how much he meant to you, but there are other fish in the sea. Just you wait and see – the boys will be queuing up to ask you out!"

Rosa glared at her mother. "That's what Danny said too. But I don't want anyone else. He's the only one I've ever wanted."

Hannah desperately wished she could find the right words to soothe her daughter's broken heart.

"Look, you'll get over him eventually. In a few months' time, you'll wonder what you ever saw in him –"

"No, I won't – I'll always love him!"

Hannah sighed. "Look, I know that young love can be very painful, and you think you'll never love anyone again, but –"

"I won't!"

Rosa was crying again. "I couldn't go back to school – they'll all be laughing at me. And I'll have to watch Danny swooning over that bitch Ivy Morton!"

"Well, maybe we could get you a place at the school in Allcott?" said Hannah, now very concerned. "It's important to finish your education. Then you can be anything you want."

"I don't want to be anything except Danny's wife!" Rosa screamed. "And now I'm not going to be that. I've had enough, Mamma – I'm never setting foot in Willow Haven again. I hate this place, and everyone in it!"

"But without an education, you'll never get anywhere! Please don't make a hasty decision – come on, let's sit down and discuss it over a cuppa."

Rosa glowered at her mother. "I'm going to London, and you can't stop me!"

"Stop this nonsense at once!" Hannah said angrily. "You're only seventeen – you can't go gallivanting round a big city on your own! Where will you stay? It's out of the question."

"I'm going, one way or another, so you might as well let me go with good grace," Rosa said angrily. "I'll get a good job in London, just you wait and see. And I'll never have to see that spineless scumbag Danny Heartley again!" She looked at her watch. "I'm catching the six fifteen train, so I'd better get going," she added gruffly.

"Please, love – don't do this!" Hannah begged her. "You'll feel different when you've calmed down. Please!"

Rosa picked up her rucksack and put it on her back. "I'll write, Mamma – I promise. You'll be proud of me some day, but right now, I can't stay here."

"Oh love, don't let Danny Heartley do this to you!" Hannah begged her.

Rosa didn't reply, but Hannah recognised that look of determination on her daughter's face, and knew there was nothing she could say that would change her mind.

"*And what'll you do for money?*"

Rosa shrugged her shoulders, and Hannah longed to throw her arms around her daughter and protect her from the big bad world outside. She had visions of Rosa ending up in a homeless people's shelter or, worse still, sleeping rough in a doorway.

"*Please, love, just wait till tomorrow. Things won't look so bad then.*"

Rosa shook her head, and Hannah knew her daughter wasn't going to change her mind.

"*Well then, hang on a minute – let me give you what cash I have . . .*"

Hannah rushed to her handbag, relieved that she'd been to the bank earlier that day. She'd taken out the money to buy a new television set, but right now Rosa's needs were far more urgent.

"*Here –*" *she said, thrusting the collection of notes into Rosa's hand.* "*Hopefully that'll keep you going for a while. And please let me know if you need any more.*"

"*Thanks, Mamma – I will,*" *Rosa promised, a lump in her throat as the two women embraced,* "*and I'll write soon – I promise.*"

"*Look, take this as well –*" *Hannah said, taking off the gold chain and pendant she always wore around her neck.* "*This was your grandmother's – it's worth quite a bit of money, so if you run into any problems –*"

"*I'd never sell it, Mamma,*" *said Rosa adamantly, slipping it around her neck.* "*But I'll wear it when I go for interviews – maybe it'll bring me luck.*"

"*Won't you please change your mind and stay?*" *Hannah asked, desperately hoping for a miracle.* "*You'll be able to get better jobs if you finish your education.*"

Rosa simply shook her head.

"*Well, give me another hug before you go,*" *Hannah begged, her eyes now filled with tears as they embraced. An hour ago, life had been simple and straightforward. Now, she was losing the only child she had. How could life change so drastically in such a short space of time? She groped for a handkerchief to wipe her eyes and, when she looked again, Rosa was gone.*

Opening the front door, Hannah watched the receding figure of her beloved daughter heading in the direction of the railway station. She wiped her eyes and hoped Rosa would soon come to her senses. When she discovered how difficult it was to survive in a big city, hopefully she'd be on the next train home again.

Chapter 25

As she came down early for dinner, Ivy found her brother sitting outside on the *stoep*, drinking a glass of wine. As she joined him, he poured her a glass too, and Ivy enthusiastically regaled him with her experiences that afternoon.

"We saw elephants, hartebeests, wildebeests, rhinos, impalas, guinea fowl – oh, so many animals that I can't even remember all their names!" she told him happily.

Owen smiled, pleased that his sister had enjoyed her first day in South Africa. He'd been scrutinising her since she'd arrived, and he was glad to see that the strain in her face had already lessened. No doubt her job was very exacting, because she'd definitely looked in need of a holiday when she arrived.

"I know you and Brian have offered to show me around – but I don't want to be a nuisance and keep you from your work."

"No problem, kiddo – we've adjusted the workload so that we can both spend time with you. Andile and his team are well able to run the place when Brian or I aren't here."

Ivy was aware that Owen and Brian had met while both were working on a bear-conservation project in Canada many years earlier. She and Danny had visited her brother in Canada, but Brian had been on holiday while they were there, so they'd never actually met him.

"Why did you two decide to move to South Africa?" she asked.

"When we knew the Canadian project was coming to an end, we started looking for another venture," Owen explained. "Brian had visited South Africa when apartheid ended, and had seen the possibilities. This was a new country, emerging from colonialism and racial segregation, and we felt that its wildlife, in particular, needed protecting during those transition years. We figured we could help both animals and local communities, and I truly believe we're doing that."

Ivy nodded.

"Neither Brian nor I could afford to undertake such a huge project on our own," Owen added, "so we pooled our resources, begged and borrowed the rest. When Siyak'atala came on the market, we knew it was exactly what we wanted. Of course, it wasn't called that back then – we changed the name to reflect what we're trying to achieve."

"Brian is a really nice guy," Ivy said enthusiastically. "He explained what you're trying to do here, and I think both of you are incredible. Oh, and we also had 'sundowners'!"

Owen grinned, raising his glass. "Yes, that's one of the few white traditions that I'm happy to adopt!"

"You and Brian seem very happy together," Ivy said, fishing.

Owen nodded. "We are. When we're working, I don't even need to mention something out loud – Brian already knows what it is and has probably taken care of it."

"Sounds like you're both telepathic."

Owen nodded again. "I couldn't find a better partner anywhere."

"When did you two actually, er, get together?"

For a moment, Owen looked puzzled. Then his face broke into a big grin. "You think –" He began to guffaw. "Oh my God, you think that Brian and I are an item!"

Ivy turned red. She'd clearly made a cardinal error.

"Oh Lord, this is hilarious! Wait till I tell Brian –"

"Don't you dare!" said Ivy, her face red from embarrassment.

The amused expression left Owen's face when he saw how upset his sister was.

"Okay, okay – I just thought it was really funny. Of course, you haven't met Charmaine yet."

Ivy felt her heart sink. A few seconds ago, although embarrassed, she'd been relieved to discover her brother and Brian weren't an item, although she couldn't logically say why. Was it because Brian was so heartbreakingly gorgeous? But she was a married woman, so she had no right to be having such thoughts anyway. Maybe she was suffering from sunstroke. And now there was Charmaine, Brian's partner, and Ivy was experiencing a lot of conflicting emotions. It must be the heat, she told herself.

"Charmaine is also our veterinary nurse, and she'll be joining us for dinner this evening."

Ivy smiled. No doubt Charmaine was as beautiful as Brian was gorgeous. Oh well, she'd make every effort to look good this evening – she wasn't going to let Charmaine hog the limelight. And she'd need to get a grip – she was only here for a holiday, not to develop feelings for her brother's business partner. Anyway, Charmaine's presence would keep her on the straight and narrow!

Owen patted Ivy's shoulder, but he was still smirking and shaking his head in amusement as he left the *stoep* to get another bottle of wine. Clearly, he found the whole incident terribly funny, and Ivy hoped he'd keep his promise not to tell Brian what she'd said . . .

* * *

Having hurried back up to her room, Ivy studied the items of clothing in her wardrobe, and was glad she'd brought far more than she needed, because now she had plenty of choice. Since Charmaine was joining them for dinner, she'd decided to change from her casual attire into something more spectacular. Would she wear the turquoise off-the-shoulder top with tight jeans? Or what about the orange sleeveless T-shirt with her white harem pants? Looking at her pale skin, Ivy wished she'd been able to get a tan – no doubt Charmaine would be a glorious mahogany. Finally, she settled on a one-piece jumpsuit in flowing green chiffon, and felt pleased as she surveyed herself in the mirror. Watch out, Charmaine, she thought, then felt mean and petty at wanting to score over Brian's partner.

Hadn't she a husband of her own, who adored her? Perhaps she was too used to the limelight back home and didn't like being upstaged by anyone else. Nevertheless, she was here as a guest, and owed it to her hosts to behave with decorum.

Downstairs in the dining room, Andile, Pumila and several others sat around the table. And at the end, beside Brian, was a very pretty blonde white woman whom Ivy assumed was Charmaine. Owen introduced Ivy to anyone she hadn't already met and, despite her initial reservations about Charmaine, she found her a friendly, bubbly woman. Although she'd snared the handsome Brian, Ivy couldn't help liking her.

Lumka, the cook, joined them at the table after she and Owen had brought in all the food that had been prepared in the kitchen. Bowls of salads, rice and vegetables were passed along the table, enabling people to help themselves. The food was delicious, and Ivy gestured her enjoyment to Lumka, who smiled back happily. Everyone was now tucking in, and the wine flowed as Owen opened several bottles and passed them along. At one point during the meal, Owen called for a toast to his "baby sister" and everyone raised their glasses in her direction. Ivy was surprised to find herself suddenly shy at receiving such attention, even though she appeared before several million people every week on TV.

After the meal, everyone retired to the *stoep* outside. The night was pleasantly warm. I could get used to this, Ivy thought. Back home, autumn was well under way, and a tough winter was forecast to follow. The thought of it made her shiver, and Brian was suddenly by her side, placing a rug around her shoulders.

"Here, Ivy – this'll keep you warm."

"Thanks, Brian, but I'm not really cold – I was actually thinking of the weather back home. It's starting to get chilly at this time of year."

Brian nodded. "I remember it well – and I'm grateful to be here. Can I get you a brandy?"

Ivy nodded, noting that Charmaine had disappeared. As Brian went to the drinks cabinet, she gazed out across the darkness of the grasslands, enjoying the sounds of the night and listening to the hum of the others' conversation. She felt lulled into a state of contentment, and was thoroughly relaxed when something made her sit bolt upright – she'd just seen Owen and Charmaine, outside in the dark, kissing!

Ivy looked around, hoping that neither Brian nor the others had noticed. Everyone was still talking and joking, and fortunately Brian was busy pouring her brandy into a balloon glass. Ivy felt very upset on his behalf, and made a mental note to tackle Owen as soon as possible. Surely her brother wasn't cuckolding his partner? How ironic, she thought. Not long ago, she hadn't wanted Brian to have a partner; now she was angry that his partner was cheating on him!

Smiling, Brian returned with two brandies and sat down beside her again. Thanking him, Ivy anxiously scanned the darkness outside, but there was no longer any sign of either Owen or Charmaine. Just at that moment, the two of them re-appeared on the *stoep* – holding hands! Ivy's jaw dropped until it dawned on her that perhaps she'd made another wrong assumption . . .

As they approached, Owen slipped an arm around Charmaine. "This wonderful woman has just agreed to marry me, so we're going to Johannesburg next week to buy the ring!" he told them, his voice filled with joy.

Happily, Ivy embraced them both, inwardly sighing with relief. Thank goodness she hadn't been offhand with Charmaine, since she would soon become her sister-in-law!

"Congratulations!" said Ivy, smiling at them both. "It's wonderful news – Mum and Dad will be thrilled!"

Everyone was now milling around, offering congratulations and making joking remarks.

Ivy pulled her brother aside. "You sneaky old devil!" she whispered. "You never told me you were seeing anyone! How long have you and Charmaine been dating?"

Owen grinned. "Not that long, really – just a few months. But I knew straight away that she was the woman for me."

He looked over at his fiancée, who was still being hugged and congratulated.

"And luckily, she seems to feel the same way."

Gradually people began leaving to go back to their own homes, and Ivy was struck, yet again, by how early everything closed down in South Africa. Perhaps the rapidly descending darkness was a factor. Although it was only around nine o'clock, Owen and Charmaine excused themselves and left, leaving just Ivy and Brian sitting alone on the veranda. Nevertheless, she felt so relaxed that no conversation was necessary, and she closed her eyes and began to drift off into a pleasant reverie . . .

Suddenly, the phone rang in the distance and, excusing himself, Brian went off to answer it. Within minutes, he was back, looking puzzled.

"There's someone on the phone for you, Ivy –"

Guiltily Ivy rose to her feet. It was probably Danny. Other than letting him know she'd arrived safely, she hadn't bothered ringing him since.

Hurrying to the phone, Ivy picked it up, expecting to hear her husband's voice. Instead, the voice she heard shocked her to the core.

"I can find you anywhere," it whispered menacingly. "Just stay away from the lake!"

Then the line went dead.

In an instant, Ivy's relaxed mood had evaporated. Since she'd arrived in South Africa, she'd forgotten all about her problems. Now, she was shaking like a leaf, although she did her best to hide it. Nevertheless, she didn't fool Brian.

"You're very jumpy," he said, a look of concern on his face.

"I'm fine," she replied brightly. Then she stretched exaggeratedly. "If you don't mind, I think I'll head off to bed – I'm exhausted."

Brian looked disappointed. "But you haven't finished your drink –"

"I'll take it with me," Ivy said, smiling as she deftly grabbed the glass and turned on her heel. She desperately wanted to be alone with her fears, because she didn't want Brian to see how frightened she was.

"Then goodnight, Ivy."

"Goodnight, Brian."

Ivy knew Brian would be watching her as she climbed the central staircase, so when she reached the top, she turned and gave him a cheery final wave.

Alone in her room, Ivy turned the key in the door, her heart thudding painfully. She'd never felt the need to lock the door before, but now she was terrified. How could the caller know where she was? She'd travelled 6,000 miles, yet still they'd managed to trace her.

Chapter 26

"Hello, Danny."

"Oh – hello, Ivy."

Danny appeared deep in thought as he walked along the main street of the village, and he'd almost collided with Ivy as she made her way in the opposite direction.

Ivy felt awkward speaking to him, but right now she had a problem, and there was only one way she could hope to make it right.

"Are you okay? You look a bit preoccupied –"

"No, I'm fine, honestly." He gave her a quick smile. *"But Dad's been giving me grief over breaking up with Rosa – Hannah is his customer and friend, and he's furious that I've made things awkward between them. I must admit it was a bit of a shock – I never expected Rosa to react so badly . . ."*

Rosa's departure from the village the day before had the girls' school buzzing with the news. Somehow, word had got out that Hannah's daughter was so devastated by Danny's rejection that she'd packed her bags and left on the train to London.

"That behaviour's a bit extreme," Ivy's mother Eleanor said worriedly when she'd heard the news. *"I know being rejected can be devastating, especially when it's your first love, but people usually manage to get over it and move on. I hope Rosa will be all*

right. I mean, London isn't all glamour, you know –" She'd looked pointedly at Ivy. *"I hope you'd never be such an idiot – you need an education before going places like that. Cities can be dangerous places for unwary young girls . . ."*

Ivy assured her mother that she'd no intention of leaving Willow Haven for London until she'd secured a place at RADA. Thankfully, her mother had no idea she'd already tried to escape from the village – and failed.

Danny interrupted her thoughts again. *"Are you alright? You look a bit preoccupied yourself."*

"I'm fine thanks – really," Ivy replied, a blush returning colour to her cheeks.

"That's better!" said Danny, smiling. *"I suppose you're going to miss Rosa too,"* he said kindly. *"She was a lot of fun, wasn't she?"* He sighed. *"I just wish I could have felt about her the way I feel about you –"*

Ivy took a deep breath. If she didn't say it now, she'd lose courage.

"Danny – I've been thinking about what you said."

Danny looked at her, shy and uncertain. *"What do you mean?"*

"Well, I've always really liked you, and now that Rosa's gone away – well, I mean, if you still want me to, I'd be happy to go out with you."

Ivy's last words were drowned out as Danny began whooping joyfully.

"Oh Ivy, you've made my day – I mean, you've made my life! I swear you'll never regret it –"

Suddenly, she was in his arms and he was spinning her around, and they were both laughing.

When he put her down on the ground again, Danny looked earnestly into Ivy's eyes. *"I'll never stop loving you. I fell for you a long time ago."*

Ivy smiled mischievously. *"It can't have been that long ago – you're only seventeen!"*

"I fell for you in junior school!" Danny told her solemnly. *"There's never been anyone else for me – I was getting up the*

courage to ask you out when I got cornered into asking Rosa. Anyway, you were always hanging out with Joe, so it wasn't easy to get close enough to ask you!"

Ivy's face coloured. "That was because Joe and I were both keen on History and Science," she lied.

Danny kissed her lightly. "At one stage, I was worried in case you fancied Joe, and I was terribly jealous of him."

Ivy's heart was pounding, but she gave him a convincing smile. "Never! I've already told you – I liked your brother – I like all your family – but I never fancied Joe, not even for a minute."

She experienced a pang of guilt at denying her feelings for Joe, and felt equally guilty for deceiving Danny. But there was too much at stake to tell the truth.

"I'm so glad to hear that," said Danny, holding her tightly, and Ivy felt sick inside as she returned his embrace. How easy it was to fool poor Danny.

"I adore you, Ivy – so you better get used to it!"

Hugging her new boyfriend, Ivy should have felt happy. But all she felt was fear.

Now, she was embarking on yet another deception. Her period was a month late, and she knew without a shadow of doubt that she was pregnant. With Joe's baby.

She'd briefly considered an abortion, but decided against it. She didn't have the money, and even if she had, it would mean travelling alone to a clinic in a city she didn't know. She'd thought of telling Owen, but what could her brother do? She didn't dare tell her parents because they'd want to know who the father was, and she could hardly tell them he was lying dead at the bottom of Harper's Lake.

Ivy sighed. Anyway, this baby was a part of Joe, the man she'd loved, and was all she had left of him. It would be wrong to destroy a life that had been conceived in love. By delivering this baby, she'd also be giving something back to Joe's parents. While she couldn't give them their beloved eldest son, at least she'd be giving them a grandchild to replace him – even though they'd believe it was Danny's. Ivy sighed. Yes, this was the best way. Now, she needed to have sex with Danny as soon as possible, and in eight months' time, she'd deliver an 'early' baby.

"I love you, Ivy Morton!" said Danny, swinging her in the air again.

"Put me down, you great oaf!" she laughed, disguising the fact that she couldn't say 'I love you' back to him.

Not yet, anyway. Maybe someday she'd feel that way, because Danny was the most decent boy she'd ever met, and the most deserving of someone's love. But for now, he'd be content with making love to her.

"There's one thing I want you to promise me," Ivy said as he put her down on the ground again.

"Of course – anything you want in the whole world!"

"You said you were leaving Willow Haven after your exams – I hope you still mean that."

Danny looked surprised. "Of course! I've already told you I have big plans – and they don't involve working for my dad!"

"Well, I'm just saying. Things change, people change, and your father is a very persuasive man. I want your word that we're going to get out of here."

"Of course – you know I want to be my own boss."

As he kissed her again, Ivy knew what she had to do next.

"Oh Danny, let's go somewhere private," she whispered.

Danny grinned happily. "I know a great spot, down beside the lake."

Ivy smiled to cover the dart of pain she felt. She knew that spot – she'd often gone there with Joe. Now she and Danny would be making love within feet of where Joe lay trapped in the car beneath the lake's murky waters. Would she ever escape from the agony of Harper's Lake?

"Let's go, then," she said, smiling up at him and taking his hand.

Chapter 27

Since she'd paced the floor for much of the night, Ivy slept late the following morning. She was unable to eat the breakfast Pumila had kindly brought to her room, and she didn't go downstairs until lunchtime. Brian was in the kitchen and offered to take her on another game drive, and Ivy was happy to agree, reasoning that her mystery caller could hardly pursue her across the wilds of the Eastern Cape. Besides, she enjoyed Brian's company, and Owen and Charmaine were on duty at the animal clinic all day.

Making a special effort to forget about the previous evening's phone call, Ivy turned her attention to the wonders of nature all around her. By now, she was becoming more adept at spotting the different animals, and recognising the habitats where they were likely to live. She was thrilled when they came close to a family of warthogs out foraging, the babies staying close to their mother's side and eyeing the jeep warily. A few miles further on, they spotted two rare black rhinos. Ivy was also intrigued by the vast numbers of termite hills, many of them eight feet or more in height.

"The termites design their towers to cope with fluctuations in temperature and the changing direction of the sun," Brian told her. "Inside, there're lots of chambers, and the top is left open like a chimney, to keep the interior cool."

Ivy smiled. "And we dare to think that humans are the most intelligent animals!"

Brian smiled back. "Certainly, termites could teach us a lot about architecture!"

The mention of architecture suddenly reminded her of Joe's dream career and the life they'd planned together, and her good spirits suddenly evaporated. Even here, thousands of miles away from Harper's Lake, she was still affected by what had happened there twenty years ago. Would she ever escape the lake's siren call?

As they drove along, they could suddenly hear a series of loud anguished roars, and Brian brought the jeep to a halt.

"That doesn't sound good. Stay here, Ivy," he warned, alighting from the jeep.

He disappeared into the trees, in the direction of the noise, then returned a few minutes later, a grim expression on his face.

"It's an old bull elephant – he's badly wounded, so please stay in the jeep."

"W-what are you going to do?"

"The only thing I *can* do – put him out of his misery."

Brian went to the rear of the jeep, and Ivy watched as he took out what looked like a high-powered rifle.

"Can't anything be done for him – I mean, to make him better?"

Brian shook his head. "He's old, and the hyenas are quick to spot any weakness. They've already injured him badly, and he could wander around in pain for days, but they'll get him in the end. It's better to let him die with dignity."

Ivy watched as he strode back into the trees once again, feeling an overwhelming sense of hopelessness. The death of such a majestic creature seemed so tragic. Her heart thudded painfully as she waited for the sound of the bullet and, when she eventually heard it, she felt bereft.

After several minutes, Brian appeared from among the trees and traversed the grassland to the jeep. He replaced his gun in the back, and climbed into the driver's seat. For a few moments they both sat in silence, then suddenly it all proved too much for Ivy, and the tears began to run down her cheeks. She clenched her teeth together in an attempt to stop her jaw from trembling, but a wail escaped from her throat, and finally she gave in to her emotions. Leaning towards her, Brian took her in his arms, letting her cry against his shoulder until she felt she'd no more tears left.

Leaning against him, Ivy wished she could stay in the comfort and protection of his arms forever, but eventually she sat up, her eyes red, and looked earnestly at Brian.

"C-can I see him?"

"Sure."

Climbing out of the jeep, Ivy felt her knees almost buckle beneath her. But Brian was there to steady her. Gripping his hand tightly, Ivy walked with him through the trees to where the magnificent creature now lay motionless. She hadn't been able to bear the thought of seeing him in pain but, now, reaching out, Ivy touched his tough and wrinkled grey skin. It was still warm, and she desperately wished she could will him back to life. She'd never felt so powerless in this cycle of life and death as she did now. But at least he was at peace.

"W-what will happen to him?"

"The scavengers will be here by nightfall, and gradually they'll devour him. But he's beyond pain, and that's the way nature does its work. Within a week, there'll be nothing left but the bones."

Ivy shuddered. In one way, nature seemed so cruel, but in another way it was the ultimate conservationist. Nothing was ever wasted. The vultures, jackals, hyenas and other assorted creatures would dine well that night.

They drove back to Siyak'atala in silence, Ivy subdued by the tragedy she'd witnessed. She was also feeling embarrassed about her outbreak of crying, and guilty about the large wet patch that her tears had left on Brian's shirt.

"I'm sorry about your shirt."

Brian smiled. "Don't give it another thought – it'll be dry in no time. You've been through a lot today, Ivy – that wasn't a situation we'd want any tourist to see."

Ivy felt stung. She didn't want to be thought of as a tourist! Yet, in essence, that was what she was. She wasn't hardened to the necessity of taking life when it couldn't otherwise be saved, and she could only admire the people who had the moral gumption to do it when the need arose.

Back in Siyak'atala, Ivy was relieved that no one else was around. She didn't feel like talking to anyone, and was thankful that after finishing their shift at the animal hospital, Owen and Charmaine had gone into Port Elizabeth for supplies, and were stopping off to visit friends on their way back. Lumka had the day off, so Brian made them both a sandwich in the kitchen, which they then ate silently at the large kitchen table. Then he led her out to the *stoep*, where he poured them each a large brandy. Already, the light was fading, and Ivy shuddered as she thought of all the creatures that were probably now feeding on the old elephant's carcass.

Brian sat down beside her. "Poor Joe – you're never going to forget him, are you, Ivy?" he said softly.

Ivy blanched. "W-what did you say?"

Brian looked directly at her. "I said, you'll never forget poor Joe. We're linked forever to those whose deaths we've been part of. Don't you agree, Ivy?"

Ivy's heart was doing a somersault at the mention of the man who'd been her first love. How could Brian possibly know about him? Suddenly, her mind was filled with pictures of Joe in his watery grave, his hair weaving in the water, terror in his eyes as he fought in vain to escape the murky depths of Harper's Lake. And for a frightening split second, Ivy wondered if Brian could be a hired assassin, sent by the mystery caller to finish her off? Then common sense intervened – he was her brother's business partner, for heaven's sake! She was just tired and emotional and unable to think straight.

"H-how do you know about Joe?" she whispered.

Brian looked surprised. "The same way *you* do! Oh, didn't I tell you? We've given names to all the elephants – that old elephant I had to shoot was called Joe. Everyone at Siyak'atala will be very sad to hear what happened to him."

Ivy's heartbeat returned to normal, or as normal as it could be, given that she'd just thought she was about to be terminated herself!

Suddenly, she realised that Brian was looking closely at her. "Why did you look so shocked when I mentioned the name Joe?"

Momentarily, Ivy looked stricken, but quickly recovered. "Oh, nothing. I'm probably still a bit emotional because of what happened."

Brian looked at her searchingly. "No – there was something else, Ivy. I felt emotional myself – no vet likes to see an animal die. But you looked really stunned – maybe even frightened – when I mentioned his name. Does the name Joe have some special meaning for you?"

Ivy struggled to find a suitable answer. "Er, that's my son's name."

"Any time you've spoken about your son, you've always called him 'Joseph', not Joe," Brian said patiently. "And that phone call yesterday had you terrified, although you tried not to show it. Come on, Ivy – tell me what's really going on."

Ivy looked down at her feet, because she didn't dare look at Brian's kind face. She knew he'd be looking worried, his brow furrowed with concern. Perhaps it was the large brandy he'd given her, but she was suddenly overcome by the most tremendous urge to unburden herself. Instinct told her that he would keep any secrets she shared with him, and she knew that Owen trusted him implicitly.

Slowly, she nodded. "It's a long story – but you don't really want to know."

He reached out and grasped her hand, his blue eyes staring intently into hers. "Oh, but I do. I can see that something is making you very unhappy."

For a while, Ivy said nothing, and Brian didn't try to hurry her.

"I think someone's planning to blackmail me – or maybe even kill me," she finally blurted out, still looking down at the floor. Her guilt wouldn't allow her to look at him yet. "The phone call last night was from the person who's called me before – I'm sure of it. But I never thought they'd manage to find me here."

Brian looked shocked. "Ivy, this is serious – have you told the police?"

She looked up at last, and despite her determination not to cry, fresh tears were filling her eyes. "The trouble is – I'm guilty. I did something terrible when I was a teenager – well, not intentionally. I thought I'd got away with it, but the hurt I've done to other people never ends – and now, I think someone is trying to get revenge."

Ivy began weeping, and silently Brian took her into his arms.

Chapter 28

Danny Heartley whistled happily to himself as he walked home, having shared a last lingering kiss with Ivy on her doorstep. They'd just made love down by Harper's Lake, and it had been every bit as magical as he'd hoped it would be. Ivy Morton was his at last! He could hardly believe his luck – he'd loved her for so long, and now they were finally a couple.

He was also relieved that Rosa wouldn't be in Ivy's class at school any longer – she'd probably have caused a scene, and he knew how much Ivy would hate that. Rosa could be volatile and unpredictable – he knew all about that too! On the other hand, maybe he should feel grateful to Rosa, because going out with her had probably helped to focus Ivy's interest on him, and enabled him to win her round at last.

As he walked along there was a spring in his step, and he felt as though he was walking on air. It was amazing how one person could do this to him! Now he knew that all the songs written about love were true – it was a wonderful feeling. He felt a momentary pang of guilt about Rosa – he'd never expected her to be so upset. But Rosa was in the past, and a glorious future with Ivy lay ahead.

As he walked home, he thought of Ivy's pretty face, her cute freckled nose and glorious long blonde hair. He also loved her quiet determination – and her sex appeal, of course. Ivy Morton was something special.

Danny grinned. Now he had every reason to study hard this year. He could get top marks when he put his mind to it, and that was what he now intended to do. And when they finished school, he and Ivy would leave Willow Haven together. He hoped Ivy would get the place at RADA that she was longing for – if not, he'd have to earn enough money from his day job to pay for acting classes, since acting was what she wanted to do more than anything. He'd attend night classes in marketing and retail management because, unlike his brother Joe, he genuinely loved working in his father's shop. But he intended surpassing his father's ambitions – owning a village grocery store might have been enough for Fred Heartley, but he intended owning a chain of supermarkets one day. He'd learned a lot in his father's store, and he'd take with him the ideas that worked, and discard those that didn't. His supermarkets would be different from those already in existence, offering new kinds of produce allied to top-quality service.

In fact, he was bursting with ideas, and all because Ivy Morton was his! He felt as though a cracker had gone off inside his head, spilling out all sorts of plans and possibilities. He suddenly felt able to take on the whole world and win.

Back at the store, even his father's sour expression couldn't dampen Danny's happiness.

"What has you grinning from ear to ear?" Fred Heartley asked grudgingly. "You look like a cat that's got the cream!"

"Even better, Dad, even better," Danny said cheerfully. "Now, let me help you with those potato sacks – you shouldn't be lifting such heavy weights at your age."

"Listen here, young man, I'm not helpless, you know!"

Danny grinned. "I know, Dad – but there's no need to do it when I'm here."

His father looked at him crossly. "You're late for your shift."

Danny gave him a look of mock outrage. "Dad – that's not fair! I'm only ten minutes late! You know I always do my fair share in the shop – and I do the stocktaking on Saturdays and a full shift on Sundays."

Fred nodded "Yes, I know. You're a good lad, Danny, a good lad. I only wish –"

As his father gazed into the distance, Danny knew he was thinking of Joe.

"I miss him too, Dad," he said softly. "And I don't think you need to worry about him – I'll bet he's off in Australia right now, living it up!"

"That's all very well," Fred said softly, "but I just wish he'd let us know."

As Danny went upstairs to the family's living quarters, his joy at being Ivy's boyfriend was briefly tempered by sadness for his brother. He missed Joe too, and he wished his father wouldn't keep clinging to hope, since he was certain Joe wasn't coming back.

Chapter 29

Aided by several more brandies, Ivy told Brian everything as they sat on the *stoep* together. It was a huge relief to share it all with someone at last. Brian didn't appear shocked, and asked pertinent questions throughout Ivy's narrative. Then he held her again, and she lay quietly in his strong comforting arms.

Ivy felt overwhelmed with relief. He hadn't seemed appalled by her duplicity. Instead, he'd assured her that she'd only done what any scared teenager might have done.

"You've punished yourself enough," Brian said gently. "You have to start forgiving yourself. You're a different person now – you were only a child when it happened. Today, the adult 'you' would make a different choice."

"But my actions have hurt so many people!" Ivy whispered, her tears starting to flow again.

Brian sighed. "We all hurt others, often without meaning to. Anyway, I think you've probably hurt yourself as much as anyone else." He looked at her sternly. "But this mysterious caller is clearly a murderer. You must go to the police – you could be risking your life if you don't."

Ivy grimaced. "I can't, at least not yet. My possessions are still at the bottom of the lake, and I need to get them back first."

Brian's blue eyes flashed angrily. "It's too dangerous – you could end up the third body in that car! Maybe telling the police would be enough to scare this person off – you mightn't need to tell them about your own involvement."

"Sorry – I can't take that risk."

Brian looked at her earnestly. "Don't you think you should tell Owen? You know he loves you, and would never judge you."

Ivy nodded. "He's the best brother anyone could have, but he's just got engaged, and I don't want to spoil his happiness."

Ivy suddenly hoped Brian wouldn't think she'd burdened him simply because he didn't have a partner of his own. "I hope you don't think –"

Brian seemed to read her mind. "No, of course not – I'm honoured that you trusted me. But this is serious – you could be in real danger."

Ivy bowed her head. She felt drained by her confession, and guilty for involving Brian, since there was nothing he could do from such a distance. But it felt good to have someone on her side – she'd felt so alone for so long. Had she betrayed Danny and his family by sharing her concerns with Brian? She felt a stab of guilt at having confided in a relative stranger. But she was well aware that a wedge had been driven into her relationship with the Heartley family a long time ago. It had been lodged there the moment her deception began.

Brian stood up. "Come on – I'll walk you to your room. I think we've both had enough excitement for tonight."

But the excitement was far from over. As they stood outside Ivy's bedroom door, both felt overwhelmed by all that had happened. And both their emotions were raw and needy. Suddenly, a goodnight kiss turned into a promise of something more.

Ivy found herself desperately wanting this gorgeous man, who now knew more about her than any other person in the world. Brian knew what she'd done yet he didn't blame her. And he wanted her, too. It was a heady feeling that she hadn't experienced since the days when she and Joe made love in Johnson's barn. She felt cleansed by Brian's desire for her – surely she couldn't be a bad person if this wonderful man wanted her?

As he kissed her outside her bedroom door, his lips were warm and urgent, and she was filled with longing for him. Quickly she opened her bedroom door and drew him inside.

"I've wanted you since the moment I first saw you," Brian whispered, kissing her again, and she felt desire course through her. Everything in her longed to make love to him. Her entire body was aching for him. For the first time in her adult life, she could make love honestly, with a man who knew the truth about what she'd done.

But she couldn't. As she thought of Danny, all passion evaporated. She couldn't do it to him. Even though her husband was thousands of miles away and would never know, she still couldn't go through with it.

Still panting with desire, Ivy broke free from Brian's embrace.

"I'm sorry, but I can't – I really want to – but I just can't."

Brian groaned softly. "It's okay, I shouldn't have even – look, you're vulnerable right now, and I wouldn't want you to think I'd take advantage of you –"

"No, I want you, too!" she whispered, aware that she'd led him to believe she wanted it to happen, and she still did. But somehow clarity and common sense had prevailed. She was a married woman, and wasn't free to make love to another man, no matter how attractive he was. And Brian *was* attractive. She longed to run her hands through his sun-bleached wavy hair and kiss every inch of his tanned, handsome face. Part of her wanted him to take control of the situation so that she wouldn't have to bear any responsibility for what happened between them. Then she felt ashamed – he'd never force her to do anything she didn't want to.

As her pulse slowed down, Ivy gave him a tentative smile. "I'm sorry, I can't expect you to understand –"

"I do – and I'm sorry, too," he said sadly. "I'd no right to assume anything. I got carried away – you're quite a woman. What man wouldn't desire you?" He kissed her forehead. "Let's forget this ever happened. I want you, but you're out of bounds, and you have my word I'll never cross that line again." He smiled tenderly. "I hope we can still be friends?"

She nodded, slipping into his arms again. But this time their embrace was simply tender and affectionate. Then, placing another light kiss on her forehead, Brian slipped out of her room. Alone, Ivy touched her skin where he'd kissed her, and wished it could have been so much more.

* * *

There were no more phone calls for Ivy and, as the days went by, she began to relax again. Brian and Owen each took her out on early-morning game drives, which necessitated getting up at five, but which were worth it because of the range of animals she saw.

Even when alone with Brian, Ivy was deeply conscious that he never again mentioned that night, and they slipped back into a relaxed and companionable friendship. But Ivy always felt the pull of her attraction to him. Sometimes, she secretly hoped he felt the same, but then she felt mean for wishing it, since it was unfair to Brian because she was a married woman and had no right to return his feelings.

Why on earth did she feel this way about him? She was well aware that being married was no guarantee that you wouldn't notice other attractive people. In the course of her career, she met them every day. But what she felt for Brian seemed deeper than any of the minor attractions she'd felt for other men throughout her life.

Perhaps it's just a holiday thing, Ivy concluded. I've been married to Danny for so long that any show of interest from another man would go to my head. Or perhaps it was simply the contrast between the two men. Danny was a businessman with a wardrobe full of expensive Saville Row suits, and he never went anywhere without a tie. In contrast, Brian was always dressed in shorts, and his tanned arms and legs would surely turn any woman's head.

Ivy spent a day at the veterinary hospital, and was astonished and humbled by the variety of Owen and Brian's work, and the speed and professionalism with which they, veterinary nurse Charmaine and their team got through their workload. Their patients that day included a crocodile, a pregnant giraffe and a rhino with a badly infected wound who'd been tranquillised in the wild and transported to the veterinary hospital by a team of rangers. Local people also brought in their animals, including a female dog for spaying and a goat with a wound that needed stitching.

"You're all amazing," Ivy said at the end of the day.

She'd watched as Owen and Brian performed operations, applied medication and reassured animals, always treating them with respect. They both nodded their thanks, smiling wearily as they stripped off their operating gowns and went to shower.

The next day, her brother took her to Port Elizabeth and showed her around the city. Ivy was fascinated and delighted to see the many Art Deco homes and buildings that comprised much of the city centre. Then Owen took her to visit the Red Location Museum, which detailed the local struggle against apartheid, and to lunch at a beach café in Summerstrand.

As they sat gazing out across the sea, Ivy watched seals cavorting in the bay. "This is such a beautiful country," she said. "I feel so lucky to be staying with you, and getting a chance to see the real South Africa."

Owen nodded. "If you'd stayed in hotels or guesthouses, you'd believe this country was entirely populated by whites. You'd never see a black face because they're the ones cleaning the toilets, washing dishes or peeling vegetables in the kitchens. Inequality here is still rife, and there seems little hope of change."

Ivy touched his hand. "I can see you're very angry, Owen. But apartheid is over – I find it hard to believe that the present government isn't trying to improve their own people's lives."

Her brother looked sad. "Then why has so little been done?"

Ivy said nothing. Since she'd arrived in South Africa, she'd been appalled at the extremes of wealth and poverty. And the wealthy seemed to feel no need to redress the inequality that existed. On the other hand, the people who suffered such poverty still maintained immense dignity and self-pride.

Back at Siyak'atala, there was only just time for a quick change of clothes before they all set out for the nearby township. First, they went to hear one of the many choirs rehearsing, then on to the

143

shebeen, where they drank, sang and danced the night away, in the company of some of the poorest of people in South Africa. Yet they had more fun than if they'd visited the most expensive nightspot. The shebeen consisted of nothing more than a few sheets of corrugated iron over brick walls, yet inside there was a well-equipped fridge for storing beers. As regulars, Owen, Brian and Charmaine knew everyone present, and Ivy was quickly introduced to them all. By the time she was leaving, she truly felt she was leaving friends.

Ivy found she didn't want to leave South Africa, but all too soon the day of her departure approached. After a quiet dinner on her last night, it seemed the most natural thing in the world for Owen and Charmaine to sit in one corner of the *stoep*, talking quietly to each other, while Ivy and Brian sat on the opposite side. No doubt, Ivy thought, they're drawing up plans for their wedding. And she was pleased to have an excuse to return to South Africa again the following year.

Ivy shivered at the thought of going back home. She desperately hoped that by the time she returned for Owen's wedding, the problem of the mystery caller would have resolved itself. Once she recovered her possessions from the lake, the caller would no longer have any hold over her.

She was still perturbed that this person had managed to locate her in South Africa – which had to mean it was someone she knew. She guessed her parents hadn't been able to resist telling everyone in Willow Haven about her trip to visit their son in South Africa, since they enjoyed trumpeting their children's achievements. A brief enquiry would easily have elicited Owen's location, and Google would have supplied the details of Siyak'atala and its phone number. Ivy couldn't really blame her parents for being proud of their children, except that in this case it could lead to her downfall.

"I wish you'd had time to see Cape Town and its surroundings," Brian said, interrupting her thoughts. "It's a beautiful city, and you can take the cable car to the top of Table Mountain, where the views are spectacular. If you're lucky, you might see some dassies too –"

"Dassies? What are they?"

Brian smiled. "They're cute little creatures – they're also called rock rabbits – and they're amazingly friendly."

Somehow, Ivy found herself holding his hand.

"You can drive out along the coast to Simon's Town, see the penguins at Boulder Beach, then travel on to baboon country at Cape Point," Brian continued enthusiastically. "That's where the Atlantic and the Indian oceans meet."

Ivy sighed. She'd have enjoyed making that trip with Brian, but she was a married woman and couldn't allow herself to reciprocate his feelings. Besides, when she returned for Owen's wedding, she'd have Danny and Joseph with her, and they'd be the ones accompanying her to Cape Town . . .

Suddenly, Brian looked serious. "I asked the staff to keep a log of every incoming phone call during your stay – and thankfully, your mystery caller hasn't tried to contact you again." He looked at her searchingly. "But please be careful – don't underestimate this person. And please don't risk your life by searching in the lake – your possessions have probably disintegrated by now. There may be nothing left to connect you to what happened."

Ivy smiled noncommittally. Her handbag had contained her passport and exam certificates – and they'd been sealed in a plastic folder, so she couldn't assume they'd been destroyed. Documents from the Titanic had survived intact, so why wouldn't hers?

Brian squeezed her hand. "I understand that you can't tell your husband about the past – but now, at least, you've got someone on your side who knows what you're going through."

His blue eyes searched her face.

"I'll always be there for you – if I can help in any way, or if you just want to talk, lift the phone and call me."

Suddenly, his eyes were sad, and Ivy was aware that there was so much left unsaid between them. Then he stood up, leaning down to kiss her cheek.

"Goodnight, Ivy, and goodbye," he said. Then he left the room without a backward glance.

As she watched his retreating figure, Ivy was still nodding, not trusting herself to speak.

* * *

The next morning, Ivy left Siyak'atala for Port Elizabeth airport in Owen's jeep. She didn't see Brian before she left, because he'd been called out at dawn to treat an injured buffalo. In a sense, she was glad not to see him, because they'd said all they needed to say the night before.

As Owen drove through the majestic landscape of the Eastern Cape, Ivy felt a deep sadness at leaving this beautiful country. South Africa had a way of getting inside you. She loved its sights and sounds – its pungent vegetation and red earth, the choirs and the shebeens, the warmth of the local Xhosa people. And of course, the majestic animals who roamed its plains.

In the airport, Owen hugged her before she boarded her plane for Cape Town, where she'd connect with her flight to London.

"It's been wonderful having you here, kiddo," he murmured. "I'm going to miss you terribly." He held her at arm's length. "And I know Brian's going to miss you, too. You two made a real connection, didn't you?"

Ivy felt so emotional she could only nod.

"Give my love to Mum and Dad," he said. "Do you think they might come out for the wedding next year? You'll come back too, won't you?"

Ivy nodded again. Now that she'd discovered the magic of South Africa, she wouldn't be able to stay away. She now fully understood why her brother had chosen to make his life there.

As her flight was called, Ivy and Owen exchanged a last quick hug, and she began walking out onto the tarmac. Waving back at her brother, her eyes filled with tears, Ivy vowed to use some of her own wealth to help the animals and indigenous people of the Eastern Cape. Poverty ruled so many lives there, and it was poverty unlike anything ever seen in the privileged world.

On board, Ivy settled herself in her seat, and waved to Owen who was still standing in the doorway of the airport departure lounge. Quickly she dabbed her eyes. It was a long time since she'd felt so emotional. All her life, she'd had to control her feelings in order to prevent herself from confessing her secret. Now, she'd confessed it all to Brian and she felt cleansed by his refusal to judge her.

And thankfully, she could now go back to Danny with an honest heart, knowing she hadn't been unfaithful to him. She'd been sorely tempted, but common sense had prevailed in the end.

Ivy wiped her eyes again as the plane taxied down the runway.

Chapter 30

In the weeks following Joe's departure, Fred Heartley realised he'd been far too hard on his eldest son. All he'd wanted was to knock all those silly notions out of the boy's head, and make him see that he could have a good life in the family business. Now, he regretfully accepted that it was his fault his son had left.

As time went by without any contact, Fred never gave up hope that Joe would return. He felt certain his son was down in London, or in some other big city, and when he tired of living the high life, he'd be glad to come home and settle back into a secure job at Heartley's Stores. Fred had long ago decided that he wouldn't even ask Joe where he'd been, or why he'd stayed away so long. He wouldn't even ask what had happened to his new Ford saloon. He'd just put his arms around his son and hug him. And if he didn't want to work in Heartley's Stores, then so be it. It no longer mattered to him how Joe earned a living, just as long as he was happy at it.

After the police had admitted defeat, Fred Heartley tried the Salvation Army tracing service and ultimately contacted the Mormons' world missing-persons database in Utah, but all to no avail. Joe had covered his tracks well, and Fred wondered for the umpteenth time why other fathers and sons managed to get along with each other, and work together in the family business. What had he done wrong to make that dream an impossibility? He'd only tried to do the best for his children.

Fred sighed. Joe's departure had affected his marriage too. Day after day, he now had to endure Julia's icy stares and snide comments. He knew she blamed him for what had happened. As each day went by without their eldest son, her feelings for him were turning colder and colder, yet he was powerless to remedy the situation. They'd become like two prisoners forced to share a cell and, as a result, they gave each other as wide a berth as possible.

Since he and Julia had to work in the shop together, the strain was almost unbearable. Julia carried out her duties in total silence, and any time he darted a glance at her, he'd find her staring back at him with accusing eyes. He could almost feel the venom emanating from her, and he carried his guilt around like a weight on his back.

By now, Julia had moved into the spare room, without even proffering an excuse. She'd simply moved all her personal possessions out of their bedroom one day, and he hadn't had the nerve to ask her why, because he already knew. She was punishing him for his role in Joe's departure, and he knew he'd spend the rest of his days sleeping alone in their great big double bed. Would either of them ever find peace again?

* * *

Fred was deep in thought behind his shop counter when Hannah Dalton approached the till with a basket of groceries. As she placed them on the counter, she had a big smile on her face.

"Oh, by the way, Fred – I got a letter from Rosa today! She's got a job in the offices of an airline, and she's moved into a flat with several other girls . . ."

Hannah was keen to let him know that, despite his youngest son's rejection of Rosa, her daughter was doing fine without him.

Fred felt a stab of pain in his heart. "I'm pleased for you, Hannah," he said, trying his best to put on a convincing smile. Hannah was lucky – he'd give anything to hear from his eldest boy.

Hannah hesitated. "Have you heard from Joe yet?"

Fred sighed. "No, Hannah, I'm afraid not. But I live in hope."

"Oh. Well, I'm sure you will, Fred, very soon."

"I hope so," said Fred, turning away. Suddenly, he couldn't bear to be in Hannah's company. He liked the woman, and he was pleased that her daughter was safe and well. But Hannah was no longer in the same boat as he was, and he felt more alone now than ever before.

Quickly, he rang up Hannah's items, took the money and packed them in her shopping bag in silence. He could barely muster up a perfunctory smile as she left the shop.

Chapter 31

Ivy felt displaced and disoriented when she arrived back in Heathrow airport. Shivering, she waited for her suitcases at the carousel, already feeling the drop in temperature. She dreaded the approaching winter, and all the standing around in the cold that would be required on the outdoor set of *Bright Lights*.

Danny was waiting for her in Arrivals, clearly delighted to see her. He talked about the two new branches of Betterbuys that had just been opened, about Joseph's sponsored walk for a charity, and Ivy was grateful for his ebullience, because she didn't feel like talking herself.

"You look tired," he said, a concerned expression on his face as he helped her into the company's chauffeured Daimler outside the terminal.

Ivy nodded. It had been an eventful trip in many ways.

"How is Owen?"

"Great – he's just got engaged."

Danny looked delighted. "Well, that's marvellous news! I'd given up on your brother in that department," he chuckled. "His fiancée must be quite a woman to prise him away from all those animals!"

Ivy nodded, smiling. "Charmaine is their veterinary nurse, so she loves the animals too."

Settling back in Danny's company car, Ivy noticed that he'd closed the glass partition between them and his driver. That in itself was unusual. Did Danny need privacy for some reason?

As if to confirm her suspicions, Danny reached for her hand and squeezed it gently.

"Oh, by the way – there were several weird phone calls for you while you were away. Each time I said you weren't available, the caller hung up and didn't leave a message."

Ivy tried to look nonchalant, but her heart was suddenly beating wildly. She longed to ask Danny for every detail about the calls, but instead she merely nodded. "Probably work-related," she said dismissively.

"No, I don't think so," Danny added, looking worried. "The person sounded, er, a little odd – they were whispering, like they were hoarse or something –"

"Well, maybe they were," Ivy said acerbically. "It was probably some deranged fan with a sore throat."

Celebrities were always getting peculiar calls, so she hoped Danny would accept that explanation. But even as she spoke sarcastically to him, Ivy felt there was more than a grain of truth in what she'd just said. Perhaps the caller was deranged enough to kill her, or hurt her in some way. Maybe it would be better if she intercepted the call next time and tried to find out what the caller wanted. Otherwise, she'd have to spend the rest of her days worrying in case this mysterious person suddenly decided to reveal her secret. If they wanted money, she'd pay them what they asked. But if they wanted something else . . . Ivy shivered and Danny slipped his arm around her.

"Are you sure you're not worried about the calls?" he asked quietly. "I have to admit I was a bit spooked by them myself. Because I haven't told you everything yet –"

Ivy held her breath, terrified of what was coming next.

"– the last time this person called, they said something about a lake. I couldn't really understand what they meant –"

"Was it a man or a woman?" Ivy said at last.

"Since they were whispering, I couldn't be sure – look, Ivy, do you think it might be worth mentioning these calls to the police? I'm not happy about weirdos ringing our home. I'll come with you to the local police station tomorrow morning –"

"Don't be ridiculous!" Ivy said angrily. "It's just some demented fan – if I ran to the police after every odd phone call, I'd look as daft as the callers themselves."

"But what did they mean about a lake?"

"How do I know – are you sure you heard him right?" Ivy said angrily. "They probably said 'cake' or 'hake', for God's sake!"

Danny looked worried. "But that still wouldn't make any sense –"

Giving an exaggerated yawn, Ivy laid her head on Danny's shoulder, and for the rest of the journey, she pretended to be asleep. But her mind was on full alert. The situation was even worse than she'd thought. If this person was willing to involve her own husband, they must be desperate, or else they were upping the ante in order to make her comply with their demands. Whatever they were.

Ivy shivered. Momentarily she thought of Brian, and how supportive he'd been. And her immediate instinct was to phone him as soon as she got home. But that wouldn't be fair to him. She'd be using him, and she respected him too much to do that.

Ivy shivered again. She longed to be back in the warmth and beauty of South Africa, but now she had to face reality again. The day after tomorrow, she was due back on the set of *Bright Lights*, and she needed to spend the time going through her script in readiness for her character's return from hospital.

And she still had to make another trip to the lake. She'd run away at the first sign of trouble, and now she was paying for her cowardly actions. She had no more weekdays free for ages, and if Colin called on her to fulfil her promise to work extra hours, she might find herself working around the clock, leaving no time at all for recovering her possessions.

At last the Daimler swept up the driveway to their house.

"Welcome home, darling – I've missed you so much," Danny whispered, hugging her as the driver stopped the car outside the front door.

As she stepped out, Ivy smiled to mask her feelings. Coming home no longer felt like a welcome. It felt more like a noose winding tightly around her neck.

Chapter 32

Fred sighed. Now, he and Julia had to face another blow – Danny had got young Ivy Morton pregnant. But he wasn't going to make another mistake and lose his second son. Although he loathed the embarrassment that young Ivy Morton's pregnancy was bringing on his family, outwardly he and Julia were behaving graciously and accepting their son's impending marriage, holding their heads high and letting people think they were delighted at becoming grandparents.

As far as Fred was concerned, if anything good came of this hasty marriage, it would be a miracle. But maybe, when Julia got over the shame of it all, a first grandchild might give her life a focus that had been missing since Joe left.

Fred wiped his brow. Danny a father at eighteen! It was ridiculously young, yet what could he do if his son couldn't keep his pants zipped up? Danny was besotted with young Ivy Morton – he'd been following her around for ages like a lovelorn puppy, despite having a girlfriend already. Ivy had led him a merry dance, and for a long time she hadn't seemed interested. But maybe that had been her way of making sure he really wanted her before she committed herself to him.

Fred felt a momentary wave of sympathy for Rosa Dalton. How humiliating it must have been for the poor girl, knowing all the while that Danny was besotted with someone else, and then to be dropped for no reason other than Danny's ongoing obsession with young Ivy. No wonder she'd left town – he could understand how impossible it would have been for her to stay.

After Danny had told them, thrilled and emotional, that he and Ivy Morton were expecting a baby, Fred decided to pay a visit to Rosa's mother. He felt bad at the way in which his son was crowing all over the village. The lad was still at school and didn't even have a job! It wouldn't surprise him to find that he and Julia were expected to help rear the child, but at least now Danny might settle down and eventually take over the running of the shop.

Rosa's mother hadn't been keen to speak to him when he'd called to her door. Nervously, her hand fluttered to her throat as she tried to finger the gold pendant she normally wore around her neck. But it was no longer there since she'd given it to Rosa.

"Really, Fred –"

"Look, I'm sorry about what's happened between Rosa and our Danny. We're neighbours, Hannah, so I don't want there to be any bad feelings between us."

"Well, I accept it's not your fault, Fred, but this wedding is really going to upset Rosa."

"I can well imagine. All round, my son has behaved like an immature pup."

Hannah began to mellow a little when it became clear that Fred didn't condone his son's behaviour. "I don't know how I'm going to tell Rosa – she was devastated when Danny dumped her. Now this news about Danny's wedding – I doubt if she'll ever come back to the village now." She bit her lip. "I miss her terribly, Fred, but at least she's doing well in London." She looked Fred in the eye. "I'm sorry about your eldest boy, Fred – I guess he wanted to get away too."

Fred sighed. "Kids can't wait to escape from a backwater like this," he said sadly. "They think the city can offer them excitement and wealth, but sometimes it just gobbles them up and spits them out when it's finished with them." He hesitated, and Hannah knew he was thinking of Joe. "What worries me most is that when things don't work out for them, their pride stops them coming home again."

Tears filled his eyes, and he angrily brushed them away.

"Well, thanks for calling, Fred," said Hannah, patting his arm. "It means a lot to me – to know that you understand how I feel."

"Thanks, Hannah – that's all I wanted to say."

* * *

Ivy's parents had been shocked to discover their daughter was pregnant. Her father had simply grimaced when told the news, but somehow his reaction had hurt the most. Ivy knew she'd disappointed him, and she desperately wanted to get a place at RADA so that she could fulfil his belief in her potential. Besides, she wanted it for herself too.

"Oh Ivy!" her mother had said sadly. "What about all your dreams of acting? You had so many plans for your future!"

"I'm still going to try for RADA – I'll have had the baby and be back on my feet by the time the auditions start."

"That's impossible," Eleanor said briskly. "You can hardly attend the interviews when you're eight and a half months pregnant!"

Ivy gulped. She'd forgotten that she was pretending to be a month later than she actually was. She knew she'd be able to attend the interviews, but no one else did.

"Sorry, Mum – I guess I got my dates mixed up. Well, I'm going to hope the baby arrives early, so that I can still go. I don't intend missing a day of school, and I'm going to keep up my dancing and singing lessons too."

Her mother was still tut-tutting. "And who's going to mind the baby? I hope you're not expecting your father and me to take on an extra child . . ."

"No, Mum – Danny and I are going to London as soon as we've finished school. Danny's going to get a job, and he'll be able to pay for a flat."

"And what if you do get a place at RADA? How on earth will you to able to look after a baby? And if you don't get a place, you'll need to get a job anyway –"

"Stop worrying, Mum. We'll get an au pair or a nanny, or we'll put the baby in a crèche. Danny and I will sort it out – it's not your problem."

Eleanor looked worried. "Oh dear, I'm not happy about any of this. Your father and I will need to have a talk with Fred and Julia . . ."

* * *

When the four parents met with Danny and Ivy to discuss their future, the young couple were adamant. Regardless of whether Ivy got a place at RADA, they were going to London after they'd both finished school.

"Well, in that event, you won't go penniless," Fred told them gruffly. "I've a few pounds put away, so Julia and I will see you sorted before you go."

"Thanks, Mr Heartley," Ivy said, hugging him.

"And since you're going to be my daughter-in-law, I think you'd better start calling me Fred," he said, his eyes twinkling.

"Okay, Mr – I mean, Fred," said Ivy, touched and embarrassed at the same time.

"Thanks, Dad," Danny said, his eyes shining. "We really appreciate it."

"We'll give them some money too, won't we, Peter?" Ivy's mother said, not wanting to be outdone in the generosity stakes.

"Of course!" Ivy's father replied quickly. "You can never have too much money in a place like London."

* * *

"I'm so thrilled!" said Peggy, leaping up from the Heartleys' kitchen table and throwing her arms around Ivy. "I'm going to be an auntie! Oh Ivy, you must be so excited!"

"Well, yes, I suppose so – it's such a big step, isn't it? Having a baby, I mean. We didn't really expect this to happen so soon. I mean, with both of us still being at school."

"Oh, I'm sure everything will work out alright. I've never seen Danny so happy – you've made all his dreams come true!"

"He's very special to me, too, Peggy. I'll do my very best to make your brother happy."

"You've done that already. When exactly is the wedding?"

"In about three weeks' time. It's going to be a very small affair

– but we're holding a party at the hotel afterwards – and I hope you'll be my bridesmaid."

Peggy jumped up and threw her arms around Ivy again. "Of course – oh thank you! I'll try to be the best bridesmaid in the world!"

As Ivy hugged her back, Peggy's face darkened. "Rosa will be devastated when she finds out you're pregnant. But you can't make someone love you, no matter what you do – and Danny's always wanted you."

Ivy grimaced, unsure of what to say. Rosa's sadness and departure from the town was an added blight on their future. Ivy feared she might always be known as the girl who stole Rosa Dalton's man.

Suddenly, Peggy brightened. "Anyway, since you're having a baby, you know all about sex! What's it like to do it?"

Ivy blushed. But at least they'd moved away from the more personal aspects of her situation.

"Oh, it's great, especially when you're in love," said Ivy, but she was thinking of Joe, rather than Danny. "It's a wonderful feeling to be as close as you can be to someone . . ."

Suddenly Peggy's expression was wistful. "I wish Joe could be here for the wedding. You and he were such good pals – I'm sure he'd want to wish you and Danny well. Do you think he might come back before then?"

Ivy felt sick. "I-I don't know – it would be great, wouldn't it?"

I'm a total hypocrite, she thought, loathing herself for the trite words she'd offered poor Peggy, who had no idea her brother was lying dead at the bottom of Harper's Lake. And I'm doubly a hypocrite, because I'm carrying Joe's baby, and passing it off as Danny's. But what else could she do? Her original deception had trapped her in a world of subterfuge from which there was now no escape. She was condemned to lie for the rest of her life, and to the people she loved most in the world. It felt like slow torture, but there was no other choice . . .

Chapter 33

With the two new branches of Betterbuys already doing well, Danny was keen to have a few days of rest and recreation.

"Let's go down to Willow Haven soon," he said enthusiastically, as Ivy arrived home after her first day back on the set of *Bright Lights*. "I'll settle for a weekend if you can't spare any more time."

Ivy bit her lip. She was terrified of returning to the village. That had to be where the mystery caller lived, and visiting there would surely put her in his or her line of fire. And with Danny in tow, there'd be no chance of recovering her possessions from the lake. On the other hand, Danny had been very understanding about her trip to South Africa, so she could hardly deny him a weekend with their families.

"Of course, love – I can manage a weekend. When do you want to go?"

"Well, the sooner the better, as far as I'm concerned. Why don't we go next weekend?"

Ivy nodded and tried to look cheerful. Since Colin hadn't asked her to work next weekend, she'd no excuse for not agreeing. "Great! Can you collect me from the studios on Friday evening – or would you prefer me to do the driving?"

Danny shook his head. "No, I'll collect *you*. I intend to cosset you this weekend, my lovely wife. You're looking very tired, so I want you to rest as much as you can." He looked at her closely. "I thought you'd be rested after South Africa, but you looked exhausted."

Ivy smiled back at him. "Having fun was hard work!"

Nevertheless, she was alarmed that Danny had noticed she was edgy, but thankfully he'd interpreted it as tiredness. "Anyway, there'll be no chance of resting in Willow Haven," she added. "It'll be the usual scrum when we get there – we'll spend all our time visiting people, and hoping not to offend those we haven't time to see!"

Danny shrugged his shoulders. "We don't have to see anyone we don't want to."

Ivy cocked an eyebrow. Their arrival was always a cause of excitement and gossip. They had found over the years that, although she and Danny gave generously of their time to the community, sometimes being so much in demand was just a pain in the neck.

Worst of all, the mystery caller would know she was back in Willow Haven. Being a celebrity made it impossible to visit without everyone in the village knowing. Of course, even if she wasn't a star, the village grapevine would soon spread the news anyway.

Danny squeezed her arm affectionately. "I'll get dinner ready, love – you go and put your feet up."

Ivy nodded gratefully, slipping off her shoes and padding into the drawing room, where she flopped down on one of the large sofas. This house was her domain, and she loved relaxing there in the evenings with Danny. Their home was an eclectic mix of antique furniture and fabrics of various textures and colours, most of them chosen by Ivy herself. She'd always felt safe there, protected from fans and the demands of work. But now, that feeling of safety had gone, since the caller had actually phoned her home while she was in South Africa, and had spoken to Danny. All it needed was for the caller to tell him what she'd done, and her marriage was over.

Ivy bit her lip. Although she'd insisted to Danny that the caller must be a deranged fan, few fans had ever managed to gain access to their private home phone number before. It was a closely guarded secret, known only to family, friends and people she worked with. Which seemed to point once again to the caller being someone she knew.

This person had also been clever enough not to risk ringing her mobile phone, since the caller ID might inform her who was phoning. On the other hand, they could simply buy a mobile for the sole purpose of contacting her, so the number would be useless in identifying them anyway.

Who on earth could it be? Ivy pictured all their friends and acquaintances in Willow Haven, but found it impossible to believe any of them would want to hurt her. Did that mean there was someone in the village who was an even better actor than she was?

Ivy racked her brains. Could the caller be someone she'd been at school with? Mentally, she ran through the names of all her classmates, and the pupils from the boys' school who had gathered at the lake during the spring and summer months. Like her, most had left the village long ago. But maybe someone had returned recently? She'd casually ask her mother if any old schoolmates were back. Perhaps one of them had seen her climbing out of the lake on the day Joe died, but hadn't realised its significance at the time. Later, if they'd discovered the car in the lake, they might have guessed at Ivy's involvement. If they'd now fallen on hard times – and saw how wealthy Ivy was – they might see benefit in blackmailing her.

Ivy sighed. But nobody had actually asked for money so far. And why would they have told her to stay away from the lake? Of course, they might be softening her up, terrorising her so much that when they finally made their demands, she'd give them anything they asked for . . .

The silence of the drawing room was pleasant after her hectic day on the *Bright Lights* set, and Ivy lay back and tried to enjoy it. She and Danny had always valued their privacy. Although they could afford a bevy of staff, they didn't like people in their home when they returned there after a busy day. So all the cleaning and gardening work was done in their absence, and a housekeeper kept the larder stocked and the washing done, and prepared their evening meal from a pre-arranged weekly menu before she went home. Then all they had to do was heat it up or do the minimum of cooking. All of which was designed to ensure that when they relaxed at home together, nothing and nobody was likely to disturb their peace.

Ivy shivered. But somebody already had. Nowhere was safe from this unknown person, since they'd found her in South Africa and even managed to breach the security of her home. With modern technology, this mystery caller seemed capable of finding her anywhere.

"Dinner's ready, love!"

Ivy smiled, feeling cherished as Danny called from the kitchen.

"Coming!" she called back, climbing up off the sofa and heading out towards the kitchen. But even as she plastered a bright smile across her face, fear gripped her insides like a vice, and threatened to engulf her again.

Chapter 34

Eagerly, Hannah Dalton looked at the letter the postman had just delivered. The envelope was typewritten and postmarked London, so she knew it was from Rosa. Her daughter's regular letters were always cheerful, filled with stories about the people she shared a flat with, and the people in her office, and already Hannah knew them all by name. She loved hearing all the details of her daughter's new life in the airline offices. Already, Rosa had been to several West End shows, and had previously regaled Hannah with amusing anecdotes about the performers and patrons.

At least Rosa was part way towards her dream – she'd always wanted to be a flight attendant, and maybe someday she'd succeed in making the transition from office to airplane. Hannah often wondered if Rosa met any pilots in the office, but she didn't dare ask. She hoped her daughter would eventually meet someone nice. Danny Heartley was a lovely fellow, but he was going to be married soon and, besides, there were plenty of other fish in the sea.

Hannah grimaced. Telling Rosa about Danny's forthcoming marriage to Ivy Morton had been the hardest letter she'd ever had to write. But Rosa's reply had been upbeat, and Hannah began to feel confident that Rosa was gradually getting over him.

Tearing open the envelope, Hannah pulled out the typewritten letter, thrilled to see Rosa's familiar swirling signature at the end of *it, followed by a dramatic row of kisses. Hannah imagined her daughter typing it surreptitiously in the office in between her allotted chores, or maybe even during her tea break. On the other hand, Rosa's boss sounded nice and kind, so he probably didn't mind her taking a few minutes of work-time to write to her mother.*

Reaching for her reading glasses, Hannah began to scan the page, hungry for every little detail of her daughter's new life. But suddenly her hand started shaking as she finished the first paragraph. It couldn't be true – could it? Her little girl had just been selected for training as a flight attendant! Rosa's dream was finally coming true – clearly, people in the airline had seen her potential. Hannah dabbed her eyes. Now, she didn't need to ask any embarrassing questions – Rosa would be meeting lots of pilots very soon!

* * *

As Fred swept the aisles of the store, Julia was silently stocking the shelves beneath the counter. Fred felt almost at breaking point, certain that soon other people must notice how coldly Julia was treating him. Indeed, she didn't treat the customers any better and Fred couldn't help wondering if her churlishness would drive customers away. He was already worried about the new store that had recently opened on the other side of the village . . .

Suddenly, the silence was broken as the shop door was flung open, and Hannah rushed in, her face wreathed in smiles. "I've just got a letter from Rosa, and she's been selected for training as a flight attendant! I knew she was never cut out for office work, and someone in the airline obviously realised that her personality was more suited to –"

Hannah stopped in mid-sentence, the words dying on her lips. She'd just seen the pain in Julia's eyes, and realised that her own joy was like a knife in Julia's heart.

Hannah's expression quickly changed. Silently she reached out and squeezed her old friend's hand.

"I'm sorry, Julia – that was thoughtless of me."

Brusquely, Julia pulled her hand back. "You've every right to be happy, Hannah – no point in us both being miserable."

Turning her back on Hannah and Fred, Julia began dragging boxes of stock to the back of the shop, and Hannah knew that she was only doing it to hide the fact that she was crying.

Fred and Hannah caught each other's eye, both startled and pained by Julia's admission of her misery. Hannah looked helplessly at Fred, all the joy gone out of her now. She desperately wished she'd curtailed her excitement, or at least had the good sense to express her joy to someone whose child wasn't still missing. But Peter and Eleanor Morton had been out when she called, and she'd been desperate to tell someone about Rosa's good fortune.

"Did you want anything, Hannah?" Fred asked pointedly.

"Er, no thanks. I'll –"

Quickly, Hannah hurried out of the shop. She was embarrassed and upset, knowing that Fred wanted rid of her so that he could attempt to console Julia in private. But she knew his efforts would be pointless, since Julia didn't seem to care if she lived or died these days. Hannah felt a spurt of anger – didn't Julia realise that Fred, Danny and Peggy were hurting too? But she reserved most of her anger for Joe Heartley – how could he put his parents through such torment? Couldn't he simply write or phone and let them know he was okay?

Hannah sighed. Young people could be so thoughtless. She felt blessed to have a daughter who kept in regular contact. Maybe that would change when Rosa was flying all over the world, but Hannah doubted it. Rosa could be volatile and attention-seeking, but she'd never put her mother through the agony that Joe Heartley was causing his parents.

Hannah also knew that her friendship with Julia had effectively been severed that day. Never again would they share confidences over a cup of coffee, or giggle together like schoolgirls about something they'd read in a magazine. Julia was lost, and Hannah felt powerless to help her. The only one who could save her was her eldest son.

Under her breath, Hannah whispered a silent prayer: "Oh Joe, please come back – we're all suffering because of what you've done."

Chapter 35

During their weekend in Willow Haven, Ivy and Danny fell into their usual pattern, whereby Danny slept in his old room at the Heartley home, and Ivy stayed with Eleanor and Peter. This enabled them to spend time with their own families, but they effectively lived between the two houses, taking breakfast in one house and dinner in another, so they were never apart for long.

Ivy enjoyed spending time with her parents and on this occasion they were keen to hear all about her trip to see Owen.

"We haven't seen you since you were in South Africa!" Eleanor said, making it sound like an accusation. "Now, come and sit down by the fire and tell us all about it!"

Peter nodded. "We couldn't believe it when you phoned to tell us Owen had got engaged."

"What's she like?" Eleanor asked, and Ivy assured her that Charmaine was a lovely woman and most definitely worthy of their precious son.

"I presume you're going to South Africa for the wedding?" Ivy asked, knowing that wild horses wouldn't hold her mother back now.

"Of course!" Eleanor replied, then she prodded her husband's girth with her index finger. "Of course, your father will have to lose a few pounds before we go. With that beer belly, he wouldn't be able to buckle his seat belt on the plane!"

"Well, who does the cooking around here?" Peter grumbled. "You'd be the first to complain if I didn't eat the meals you put in front of me!"

Ivy hid a smile as her parents bickered back and forth. Eventually they agreed that Eleanor would serve smaller portions and Peter would do his best to like salads.

"What's the South African countryside like?" Peter asked when the bickering had finally died down.

"It's magnificent!" Ivy told him fervently. "The earth is red, and the vegetation is amazing. You're going to love it!"

"And this fellow Owen's in business with – what's he like?"

Ivy could feel herself blushing. She was remembering the time she'd thought Brian and Owen might be a couple, until Brian's kisses had assured her they were not.

"Oh, he's very nice too," she said, as nonchalantly as she could manage. "In fact, all the people working at the nature reserve are great."

"I'm looking forward to seeing all the animals," her mother added.

"They're amazing!" Ivy told her enthusiastically. "It's an incredible experience to see them in their own habitat, the way nature intended them to be."

"And this apartheid business?" Peter asked. "Are the people really free now?"

Ivy grimaced. "Well, politically, apartheid is gone, but economic and social apartheid still exists for millions of people. But you'll see for yourself when you get there."

Momentarily, her father looked sad, then he brightened as he pointed to the mantelpiece where he'd placed the postcard Ivy had sent them from South Africa.

"This time, we got our own back on Hannah!" he said, chuckling. "We had a postcard of our own to stick under her nose!"

At the mention of their neighbour, Eleanor's face grew serious.

"You'll have to visit her while you're here, Ivy," she said, pursing her lips.

Ivy knew by her mother's tone of voice that she was issuing an edict, not a request.

"Of course, Mum – but you know I always make a point of dropping in."

Eleanor pursed her lips. "I'm not saying anything, but I don't think she's well."

Peter shrugged his shoulders to let his daughter know he didn't share Eleanor's scaremongering.

None the wiser, Ivy made a mental note to visit Hannah. Otherwise, she'd never hear the end of it.

"By the way, Mum," she asked, as casually as she could manage, "have any of my old school chums come back to live in the area lately?"

"No, not that I've heard. Why do you ask?"

Ivy shrugged her shoulders. "Oh, nothing. I just wondered, that's all."

Chapter 36

The wedding took place on a dull and blustery afternoon. Luckily, the wind died down while photographs were being taken in the church grounds after the ceremony. Danny had also brought along his camcorder, and Ivy watched as her new husband laughed and joked with friends and family as he filmed them in their finery. It was clear that he was enjoying the day immensely, and Ivy felt a mixture of relief and sorrow as she contemplated her future.

Eventually, the rain began to fall, and everyone hurried into the hotel. As people gathered in the foyer, Ivy darted a glance at her parents. She knew she'd disappointed them, and that this hurried ceremony wasn't what they'd had in mind for their only daughter. It wasn't something she'd envisaged for herself either. After she and Joe got together, she'd often daydreamed of marrying him, and in those daydreams the sun had always been shining, and all the guests had been smiling and wishing them a happy future together. Now, she was well aware that everyone present knew that this was a shotgun wedding. They just didn't know that the father of the child she was carrying was now at the bottom of Harper's Lake.

Ivy smiled as people approached her, offering their congratulations and telling her how wonderful she looked. She was well aware that the matrons of the village simply wanted to get close in order to check if her pregnancy was showing yet. But she wasn't showing, so she'd been able to wear a tight-fitting cream taffeta dress that fitted her like a glove. She knew she looked good, and Danny's adoring glances confirmed it. On the other hand, Ivy knew that Danny would view her favourably even if she was wearing a sack. She supposed it was an advantage to be marrying someone who was crazy about her, but as yet she could only feel gratitude towards him since he'd saved her from a worse fate. Hopefully, love would come later.

"Kiddo, are you okay?"

Ivy smiled as her brother touched her arm.

"Yes, I'm fine, Owen."

"You look gorgeous, by the way – I didn't get a chance to tell you at home, with Mum fussing so much!" he said. "Danny's a lucky man – if he doesn't treat you right, he'll have me to deal with!"

Ivy smiled, but inside her heart was beating uncomfortably fast. Dear Owen, she thought, if only he knew that I'm the one who's not playing fair. But I'll do my best to make Danny happy.

"You look sad," Owen said, looking closely at his sister. "Are you sure you're okay?"

"I'm fine – honestly. I'm just a bit tired after all the preparations for the wedding."

"I'm going to miss having you around – I never expected to be losing my sister so soon."

Ivy grimaced. "To tell you the truth, I wasn't expecting this to happen either."

Brother and sister shared a knowing look, and Owen shuffled his feet. "I wish you'd told me, kiddo – I'd have helped you. You didn't need to do this . . ."

"Yes, I did," she said softly. "Anyway, it'll all work out."

Her brother squeezed her hand. "Just because you're married now, it doesn't mean we can't still be close. You know I'll always be there for you, Ivy."

Ivy couldn't speak because of the lump in her throat.

"Thanks, Owen," she managed at last.

As Owen left, the guests began moving from the foyer into the *large conference room where the wedding reception would be held. As Ivy made her way across the foyer, she couldn't help wondering how the Heartleys were feeling. Only a short while ago, in this same room, they'd held that fateful eighteenth birthday party for Joe. And they must still be hoping he'd get back in time for the wedding reception.*

Ivy blinked back a tear. But if Joe was here, she thought, I'd be marrying him instead . . .

Just as she entered the conference room, Hannah Dalton approached her, and Ivy squirmed with embarrassment as the older woman hugged her. This day should have been Rosa's – Hannah's daughter should have been the one marrying Danny – but Hannah appeared to bear her no ill-will.

"You look lovely, Ivy," she said, genuine warmth in her voice. "I hope you and Danny will be very happy together."

As she hugged her back, Ivy suspected that the effort of attending the wedding was costing Hannah dearly.

As the guests took their places at the tables, Ivy glanced at Fred and Julia Heartley. They were doing their best to appear happy, but Ivy was well aware that they, like her own parents, were probably wondering if the marriage was a mistake from the outset.

The meal passed in a blur for Ivy, and she hardly tasted anything she was eating. Glancing over at Peggy, she saw that her new sister-in-law was also deep in thought. Ivy's heart went out to her since she knew exactly what Peggy was thinking. She was wishing Joe could be present at the wedding of her younger brother and her best friend. Some close friend I am, Ivy thought bitterly.

The meal was followed by speeches, a toast to the bride and groom, and a few bawdy jokes. Then Danny made his speech about Ivy making him the happiest man in the world, and gratefully, Ivy glanced at her new husband. He was undoubtedly the most elated person in the room. At least I've made one person happy today, Ivy thought. And I've saved Joe's baby. Maybe it will all work out in the end.

Chapter 37

Hannah Dalton smiled happily as she opened another of Rosa's letters. She was so proud of her high-flying daughter! Sometimes just a postcard arrived, with a scribbled greeting from some far-off exotic location. But Hannah loved Rosa's letters the best, since they were always full of news and gossip about her colleagues and her travels.

Unfolding Rosa's letter, she found photographs and the money her daughter always included. Clearly Rosa was doing well, Hannah thought, as she counted the notes. Her daughter had been including money ever since she'd become a flight attendant. Hannah was grateful for it, since she only had a small pension, and that didn't go very far. Of course, she always put some of the money aside, in case Rosa ever announced she was getting married. Then Hannah intended buying a spectacular mother-of-the bride outfit . . .

Leaving aside the bundle of photographs, Hannah began reading Rosa's letter. As always, its tone was upbeat, and it was obvious that Rosa was leading a wonderfully varied and exciting life. She'd just been transferred to the Jamaica route, and was hoping to top up her tan on the beach while there.

Gazing at the familiar swirling signature at the end, a dart of pain flitted across Hannah's face. What a pity Rosa wasn't the one getting engaged! How ironic that her old school friend Clara Bellingham, who'd never even left the village, should have recently found herself a husband, yet her own high-flying daughter couldn't. Surely Rosa must meet dashing pilots and foreign diplomats on her travels? She couldn't still be hurting over Danny's rejection all those years ago! Hannah longed to ask her daughter if there was a special man in her life, but it might seem too pushy. All the same, it didn't stop her hoping for that special letter. She'd love to hear the patter of tiny feet before she died . . .

As she reached for the photographs, Hannah's heart filled with pride. Rosa often sent photographs of the places she visited. Over the years, Hannah had received an assortment of pictures showing Rosa and her friends rubbing in sun cream on a Florida beach and on a hovercraft in the Everglades, skiing in Aspen, Colorado, dining in an open-air restaurant in Hawaii, and waving from a speedboat on one of the Italian lakes. These latest photos had obviously been taken recently during her time on the Australia route, and showed Rosa and friends outside Sydney's Opera House, and in the Blue Mountains surrounded by amazingly tall trees. Clearly, Rosa was living the dream. In all the photographs, Hannah noticed the same dark-haired man at her daughter's side – could this be someone special?

Hannah desperately hoped so. It was years since Rosa had left Willow Haven, humiliated and defeated by Danny Heartley's rejection. Surely it was time she found happiness with a nice man? Hannah didn't care where he was from, what nationality, colour or creed he was, as long as he made Rosa happy.

As she wandered into the kitchen and turned on the electric kettle, Hannah was still daydreaming. If Rosa and this dark-haired man decided to wed on a beach, or in some exotic location, Hannah was determined to be there at all costs.

But what she really wanted was for Rosa to come back to her roots in Willow Haven, and hold the reception at the local hotel. Surely, if she'd found the man of her dreams, she wouldn't be worried about Danny Heartley? Marrying in Willow Haven would let everyone know that he didn't matter any more. Undoubtedly her gregarious and glamorous daughter would also have a bevy of international friends, and their exotic presence in Willow Haven would be an eye-opener for the locals!

Hannah longed to show off her daughter, just like the Mortons did theirs. She was tired of being the one who had to pack her suitcase and go to London. But she'd no other option since Rosa had vowed she wouldn't set foot in Willow Haven ever again.

Hannah bit her lip. She'd another motive for hoping Rosa might marry soon. She'd recently visited the doctor because of unexplained tiredness, but had been subjected to a barrage of questions and a speedy hospital appointment. All she'd wanted was a tonic or some kind of pick-me-up, but at the hospital she'd been poked and prodded, and put through all sorts of tests, while the doctors spoke in hushed tones and used euphemisms in her presence.

Hannah suspected that something wasn't quite right, but no one was prepared to tell her anything until they'd got the results of the tests. Such focused attention could only mean that something was definitely amiss. Hopefully, it wasn't anything too serious.

Chapter 38

Ivy made no mention of her mother's remarks to Danny – she'd wait and judge Hannah's health for herself. But when she and Danny arrived at their old neighbour's house, Hannah looked much the same as usual, and Ivy dismissed her mother's warnings as fanciful.

In Hannah's hallway, Danny hugged the elderly woman warmly. "It's great to see you, Hannah!"

"Danny! Oh my goodness, don't you look smart!"

Hannah's face was pink with delight as she beamed happily up at him. She'd always been genuinely fond of Danny, and Ivy had little doubt that Hannah still wished it had been Rosa he'd married instead of her. Nevertheless, Hannah was always gracious and kind to Ivy as well, so it was obvious she'd long ago decided to make the best of the situation.

Hannah began bustling around, filling the kettle and making tea. And despite their protestations, she insisted on buttering some scones that she'd just taken out of the oven.

As always, it didn't take Hannah long to bring the conversation round to Rosa, how wonderful her job was, and how many exotic places she'd visited. As Ivy and Danny began drinking their tea – and nibbling a scone so as not to offend their old neighbour – Hannah carried over an old tin box.

"Look at these letters and postcards, Danny," she said eagerly, taking out a bundle and pressing them into his hands. "I never thought my little girl would end up seeing such amazing places – it's wonderful, isn't it?"

Danny nodded, studying the items in the box, and passing them along to Ivy. "You must be so proud of her," he told her. "With such an outgoing personality, it was obvious that Rosa would do well."

Nodding, Hannah sighed. "I suppose it's selfish of me, but I wish she could write more often. I know she's busy and doesn't get the time. I mean, with such a great job, I suppose I'm lucky she keeps in touch at all!"

Danny patted her shoulder. "Why don't I get you a computer, Hannah, and show you how to use it? I'm sure Rosa has an email address. That would make it a lot easier to keep in touch with her."

Ivy nodded in agreement, touched at her husband's kindness to their old friend.

"I couldn't let you do that!" Hannah said, looking shocked. "I mean, it's very good of you, Danny, but you haven't time to spare for an old dunce like me!"

Danny grinned. "Good. I'm glad we've got that sorted! Next time I'm back in Willow Haven, I'll bring a laptop for you, and honestly, you won't be long getting the hang of it." He smiled at Hannah's worried expression. "Don't worry, I'll set it up with the software you need, and give you your first lesson."

"No, Danny, I couldn't let you do that."

But already, Ivy could see the faint glimmer of something like hope in Hannah's eyes. The older woman was considering taking a step into the digital age, and Ivy could see she was frightened and excited in equal measures. She was willing to try anything that would give her more contact with Rosa.

A short time later, as they were leaving, Danny kissed the older woman's cheek.

"I'll see you very soon, Hannah, so be ready for your first computer lesson!" he told her, and she was beaming happily as she waved them off.

Once outside, Ivy linked her husband's arm. "That was really nice of you, love – I wish *I'd* thought of getting Hannah a computer.

It'll be perfect for her, and Rosa will be able to keep in touch even when she's abroad."

Danny nodded. "I'll get a laptop and printer as quickly as I can. I'll be visiting the site for the new Coulton branch next week, so I won't be a million miles away from the village. I'll pop in before I drive home, and give Hannah her first lesson."

Ivy nodded. Danny was a real sweetie.

"Hannah looked well, didn't she?" he said, smiling. "She'll master the computer in no time!"

Ivy smiled in agreement, glad she hadn't dampened Danny's good spirits by relaying her mother's dire warnings. Sometimes, her mother could be too pessimistic for her own good.

* * *

"Hannah seemed fine," Ivy told her mother when she returned from their visit to Hannah's house. Danny had already gone off to see his father, after which he was calling in to see Peggy and Ned.

"Well, that's as may be, but . . ." Eleanor's voice trailed off.

"Mum, I don't know what you're talking about," Ivy said crossly. "Danny's getting Hannah a computer, and she's all fired up about learning how to send emails."

"Have it your own way." Eleanor shrugged her shoulders and walked out of the room.

But her mother's remarks left Ivy feeling unsettled.

* * *

By Sunday afternoon, Ivy was relieved to be leaving the village. The mystery caller had robbed her of any joy she might have felt at being back in the place where she grew up. Since they'd arrived she'd been on edge, wondering if she was being watched, or if the caller had actually been talking to her?

Ivy shivered, and Danny, who was driving them home, leaned over and squeezed her hand.

"You okay, love? You're still looking tired – why don't we get a Chinese takeaway tonight, and watch that new movie I got?"

Ivy nodded gratefully. A movie meant she wouldn't have to

make small talk for an hour or two – as long as Danny didn't want
to discuss the ins and outs of the film afterwards. He still maintained
an interest in photography even though he'd little time to indulge in
it any more. And when they went to the cinema, Danny could never
resist airing his views on every camera shot and special effect used.
Ivy often thought that if he hadn't gone into the retail trade, he'd
have made a great director. She smiled, wondering what it would be
like working with him on the set of *Bright Lights*. Probably better
not to mix business and pleasure!

"You alright?"

"Yes, of course." Ivy made an effort to sit up and look happy.
There was no point in arousing Danny's suspicions, especially now
that they'd left Willow Haven behind.

Chapter 39

When Julia didn't appear in the shop one morning, Fred had an uneasy feeling. Although they barely spoke nowadays, Julia was always punctual and, despite the tension between them, she still took pride in seeing that all the shelves in the shop were fully stocked.

Since they didn't sleep in the same bedroom any more, Fred always made a point of having an early breakfast and taking a short walk. By the time he returned, Julia would have showered, had her own breakfast and opened the shop. That way, intimacy was avoided and embarrassment and hostility kept to a manageable level.

But this particular morning, the shop was still closed when Fred returned from his walk. He could see the retreating figure of one of his regular customers, and he cursed beneath his breath. What was Julia thinking of? They couldn't afford to turn away business . . .

Opening the door with his own keys, Fred surveyed the empty shop. Where on earth was Julia? He had a bad feeling in the pit of his stomach, but before he could consider the matter any further, two more regulars entered the store and Fred quickly served them. By now, he was very worried. Could Julia have left him? Things had been strained between them for so long that he wouldn't be surprised.

At the first opportunity, Fred locked the shop's outer door and headed upstairs to their living quarters, two steps at a time. He might as well know the truth; perhaps she'd left him a letter . . .

There was no letter on the kitchen worktops or dining-room table, and Fred felt a momentary sense of relief. But now he had to approach the spare room that was now Julia's fiefdom. The door was closed, and Fred knocked tentatively. He didn't dare invade the space that Julia now guarded so zealously. But there was no answer, and Fred was filled with a horrible sense of foreboding.

Reluctantly, he opened the door, and immediately knew that Julia was dead.

She still looked as though she was sleeping, but he could see that her skin had taken on a pale and almost translucent sheen. Her heart was no longer beating, and he was stricken as he touched her cold, lifeless body as she lay in eternal sleep. Tears welled up in his eyes, and he thought of all the things he'd longed to say to her, but had avoided, fearing a row. Now it was too late. Oh Julia, dear Julia, he thought, I've failed you. You haven't known a moment's happiness since Joe left, and you were right to blame me for it. Now I'll never have a chance to make it up to you. Maybe I've killed you by what I did to Joe . . .

An emotional Fred rang their family doctor, and before long the wheels of officialdom were in motion. Peggy arrived back from school shortly afterwards. Weeks earlier Fred had explained to Peggy and Danny that Julia had moved into the spare room because she was having trouble sleeping, and hadn't wanted to wake him. Fred doubted that anyone would believe him, but he didn't want the recent coldness between him and Julia to blight what had essentially been a good marriage. Nor did he want outsiders speculating about their relationship, since they themselves had never had to deal with the loss of a child like he and Julia had.

As father and daughter clung to each other, sobbing, Fred felt numbed by his loss.

Two of the people he'd loved most in the world were gone, and in each case they'd parted from him in anger. Joe had been particularly close to his mother – how he wished he had some way of contacting him and letting him know about her death.

The official cause of Julia's death was given as a heart attack, but Fred knew that his wife had died of a broken heart. She'd never smiled again since the day Joe left, and he now realised that her aloofness had been the only way she could cope with the pain of loss. She'd bottled it all up inside her, and if she'd tried to speak it would probably have emerged as one long howl of anguish.

At least she hadn't chosen to leave him, and Fred took solace from that fact. Julia had her own money, so she hadn't been trapped in the marriage. Perhaps, in some small way, she'd still loved him right to the end . . .

* * *

Everyone in Willow Haven turned out for Julia's funeral. Danny was distraught, so Ivy left her young husband free to spend as much time as he needed with his father and sister.

But Ivy was beginning to worry in case this change of circumstance would put pressure on them to stay in Willow Haven. While she supported Danny's dream of launching his own supermarket chain, she was well aware that Fred Heartley still exerted an immense pull over his son through their combined love of the retail trade. Ivy desperately hoped he wouldn't make Danny feel obliged to stay in Willow Haven by dangling the prospect of taking over Heartley's Stores. If that happened, Ivy wasn't sure what she'd do. She didn't want to give up on her own dream, but she was also a married woman, and she'd have little choice if Danny wanted to stay.

She also knew that her own parents would be thrilled to have her stay in the village and, despite her protestations, her mother would be a willing baby-sitter when the baby arrived. Ivy knew she could have a pleasant, if dull, life in the village. Obviously, this kind of life suited many people, but Ivy longed for something more. She felt deeply sorry for Fred, but she didn't feel like sacrificing her own ambitions. Besides, Danny had ambitions too, and they weren't likely to be fulfilled in a small village like Willow Haven.

Much to her relief, Danny still seemed keen to go to London, and he made no suggestion that they remain in Willow Haven. However, they couldn't leave until after the baby was born and until they'd sat their exams, and Ivy feared there was still time for Fred to work on Danny and convince him to stay.

Chapter 40

Ivy was relieved to be back at work on *Bright Lights*, and her fears about the mystery caller were already beginning to fade. In the absence of any calls the previous week, she was managing to convince herself that the caller was just a random crackpot, and that the calls had nothing whatsoever to do with her or Harper's Lake. There was no second body in Fred's car – she'd simply allowed her own fear to create a monster that didn't exist except in her imagination.

She also managed to convince herself that the phone call in South Africa had simply been someone playing a prank on her, and that her own fear had made her jump to the wrong conclusions. Ivy didn't intend to scrutinise the situation any more closely – that would mean giving power to this crackpot and diverting her energy from the professional performances she was expected give on the set.

Being back in the company of her acting colleagues and film crew also lent an air of normality to things, and by lunchtime Ivy had rationalised away most of her fears. She was in top acting form, and enjoying the new storyline. After her spell in hospital, Ivy's character Isabella was keen to resume the affair that had been interrupted by the nightclub fire. But she was under scrutiny by her husband, who'd almost caught her and her young lover in an embrace just before the fire started. Now he was determined not to let her out of his sight, and Isabella was beginning to wonder if her own husband could have been the person who started the fire . . .

As they shot the next scene, Anton, as Ivy's stern older husband, was at his irascible best, and he and Ivy hurled insults and accusations at each other with all their might. Once the angry scene was over, cast and crew relaxed, and the director called for a tea break.

Ivy gave Anton a quick hug, then they headed to the catering van for a well-earned cup of coffee. "You were superbly nasty – as usual!"

Anton laughed. "Thank God I'm not married to a woman like Isabella – I'd probably have a heart attack and die before the honeymoon was over! Imagine all that constant aggression – at least, Ivy, we get paid to have such stupendous rows!"

The cast from the previous scene were already milling around the catering van, and Ivy and Anton waited in line for their coffees.

Suddenly, Alison, the director's PA, appeared at the door to the studio offices.

"Ivy – there's a call for you!"

Excusing herself, Ivy left the queue and headed into the studio offices. She was angry at the intrusion, and ready to be livid with the caller. Family and friends knew never to phone her at work. The *Bright Lights* set was sacrosanct, and she'd chew the ear off whoever was phoning her.

Suddenly, she felt stricken. Could something have happened to Danny, Joseph or her parents? Suddenly she was running, and without even a nod to the director's PA, she snatched up the phone from the desk and pressed it to her ear.

"Hello?"

"You were in Willow Haven at the weekend," a voice whispered. "I hope you stayed away from the lake!"

"Who the hell *are* you?" Ivy shouted.

But the caller had already hung up, and Ivy found herself listening to the dial tone. She was now shaking from head to toe, and the concerned PA rushed over to offer her a chair, since she looked as though she was about to faint.

"Are you okay, Ivy? Here, let me get you a drink of water –"

"No, no, I'm fine thanks, Alison. Do you think you could trace that last call?"

Alison lifted up the phone and dialled a number, then looked sadly at Ivy. "Sorry – it just says: Private Caller."

Ivy grimaced, feeling powerless and frightened. Her earlier certainty that the calls were a mistake had evaporated once again. What did this person want from her? So far they'd asked for nothing, except that she stay away from the lake, and the calls only seemed hell-bent on terrorising her. Ivy wished she could go to the police, but if they put a tap on her phone, they'd hear the caller talking about the lake, and they'd want to know what that meant.

"Ivy, should I ask Doug to hold off shooting the next scene for half an hour? You don't look well –"

Rising to her feet, Ivy shook her head. "No thanks, Alison, I'm fine."

Alison looked at her perceptively. "If that caller was giving you hassle, don't forget we have a legal team to take care of things like that."

"No, no – I think it was just a wrong number."

Alison gave her a sceptical look, but said nothing more.

Outside, Ivy headed for the catering van, a smile firmly plastered on her face once again. But inside, her stomach was churning. The caller said they "hoped" she'd stayed away from the lake – did that mean they hadn't actually been watching her? She supposed they couldn't follow her everywhere, which also seemed to confirm it wasn't anyone she knew well, because friends and family had been constantly in her company. Or could it mean that the caller hadn't been in Willow Haven at all? But that would widen the net of possible perpetrators even further . . .

Back on the set, Ivy's good humour had dissipated, but she got through the rest of the shoot by concentrating on how Isabella was feeling, and making a real effort to put her own concerns aside. Luckily, the afternoon was spent filming several montage sequences, and the lack of script enabled Ivy to gradually gain her composure once again and, by the end of the day, she was feeling a little more in control. But this latest phone call didn't augur well for her next trip to the lake.

* * *

That evening when she returned home she found a cheerful Danny already in the kitchen heating up their evening meal.

"How was your day, love?"

"Oh, fine," Ivy said, as nonchalantly as she could manage. "And yours?"

"Very good, as a matter of fact. I was down at the site in Coulton, and it's perfect for what we want. I also got a new laptop and printer for Hannah and called in to see her – you know, despite her claims of being a technophobe, she's mastered the computer very quickly."

Ivy smiled. Danny had been true to his word. But then, he always was, because he was such a kind and decent man.

Then it suddenly occurred to her that if the mystery caller lived in Willow Haven, Danny might actually have passed them in the street that very day, or they might even have spoken to him, before or after they'd made their threatening phone call. Ivy's blood ran cold as she envisioned this person toying with Danny, maybe even dropping hints during their conversation with him, hints he might later add together and suddenly discover the depths of her cruelty and deception.

"D-did you talk to anyone else while you were there?"

Danny shook his head. "No, I'd only time for a flying visit – the surveyor was late so we got delayed at the site. Luckily, Hannah was amazingly quick on the uptake – I doubt if she'll need any more lessons." He smiled ruefully. "I'd hoped to see Dad but, if I hadn't got out of the village early, I'd still be stuck in traffic on the M25!"

"So you didn't talk to anyone else?"

Danny looked puzzled. "Are you okay, love?" he said, looking closely at her as he poured her a glass of wine.

Taking the proffered glass, Ivy nodded, too tired and too worried to speak. Anyway, if she opened her mouth, she feared only a squeak would come out. Instead, she sipped her wine and said nothing.

"You look tired," Danny said, stirring the pan on the stove. "Why don't you sit down at the table and take it easy – I'll have dinner ready in five minutes – okay?"

Ivy nodded, trying to muster up a smile. Danny didn't deserve her churlishness. Nor did he deserve what she'd done to his family. Looking at his eager face, always anxious to please her, she wanted to cry. Or beg his forgiveness for what she'd done. But she could never confess, because she'd lose the most important person in her life if she did. And Fred and Peggy, whom she also cared about deeply. And Joseph, her son, would be appalled and devastated at the depths of his mother's duplicity.

Ivy sighed as she took her place at the table. Why do we always hurt the ones we love?

Chapter 41

"Hello, Mamma? It's Rosa. The line is very bad – I'm in Hawaii. Oh, damn –"

The line went dead and Hannah sighed. It was great to hear her daughter's voice.

Rosa didn't ring very often, and when she did, there was invariably a problem with the line. Hannah could understand that some places still had primitive telephone systems, but she'd been longing to tell Rosa that she now had a computer, and to ask for her daughter's email address.

Hannah glanced across at her new laptop and printer. Danny had shown her how to create a Word document in order to write a letter to Rosa and how to print it off when she'd typed it. Then she'd add her signature to the end, just like Rosa did. She'd also be including the new email address Danny had set up for her – wouldn't Rosa be surprised to discover how technologically advanced her mother had become! From now on, neither of them would need to send bulky letters – they'd simply be able to email each other! Danny had also explained that she could receive photos from Rosa on her computer, and she was thrilled at all the possibilities opening up to her. She was also inordinately proud of herself – she'd only needed one lesson, and Danny had been delighted at how quickly she'd got the hang of everything.

As Hannah replaced the receiver, she glanced at the picture

frame on the telephone table. In the photograph, Rosa was standing in the middle of a group of newly qualified flight attendants. Flanked by the captain and first officer, a large Boeing 747 behind them, the new recruits smiled happily at the camera.

Rosa looked so elegant in her dark-blue uniform, Hannah thought proudly. They all looked so happy that day, on the threshold of a new and exciting career. The picture always reminded her of how well Rosa's life had turned out. And how blessed Hannah was compared to the poor Heartleys.

But her joy turned to concern as she remembered where she was going later that afternoon. She had an appointment at her GP's surgery, where she'd get the results of her recent hospital tests. Hopefully, they'd just give her a tonic that could alleviate the awful tiredness she simply couldn't shake off. Luckily, learning about computers hadn't involved expending much energy . . .

* * *

Hannah Dalton's lip trembled as she let herself into the house and closed the front door. The news that she had cancer had come as a terrible shock. She'd known something was wrong, but she'd blithely assumed her tiredness was due to getting older, or at the very worst, an ulcer or anaemia – something that could be cured by a few pills or a bottle of medicine.

But as she'd sat facing her doctor across his desk, his expression had been grave.

"I'm sorry to have to tell you, Mrs Dalton, they've found cancer – colon cancer."

Hannah's heart almost stopped, but she had a question to ask.

"Is it, I mean –?"

The doctor shuffled the papers on his desk, confirming what Hannah already suspected.

"Hrrmph, er, well yes, I'm afraid it's fairly advanced. Of course, we'll do the best we can for you, Mrs Dalton. I know this is a shock to you, and we'll arrange treatment right away. We can do a lot to make people comfortable these days. At some point later on, I'll need to talk to you about hospice care . . ."

Hannah had stumbled out of the doctor's rooms. She didn't remember anything he'd said, except the word cancer, cancer, cancer . . .

Her first impulse had been to contact Rosa, because she'd felt a primal urge to lean on someone who loved her. But by the time she'd got off the train and walked home from the station, she'd decided that telling Rosa would be unfair on her. She didn't want to be a burden. People often expected their children to look after them in their old age or during terminal illness, but she'd no intention of imposing herself on her daughter. Rosa had made a great life for herself flying all over the world, and she'd even bought a house in Hampstead and become a landlady herself. There was no way Hannah was going to expect her to come back to the village she hated, in order to nurse her dying mother. Hannah didn't flinch from the fact that she was dying. Instinctively she knew she didn't have too long to live.

Well, for now she wouldn't say anything to anyone. That way, she could still pretend that everything was normal. Hannah was well aware how people reacted when someone they knew became ill. Their lives suddenly became filled with appointments and other activities that left no time to spare for their dying friend. People seemed to develop an almost primitive belief that terminal illnesses were contagious, or perhaps they just didn't know what to say. Even the greeting 'How are you' became loaded with innuendo. Terminal illness became an embarrassment that changed relationships, and friends pussyfooted around, fearful of saying anything that might remind the dying person of their mortality. In doing so, they isolated them even more.

Hannah sighed. Nor did she want to tell her sister Joan, at least not at present. She knew that her sister would react badly to the news, and she couldn't bear the thought of watching Joan go to pieces. There'd be time enough for that when she became seriously ill. Right now, she intended carrying on just as before.

Hannah wandered into the kitchen. As she made a pot of tea, she felt a sense of unreality and detachment from everything around her. It felt strange to think that your own body could turn against you so cruelly. Somewhere inside her, rogue cells were multiplying and taking over the work of her normal cells. Eventually, they'd take her over completely. What would it feel like? She'd forgotten to ask the doctor about the progression of the disease. She'd been so stunned by the news that her brain had turned to mush and she hadn't asked the questions she needed to.

Suddenly, Hannah felt a surge of anger. She wasn't ready to go yet! She was only sixty-five, and had lots of living still to do. She wanted to be around to see Rosa married – maybe to the dark-haired man in the photos – and become a grandmother too.

She wiped away a tear. Later on, when she'd become used to the idea herself, she'd tell a few close friends she could rely on, like Eleanor and Peter Morton. At some point she'd have to tell Rosa, but she'd wait until there was little time left for long drawn-out goodbyes. She didn't want her daughter putting her career on hold – or maybe even ruining it – by coming back to nurse her dying mother.

Angrily, Hannah pushed her mug of tea away. It brought her no comfort today.

Chapter 42

It felt strange being married, yet still in school. When Ivy returned to class after her wedding, she could see that her teachers and classmates viewed her very differently. Some of her classmates avoided her, and Ivy wondered if they feared that they, too, might become pregnant by association. She also found herself the victim of occasional barbs about stealing Rosa's man, but in general, her classmates ignored her, which suited Ivy well. She was here to study and pass her exams, not to be popular. She understood the other girls' reticence – she now inhabited a very different world from theirs. She was the only pupil wearing a wedding ring, and the only one who walked home from school with her husband.

Despite Ivy's isolation from many of the other girls, her classmate Clara Bellingham was loyal and supportive, as was her new sister-in-law Peggy, in the class below her. It felt strange not having Rosa in school any more, and Ivy occasionally wondered how she was getting on in London. By all accounts, she was doing very well, and Hannah was always quick to let people know that her daughter had survived Danny's rejection and was building a new life for herself.

Sometimes, Ivy felt unreasonably jealous of Rosa; she'd escaped the small-town mentality of Willow Haven, whereas Ivy was still trapped there until she and Danny could leave school and move to London too. At times, Ivy felt like urging Danny to leave the village *with her immediately. After all, Rosa appeared to be doing well without any qualifications. But then she'd remember her pregnancy, and the help she'd need delivering her baby. And of course there was her application to RADA – she wasn't prepared to give up on her dream.*

It also felt strange to be living in Danny's bedroom at the Heartleys' home above the shop. But Fred had been adamant that there was plenty of room, especially since Julia and Joe were no longer there. Ivy would have preferred to stay with her own parents, but it was assumed that a married couple would want to be together, and both families agreed that it made sense for them to stay at the Heartley home.

Danny's room already contained a double bed, so there was little room for Ivy's clothes and personal possessions, and sometimes she wanted to scream. Several times she begged Danny to move his photographic equipment to someplace else, but his answers were always evasive. Finally, he'd suggested that Ivy store her possessions in his late mother's bedroom next door, but Ivy had no intention of using the room in which Julia had been found dead. On her way to and from their bedroom, she'd creep past Julia's room, never daring to go inside, wondering if death lingered in the atmosphere long after a person was gone. Ivy was now uniquely privy to the knowledge that Fred and Julia had inhabited separate bedrooms though, like most people in the village, she was already well aware that the Heartleys' relationship had been deteriorating for a long time prior to Julia's death.

Neither Danny nor Fred ever suggested she use Joe's bedroom, presumably because they still hoped he'd return home someday soon. For that Ivy was grateful – she knew she'd never cope with the pain of loss she'd feel each time she had to see Joe's possessions, and especially the bed where he'd slept the night before their ill-fated trip . . .

One evening, after she'd finished her homework, Ivy decided to clear a space beneath Danny's bed once and for all. She figured that if she pushed his possessions over to one side, she might be able to store her hairdryer and some of her shoes there. Down on her hands and knees, she'd just begun moving Danny's photographic equipment to one side when her husband returned to the room. In an instant, his usually happy face contorted into rage.

"Hey – don't you dare touch any of my stuff!" he shouted angrily, scrambling beneath the bed, checking to see what she'd moved.

Ivy burst into tears, and Danny was instantly contrite.

"Sorry, Ivy – I didn't mean to be short with you," he said softly, as he kissed her tear-stained face.

"Then why did you shout at me?" Ivy whimpered. It was the first time Danny had ever spoken sharply to her, and she didn't like it. She was also furious with herself for crying. No doubt her overreaction was caused by all the pregnancy hormones racing round inside her body.

Danny looked at her sheepishly. "Look, I'm really sorry, love – but I've hidden a surprise for you under the bed, and I don't want you discovering it yet!"

"Why can't I have it now?" Ivy said petulantly. "Why are you making me wait?" She knew she was being unreasonable, but she intended making Danny pay for his hurtful outburst.

"It's not the right time yet, but you'll get it soon," Danny promised her. "I hope you'll feel it was worth waiting for. But please, in the meantime, don't go near my stuff under the bed – promise?"

Ivy nodded. "Promise."

* * *

The following Saturday Danny brought Ivy breakfast in bed.

"Wake up, sleepyhead!" he called, a silly grin on his face.

Yawning, Ivy sat up. This was a lifestyle she could happily get used to . . .

"Happy anniversary!" Danny whispered, placing the tray beside her. "I'm the luckiest man in the world – we're married three whole months today!"

Ivy smiled. "Is that why you've been keeping my surprise under the bed?"

Danny nodded. "I've been saving it especially for today. But you'll have to eat your breakfast first, Mrs Heartley."

Ivy smiled. She liked being called Mrs Heartley. Even if the Mr Heartley she'd married wasn't the one she'd originally wanted . . .

"What's my surprise, Danny?"

"Don't be so impatient!" he teased. "It's still under the bed – I'll give it to you when you've cleared your plate!"

As Ivy munched her toast, she was genuinely excited. Danny was unbelievably romantic – how many other men would think of a three-month anniversary? While she couldn't claim to love him yet, she was definitely feeling a lot more positive about their future together . . .

When Ivy finished her breakfast, she put her tray on the bedside table and looked expectantly at her husband. Grinning, Danny crawled under the bed and brought out a small box from behind his photographic equipment, and handed it to Ivy. Opening it, she was astonished to find a diamond ring inside.

"It's not a very big diamond, but it's all I could afford," he explained. "I wanted you to have an engagement ring – I know the wedding ring came first – but I wanted everything to be right for you, Ivy. I love you so much."

Gently he slid off her wedding ring, slipped on the engagement ring then replaced her wedding ring over it. It fitted perfectly.

"Someday, I'll get you a really big diamond," he whispered.

Vehemently, Ivy shook her head. "This is all I want – no other diamond could ever mean as much as this one does," she whispered.

Instinctively, they reached for each other, and slowly and languidly, they began to make love.

Chapter 43

After a month of exhausting days on *Bright Lights*, which involved working late several nights during the week and at weekends as well, Ivy was regretting the two weeks' free time she'd blagged from Colin. He was now making her pay by working her to death! But she was well aware that the filming schedule for a television soap opera was relentless. Episodes were broadcast five nights a week, so there was no time for slacking or for hissy fits from either cast or crew. It was work, work, work, with everyone pulling together as a tightly knit team.

Despite her workload, Ivy made sure to anonymously phone the offices of the local Council for Willow Haven each week, and had been relieved to discover that the proposed work on Harper's Lake was still out to tender. Her most recent enquiries had elicited the best news of all – on this occasion, the woman at the Council offices had been in a chatty mood, and had expressed doubts that the project would get started before the end of the year. "The tenders are all way over budget," she'd confided. "So there's a lot of bickering going on at Council meetings."

Finally, Ivy had a weekend free. And since Danny was up north on a fact-finding mission with two other Betterbuys directors, she'd decided to return to Willow Haven. A weekend wasn't ideal, but she was nevertheless going armed again with a swimsuit and goggles. She'd have to risk being spotted by the mystery caller, but it would all be worth it when this person no longer had any hold over her.

But when she arrived in Willow Haven, Ivy discovered that her mother had other plans for her time.

"If you're expecting us to go to South Africa for Owen's wedding, you'll have to do something about your father!" Eleanor told her daughter, a determined look on her face. "Assuming you'll be jogging each morning, you'll have to take him with you – he'll never lose weight if he doesn't get out there and exercise."

Reluctantly, Ivy agreed. Much as she loved her father's company, having him in tow would make it impossible to carry out her plan. She'd been relieved by the comments of the woman in the Council offices, but she couldn't take them as Gospel. And once the tender was awarded, work on the lake could start immediately.

"You'll also have to visit Hannah," Eleanor informed her. "I was right, you know – of course, you wouldn't believe me that anything was wrong, would you?"

Ivy acknowledged her mother's astuteness with a nod of her head.

"Your father and I are the only ones she's told – she doesn't want people knowing she's got cancer yet. I'm only telling you because, well, you might be able to talk some sense into her."

"About what?"

Her mother gave an enigmatic smile. "Just go and see her."

Ivy nodded. Her weekend was unravelling by the minute.

* * *

"Hannah – it's so good to see you again!"

Hugging her old neighbour, Ivy had to call on all her acting skills so as not to let her dismay show. The once well-built and rosy-cheeked woman had already lost weight, which didn't suit her at all. She looked gaunt, and it was only when she smiled that Ivy saw the old Hannah she knew so well.

Ivy placed a bouquet of flowers and a large box of chocolates on the coffee table, wondering guiltily if Hannah was still capable of swallowing anything like a sweet, since she looked very frail. Then she sat down beside Hannah and took the elderly woman's hand in hers.

"How are you, Hannah?" she asked, although it was a rhetorical question. Hugging Hannah's fragile frame had told Ivy all she needed to know.

"I'm fine," Hannah told her, her eyes filling with delight. "Thanks for dropping in, Ivy – it's not everyone who has a TV star calling to see them! And thanks for the chocolates – they're my favourites! But you really shouldn't have –"

"Of course I should – you deserve a treat," said Ivy brightly, trying to dispel the lump in her throat. She hoped she wouldn't start crying, but she was shocked at Hannah's shrunken appearance.

"So your mother told you."

Ivy nodded.

"Well, I'd be grateful if you'd keep it to yourself," Hannah said. "The only people I've told are your parents – in fact, I think your mother guessed something was wrong even before *I* did."

"Why don't you want anyone to know?" Ivy asked, exasperated.

Hannah's mouth was taut. "Because people's attitudes change when they know you're terminally ill," she replied. "People start pitying you, and I don't want anyone changing their behaviour towards me." She smiled impishly. "I've explained the weight loss by telling people I'm on a diet. So please, Ivy – don't tell anyone, not even Danny."

Reluctantly Ivy agreed. "If you're sure, Hannah . . ."

Seeing Ivy glancing at her computer, Hannah's face lit up. "It was so good of Danny to give me the computer and the lesson, Ivy. Luckily, I got the hang of it very quickly."

"He told me you were a brilliant pupil!"

Hannah smiled in acknowledgement. "I've just had a lovely email from Rosa," she said. "Here, come and read it, Ivy."

With a look of pride, Hannah sat down and scrolled down her computer screen, opening the most recent email. Ivy was pleased that Hannah had taken to the computer like the proverbial duck to water. Being able to use it gave her and her daughter a lot more flexibility.

According to the email, Rosa was now flying the New York to San Francisco route, and was enjoying it immensely. Her bubbly email was filled with news about a recent visit to San Francisco's Golden Gate Bridge, and a boat-ride to the once infamous Alcatraz prison, now a museum. The email seemed to indicate that Rosa was happy with her life, and enjoying the opportunities her job offered for travel.

Ivy felt a brief surge of warmth towards Rosa. She was glad she kept in touch with her mother regularly, even though she had never been back in Willow Haven since that fateful day she'd left for London. Hannah was the one who made all the journeys to London and elsewhere to visit her daughter. Suddenly Ivy felt annoyed for poor Hannah. Surely, now that her mother was ill, Rosa would come and visit *her*?

Then it suddenly dawned on Ivy – Hannah hadn't told Rosa about the cancer! It would be typical of Hannah to keep her illness to herself, for fear of being a burden on Rosa. She wouldn't want to curtail her daughter's life by being needy.

"You haven't told Rosa, have you?"

Hannah shook her head. "Please – I don't want Rosa to know, Ivy. Not yet, anyway. Look, I'm fine at the moment – if Rosa finds out, she'll feel obliged to come back here, and you know how she hates this place."

"She can hardly still feel bad about what happened with Danny – Hannah, that's years ago!" said Ivy in exasperation.

"Be that as it may, I don't want to disrupt her life. If she took time off, she could jeopardise that great job she has . . ." Momentarily, Hannah looked sad, and her voice dropped so low that Ivy could barely hear what she was saying, "although I'd hoped she might have married and had children by now . . ."

"Hannah, you're not well," Ivy said crossly, realising that this was why her mother had wanted her to 'talk some sense' into Hannah. "You need your family around you at a time like this."

"Look, I'm fine, Ivy," Hannah assured her. "I don't intend telling my sister Joan yet either – she's a terrible fusspot. I just want to get on with what's left of my life in peace."

"Hannah, Rosa would want to know."

"I'll tell her later, when I'm a bit further along the road –"

They both knew Hannah meant when she was a bit closer to death.

"Okay, Hannah," said Ivy resignedly. "If you're sure everything is okay –"

"Oh yes, everything's fine!" Hannah replied, relieved that Ivy wasn't going to browbeat her any further.

Well, something has to be done about the situation, Ivy thought to herself. She couldn't let Hannah's pride and Rosa's ignorance keep the two of them apart. Hannah didn't look at all well, and Ivy suspected the end might be closer than even Hannah realised. How awful for Rosa if her mother ended up in hospital – or dead – without her even knowing she was ill, and how awful for Hannah to die without the comfort of her daughter beside her.

Ivy looked closely at the email, but of course there was no address or phone number on it. She supposed she could email Rosa, but she felt that news as devastating as Hannah's illness should be delivered in person. It would be easier to convey the seriousness of her mother's situation face to face. Ivy felt certain that when Rosa was made aware of the situation, she'd come back to Willow Haven immediately.

"Did I tell you that Rosa bought the Hampstead house?" Hannah asked, her gaunt face filled with pride. "The landlord wanted to sell, so Rosa took out a big mortgage, and now she's a landlady herself!"

Smiling, Ivy nodded. She'd heard this story from Hannah at least a dozen times over the last few years but, since it made Hannah happy to tell it, Ivy didn't mind hearing it over and over again.

Hannah began to rise with difficulty from her chair, and Ivy rushed to help her.

"Maybe you'd put on the kettle, Ivy? I'll be back in a minute . . ." Hannah said, as she headed off to the bathroom.

Ivy wondered guiltily if she should be helping Hannah in some way, but her old friend seemed fiercely determined to be as independent as possible.

"Of course, Hannah."

When Ivy heard the bathroom door close, she began looking frantically around the room. Before Hannah got her computer, Rosa wrote regular letters to her mother. Ivy knew that Hannah kept them in a tin, which she'd produced the last time she and Danny had visited her – where on earth did she keep it? If she could locate the letters, there might be an address for the Hampstead house on one of them.

Quickly, Ivy went to the dresser in the living room and began rummaging through each drawer. She was in luck! In the third drawer, she found the tin box full of postcards and letters. Grabbing one of the letters, she noted Rosa's dramatic signature and kisses – and the address of her Hampstead home at the top.

As Ivy was memorising it, she heard the bathroom door open, and quickly slid the tin box back into the drawer and hurried into the kitchen. She was taking down mugs and preparing a tray when Hannah reappeared.

A short time later, as the two women sat drinking tea, Ivy tried to offer her help.

"Is there anything you need, Hannah?" she asked. "If you need any extra medical care, I'm more than happy to pay for it."

"Thank you Ivy, that's very generous of you, but I'm fine," Hannah assured her with a quick smile. "Your mother and father call regularly to see if I need anything, and Meals on Wheels bring me lunch every day. Social Services send a home help once a week, and the Macmillan nurses are wonderful . . ."

Briefly, Ivy thought of mentioning Owen's engagement and his wedding the following year, but no doubt Hannah already knew about it from her parents. Anyway, talk of the future would only remind Hannah of a time when she wouldn't be there any more. Then Ivy realised that this was precisely why Hannah wanted to keep her illness quiet – people began editing their comments and conversation, as she'd just done herself. Silently she applauded her old friend, and vowed to treat her as she'd always done. So she told her about Owen's fiancée Charmaine, the thousands of acres of the nature reserve that allowed the animals to live in their natural habitat, and the warmth of the indigenous people of South Africa.

It was obvious that Hannah enjoyed Ivy's first-hand account of her visit, and Ivy was surprised when she looked at her watch and discovered that she and Hannah had been talking for over two hours!

As she stood up to leave, Ivy kissed the older woman's cheek and hugged her as she said goodbye. Urging her to stay in her chair and rest, she let herself out of Hannah's house, making a mental note to send her a large hamper of Betterbuys' luxury range of foods. She hoped Hannah was still able to enjoy her food, and would relish being spoiled a little, since there seemed little else that she could do for her. It was obvious that the poor woman was seriously ill.

Which made her trip to see Rosa all the more urgent.

Chapter 44

It was dark as Ivy parked her car opposite 6 Cherrywood Road, Hampstead. She was nervous since she didn't like being the bearer of bad news. There was also the fact that she'd been the victor where Danny was concerned, so there would always be tension between her and Rosa.

Ivy surveyed the darkened street. Rosa might still be away, but calling in person was the only option she felt was appropriate. If Rosa wasn't home today, one of her tenants would probably know when she was due back, and Ivy would make a return trip to see her. She'd only email Rosa if she discovered that she was going to be away for several more weeks. Since Hannah was going downhill fast, time was critical.

Ivy shivered. Even though she dreaded facing her nemesis, right now it was preferable to diving into Harper's Lake again. Ivy had been only too glad to postpone her next trip to Willow Haven and concentrate on locating Rosa instead. At least the tender for draining the lake hadn't been awarded yet.

Ivy vividly remembered the look of horror on Brian's face when she'd told him about the need for one more dive. He'd begged her not to do it, and she shivered as she remembered his comment that she could become the third body in the car.

As Hannah requested, Ivy hadn't told Danny how ill she was,

and she'd arranged delivery of the Betterbuys hamper herself. She knew Hannah didn't want people's sympathy, and knowing Danny, he'd insist on going down to Willow Haven, fussing and trying to help, and making poor Hannah's life miserable in the process. He hadn't seen her since he'd given her the computer lesson, and Ivy had no doubt he'd be shocked and upset when he eventually found out about her condition. She felt bad about not telling him, but she had to respect Hannah's wishes.

Of course she hadn't told him about her plan to contact Rosa either. In a sense, it felt like a betrayal of Hannah, and she didn't want Danny trying to dissuade her. But Rosa needed to be told, and when she came back to Willow Haven they could all work out a plan to help Hannah through the final days of her illness. As Hannah's next-of-kin, Rosa had to be the one to decide what was needed. Perhaps she could take compassionate leave from the airline for a while?

Reluctant to face Rosa, Ivy sat in the car, biding her time. To ease her tension, she massaged her temples. She'd no idea what hours flight attendants worked, but she hoped Rosa might be on a break after her stint on the New York-San Francisco route. She was dreading this awkward meeting, but she owed it to Hannah to ensure that mother and daughter had some quality time together before she passed away.

Ivy sighed. Maybe, in fairness, she ought to let Danny know. He really cared about Hannah, and perhaps it wasn't right to keep such devastating news to herself . . .

As she unbuckled her seatbelt and prepared to get out of the car, Ivy failed to notice two people approaching until they were almost level with her car.

Startled, she peered out the car window. In the gloom, she spotted a woman with shoulder-length fluffy blonde hair, in the style Rosa had always worn, and holding her hand was a small boy of about ten. Ivy's heart did a somersault. She hadn't seen Rosa in years, but there could be no doubt that this was her. She looked slightly older, and a little heavier than the Rosa Ivy remembered, but that was only to be expected with the passing of time.

Who was the boy? Rosa didn't have any children – at least none that Hannah had ever mentioned. As she watched, the duo turned into Number 6, opened the door and stepped inside. A light came on in the hall, and Ivy decided she'd wait five or ten minutes until they'd had time to take their coats off and settle in for the evening.

As she waited in her car, Ivy puzzled over the boy's presence. Maybe Rosa was minding a friend's child, or it belonged to one of her tenants. It could hardly be her own child, could it? Surely Hannah would know if she had a grandchild?

Ivy was about to step out of the car when she saw a man approaching on the same side of the road, his head down, bracing himself against the wind. She decided to wait until he'd passed by, but her heart gave a jolt as she suddenly recognised him. It was Danny! What on earth was he doing here, walking along a road in Hampstead?

As she stared out the car window, he reached the gateway of Number 6 and turned in. Uncomprehending, Ivy watched as he took a key from his pocket, opened the door, stepped inside and closed the door behind him. What on earth was going on? Why did he have a key to Rosa Dalton's house? Like a ton of bricks, it suddenly hit her, leaving her gasping for air and clutching her chest. Danny was having an affair with Rosa – and the young boy was probably their son!

Ivy felt sick. How long had this been going on? If the child was Danny's, then the affair must have started more than ten years earlier. How could Danny do this to her? How could he look at her, affection in his eyes, while all the time he was carrying on with Rosa behind her back?

Ivy stifled a sob. Her whole world was starting to unravel and fall apart. Her hands were shaking, and she wondered if she was about to have a heart attack. Could it just be a bad dream, from which she'd soon wake up? Briefly, she closed her eyes, but nothing had changed when she opened them again. Her husband was still inside Rosa's house.

Now she knew where Danny went when he claimed to be making impromptu visits to Betterbuys branches around the country. Of course, she'd always believed him, but now she realised he'd been bedding Rosa instead. How could he have been so deceitful?

All sorts of thoughts were racing through Ivy's brain. When had Danny and Rosa rekindled their relationship? Did that mean Danny regretted marrying her, and wished he'd chosen Rosa instead? Or had he simply wanted to have his cake and eat it? Ivy wiped away a tear as she sat staring across at Number 6. Were Danny, Rosa and the child sitting round the kitchen table at this very minute, eating together, laughing together, and playing happy families?

Ivy bit her trembling lip. But who was she to talk about honesty? She'd claimed to be expecting Danny's child in order to hide the fact that she was pregnant by his brother. Eventually, she'd grown to love him, but she'd deceived him about her feelings at the very start of their relationship. Was she now paying the price for her own deception? Suddenly, she recalled the saying: '*What goes around comes around.*' Was it now her turn to pay for the lies she'd told in the past?

Ivy took a deep breath and tried to calm herself. No wonder Rosa hadn't told her mother that she had a child – she could hardly tell Hannah who the father was! Of course, she could have lied, like I did, Ivy thought, but maybe Rosa is a better person than me. She felt a fleeting stab of sadness for Hannah, who'd be overjoyed to know she had a grandson . . .

Suddenly, Ivy felt almost hysterical. She needn't have tried to contact Rosa at all – if she'd simply told Danny about Hannah's illness, he could have told Rosa himself!

Ivy buried her face in her hands. It was all too much for her to take in, and there were so many questions to which she had no answers. But central to everything was the fact that Danny was cheating on her, and with the woman he'd originally dumped to be with her.

Ivy glanced at her watch, realising that she'd been sitting opposite Rosa's house for almost fifteen minutes. She needed to get away before anyone spotted her – she'd die if Danny or Rosa came out and found her sitting there. She needed time alone to recover from the shock of what she'd just found out, and time to decide what she intended to do next.

Starting the engine, Ivy began driving away. Everything felt strangely unreal as she changed gears. Danny's affair had stunned her, because she'd always believed he adored her. You silly, complacent fool, she told herself. All his protestations of love were clearly lies.

No, Ivy thought, surely no one could fake the genuine affection she'd seen so often in Danny's eyes? The pride and delight he'd displayed when she'd won an acting award, the tenderness he showed when they were making love?

On the other hand, weren't there men who succeeded in living two or more separate lives? And weren't successful men supposed to have higher sex drives than ordinary men? Maybe Danny was one of those men, and felt that his success entitled him to step outside normally acceptable boundaries.

Angrily, Ivy brushed away the tears that were preventing her from seeing the road ahead. How ironic if she crashed her car at the corner of the street where her husband had his love nest, and how humiliating to be caught spying on him! Of course, she hadn't come to spy on him at all, but no one would believe she'd only come to urge Rosa to visit her dying mother.

By now, Ivy's heartbeat was returning to normal, and some of the confusion in her mind was clearing. Since I know about the affair now, she thought, I've nothing to lose any more. But before I confront Danny, I'll go and see Rosa myself – she and I definitely need to clear the air.

Suddenly, an image of Brian crept into her mind, and now Ivy felt angry that she'd turned down his advances. Clearly, Danny hadn't deserved her devotion or her loyalty! She felt certain that if Brian was her husband or partner, he'd never cheat on her. Then Ivy realised she'd believed the same of Danny until a short time ago.

Nevertheless, a sense of peace enveloped her as she thought of the South African wilderness, and thinking of Brian also calmed her nerves a little. Maybe she'd phone him soon, just to say hello. Right now she needed to feel that someone was there for her, because she felt totally alone and frightened.

Chapter 45

Eleanor, Peter and Fred were all keen for the couple to stay in Willow Haven, and Ivy and Danny conceded, at least for the present. Ivy was well aware that the baby would arrive before the end of the year – not in late January as everyone else believed – and she and Danny intended sitting their A-levels the following June.

Ivy suspected that Fred Heartley was hoping the baby would ground her, and that she'd abandon her dreams of going to RADA, and she and Danny would stay permanently in Willow Haven. Now that Julia was dead, Fred would welcome having what was left of his family around him. Ivy felt deeply sorry for her father-in-law, but she and Danny would be leaving as soon as their exams were over.

Ivy refused to attend the maternity hospital in Allcott, fearing that any medical intervention might discover she was further on than expected. She intended her 'early' delivery to be a complete surprise to everyone, and she'd play the part of an astonished new parent herself. With all this in mind, she'd opted for the local midwife, an elderly no-nonsense sort of woman who'd delivered hundreds of babies in the area. Hopefully she wouldn't scrutinise the new delivery too closely and, if she did, Ivy hoped she'd keep her opinions to herself.

It was also difficult to curb Peggy's enthusiasm about the pregnancy, since her sister-in-law wanted to know all about the different stages Ivy was going through. Therefore Ivy had to be constantly on her toes, never able to forget her pretence even for a minute.

As December approached, Ivy knew her due date wasn't far away. She hoped to give birth during the Christmas holidays, which would mean she could return to school for the new term while her mother looked after the baby. As the school holidays approached, Ivy was amused when Clara told her that her classmates were hoping she'd go into labour during the following term, and that the disruption would get them a few free class periods. Well, Ivy thought, you're all going to be very disappointed!

* * *

A week before Christmas, while Danny was in Heartley's Stores helping his father to get the Christmas orders ready, Ivy experienced her first contraction.

Having just made the Christmas puddings, she and her mother were relaxing before a blazing fire in the Mortons' drawing room when Ivy gave a sudden shriek.

"I think I've started, Mum," she groaned, but her mother was sceptical.

"I doubt if you could be in labour so early," she said firmly. "You're not due for another whole month –"

"Well, it certainly feels like labour," Ivy told her tersely. "I've never experienced anything like this before. Ow!"

Ivy groaned as another spasm rippled through her.

"I think you could be right," her mother finally agreed. "Maybe it's time to ring Mrs Grant –"

Ivy gripped her mother's arm. "Please, Mum, don't ring Danny," she whispered. "I couldn't bear to have him fussing around."

Her mother nodded. In her opinion, men were useless at a time like this.

By the time the midwife arrived, Ivy was having regular contractions, and Mrs Grant was surprised at how well she was doing and how far she'd already dilated.

"I don't think it'll be very long," she announced.

Ivy's mother proved to be a tower of strength, and didn't grimace or comment when Ivy squeezed her hand too tight or cursed and swore as labour progressed. A few hours later, an exhausted Ivy pushed her son into the world.

"It's a fine, healthy boy!" said the midwife, smiling broadly as she handed the screaming bundle to his mother.

"This little fellow – or should I say, big fellow – is perfect! My goodness, he's amazingly big for a premature baby! Are you sure –"

"We always had big babies in our family," Eleanor said firmly. "Both my babies were the biggest in the hospital nursery!"

Ivy was deeply grateful for her mother's intervention, which had quickly stopped the midwife in her tracks. Ivy had no idea how much she and Owen had weighed at birth or whether her mother had guessed the true situation and decided to take remedial action. Either way, a potentially embarrassing situation had thankfully been averted.

A phone call brought Danny hurrying back to the Mortons' house shortly afterwards. His face was wreathed in smiles as he gazed at the baby.

"You're amazing, Ivy!" he whispered, kissing her forehead. "He's gorgeous, isn't he? Look, he's got the Heartley nose!"

Ivy smiled, relieved that Danny didn't realise which Heartley the baby had inherited it from.

For a moment, Danny looked serious, and Ivy's heart skipped a beat, not sure what was coming next.

"Ivy – would you mind terribly if we called him Joseph? I know it's a lot to ask, so think about it for a while – but it would mean a lot to Dad, now that Joe's gone away . . ."

Ivy's heartbeat returned to normal. "I don't need to think about it – I think it's a lovely idea," she said warmly.

She gazed down at the baby in her arms, and tenderly caressed his wispy blond hair. Personally, she couldn't think of a better name for her son. In a way, it was almost like having Joe back again . . .

Chapter 46

When she reached home, Ivy went straight to the study and turned on her computer. She intended checking the ownership of 6 Cherrywood Road, Hampstead. Hannah was always proclaiming that Rosa bought it herself, but Ivy was beginning to suspect that Hannah didn't know the full story.

Trying to stay calm, she clicked on the Land Registry site, typed in the Hampstead address and paid the required fee by credit card to view the information she wanted.

Ivy felt the urge to be sick as she looked at the computer screen, and had her worst fears confirmed. The owner of 6 Cherrywood Road was her own husband! Although her hand was shaking, she scrolled further along and discovered that Danny had bought the house only a few years after they'd gone to London. They hadn't even had a house of their own back then – they'd lived in a rented flat and Danny had just taken out a mortgage to buy his first small supermarket – so why would he secretly buy a house for Rosa? And since they'd had no money, he'd have needed a mortgage to buy it. Why would he have bought a house for his mistress rather than for his own family? Since Rosa's child was only ten, it wasn't as though she was pregnant back then . . .

Momentarily, Ivy forgot her own pain as she racked her brain to make sense of it all. Since Rosa seemed to be the beneficiary, why hadn't Danny put the house in her name? Then again, he probably needed to use it as collateral for the purchase of the next Betterbuys store . . .

Everything felt weird to Ivy. Why on earth was she wasting time wondering why her husband hadn't put the deeds of a secret house into his mistress's name? Was she going crazy? Maybe if she just closed her eyes and counted to ten, everything would be back to the way it had been. There would be no secret house in Hampstead where her husband was conducting an affair with his childhood sweetheart, who lived there with his child. There would be no need for her to feel betrayed, demoralised, weepy, and very afraid.

Then anger filled her. How dare Danny and Rosa destroy her happy and comfortable life! Everything had been fine until she'd decided to go and do a good turn for Hannah. If only she hadn't gone to the Hampstead house!

No, Ivy told herself, ultimately I'd rather know. I've clearly been deceived for a very long time. Then a horrific thought entered her head. Did other people know about Danny's affair? Did Peggy know, or even Hannah herself? Had any of them known that Danny had bought a house for Rosa? Maybe they all knew he visited her regularly. Ivy's face flushed crimson at the thought of such humiliation. She couldn't bear to think that people she cared about might be feeling sorry for her behind her back.

And how the newspapers would love it if they found out. The paparazzi had been following her for years without ever digging up any salacious gossip about her. Now, they'd finally have their scoop.

Drying her tears, Ivy closed down her computer. She'd never expected her marriage to end, and certainly not this way. She'd expected that she and Danny would grow old together, and only be parted when one of them passed away.

Ivy buried her head in her hands. She'd no tears left, and a pounding headache. She felt drained and used, like an old threadbare kitchen cloth that had been wrung out so tightly that there was no moisture left. For the first time in her life, she felt old and tired. In place of the vibrant and dynamic actress was a shell of the woman she'd previously been. Had it been only this evening that her world had fallen apart? She felt as though she'd lived a lifetime in the last few hours.

Ivy massaged her temples to ease the throbbing in her head. She needed to direct her energies into some sort of plan, otherwise she was in danger of moping, crying, and challenging Danny when he got home – which was definitely not something she wanted to do. Not yet anyway. Her situation was so new and frightening, and the prospect of breaking up with Danny was heartbreaking. But it seemed he had a whole other life and an enduring relationship with another woman.

Ivy gave a hysterical laugh. It was amazing how the business of the lake had suddenly paled to insignificance. For months, it had been uppermost in her mind. But right now, she was hurting so badly over Danny's betrayal that the mystery caller and her search in the lake might as well be happening on another planet. The very foundations of her life were crumbling, and nothing else seemed to matter any more.

Ivy headed towards their bedroom. Luckily, Danny wouldn't be back that night – it was supposedly one of his nights for making impromptu visits to Betterbuys stores – so she could cry herself to sleep in private. No doubt at this very moment, he and Rosa were snuggled up in bed together, probably making love, and maybe even laughing at poor easily deceived Ivy.

As she climbed into bed without bothering to wash her face or clean her teeth, Ivy felt overwhelmed by all that had happened that evening. Her entire marriage was a lie, since there was no longer any part of it that had truly belonged to her and Danny. Rosa had always been there in the middle. Each night as he'd lain beside her, or made love to her, had Danny been thinking of Rosa? It was frightening to review the life she'd considered near-perfect, and discover all its flaws and hidden innuendos. With hindsight, it was possible to read all sorts of meanings into simple events that had seemed so wonderful at the time.

Ivy knew she was making herself sick with all the permutations and combinations that her brain kept coming up with. At times, she felt that her head would explode. But she had to know the truth, and she wanted to work everything out before confronting Danny. If she didn't know the full story, he'd sense it and try to convince her it wasn't true. And she wanted so much to be convinced . . .

No, she needed to know every little detail before she confronted him. And the only way to find out the truth was to go and talk to Rosa.

As she tossed and turned, unable to sleep, Ivy imagined confronting her nemesis. Out of courtesy, she'd tell her about Hannah's illness. Then she'd demand answers to the questions that Danny would probably refuse to answer. She intended being informed about every detail of the affair by the time she finally confronted Danny.

Ivy could feel anger boiling up inside her. What sort of woman would steal another woman's husband? She bit her lip. But hadn't she herself been the one to take Danny from Rosa in the first place? Was this Rosa's revenge? Whatever the reason, Ivy felt that first and foremost, her duty was to Hannah. The least Rosa could do was look after her terminally ill mother. Hannah deserves better treatment than she's getting, Ivy thought angrily. And so do I.

Eventually, she drifted off into an exhausted sleep.

Chapter 47

The following evening, when Danny returned home from work, he was in good spirits as he walked into the drawing room, where Ivy was pretending to read the daily newspaper.

"Well, pet – did you miss me?" he asked, leaning forward to plant a kiss on her lips.

"Of course!" said Ivy lightly, deftly turning her head so that his kiss landed on her cheek instead. Inside, she was livid but, being a talented actress, she was adept at hiding her feelings. Truthfully, she wanted to strangle him. She couldn't bear the thought of him touching her, and she longed to challenge him about his affair. But she was determined to wait until after she'd confronted Rosa.

Later that night, Ivy claimed to have a monumental headache in order to avoid Danny's advances. As she lay rigidly on her own side of the bed, a damp towel covering her eyes, she groaned for effect as Danny hovered anxiously, offering to bring her tea, painkillers or anything else she needed. Ivy longed to shout that what she wanted was the truth, but after years of deceiving her he was hardly likely to give her that now.

Stupidly, she'd felt immune from extra-marital affairs. Everyone viewed her and Danny as one of society's golden couples, and Danny had always shown his devotion with every little gesture, smile and unexpected gift. It just shows what a good actor he is too,

Ivy thought wryly. And if it weren't for Hannah's illness, I might never have known what was going on.

The following morning, Danny had an early meeting, so he was up and gone from the house by eight o'clock, for which Ivy was very grateful. She doubted if she could have made any attempt at civility over breakfast.

Fortunately, it was one of Ivy's late days, so she didn't have to be on the set of *Bright Lights* until the afternoon. She had only a few lines to speak today, and she knew them off by heart already. As she shuffled around in dressing gown and slippers, a cup of coffee in hand, she wondered how she would fill her morning. She was still reeling from the impact of her discoveries, and she longed to have someone she could confide in. But celebrities rarely had trusted friends, since their secrets were too tempting for others to keep to themselves.

Ivy sighed. Her own secret was so heinous that she was destined to be alone forever. She couldn't even confide in Peggy, her closest woman friend, because Peggy herself was a victim of her deceit. Anyway, how could she talk to her sister-in-law about her own brother's infidelity?

Ivy longed to ring Brian, and tell him what she'd found out. But what exactly would she say? Somehow it didn't feel right to burden a man for whom she still had such warm feelings. Besides, he might consider her pathetic because her husband had managed to fool her so easily. And she'd be embarrassed if he thought she was looking for more than she had a right to ask for, or more than he wanted to give.

But she could ring Owen and, if Brian was there, she felt sure he'd want to say hello to her.

Quickly, she dialled the phone number of Siyak'atala, and was pleased when Owen answered.

"Hello, brother – how are you?"

"Kiddo – it's great to hear your voice!"

"Just thought I'd give you a call – I miss you all so much!"

Suddenly, Ivy had tears in her eyes as she realised just how true her statement had been. She really missed South Africa, and all the wonderful people she'd met there, and one man in particular.

"Are you okay, sis? You sound a bit – I don't know, not quite your usual cheery self –"

"I'm fine," Ivy told him firmly, making an effort to inject some gaiety into her voice. "I hope you and Charmaine are well too?"

"Yep, we're up to our eyes in plans for the wedding – originally, we were going to hold it in Knysna, where Charmaine's family live, but we've finally decided to hold it here at Siyak'atala. It'll be easier for friends and family to fly into Port Elizabeth. Lumka says she can handle all the catering, but I don't think it would be fair to burden her. Charmaine thinks we should get outside caterers to handle the food –"

"Whatever you decide, I'm looking forward to seeing you all again," Ivy told him, hoping her voice didn't sound too shaky or emotional. She was pleased that her brother had found happiness at last. But the irony of their situations wasn't lost on her. Just as his life was getting on track, her own was falling to pieces . . .

"Have you seen the parents lately?" Owen asked.

"Yes, we were down in Willow Haven last weekend," Ivy told him, avoiding mentioning Danny's name. "They're both fine – as usual, Dad is trying to avoid taking any exercise, and Mum is determined to get him fit!"

Owen chuckled. "I hope they're coming out for the wedding?"

"Definitely," Ivy told him. "Mum's been hassling Dad about getting into shape for South Africa, and I've had to take him jogging with me!"

"That sounds positive – it would mean a lot to have them here with us. I think I'm turning into a sentimental old fool in my dotage!"

Ivy laughed back, although it was the last thing she felt like doing.

"How's everyone in Willow Haven?" Owen asked.

"Oh, fine."

It suddenly occurred to Ivy that Hannah would probably be dead by the time Owen and Charmaine got married. But she didn't want to burst Owen's bubble of happiness by mentioning Hannah's illness, because he'd always been fond of Hannah too.

She also longed to tell him about her own situation, but

somehow she just couldn't bring herself to do it. Why ruin his happy mood when he couldn't do anything about it? Besides, she needed to acquire a lot more information before she was in a position to make a definitive judgement on Danny's behaviour. A tiny part of her brain was still hoping there was some other explanation for what he was doing in Hampstead.

"How's Joseph?"

"Oh, he's fine – he's hoping to come out for the wedding too."

"Great! Hang on, Brian's just come out of the operating theatre. I'm sure he'd like to say hello . . ."

Ivy could feel herself blushing at Owen's words, and was relieved that he couldn't see her.

She could hear mumbling voices, then the sound of a closing door, and she realised that Brian was ensuring they had privacy for their chat. Then she heard the phone being lifted, and she found her heart beating faster.

"How are you, Ivy?"

"Fine thanks, Brian," she replied, which was a total lie.

He lowered his voice. "I hope you haven't received any more of those phone calls?"

"No," Ivy lied. Right now, the phone calls were just one of the many problems she had to cope with. If only Brian knew what else was going on!

She guessed he was smiling at the other end of the phone.

"Well, that's got to be a relief," he said cheerfully. "Hopefully, whoever it was has given up."

"Yes, I'm sure you're right," Ivy said dully.

"And the lake – I hope you've decided against diving in there again?"

"Yes, of course I have," Ivy replied, depressed at being reminded of yet another problem she still had to deal with.

"Ivy, are you okay? You don't sound great –"

"I'm fine," Ivy assured him. Suddenly, she wished she hadn't phoned at all. She couldn't bring herself to tell Brian what she'd discovered about Danny. Besides, she'd already burdened him with all her past history – it simply wasn't fair to use him as a sounding board and repository of all her fears and insecurities. And anyway, she still didn't know for certain if Danny was cheating on her. Maybe she was being unfair to her husband, and there really was a simple explanation for what he was doing.

It seemed that Brian could also sense her change of mood, and he quickly directed the conversation to a more neutral topic.

"How's work going?"

"Oh, it's fine. We're shooting a complicated storyline at the moment," Ivy replied, now feeling that he was humouring her, and that the magic had somehow been lost.

"Oh. Well, I hope it works out okay."

Suddenly, Ivy felt the distance of each and every mile that separated them. Brian knew nothing about her world, and she felt overwhelmed by all the differences between them. How had she ever thought that they had a special bond?

It was clear that Brian could also feel the strain.

"Will I get Owen back to say goodbye to you?"

"No, it's okay – I just rang to say hello."

"Well, that was nice of you, Ivy. And I'm glad things are working out okay for you. You'll be out for the wedding?"

"Yes – see you then."

Ivy hung up, wanting to scream with frustration, a dull pain in the pit of her stomach. *Nothing* was working out for her! And phoning seemed to have made everything worse. She desperately wanted someone to realise how hurt and frightened she was, but she also knew she was asking too much. Had she expected Owen or Brian to pick up on her mood by osmosis, and instinctively know that she was suffering? She couldn't expect either of them to be mind readers. She'd had every opportunity to tell them how much she was hurting, but her pride had prevented her. It was as though an invisible barrier had formed between her and everyone else.

As for Owen's wedding – right now she suspected she'd be going to it alone, or just with Joseph. If Danny was having an affair with Rosa, he certainly wouldn't be accompanying her.

Chapter 48

As she waited on the set of *Bright Lights* for her scene to commence, Ivy was shivering. She dreaded the thought of losing Danny, but if he was bedding Rosa, there was no way she could stay married to him. Not for an instant. She'd file for divorce and they'd split their assets in a fair and equitable manner. The only favour she'd ask of him was that he keep the details of his affair under wraps. She didn't want to be portrayed in the newspapers as a victim.

How and when had Danny and Rosa got together? Ivy knew she was torturing herself, but somehow she couldn't stop her mind running riot as she kept going over every detail. Initially, she'd wondered if they'd become reacquainted on a flight, when he was en route to one of the retail conferences he attended abroad. But Danny had bought the house in Hampstead a long time ago, so he and Rosa must have stayed in contact even after she'd left Willow Haven. Could Danny have felt guilty and gone to London to find her? Maybe he'd secretly regretted being forced into marriage so young, and he and Rosa had resumed their relationship behind her back . . .

Suddenly, Anton, Ivy's screen husband, appeared by her side and slipped an arm around her, immediately shaking her out of her reverie. But not quickly enough to dispel Anton's concerns.

"Are you all right, Ivy?" he asked, a quizzical look on his

wrinkled old face. He looked so kindly and father-like that Ivy longed to confide in him. But the instinct for self-preservation immediately kicked in – she'd been relying on herself for a lifetime, and she wasn't about to let down her guard now.

"I'm fine thanks, Anton," she replied, smiling.

"You look tired – are you sure you're okay for this scene?" he asked. "We've only got two shots at getting this coffee scene right, Ivy, because Props have only two identical jackets for me."

"Stop fussing, we'll be fine," Ivy said crossly, annoyed at having her thoughts interrupted. She didn't want to be on the set of *Bright Lights* at all – there were far too many other things needing her attention.

Anton moved off, and Ivy immediately felt contrite. She hadn't meant to be abrupt with him. Of all the people she knew, he was least deserving of her ire. But quickly her thoughts reverted to Danny and his relationship with Rosa, and another shocking thought occurred to her. All those business trips Danny had been going on for years – maybe they'd been nothing of the sort, merely excuses to meet up with Rosa in exotic locations. Perhaps Rosa had let him know her schedule in advance, then he'd tell his wife he had a conference to attend. And when Rosa was back in London, they'd use the Hampstead house for their trysts . . .

Ivy made a mental note to check Danny's passport. Now that she thought about it, she couldn't recall ever being shown a single programme for any of the conferences Danny supposedly attended. He'd always been dismissive when he'd returned home, claiming that the conferences had been full of shoptalk that would bore her. Now, Ivy realised he'd probably been lying.

God, what a fool she'd been. Never once had she checked up on him – she'd always assumed he was telling the truth.

Ivy chewed her lip. When she and Danny first moved to London, it would have been convenient for him to meet Rosa regularly. Looking back, she recalled all those occasions when Danny claimed to be working late in the small supermarket he managed, supposedly to secure their future. Now she wondered if he'd been spending the time in his mistress's boudoir.

Suddenly, Ivy had a startling thought. Could Rosa be the mystery caller? It made perfect sense. Perhaps she was getting tired of being Danny's mistress, and wanted him all to herself. Perhaps the price of her silence over the car in the lake would be Ivy's agreement to give Danny a divorce? By telling her to stay away from the lake, Rosa had been letting her know that she knew what was down there. That would also explain why the mystery caller had managed to contact her in South Africa. No doubt Danny had been with Rosa while she'd been away, so she'd have known exactly where Ivy was.

The more she thought of it, the more plausible it seemed. Rosa had still been living in Willow Haven when Fred's car plunged into the lake. Could she have seen what happened, and kept quiet about it? On the other hand, Rosa had been dating Danny at the time, so wouldn't she have told him if she'd witnessed his brother's death? And how would Rosa know that Ivy had recently dived into Harper's Lake? If Rosa had been back in Willow Haven, surely she'd have visited her mother? Ivy shook her head. Rosa might be a husband-stealer, but she couldn't see how she could be the mystery caller, unless she had some other agenda. Nevertheless, she felt certain that Rosa was out there somewhere, pulling her strings like some master puppeteer.

Momentarily, Ivy thought of ringing Brian again when she got home, because she desperately longed to talk the situation through with someone she could trust. But just as quickly she changed her mind. Their last phone call had been far from satisfactory, and Ivy knew it was her fault.

"Ivy, are you okay?"

Ivy turned round to find Emily beside her.

"Yes, of course, Ems. Why do you ask?"

"You looked a bit sad – are you sure there's nothing bothering you?"

Ivy switched into acting mode immediately, recalling how observant Emily had been at her dinner party some months earlier. Much as she was fond of her kind-hearted colleague, Emily was far too astute for her liking!

She leaned down and whispered conspiratorially. "I'm just

getting in form for my next scene – I'm deliberately putting myself in a sad mood for my row with Anton."

"Oh, okay," said Emily, looking doubtful. "It's just that Colin mentioned you'd been to see some medical guy – I hope nothing's wrong, Ivy?"

"Thankfully no," Ivy replied. "It was a false alarm, and I'm fine." She hated lying to her friend, but she'd no other option. The cast and crew were a great bunch of people, and she didn't want them worrying about her, especially since all her actions were designed to cover up her own unsavoury past.

Ivy smiled down at her diminutive friend. "By the way, Ems, I meant to congratulate you on Marina's affair– Colin gave me a look at the rushes when I got back after my hol – break –"

She'd been about to say holiday, but just caught herself in time.

"The scenes between you and Tony are incredible. You really look as though you're crazy about him!"

Emily made a face. "You've no idea how difficult those scenes were, Ivy – between his bad breath and his wet kisses, I wanted to kill him or commit suicide – I just couldn't decide which!"

"Well, it just shows what a professional you are," said Ivy, smiling. "I'll be watching again tonight when the affair airs on TV. You know, it wouldn't surprise me if the writers decided to make Marina a much more prominent character."

Emily coloured, looking pleased. "Do you really think so, Ivy? But I'd never want to usurp Isabella –"

Ivy patted her friend's shoulder. "Sometimes, we all need a change," she said enigmatically.

Suddenly, there was a shout from the director.

"Ivy and Anton – you're on!"

Quickly, Ivy rose to her feet and hurried to the indoor set, where Anton gave her a discreet thumbs-up as she joined him at their dining-room table. She returned Anton's greeting with a nod as she sat down opposite him. Her and Anton's explosive row would culminate in Ivy throwing a pot of hot coffee over him.

As the scene progressed and the atmosphere became more heated, Ivy finally hurled the coffee pot, screaming at Anton as the coffee dripped down his shirt, tie and jacket. In reality the coffee was cold, but Ivy found herself pretending that Danny was the recipient of the coffee, and the hotter the better as far as she was concerned.

"Brilliant, folks – we got it first time!" the director called, as people from the make-up and wardrobe departments stepped forward with towels to wipe the coffee from Anton's hair and face and to relieve him of his now very wet shirt and jacket.

Ivy looked apologetically at her screen husband as he grinned back.

"Well done, Ivy – my word, that's some temper you displayed!" Anton said, laughing. "I wouldn't like to be in Danny's shoes if he ever did anything to upset you!"

Ivy smiled back at him, but her smile turned to a grimace as soon as she turned away. Yes, she thought to herself, Anton was right. Danny has no idea what he's taken on. But very soon he was going to find out.

Chapter 49

On a warm June afternoon, Willow Haven train station was crowded as the 2.15 to London prepared for departure. People were opening and closing carriage doors, loading on luggage and shouting to family and friends.

Danny was laughing, excited to be setting out on such a big adventure.

"Ivy and I are going to be rich and famous – just you wait and see!" he told his father and Ivy's parents.

Although smiling in agreement, Ivy secretly wished that Danny would keep his mouth shut – it almost seemed like tempting fate. They'd only just sat their A levels, and wouldn't get their results for ages yet. Nevertheless, Ivy had already received confirmation of a place at RADA, so her A levels would just be the icing on the cake. Neither she nor Danny were short on ambition, so she'd little doubt they'd be successful in their chosen fields. But there was no point in boasting about it in advance.

As Fred stood on the platform, he seemed like a zombie, unable to say anything, his face frozen into a ghastly white mask of grief. As Ivy's father glanced at him, he was acutely aware that, for Fred Heartley, Danny's departure must seem like losing yet another son.

Outside the carriage, Eleanor Morton was struggling to make herself heard over the din of voices and engine noise.

"Safe journey, Ivy – phone us as soon as you and Danny get settled!"

Ivy nodded as she stepped on board, following Danny who was now carrying on their suitcases, his photographic equipment and Joseph's buggy, stacking them all on the luggage rack inside. Reaching down to take little Joseph from her mother, Ivy could see that there were tears in her mother's eyes as she handed him over.

"I'm going to miss him terribly," Eleanor whispered, trying to smile. "I've grown so attached to him, you know. Are you sure it wouldn't be better to leave him here with us – at least until you get settled in a flat, and Danny gets a job?"

Ivy smiled at her mother. "I seem to remember – not all that long ago you were adamant that you and Dad didn't want to be saddled with a baby."

"That was before we knew him!" her mother replied, desperation in her voice. "Now the house is going to be so empty, with Owen away at university and you gone to London . . ."

Ivy's father intervened. "We'll gladly look after him any time you need us, pet," he said, "but we know you want to make your own lives – don't we, Eleanor?"

"Yes, yes, of course we do. It's just that –"

Peter Morton closed the carriage door firmly. "Safe journey!" he called out, just as the whistle was blown and the train began to slowly move off. Danny and Ivy were waving frantically while a bemused Joseph looked on.

Eleanor was now weeping quietly, tears running down her cheeks. The day she'd dreaded for so long had now come, and she was bereft. Fred Heartley was still wearing a haunted expression on his face. Peter sighed, slipping an arm around his wife. Earlier, he'd assumed the role of jovial conversationalist in an attempt to keep everyone's spirits up, but now he had nothing left to say either. But as the silence deepened, he felt the need to make some comment or remark.

"Why don't you come back to our house for tea?" he said, addressing Fred as the train finally disappeared into the distance. "Or why don't I open that bottle of brandy I got last Christmas? You look like you could do with a strong tipple, Fred."

Fred Heartley seemed oblivious to what was being said, and Peter had to repeat himself before he got a response. But Fred merely shook his head and began to walk away.

Peter sighed, understanding that Fred didn't dare risk crying in public. He regarded himself as a pillar of the local community, so he couldn't allow himself to demonstrate human weaknesses.

Eleanor was puzzled by Fred's sudden departure.

"What's wrong, Peter? Where's Fred gone?"

"Come on, let's get home," Peter Morton said softly. "I think Fred wants to be left alone."

Eleanor nodded, and they began walking home arm in arm. Already, Peter was missing Ivy, but he was well aware that parents had to let their children go in order for them to fulfil their own destiny. Wasn't Owen already away at university, and talking of going overseas when he qualified? But Peter knew his own feelings of loss were nothing compared to the agony that poor Fred Heartley was experiencing – having already lost a son and a wife, he was now watching another son leave.

Peter sighed. Nothing could be worse than dealing with heartache all alone. At least he and Eleanor could share their pain with each other.

* * *

As the train trundled along, Ivy glanced across at Danny, who was singing a nursery rhyme to Joseph. Suddenly, she felt fearful for their future. She and Danny were two jobless teenagers with a young baby – how on earth were they going to survive? They'd need to find a flat quickly, preferably one with a garden for Joseph – and she'd need to get him settled in a crèche before she started classes at RADA. They had the money Fred Heartley and her parents had given them, but that wouldn't last for long. The cost of their first few nights in a B&B would make quite a dent in their funds. Danny would need to get a job as soon as possible. And since Rosa lived in north London, Ivy had decided they'd live south of the river. She'd buy a newspaper as soon as they arrived and start looking at the ads for accommodation.

She sighed. Going to London was a huge undertaking, and she was beginning to wonder if she'd been wrong to insist on going. Danny had been fully in agreement, but Ivy also knew he'd do anything to please her. If she'd wanted to stay in Willow Haven, he'd happily have gone to work in his father's shop. Would her determination to act be the undoing of them all? And little Joseph deserved a proper upbringing – if they'd stayed in the village, he'd have had three grandparents and a doting aunt, all willing and able to give him lots of love and attention. Ivy knew how deeply it had distressed her mother to say goodbye to him . . .

Ivy sighed again. On the other hand, she and Danny were on the brink of a big adventure, and it was nice to have someone who adored you and would take care of you. Even if he wasn't the one you'd originally wanted.

The movement of the train soothed her, and gradually she felt herself drifting off into sleep.

* * *

As Danny stared out the window of the train, watching the countryside rush by, he felt a surge of excitement inside him. Against all the odds, he'd succeeded! It had all been worth it, to finally win the woman he'd always wanted.

As he bounced little Joseph on his knee, he glanced across at Ivy, who'd already dozed off, lulled into sleep by the warmth of the carriage and the monotonous clacking of the train. He gazed at his wife's sleeping face, her golden hair lit by the sun, and the smattering of freckles across the bridge of her nose giving her a look of childlike innocence in repose. She was so beautiful, and he adored her! He'd support her one hundred per cent as she fulfilled her dream of becoming an actress. He'd be the rock she'd lean on as she made her way up the ladder of success.

And he'd be successful himself – he didn't intend lagging behind his lovely wife. His success would match hers, albeit in a different field. He was taking with him all the knowledge of the retail trade that he'd learnt from his father – both the good and bad – and he intended ultimately turning the retail world on its head. He was *buzzing with ideas for a new kind of shopping experience, and one day he'd create a new kind of supermarket. He'd give himself five years to get his dream up and running . . .*

He'd never told Ivy that after his mother's death Fred had offered to retire and sign over Heartley's Stores to him. But he'd turned it down, because he had ambitions he could never achieve in Willow Haven. There was also another reason why he needed to be in London, but it had nothing whatsoever to do with his or Ivy's career. It was a personal matter, one that Ivy must never find out about . . .

Despite the warmth of the sun shining in the window, Danny suddenly shivered. Things could have turned out very differently. At one point, it had looked as though he might lose everything. But that was all in the past now, and an exciting future was beckoning.

Joseph was now asleep in his arms and Danny gazed down at him in wonderment. Would he take after Ivy, and end up in the theatre or on television? Or would he favour the retail business? Or maybe he'd want to do something else entirely? Well, whatever he wanted to do, Danny intended making sure that the world was his son's oyster . . .

* * *

"Ivy, we're in London!"

She awoke with a jolt, just in time to see the train glide into Kings Cross station.

Danny was smiling cheerfully and even Joseph was looking interested in what was happening all around him. Throughout the carriage, people were collecting their belongings and queuing for the doors.

Ivy felt disoriented and wrong-footed. She'd been asleep for three hours!

"Why on earth didn't you wake me?"

Danny grinned. "You looked so cute – I couldn't bear to disturb you!"

His good humour was infectious, and Ivy found herself smiling too. They were in London at last, and their adventure was just beginning.

Chapter 50

At the earliest opportunity, while Danny was working late at the Betterbuys head office, Ivy opened the wall safe in the drawing room where the family passports were kept. Then armed with pen and paper, she retired to the coffee table with Danny's passport, and began writing down the countries he'd visited and the dates on which he'd arrived and departed.

Her heart was beating uncomfortably. As far as she was aware, Danny had told her he'd visited cities like New York and Philadelphia for his retail conferences. He'd never told her he was going to the Seychelles, Barbados, the Bahamas, Florida and Hawaii. Danny had also made a brief visit to Sydney in the last year, but Ivy had no recollection of ever being told he was going to Australia. Fleetingly, she pictured her husband and Rosa relaxing on Bondi beach, drinking pina coladas in a beachside café before hurrying back to the privacy of their hotel to make love . . .

Having written a detailed list covering the eight years of travel on his passport, Ivy had mixed feelings as she returned it to the safe. She'd proved, without a shadow of a doubt, that Danny had lied to her. But while she had the satisfaction of being right, that proof was leading inexorably and frighteningly to the disintegration of her marriage.

Next, she had to undertake the most difficult part of her

investigation. She needed to check Rosa's letters and postcards to Hannah. If these dates coincided with Danny's visits abroad, then she'd have the proof they'd spent the time together. But first, she had to visit Willow Haven again, and somehow gain access to the drawer where Hannah kept Rosa's correspondence. Could she sneak in at night, while Hannah was asleep? Ivy shuddered. If she was caught, she couldn't imagine explaining herself out of that one. Ideally, she needed Hannah to leave the house, but wasn't an ill woman more likely to stay close to home?

At last, Ivy had an idea. She'd treat her parents and Hannah to a visit to the cinema in the nearest town. A new blockbuster movie had just been released, and every cinema had queues to see it. She'd have a word with the manager of the cinema in advance and ensure that Hannah and her parents got VIP treatment. Her celebrity would be enough to ensure his cooperation. She'd also book and pay for a meal for her parents and Hannah at a top local restaurant, ensuring they'd all be away from Willow Haven for at least several hours. Enough time to find out what she needed to know.

* * *

In the end, it had all been so easy. She'd visited Willow Haven that weekend, convinced Hannah and her parents to visit the cinema and have dinner, but pleaded lines to learn as the reason she couldn't accompany them herself. When they'd all left, she'd let herself into Hannah's house with the back-door key that was always hidden under the mat, and gone through everything in Hannah's tin box.

Since Hannah kept all Rosa's letters in their original envelopes, Ivy was able to jot down the dates and destinations quickly. She did the same with the numerous postcards. She'd put them in date order later, then check them off against the entries in Danny's passport. She completed her task in less than half an hour, and was back sitting in the kitchen, reading through her script, when her parents returned.

"That was a great movie, Ivy," her mother told her approvingly. "What a pity you couldn't have joined us – I know you'd have enjoyed it."

Ivy shook her head ruefully. "I wish I could have gone with you, but you know how urgent it is to get these lines learnt. Maybe I'll catch it on DVD later."

Her father touched her arm. "Thanks, love – it was a great night out, and Hannah enjoyed herself immensely. It was nice of you to include her – she hasn't been out much since she became ill."

Ivy nodded in acknowledgement. "I'm glad she had a good time," she replied, feeling a total hypocrite. "You all deserved a little treat – was the restaurant okay?"

"Yes, the food was wonderful!" Eleanor chimed in. "I was amazed at how much Hannah managed to eat – since she got the cancer, she hardly eats anything at all."

Peter grinned. "Of course, we had to listen to her waffling on about how wonderful Rosa is."

Ivy instantly felt angry at the mention of Rosa, but outwardly she laughed. "Surely you feel the same about Owen and me?"

Her father chuckled. "Of course we do, love – but we try not to bore people about it."

Ivy smiled to herself. Her parents were forever boasting about their children's achievements. They could certainly give Hannah a good run for her money!

Eleanor grimaced. "I could put up with Hannah's ramblings if Rosa showed a bit more responsibility towards her mother," she said, her eyes glittering angrily. "And I can't understand why Hannah won't let her own daughter know that she's dying."

"Look, it's Hannah's decision," Ivy said gently. Inwardly she wanted to kill Rosa, and she longed to tell her parents that Hannah's daughter was doing a lot more harm than just neglecting her mother. But she kept quiet, and let her mother ramble on about the neighbours, the new factory and Clara Bellingham's forthcoming wedding.

"I wouldn't be surprised if she's in the family way," her mother snorted. "She's only just got engaged, so why else is she rushing to the altar so quickly?"

Ivy laughed. "So what, Mum? In this day and age, no one cares. If she's pregnant, then good luck to her!"

Eleanor pursed her lips, and Ivy wondered if her mother was still smarting from Ivy's own unplanned pregnancy years earlier. At least attitudes were a lot more tolerant now, and anyway, her parents were thrilled to have a grandson. They'd even hinted on several occasions that it would be nice to have more than one grandchild.

Ivy herself had been puzzled that she and Danny had never managed to have a child together. Of course, Danny believed that Joseph was his son and, to all intents and purposes, he was a good father. But Ivy had often wondered why she'd never conceived again, especially since she'd never bothered with contraception throughout her marriage, not even after winning the coveted role of Isabella in *Bright Lights*. A pregnancy could always be written into the storyline, and she'd have welcomed another child, even at the price of her career.

Now, of course, Danny was the last man on earth she'd want a child with! It was obvious he'd had child with Rosa, and had been hoping to keep her from finding out about his second family. Ivy sighed. She knew her parents would love more grandchildren, so she could only hope that Owen would increase the family quota when he and Charmaine got married.

"I wonder if Rosa will come back for Clara's wedding?" said her mother, interrupting her reverie. "They were always good friends, weren't they, Ivy?"

Ivy nodded. Clara and Rosa had been friends in school, but she doubted Rosa would never willingly set foot back in Willow Haven. Since she couldn't be bothered to visit her own mother, it wasn't likely she'd come back for a wedding. Ivy still occasionally wondered if Rosa could be the mystery caller, and she'd quiz her about the calls when they finally met.

She bit her lip. She'd need to start thinking of a nice wedding gift for Clara and Bill . . .

* * *

The following morning, as she jogged past the new factory, Ivy heard tapping on a window. Looking up, she saw Clara Bellingham gesturing for her to wait, and within minutes Clara was at the entrance to the factory offices, where she worked as PA to the managing director. The two women embraced.

"Oh Ivy – how wonderful to see you!"

"Clara – congratulations, I hear you're getting married soon."

Clara blushed. "Yes, on the 19th of next month, to Bill Huggins of all people! We never expected to end up together – we were always arguing when we were kids."

Ivy smiled, pleased to see Clara so happy. "Perhaps the attraction was there all the time?"

Clara laughed. "Maybe you're right. But we certainly took our time getting together – I'll be thirty-eight next birthday. Not too late to get pregnant, I hope – Bill and I intend trying for a baby as soon as we get married."

Ivy smiled to herself. So her mother was wrong, and she'd enjoy telling her so.

"Well, I wish you the best of luck," Ivy told her. "I hope you'll have lots of fun trying!"

Clara hesitated. "I don't suppose you'll be around for the wedding, Ivy? It's in the Allcott Arms Hotel, and we'd be delighted if you and Danny could come, but I know you both lead such busy lives . . ."

Ivy patted her old friend's arm. "Thanks, Clara, but unfortunately I'll be filming steadily all next month," she lied, "and Danny is opening another new store, so he's up to his eyes."

Ivy had no intention of accompanying Danny anywhere right now!

"But I'd intended phoning you anyway, to ask what you'd like for a wedding present –"

Clara turned pink. "Oh, Ivy, that's not why I invited you – oh dear –"

"Of course not – we'd be sending you a gift anyway. What about, say, a cooker, or a fridge freezer?"

"Oh Ivy, they cost far too much! We couldn't possibly –"

Ivy laughed. "You'd better tell me which one you want – otherwise the wrong one could turn up at your door!"

"Oh my God, that's very generous of you, Ivy – a fridge freezer would be wonderful! But are you sure?"

Ivy nodded. "Is there any particular make or size of fridge freezer you want? What about one of those big American ones, with drink dispensers in the door?"

With promises from Clara to provide her kitchen measurements, Ivy was about to leave when Clara tugged at her sleeve.

"I was thinking of inviting Rosa Dalton to the wedding, but I expect she's away in some exotic location, as usual." Clara hesitated. "The *Bright Lights* studios are in London, aren't they, Ivy? I don't suppose you ever run into Rosa there? Then again, maybe you wouldn't want –" She turned puce. "I mean, you and she didn't, I mean, after Danny chose you –" Abruptly, she closed her mouth.

"No, I haven't seen Rosa since she left Willow Haven," said Ivy dryly. "But she did send me a congratulations card when I got the part of Isabella – which I thought was rather nice of her."

"I still miss her," Clara added wistfully. "She was such fun. But then, we all move on, don't we? She leads such an exciting life now . . ."

Ivy nodded, handing Clara her business card. She was anxious to avoid any further discussion of Rosa's merits, since she wasn't sure that she could continue to maintain an equable demeanour. "Phone me at any of these numbers when you measure your kitchen, Clara. Or you'll catch me at Mum and Dad's until tomorrow morning. You remember their number?"

Clara nodded, and Ivy marvelled at how little the village had changed in twenty years. Same phone numbers, same people. But soon, Harper's Lake would be due for the biggest change of all.

* * *

That evening, Ivy paid a visit to Hannah Dalton. She always made a point of calling to see her old neighbour when she was in Willow Haven, but on this occasion, she had a decidedly ulterior motive.

Once again, Ivy was saddened to see that Hannah had deteriorated further, even in the short time since she'd last seen her.

"Ivy – how lovely to see you!" Hannah said as she opened the door, her gaunt face wreathed in smiles. "Thank you so much for the trip to the cinema and meal out – it was a lovely treat!"

"You're very welcome," Ivy told her, hugging her warmly.

"Mum said it was a very good movie. How are you feeling, Hannah?"

The older woman slumped into a chair.

"Oh, I'm managing alright. I have good days and bad days."

"How's Rosa?" Ivy felt she had to ask.

Hannah's face became animated. "Oh, she's great – she's on the New York-Bahamas route at the moment, standing in for a colleague for the next week, and she says it's an amazing place. According to her, the nightlife is fantastic."

"She's obviously having a wonderful time," Ivy said, smiling, still inwardly livid with Rosa. Hopefully after her latest stint, Rosa would be back in Hampstead, and Ivy would finally have her showdown.

Briefly, Ivy wondered who looked after the boy while Rosa was away. Was there a housekeeper or childminder in residence? And did Danny drop by regularly to see his son? Presumably Danny's wealth would ensure that this child was well looked after – in fact, Rosa didn't need to work at all. But perhaps she was the kind of woman who needed her own career and independence. Rather like me, Ivy concluded. Danny obviously liked strong independent women.

"You still haven't told Rosa about your illness."

Hannah looked defensive. "I'll do it when the time is right, Ivy."

As the two women sat in silence, Ivy ventured the question that was the true purpose of her visit.

"Hannah, didn't you have a mysterious caller several years ago?"

Hannah nodded. "Yes, it was very weird – the whispering voice on the phone kept telling me to leave the village, or 'face the consequences'. I was very scared, I can tell you!"

"What did Rosa make of it?"

"She was very worried, and felt I might be safer if I moved nearer to my sister Joan."

"But you didn't."

"No, all my friends are here. Besides, I didn't fancy starting over in another town where I wouldn't know anyone. Why should I let some voice on the phone drive me out of my own home?"

"So the police never found out who it was?"

"No, they assumed it was some crackpot. Anyway, the calls stopped as soon as the police got involved." Hannah looked at Ivy quizzically. "Why the sudden interest?"

"Oh, *Bright Lights* may be doing a scene involving abusive phone calls," Ivy lied. "It just reminded me of what happened to you."

Hannah seemed satisfied with Ivy's explanation. "Of course, Rosa is still encouraging me to move nearer to Joan – she thinks I'd be happier being close to my sister. But to tell you the truth, Joan can be a bit clingy. And if she knew I was ill, well, she'd drive me crazy with her fussing. No, I intend staying here right to the end."

There was little more Ivy could say. But she began to wonder if Rosa could have been her own mother's mysterious caller? Perhaps she felt that if her mother moved to a new location, she could introduce Danny as her partner without the attendant scandal that would ensue in Willow Haven. Ivy had mixed emotions at the thought. On the one hand, she wished Hannah the joy of knowing her daughter had found someone special, and had a child. But on the other hand, Hannah would undoubtedly be shocked to discover who that special person was!

Hannah struggled to her feet. "I'll make us both a cup of tea," she said, and Ivy didn't demur since making tea would probably help Hannah to feel useful.

While Hannah was filling the kettle in the kitchen, the landline rang and Ivy crossed the room to pick up the receiver.

"Hello?"

"Hello, Mamma, it's Rosa. I'm in the Bahamas –"

Ivy almost dropped the phone, feeling as though she'd lost the power of speech. She hadn't heard that voice in years! Suddenly, she was transported back to her schooldays, when Rosa had been the centre of attention with her risqué antics and jokes. This was the woman who'd always adored Danny, and who was now sleeping with him!

"Hello, Mamma?"

Ivy shuddered. She should probably identify herself, but she found she couldn't form any words, and her heart was doing uncomfortable somersaults.

"Hold on a moment –" she eventually managed to say, as the receiver slipped from her fingers and dropped to the floor. Placing it back on the table, she hurried out to the kitchen.

"Hannah – Rosa's on the phone!"

Hannah came rushing in, her eyes aglow as she picked up the receiver.

"Hello, Rosa!" she said cheerfully. Then her expression changed to one of disappointment. "Oh dear, the line's gone dead," she said sadly. "What a pity – I was looking forward to a chat. And you could have spoken to her too, Ivy."

Ivy nodded, secretly furious with herself. She'd missed the opportunity of telling Rosa about Hannah's illness. There would have been ample time to explain the situation before calling Hannah to the phone, but she'd bungled it by letting her own emotions get in the way. Then she'd dropped the phone, cutting off the call before Hannah could talk to her daughter.

In the silence that followed, Hannah returned to the kitchen to finish making the tea. Ivy wondered if Rosa had been just as shocked at hearing *her* voice after all these years. Perhaps Rosa had ended the call herself, rather than have to speak to her? If so, Ivy hoped she'd ring Hannah back later, because the older woman was clearly disappointed.

When Hannah returned and the two women began drinking their tea, Ivy remembered another reason she'd called around. She hadn't wanted to pique Peggy's curiosity any further by asking her about the draining of the lake yet again. This time, Hannah might be able to tell her what she needed to know.

"Hannah, have you heard how the plans for draining the lake are coming along? Have the tenders been awarded yet?"

Hannah shook her head. "According to last week's local newspaper, members of the Council are still squabbling over the scale of the project. The cost is a lot higher than they expected. Some councillors want to go ahead immediately, but others are keen to delay it and push for a grant from central government." Hannah shrugged her shoulders. "I wouldn't hold my breath – it could be ages before anything happens."

Ivy nodded, trying to look nonchalant, but inwardly she was hugely relieved. Time was still on her side. But it wasn't on Hannah's, and Ivy realised that her old friend might well be dead by the time the project got underway.

Quickly, she changed the subject. "Oh, by the way, Hannah, I've arranged for another Betterbuys hamper to be delivered to you next week –"

Hannah raised her bony hands in protest. "No, no Ivy, you're far too generous! There's no need –"

"Of course there is!" said Ivy briskly. "You're a dear friend and neighbour, and I like being able to spoil you a little. I've arranged for the same contents as before – unless there's anything in it you'd like to change?"

"No, no – everything in it was wonderful," Hannah said. "You're so kind, Ivy. I just wish –"

As Hannah gazed into the distance, Ivy waited, not sure what was coming next. If it was within her power, she'd see that Hannah got it.

The older woman looked down at her hands. "I'm sorry the way things worked out, I mean, over Danny. I hope that when I tell Rosa – you know, about the cancer – you'll both be able to put the past behind you, because you're bound to bump into each other, even if it's only at my funeral –"

"For goodness sake, Hannah, Rosa and I will be fine!" Ivy lied. "Please don't worry about the past – bygones are bygones as far as Rosa and I are concerned."

Gratefully, Hannah reached for Ivy's hand. "Thanks Ivy, you've no idea how much that means to me."

By now, Ivy felt she'd spent enough time being outwardly supportive of Rosa, and it was time to leave. Otherwise, she was in danger of exploding with anger, and that wouldn't do Hannah any good.

"I'd better be going, Hannah," she said, feigning a yawn and rising to her feet.

"Of course, Ivy – it was good of you to spend so much time with an old fossil like me."

Ivy hugged her as they reached the front door. "Hannah, I *enjoy* spending time with you. Hopefully, I'll see you again soon."

As she left, Ivy wondered if, indeed, she'd ever see Hannah again. And as she walked in the direction of her parents' house, she had tears in her eyes.

* * *

The following morning, after a leisurely breakfast, Ivy kissed her parents goodbye.

"I wish you could stay longer, Ivy," her mother said plaintively as she placed her travel bag in her car.

"Yes, love," her father affirmed, as he hugged her. "You're only ever here on flying visits lately. Come and stay a bit longer next time."

Ivy nodded, her eyes bright with tears. Her parents were the best in the world, yet she always seemed to be using them to cover up something else. Next time, she'd stay as long as she could, and she'd hopefully make her final dive into the lake.

Several times over the weekend, she'd been on the brink of telling her patents what was going on between Danny and Rosa. But in the end she'd decided it wouldn't be fair on them, or on Hannah, who relied on their friendship as she coped with terminal illness. It would drive a wedge between old neighbours, and besides, she intended to confront Rosa first, then Danny, before altering other peoples' lives.

"Bye Mum! Bye Dad!" Ivy called, waving as she drove off. In her rear-view mirror, she watched as her parents grew smaller and smaller, then she turned the bend that took her out of the village, and she couldn't see them any more.

Ivy shivered, even though the heater in the car was set on high.

Chapter 51

Back home, Ivy didn't even bother to unpack. She went straight to her bedroom where she'd hidden the list of entries she'd taken down from Danny's passport. Sitting at her dressing table, she meticulously went through all the dates on Rosa's letters, and checked the postmarks on the postcards, and aligned them with the dates of Danny's visits abroad.

Ivy felt sick as she confirmed each location and date. Clearly, Rosa and Danny had been meeting up at exotic destinations for years. Did Danny intend leaving her and going back to Rosa? Or were he and Rosa happy to carry on their affair in secret? On the other hand, if Rosa *was* the mystery caller, she clearly wasn't happy with the present situation, and was upping the ante behind Danny's back.

Suddenly Ivy's hand flew to her mouth. Could Danny have guessed that Joseph wasn't his son? Maybe, having discovered her deception, he'd turned to Rosa to create his own family?

Her legs felt weak, and she was developing a headache. All this stress was making her feel ill. Her world was unravelling by the minute, yet she still needed to present a calm public face. She had to get up each day, shower, dress and become the elegant woman people expected to see. And she still had to learn her lines and give her usual professional performance on the set of *Bright Lights*. But despite all her efforts, she sometimes felt her composure was cracking – already Anton and Emily had expressed concern. Yet there wasn't a single person she could talk to.

Several times, she thought of ringing Brian, but dismissed it each time because she feared she'd lean on him more than was fair. Thinking of him always brought back happy memories of her time in South Africa. She'd made a decision to help the animals and people of the Eastern Cape, and she wouldn't forget her promise. As soon as all this business with Danny and Rosa was sorted out – and she'd retrieved her possessions from the lake – she'd talk to Brian and Owen about how she could help best.

But in the meantime she had to prepare for the following day when the *Bright Lights* week started again. She'd have to practise iron discipline when she went on the set, leaving her broken heart and disintegrating marriage firmly behind as she stepped once again into the role of Isabella.

Chapter 52

When Fred Heartley received his diagnosis of pancreatic cancer, his reaction was far from typical. Allied to the shock was a strange sense of relief. In a way, he almost welcomed it, because it meant that his earthly torment would soon be over.

As the years had slipped by and Joe's trail had gone cold, people in the village had assumed he'd emigrated to Australia or somewhere equally far away and hadn't wanted to see his family again. After a while, the locals stopped mentioning him any more, fearing that their enquiries would only remind the Heartleys of their loss.

But Fred never forgot, not even for an instant. And in his mind, every day brought him nearer to seeing his son. One day soon, Joe would walk into the shop and all those sad and lonely days would disappear, as though they'd never happened. He had to believe it, or he wouldn't be able to go on.

He'd never known a day's peace since Joe disappeared. It was funny how you never realised how much you loved someone until you'd lost them. All those stupid arguments he and Joe had, when all Fred wanted was for his eldest son to benefit from the business he'd built up. In rejecting his father's offer, Fred felt his son was rejecting him too, so he'd reacted with anger, threats and violence. Easy to be wise afterwards, Fred thought bitterly. All Joe wanted to do was to follow his own star, and I tried to stop him.

Fred's expression softened as he thought of his eldest son. Perhaps he'd subconsciously realised that Joe's charm and personality could build the business into something greater than it was. Funny how Danny became the one who'd made a spectacular success of his life in retail. Fred was hugely proud of Danny, but the ache over Joe's disappearance would never leave him as long as he lived. Which wouldn't be for much longer now.

Fred knew he wouldn't linger, since pancreatic cancer was a silent insidious killer and it was usually too late by the time it was detected. He'd listened to all the platitudes from the doctors and nurses but, even if he adopted the most positive attitude in the world, it wouldn't change what was happening inside him.

He wondered what type of cancer Hannah Dalton had. She'd never mentioned it to him, but he could see there was definitely something wrong, and each time she came into the shop, she seemed to have deteriorated even further. Then again, he could hardly blame her for her obstinacy – he hadn't told anyone about his cancer yet either. He and Hannah were both fiercely independent people, and neither of them would want other people's pity. On the other hand, it was sad that they couldn't confide in each other, since there were some things that only a person of your own age could understand. He supposed her daughter Rosa must have been told by now, and he wondered why he hadn't seen her back in the village yet. He'd have to let Peggy and Danny know about his own situation soon.

Fred sighed as he thought of the difficult days ahead. No doubt he'd be given strong painkillers when things got bad. Fred wasn't a particularly brave man, and his initial instinct had been to take an overdose rather than wait for the disease to eventually claim him. But if he did that, he might miss Joe's return. For while there was life, there was hope, and he wanted to be there to tell his son that nothing really mattered but his happiness.

Fred sometimes wondered if he could send Joe a telepathic message. He'd always been sceptical about things like that, but when a man became desperate, he was willing to try anything. Besides, what harm was there in trying? The rest of the family would laugh at him if he told them what he was contemplating – therefore he'd keep his thoughts to himself. But it was a known fact that animals had more highly developed instincts than humans, and knew about forthcoming weather changes – even earthquakes and tsunamis – long before they happened. Who was to say they didn't achieve this by some form of telepathy? He'd also read that twins were capable of picking up on each other's physical and mental pain, even across continents. If animals and twins could do it, then there was a hope, albeit a faint one, that he could somehow make contact with Joe. Surely his abiding love, combined with their genetic link, would help him?

Fred sat down in his favourite armchair, hoping that the silence of the parlour would be a good setting for his experiment. He tried to clear his mind of all extraneous thoughts, then closed his eyes and tried to picture his son. But all he could see was Joe's face contorted in anger, and the more he thought about it, the more Fred realised that all his contact with Joe in the year before he left had involved angry exchanges. Father and son hadn't shared a smile in a very long time before he left. Now Fred longed for the chance to put things right and say he was sorry.

In the silence of the parlour, he once again begged his son to return. *Joe, if you can hear me, please come home soon, because I haven't got long to wait for you . . .*

He wondered if he needed to practise in order to make the connection. If that was the case, he'd keep repeating his messages daily to Joe, and maybe someday his eldest son would pick up on his words, think kindly of his old dad, and take the bus, train, plane or boat home . . .

Chapter 53

It was another week before Ivy was in a position to visit Hampstead again, and she hoped that Rosa would be back from the Bahamas by now. She was still angry with herself for behaving so stupidly when Rosa had phoned her mother. She could have saved herself the journey to Hampstead, and Rosa could be back in Willow Haven with Hannah by now.

Her meeting with Rosa was becoming more and more urgent – Hannah was continuing to deteriorate, and her own relationship with Danny was becoming increasingly difficult to maintain. Despite her protestations that everything was fine, she'd caught him watching her surreptitiously several times.

Initially, Ivy had considered arriving at Rosa's house in her own BMW, and dressing glamorously and ostentatiously to intimidate her rival. But she quickly realised that the brief satisfaction she'd get would be offset by the twitching of local curtains, and before long the paparazzi would be parked outside Rosa's door. How embarrassing to be caught in the act of confronting your husband's mistress! Rosa might be happy to tell them she was being stalked by her lover's wife, who just happened to be a well-known soap star . . .

Ivy shuddered at the thought. No, she'd wear something dowdy so she wouldn't be recognised. Besides, the front door might have one of those spyglasses and, if Rosa realised it was Ivy outside, she might refuse to open the door. And this time Ivy wanted answers. She wasn't going to be ignored.

On the evening of her visit, Danny was attending a sailing-club dinner, so she knew he'd be safely out of the way. After showering and changing, he'd asked her advice about what tie he should wear, but she'd pleaded inability to help him, and had lain on the bed claiming to have yet another headache.

"You really ought to see the doctor," Danny said worriedly as he selected a pale blue tie. "You've had a lot of headaches lately, love – it might be worth having them checked out."

Ivy nodded, feigning a sudden violent pain that saw her rolling onto her side and clutching her head. She felt a fraud, but on the other hand she felt perfectly justified since what Danny was doing was even more deceitful. Since discovering his infidelity, she'd been finding it difficult to behave normally when she was with him, and she'd avoided making love by blaming her ongoing headaches any time he approached her. Fortunately, Danny seemed to accept her excuses. Perhaps, Ivy thought angrily, he was actually relieved – it must be difficult keeping two women satisfied!

Before he left, Danny bent down and kissed her cheek, and Ivy longed to scream at him that he was a liar and a hypocrite. Instead, she mumbled a farewell, and lay on the bed until she heard him drive off. Then she leapt up, dressed and applied slightly different make-up before pinning back her hair and adding a long hooded jacket. Rather than the BMW, she decided to use Joseph's Fiat Punto, which he stored in one of the garages during term-time. She'd have preferred the comfort of her own car on the drive from Sussex to London, but she didn't want to draw unnecessary attention to herself.

When she finally arrived at Cherrywood Road, Ivy saw that the lights were on in Rosa's house, and suddenly she felt terrified at what she had to do. But she needed to make Rosa aware of how ill her mother was. Surely they could put their personal differences aside, albeit briefly, for Hannah's sake? Ivy shivered. And then, she'd challenge Rosa about Danny . . .

Checking her appearance in the car mirror, Ivy climbed out and pulled up the hood of her jacket. She was shaking with fear as she thought of the confrontation ahead.

Hopefully the boy would be in bed by now, and she and Rosa could conduct themselves with dignity and decorum. She hoped their emotions wouldn't get out of hand and reduce them both to squabbling, screaming harridans.

Walking up the path, Ivy felt an overwhelming urge to turn and run back to Joseph's Punto. She didn't need to do this. Hannah's illness and Rosa's ignorance weren't her responsibility. She could simply tell Danny and leave him to tell Rosa. Besides, Hannah would be furious if she knew what Ivy was about to do! On the other hand, Ivy wanted to see close-up the woman who'd managed to keep her husband so captivated all these years. Rosa had been a pretty coquette in her schooldays – had this been enough to keep Danny interested?

Her finger poised over the doorbell, Ivy allowed herself a few seconds' reflection. She could walk away now, and no one need ever know she'd been here. She could simply go home, confront Danny, and end her marriage with as much civility and dignity as she could manage.

Pressing the bell, Ivy took a deep breath. She'd done it, and now it was too late to run away.

Suddenly, the door opened, and Ivy found herself facing the woman she'd seen entering the house the previous time. But now, in the light of the porch, Ivy could see that she wasn't Rosa at all. There was a close resemblance and, if Rosa had a sister, this woman might well be her. She wore her hair in a similar style to Rosa, and she was around the same age.

Ivy peered at the woman in the dim porch light, and quickly decided to adopt a slightly foreign accent. "Oh. Excuse me, is Rosa Dalton here?"

The woman looked momentarily surprised. "Er – no, she's away at present."

Ivy grimaced. "When will she be back?"

The woman looked uncomfortable. "I'm not sure. She didn't say –" Then the woman galvanised herself into action. "Can I take a message?" she asked eagerly. "If you'd like to leave your phone number, I'll pass it on to her – "

"No, it's okay – I'll catch her later. Thanks."

As she walked back to her car, Ivy was puzzled, disappointed and angry. She'd been denied her confrontation. Should she have said something to the woman about Hannah? And what was this look-alike's connection to Danny?

Ivy's brain seemed to have deserted her, and she was annoyed with herself for not asking the woman more pertinent questions. She'd seen her own husband going into this house, so was he having an affair with this woman, rather than Rosa? No, that wasn't possible – she'd already confirmed that Danny and Rosa met up in exotic locations abroad and she knew the house was Rosa's address. But why had he visited the house when Rosa didn't seem to be there? Perhaps he was visiting his child, and the woman was the childminder? Or could she be one of Rosa's tenants that Hannah was forever boasting about? Did this woman, whoever she was, know all about Rosa and Danny's affair?

* * *

After an exhausting drive back home, Ivy was in bed and feigning sleep when his driver dropped an inebriated Danny at the front door. Jumping up, she peeped out the window, and could hear him cursing at his inability to get the key into the lock. At any other time, she'd have gone downstairs and let him in, then lovingly guided him upstairs to bed. But now she felt nothing but anger. Let him sit outside all night, she thought viciously. Hopefully, there'll be a snowstorm while he's stuck out there. Feeling self-righteous, she got back into bed and eventually drifted off to sleep.

In the morning, Ivy awoke to discover that Danny was already in the ensuite shower and singing at the top of his voice. Angrily, she turned over to block out the daylight. She'd hoped he'd have a monumental hangover, but he didn't seem remotely out of sorts.

Shortly afterwards, Ivy could hear Danny moving around the bedroom. She knew he was dressing, and before he left the room he leaned over and kissed the top of her head while she pretended to sleep. A few minutes later she heard the front door close and his driver start the car. Only then did Ivy finally open her eyes.

Now, at last, she had time to think about what had happened the night before. She'd been mystified as she'd driven home from Hampstead. Perversely, she'd felt cheated by Rosa's absence, but it was clear that Rosa lived there and that Danny was a regular visitor. He was definitely playing happy families in that house, and Ivy was determined to get to the bottom of it.

Suddenly, Ivy sat up in bed with a jolt. She'd just come up with the perfect way of doing it. She was an actress, for heaven's sake – all she had to do was act!

Over the years, she had perfected the art of disguise. It was essential if she was ever to go for a walk, shop or dine out in peace. In the early days of her career, it had been exciting to be recognised by the public, but gradually it became a millstone, and she longed for at least occasional privacy.

She'd also proved how little actual change was needed to fool the public and the paparazzi. It simply required the tweak of a scarf, or wearing glasses without prescription lenses, or a dark wig like the one she'd worn en route to South Africa. Most people were woefully unobservant, and Ivy sometimes managed to spend a blissful morning buying clothes, followed by lunch in town, without anyone recognising her. Now, she intended putting those skills to practical use when she next visited Hampstead.

Ivy had a tight filming schedule for the rest of the week – unfortunately Colin was still holding her to her promise to work late if needed, so she'd be spending several evenings on the set. But it gave her time to think up a suitable role to play for visiting Rosa's house and, in between scenes, to raid the props department for clothing to go with her new identity.

She borrowed a selection of dresses, jackets and suits from the wardrobe department, and a box of wigs of assorted lengths and colours. Back home in the privacy of her bedroom, she tried on all the clothes, revelling in the changes she could make with just a different colour or shape of a jacket.

She also tried on all the wigs, and was pleased to see how

different she looked in each one. The red-haired wig made her look wild and tempestuous, and the long dark-haired wig instantly turned her into a sultry vamp. Last out of the box was a blonde wig, with fluffy shoulder-length hair, and when she put it on, Ivy was shocked to discover how like Rosa she looked. They had the same pale skin, and she gazed, horrified, at her reflection. Maybe this likeness was one of the reasons Danny had rekindled his relationship with Rosa – perhaps they both shared some indefinable quality that appealed to him? Angrily, Ivy pulled the wig off and threw it back in the box.

It was becoming increasingly difficult to maintain a cool and distant relationship with Danny. An added difficulty was Fred Heartley's recent diagnosis of pancreatic cancer, and Ivy had found it difficult to be unsympathetic to Danny when he told her. Instinctively, they'd hugged, but Ivy quickly moved away from him, afraid that he'd use the opportunity to kiss her, or initiate sex. Right now, she'd never let him touch her that way. She felt sorry for him and for Peggy, since they faced losing their father very soon, but there was no way her sympathetic gesture was going to lead to the bedroom.

Ivy was deeply fond of Fred herself, but her concern was also tinged with relief – soon the poor man wouldn't need to hope any longer for Joe's return, and she herself would have one less person to feel guilty about. He'd also be saved the heartache of learning about Danny's impending divorce.

Chapter 54

Ivy looked in her bedroom mirror and gave a satisfied smile. She didn't look remotely like Ivy Heartley any more. She could almost enjoy playing this role if the reason for doing so wasn't so critical. Today she had a day off from Bright Lights, so she intended using it to find out what was going on at 6 Cherrywood Road.

After trawling through all the props she'd borrowed from the *Bright Lights* wardrobe department, she'd finally decided on a dark, severely cut suit, and teamed it with a high-necked white blouse and sensible shoes. She had also selected a short grey-streaked wig, and it completed the ensemble perfectly, making her look like the competent official she intended playing that day.

It was a week since she'd called to see the absentee Rosa – a tension-filled week during which she'd had to find numerous excuses to keep her distance from Danny. Ivy hoped that Rosa would be back from her travels by now. If not, she intended playing a role that would enable her to get inside the house, however briefly, so that she could get some understanding of the living arrangements there.

She also needed to call at a time when someone was in. She didn't want to go to all the effort of dressing up and preparing herself mentally, only to find that no one was there. She decided that late afternoon would be the best time to call, since the ten-year-old boy would be home from school, and he'd need looking after.

But if he was home alone, so much the better. She might get some straight talking from him. Maybe he could confirm if Danny was his father, but how on earth would she bring the conversation round to such a question?

After the drive to Hampstead, Ivy arrived with time to spare, which she used to mentally prepare herself for the role. Briefly, she checked her utilitarian watch – which she'd substituted for her usual Tag Hueur – confirming that the boy and the Rosa look-alike would hopefully be home by now. It was time to begin playing the most important role of her life.

Clutching a folder, Ivy made her way up the garden path and rang the bell. If Rosa answered the door, she'd abandon her disguise and get straight down to business. Her heart thumping, she took another deep breath to calm herself.

Suddenly, the door swung open, and Ivy found herself facing the woman she'd spoken to on her previous visit. Instantly, she sprang into action.

"I'm from the local council education department – school attendance section," she said. "May I come in?" She took a step forward, doing her best to portray someone who wasn't going to take no for an answer. "There's a boy living here, aged around ten –"

As if to prove her right, a small boy rushed out into the hall and stared briefly at her. Then he turned to the woman. "Mum, can I have those crisps now? I've finished my dinner."

"Okay, Sean," said his mother, and he raced off into the back of the house.

Ivy felt an overwhelming sense of relief – the boy wasn't Rosa and Danny's son!

She stepped a little closer. "It's about your son," she whispered. "He's been missing school."

"What?" the woman looked startled. "But he loves school, and he always gets top marks!"

"Please, may I come in?" Ivy insisted. "Maybe we can clear this up quickly. And I'd rather the boy wasn't present." She looked at her chart. "Sean, isn't that his name?"

"Er, yes – okay, you'd better come in."

Ivy sighed with relief. Obviously the woman hadn't realised that she herself had already supplied the boy's name!

The woman was looking puzzled and concerned as Ivy stepped into the hall. "I don't know how Sean could be truanting. I meet him most days after work, and we walk home from school together."

As they moved into the cosy sitting room, Ivy consulted her file once again. How on earth was she going to bring the conversation round to Danny?"

"Do you have a husband, Mrs er –"

"Brampton," said the woman. "And no, I don't. I'm a widow."

Ivy peered at her chart again, making sure the woman couldn't see the blank pages. She was also relieved that Mrs Brampton hadn't realised that a school-attendance official should already know her name.

"Ah yes, I've Sean Brampton down here for truancy. But you do have a man who visits you, don't you, Mrs Brampton? Our investigations team has seen a man coming here on a regular basis."

The woman looked surprised, then gave a tinkly laugh. "Oh, you must mean Mr Heartley!"

Ivy felt both triumph and pain in the same heartbeat.

"To what purpose is he here, Mrs Brampton?" she asked, dreading the answer. In reality, Mrs Brampton was perfectly entitled to have a male caller, and didn't need to tell some stranger who came to the door about her private life.

The woman frowned. "That seems a very personal question, and has nothing to do with Sean truanting from school," she said, looking suspiciously at Ivy.

"Oh, I do apologise," Ivy improvised. "It's just that I need to list the most influential males in your son's life. After all, these people have a direct bearing on his development –"

Ivy knew she was talking rubbish, but she hoped that in some vague way it made sense to the woman. She desperately needed to know what the woman's connection was to Danny.

Mrs Brampton thought for a moment. "Well, there's my brother Tommy – he's very good with Sean, and often takes him to football matches at the weekend, and my sister's husband Andy is good with him too –"

Ivy pretended to be writing these people's names down, but appearing calm was calling on all her acting skills.

"And what about Mr Heartley?" she asked, then realised she was holding her breath.

"Oh, we don't see him very often."

"Sorry, I don't quite understand –"

Suddenly, Mrs Brampton laughed. "My goodness – you think he's my fancy man!"

She burst into her tinkly laugh again, and Ivy found it difficult to maintain her composure.

Nevertheless she smiled reassuringly. "Well, yes, I did assume he was your partner – and of course, you're entitled to have a man friend if you wish – my only concern is your son's education."

Ivy spoke evenly and calmly, although her heart was pounding. She was hoping that Mrs Brampton might explain her relationship to Danny, because she'd no idea what direction her questioning could take next.

"Well, he's not," said Mrs Brampton snootily. "Mr Heartley uses the flat upstairs."

Seeing Ivy's look of surprise, she smiled. "Oh, didn't you realise? This house is divided into two separate flats."

Ivy then remembered that many houses in London, even quite modest ones, had been divided into two or more apartments where possible. Anyway, hadn't Hannah told her repeatedly that Rosa was also a landlady? This other flat was probably where Rosa lived when she was back in London. And when she wasn't travelling, Danny came by to be with her.

"How often is Mr Heartley here?" Ivy asked, before realising that that wasn't the sort of question an education official would ask.

"I don't really know," said Mrs Brampton, shrugging her shoulders. "I don't keep track of his movements."

"Is Mr Heartley your landlord?"

Mrs Brampton nodded. "He only charges us a nominal rent. He just needs someone to keep the place lived in, which suits Sean and me perfectly. We were very lucky to answer his newspaper ad."

But Ivy was still puzzled. Mrs Brampton had said *Mr Heartley* came here. She hadn't mentioned Rosa. Yet Hannah claimed that Rosa owned the property, although Ivy knew she didn't. There was clearly something mysterious going on at 6 Cherrywood Road, and Ivy was desperate to find out what it was.

"So does Mr Heartley come here on certain days?" she asked, trying a more roundabout way of eliciting the information she needed.

Mrs Brampton's lips were pursed. "What has that got to do with Sean?" she asked tersely, and Ivy realised she'd taken a step too far.

"Oh, nothing. I just meant that not having neighbours present all the time would be a bonus," she said. "Noisy neighbours overhead can be a terrible nuisance."

Mrs Brampton nodded silently, clearly basking in her good fortune.

But Ivy wasn't finished yet. She had one more question to ask. On her previous visit to the Hampstead house, the woman had confirmed to Ivy that Rosa lived there, and had offered to take a message for her.

"By the way, Mrs Brampton, who else is living in the house?" She consulted her blank file again. "It says here that there's also someone called Rosa Dalton in residence –"

Mrs Brampton bridled again. "I don't see that it has anything to do with Sean's school attendance!"

Ivy gave a placatory smile. "Sorry, I'm just assuming she might be a good influence on your son. So Ms Dalton *does* live here?"

Mrs Brampton pulled her cardigan tightly around her. "You'd better speak to Mr Heartley about that," she said.

Ivy knew by Mrs Brampton's attitude that she wasn't going to get any more information. Was the Rosa look-alike involved in covering up Danny's affair? It was time to conclude the interview.

"Now, about Sean truanting from school – oh dear!" she said, looking at her file again.

"What is it?" asked Mrs Brampton, looking alarmed.

"Mrs Brampton, I've made a terrible mistake – please forgive me!" said Ivy, looking aghast. "I've come to the wrong address! It's another Sean Brampton I'm looking for. I'm so sorry for wasting your time!"

Rising to her feet quickly, she headed towards the door.

"So Sean hasn't been truanting? I thought not, because he's such a good boy –"

In the hall, Ivy surreptitiously peered up the stairs to the door of the upstairs flat. Then she turned earnestly to face Mrs Brampton. "Please, Mrs Brampton, I'd be grateful if you wouldn't mention my visit to anyone – I could get into trouble for bothering you and not getting through my daily quota of cases."

"Of course I won't!" said Mrs Brampton warmly as she opened the front door, relieved and delighted that her Sean wasn't in serious trouble.

Smiling, Ivy turned to face her. "You mentioned earlier that you go out to work, Mrs Brampton?"

"Yes, I work until three each afternoon, at the local doctor's surgery," she replied, prepared now to be chatty. "Which means I can meet Sean after school, and we usually walk home together. If there's an emergency and I'm delayed, he knows where the front-door key is hidden in the garden."

Ivy nodded eagerly. "That bond with your child is so important, isn't it? Well, thanks again, Mrs Brampton, and apologies for intruding on your time."

Grimacing, Ivy walked down the garden path and out onto the road. She felt sorry for the brief distress she'd caused the woman over her son. But her evasive answers about Rosa seemed to indicate that she'd been sworn to secrecy about their affair.

As she got into her car and turned on the ignition, Ivy was already planning her next move. She could challenge Danny face to face about the house he secretly owned and its connection to Rosa, but she knew she'd never get the truth from him. She'd just made the decision to break in next time.

Chapter 55

Ivy's plans for gaining entry to the Hampstead house were put on hold the following day. A call from Peggy informed her that Fred was close to death, and her sister-in-law suggested that she and Danny should visit sooner rather than later.

Fred was adamantly refusing to go to hospital, and had announced his intention of dying in his own home. The shop had been closed until further notice, but Fred was still worrying about his customers, and Peggy had found it necessary to lie to him about re-opening the shop as soon as possible.

Danny opted to leave for Willow Haven immediately. But Ivy didn't dare ask for extra time off from *Bright Lights*, since she'd had more than her fair share recently. Anyway, the less time she had to spend in her husband's company, the better, as far as she was concerned.

When she eventually arrived at Fred's home above the store, Ivy was greeted by Peggy, who'd moved in to care for him during his final days. As the two women hugged, Peggy quickly let her know that Danny was dining with her husband Ned and the children over at their own house. Ivy nodded her thanks. At one time, she might have cared where Danny was – right now she didn't give a damn.

On the landing outside Fred's bedroom, Peggy wiped her eyes.

"He doesn't have long," she whispered, her eyes red-rimmed as she gestured for Ivy to enter the bedroom. "Call me if –"

Peggy left the sentence unfinished, and Ivy nodded as she opened the door and entered the room.

Over the years, she'd grown to love the irascible Fred Heartley, and counted herself lucky that she'd had the opportunity of loving both his sons. And of being best friends with his daughter. But she dreaded meeting those piercing eyes that hadn't dimmed despite his advancing years. Sometimes, Ivy wondered if he could see right through her, to the very heart of her guilt.

Stepping into the bedroom, Ivy found Fred wide-awake, and she planted a kiss on his forehead.

"How are you, Fred? Is there anything I can get you?"

"I wish you'd all stop fussing," Fred grumbled. "I'm not shuffling off my mortal coil just yet. I'm worried that no one is running the shop – all my customers will start going to that new-fangled hypermarket across the village. Of course, they won't get the kind of service they've always got at Heartley's Stores –"

Ivy nodded. "You're right about that, Fred, but for now you need to think about yourself and leave the others to worry about the shop. Will I fluff up your pillows? Then maybe you could try to get some sleep?"

Fred grunted. "I'll be in eternal sleep soon enough," he said testily, "but right now, I need to talk to you."

Ivy was surprised, and more than a little concerned.

"Come closer," he whispered, as she pulled up a chair beside his bed. Although close to death, Fred's grip was surprisingly strong.

"Ivy," he whispered, "I know I can depend on you."

Ivy nodded guiltily, not sure what was coming next.

"The family needs closure, and I'm not going to be around to get it for them."

Raising his hand, he silenced any protests about his longevity. "Ivy, will you please keep up the search for Joe? Danny and Peggy need to know what happened to him."

Ivy nodded, her eyes filling with tears.

"And when you find him, tell him how much his old dad loved him? And that he doesn't need to feel guilty about making his own life elsewhere." He squeezed Ivy's hand. "I've left a letter for Joe in the drawer of my bedside table. I wrote it a while ago – while I was still capable of writing legibly. My hands are far too weak now. I'm asking you to make sure he gets it."

Ivy nodded, unable to speak because of the lump in her throat. At least Fred would die still believing that his eldest son was alive. Surely that was a good thing? Inadvertently, she'd given him hope – how could she be pilloried for that?

She did her best to smile. "Of course, Fred. I'm sure Joe will turn up one of these days. Then I'll give it to him." Her voice wavered. "Don't worry – I'm sure he knows you've always loved him –"

Fred grimaced. "I hope so. I wish we hadn't always been at each other's throats."

Ivy touched his wrinkled hand. "Lots of families have rows – but that doesn't mean they love each other any less."

Fred nodded. "I hope you're right, Ivy. It's funny how approaching death makes you realise how unimportant most other things are. Right now, I couldn't care less how Joe makes his living, but years ago I thought I knew what was best for my family. I didn't treat them as individuals, with needs and dreams of their own."

"But Danny followed you into the retail business," said Ivy affectionately, "and you have to admit he's made a great success of it. And Joseph looks like following in his footsteps. In *your* footsteps. I think you've had more influence – good influence – than you could possibly imagine, Fred."

Fred smiled, but Ivy knew his thoughts weren't focused on Danny and Joseph. He was longing for one final chance to make things right with Joe, but of course Ivy knew it was never going to happen.

* * *

Fred Heartley died three days later. He passed away peacefully in his sleep, and Ivy hoped his last dreams were of being with Joe. And if there was an afterlife, father and son would be reunited at last.

Ivy drove back to Willow Haven the night before Fred's funeral. Joseph was already there, having taken the train down from university. On arrival at Fred's house, Ivy quickly hugged her son, then was absorbed into the crowds of people visiting the Heartley home. She nodded across the room to Danny, who was hugging a newly arrived tearful neighbour, before making her way to her sister-in-law Peggy.

As the two women embraced, both began to weep. But Ivy knew that not all of her tears were for Fred; some of them were for the precariousness of her own situation. She was now back in the mystery caller's territory, and she wondered if she was already under scrutiny. Was this person here, among the mourners, in this very house? Right now, she'd prefer to think it was Rosa!

As she kissed Peggy's cheek, Ivy also hoped that she and Peggy would remain friends even after she and Danny divorced.

"Poor Dad," Peggy whispered. "He waited all his life for Joe to come back. But I don't think he ever will, do you?"

Ivy gave a noncommittal shrug of her shoulders.

Peggy scrunched up her face, and Ivy could see that she was getting angry. "If Joe ever dares to come back now, he won't be welcome here – not after all he's put our parents through! I'll personally show him the door – I can't believe he could be so cruel!"

Ivy hugged her again, because she couldn't think of anything to say.

"You know, I'm sure Dad got cancer because of all the worry over Joe's disappearance," Peggy confided. "He was never right after Joe left. It wouldn't surprise me if all the pain he kept inside him turned into tumours. Some people say there's a cancer personality, you know."

Ivy nodded, but inside she wanted to scream. Dear God, she thought, am I also responsible for Fred's death? Sometimes the guilt she carried was almost too much to bear.

* * *

The following morning, everyone in the village gathered in the tiny church to mourn Fred Heartley. Many people's thoughts turned to Joe once again, and how he'd never returned to Willow Haven. There was now an undercurrent of relief, because people felt his father was finally at peace.

A frail Hannah Dalton insisted on attending, accompanied by

Ivy's parents, who walked on either side of her, gripping her tightly to prevent her falling. Her skin was taut and yellowed, and she looked as though she might collapse at any time. People looked at her, embarrassed; it was obvious they were wondering how long it would be before they'd be attending *her* funeral. But Hannah was determined to make her way up the aisle of the church, and aided by Eleanor she placed a bunch of flowers from her garden on Fred's coffin.

Leaning on Eleanor as she turned to make her way back to her seat, Hannah walked past the front pew where Danny and Ivy were sitting. Danny looked quizzically at her, then sat bolt upright. He turned to Ivy, an incredulous look on his face.

"Good God – is that Hannah?" he hissed. "What on earth has happened to her? She looks dreadful!"

Ivy shrugged her shoulders. "She's got cancer too."

"Jesus! I hardly recognised her! How long have you known? Why didn't you tell me? Maybe I could have done something to help!"

Danny looked almost in tears, and for a moment, Ivy felt a surge of affection for her husband. He'd always been fond of Hannah.

"You know how she hates anyone fussing over her," Ivy replied. "She didn't want anyone to know."

"But *you* knew! Besides, I'm not anyone – I'm your husband! Surely you could have told *me*?"

Ivy said nothing. How dare Danny presume she should have told him? How dare he assume that being her husband made him a worthy recipient of her confidences, while all the time he was conducting his own secret affair with Hannah's daughter? The gall of him!

It also occurred to Ivy that since Danny now knew about Hannah's cancer, he'd be able to tell Rosa. In fact, if Rosa came back to Willow Haven anytime soon, it would be further proof of Danny's affair with her.

Nevertheless, Ivy was still determined to confront Rosa, and to find out what was going on in the upstairs flat in Hampstead. Why had Mrs Brampton originally confirmed that Rosa lived there, but the second time she'd been evasive about her? And why would

Danny need a tenant in the house? He certainly didn't need the money. Did Mrs Brampton act as some kind of cover for his and Rosa's clandestine activities?

The answer had to lie in that upstairs apartment. If she could just get in there, she'd be able to get proof, once and for all, that Danny was cheating on her. Assuming the flat was a love nest, she'd take photographs and confront him with them before demanding a divorce.

Ivy envisioned the upstairs apartment with plush red sofas and a big four-poster bed, where Rosa strutted her stuff in suspender belt and stiletto heels. Maybe she and Danny used sex toys? Ivy had always found the idea quite tawdry. Her sex life with Danny had always been wholesome and straightforward, and they'd never felt the need for anything else. But maybe Danny had tired of their routine coupling and decided he needed something more?

Ivy shivered involuntarily, and Danny reached for her hand, squeezing it gently. Seeing the tender expression on his face as he looked at her, Ivy could almost forget that he was cheating on her. This was the old Danny, the Danny she still loved, and she found herself smiling back at him. Then she felt angry with herself and snatched her hand away. There was no such thing as the old Danny, because even then he'd been cheating on her.

As people prepared to leave the church for the cemetery, Ivy and Danny left their pew and along with Joseph, Peggy, Ned and family, led the crowds of mourners out into the sunshine. Ivy made an effort to put her own problems aside and concentrate on how the Heartley family were feeling. Right now, there weren't many of them left – only Danny and Peggy represented the present generation. And Joseph would be the only one to carry the Heartley name into the next generation, since Peggy's children had taken Ned's surname.

Outside the church, Ivy and Peggy silently hugged each other again, finding solace in each other's warm embrace.

* * *

After the cemetery, family and friends made their way to the local hotel, where a buffet lunch was available in the lounge, courtesy of the Heartley family.

Being in the village hotel again brought back bittersweet memories for Ivy. The bar was just across the corridor from the conference room where Joe's eighteenth birthday party had taken place. Her own wedding reception had also been held there, and she recalled how Danny had been the only person who was happy that day. Or had he been? As soon as they'd got to London, he'd obviously started bedding Rosa once again. Would Joe have cheated on her if they'd married? Ivy doubted it. Their relationship hadn't been flawed in the way hers and Danny's had been right from the very start.

And Brian – dear Brian – even when he learned the truth about what she'd done, he hadn't turned against her. Momentarily, Ivy allowed herself to daydream about what might have been. She closed her eyes and imagined the touch of his lips on hers, his strong tanned arms around her, and she wished more than anything that they'd made love that night in her room in South Africa. Maybe when she and Danny divorced, she'd go back to Siyak'atala and see if that spark was still there . . .

For the rest of the day, Ivy spent her time in the company of her parents and some relatives of the Heartley family. Hannah hadn't been well enough to join the others, so Peter and Eleanor had taken her home before returning to the hotel themselves.

Watching Danny as he mingled with the assorted guests, Ivy knew how devastated he would be by his father's death, and momentarily she felt sorry for him. He'd tried all his life to outshine Joe in his father's eyes, but he'd never succeeded, because all Fred's thoughts had been focused on the son he'd lost rather than the one who'd surpassed his own dreams. Even running one of the country's largest supermarket chains hadn't won Danny the adulation he craved, and now it was too late.

Joseph, as the oldest of the cousins, was making a special effort with Peggy's much younger children, who were bewildered by the loss of their grandfather, and were becoming obstreperous. Ivy smiled as she watched her son calm them by involving them in guessing games, and it pleased her to see what a kind and considerate young man he'd become.

Her heart contracted at the thought of telling him she was

divorcing his father. He'd be devastated, but she hoped he'd understand. He was an adult now, so hopefully he'd accept that she couldn't stay married to a man who'd been cheating on her for years. Anyway, if Danny agreed to a quick and discreet divorce, there mightn't be any need to tell Joseph the reason why they were splitting up. Ivy didn't want Joseph to hate Danny – he'd always been a good father. And since Joseph was following him into the retail trade, it was imperative they remain close.

Suddenly, Ivy noticed that Danny wasn't in the hotel lounge any more. And half an hour went by before she saw him enter the room once again.

"Where have you been?" she said, then felt annoyed with herself for asking. She didn't want Danny thinking she cared any more.

"I went to see Hannah."

Ivy pursed her lips. Danny looked scared and worried, and briefly her heart went out to him.

"Are you aware that Hannah hasn't told Rosa how ill she is?" Ivy ventured, watching Danny closely. "I think it's time someone let her know, don't you?"

Danny's face went white. "If Hannah doesn't want Rosa to know, surely we should respect her wishes?"

Ivy stared at him. "Isn't it obvious that she doesn't have long to live?"

Danny looked at the ground. "Yes – but I still don't think we should interfere."

"Well, in that event, I'll try to locate Rosa myself," Ivy announced. "I'll call to that house of hers in Hampstead."

Danny looked distraught. "No, no – I'll contact her. Please, Ivy – leave it to me."

Then he turned and walked over to the bar, where he ordered himself a large whiskey and downed it in one go. As Ivy stared at him, she was acutely aware that he hadn't said he'd *try* to contact Rosa. It was clear that he knew exactly where she was.

Chapter 56

Despite Danny knowing about Hannah's illness, there was still no sign of Rosa in Willow Haven a week after Fred's funeral. Ivy knew that if Rosa had appeared, her mother would be on the phone to her immediately. Rosa's arrival would be a nine-day wonder in the village, and Eleanor would relish passing on every little detail. But Ivy's mobile phone remained resolutely silent.

She guessed that Rosa must be stuck in some location from which there were limited flights out. No doubt she'd return as soon as possible, and if she was at Cherrywood Road when Ivy got there, she'd give her a piece of her mind. Anger had been building up inside her for weeks, and Rosa's callousness towards her mother, and towards Ivy herself, would give a focus to her fury.

One way or another, Ivy planned on visiting the house while Mrs Brampton and Sean were out. The woman had mentioned working at the doctor's surgery until three and the boy was at school, so Ivy intended arriving around lunchtime. Assuming Rosa wasn't back yet, she planned on getting into the upstairs flat, and taking as many incriminating photos as she could, before confronting Danny with them. Despite her heartache, she intended getting proof of Danny's clandestine activities. Their divorce would be on *her* terms.

As she dressed for her trip to Cherrywood Road, Ivy looked completely different from the school attendance officer she'd posed as before, or the woman with the foreign accent whom she'd portrayed the first time she'd called. This time, she was wearing a different wig, a casual jacket and jeans, and she'd applied make-up that made her look very different from the Ivy Heartley the public knew.

As she drove to Hampstead, Ivy hoped that Mrs Brampton wouldn't return early and find her upstairs. At which point she'd have to say that Mr Heartley told her where to find the key, and that she was collecting something for him. Then her cover would be blown, because Mrs Brampton would be bound to contact Danny, or at least mention it next time she saw him. Of course, it mightn't matter by then, since she'd already have filed for divorce.

* * *

Ivy rang the doorbell at 6 Cherrywood Road. No one seemed to be in, so she began searching the small garden, overturning flowerpots and stones in search of the spare front-door key that Mrs Brampton had confirmed was hidden in the garden. Suddenly, she heard a voice behind her. Her heart racing, she turned around.

"Excuse me, dear – can I help you?"

Ivy saw an elderly woman leaning over the garden fence from next door. Oh Christ, she'd been caught in the act! But she wasn't an actress for nothing.

Straightening up, Ivy gave the woman a friendly smile. "Oh hello!" she said. "It looks as though Mrs Brampton has forgotten to leave the key out for me! She said it would be under a stone near the door, but I can't find it anywhere."

The older woman smiled. "Don't worry, dear, I always keep a spare key for Patty's house, and she keeps one for me – it's handy if either of us loses our keys, or we accidentally lock ourselves out. Just a moment –"

Leaving an astonished Ivy standing in the garden, the woman went into her own house and reappeared a few seconds later brandishing a Yale key. Clearly, the fact that Ivy knew Mrs Brampton's name had been enough, in the older woman's mind, to assume that Ivy was a friend of hers. And now, courtesy of the older woman, she'd also learnt Mrs Brampton's first name.

"Here you are dear," said the woman. "Just drop it in my letterbox when you're leaving."

Ivy couldn't believe her luck.

"I'll do better than that," she said, taking the key and opening the Bramptons' front door. "Now you can have the key back, and I'll just close the door on my way out. Thank you so much for your help – Patty's lucky to have such a lovely neighbour as you next door!"

The old woman turned pink with pleasure at the compliment.

Ivy was just stepping inside the door when she thought of something else.

"Excuse me, do you know the other woman who lives here – Rosa Dalton?"

The old woman looked flustered. "I'm not really sure, dear. Is she the blonde lady who goes swimming with Patty? I get a bit confused sometimes. But I do know there's a nice man who visits – he always says hello."

Disappointed, Ivy smiled at the woman. "Well, thanks anyway."

Quickly, she stepped inside and closed the door. Now, she needed to move fast, since she'd already lost valuable time searching in the garden for the key. And if the older woman met Mrs Brampton as she arrived home, she'd undoubtedly mention that she'd lent someone the key.

As Ivy climbed the stairs towards the rooms Danny used, fear coursed through her. What if another neighbour had seen her creeping around outside and had already called the police? If that happened, she'd have to tell them her real name, reveal that her husband was the owner of the property and that she was perfectly entitled to be there. At which stage the press would probably get hold of the story, and a light-hearted piece would explain how the neighbours thought she was a burglar, because no one recognised her as *Bright Lights* actress Ivy Heartley. Worst of all, Danny would learn that she'd been sneaking around behind his back.

By the time she'd reached the top of the stairs, Ivy had worked herself into a state. But she couldn't afford to indulge in the kind of drama her soap character got involved in. She'd a job to do, and she needed to do it quickly and efficiently.

Fortunately, the key for the upstairs flat was on the landing window, so Ivy didn't need to try her credit-card trick. As she'd suspected, Danny wouldn't keep the key on his personal key ring. She quickly opened the main door and slipped inside.

The landing had four doors, and the two smaller rooms consisted of a bathroom and a small galley kitchen. The kitchen looked as though it was never used, since there was nothing there but a kettle and a few upturned mugs on the draining board. Ivy supposed it was hardly surprising – since Danny and Rosa were using this place as a love-nest, they'd hardly waste their precious time together drinking tea! She opened some of the cupboards but there were few provisions inside. She found sugar and tea bags, but nothing else. Presumably each time Rosa returned from her travels, she and Danny went shopping, and stocked up on fresh provisions.

The bathroom was even more surprising, and Ivy was puzzled to find no toiletries or towels in there. Surely, after slaking their passion, Rosa and Danny would want to shower afterwards? Suddenly, she felt more hopeful. Maybe Danny wasn't having an affair after all . . .

In the third room, Ivy found a double bed over against the wall, made up with bedclothes she recognised had gone missing from their home in Sussex. In a cupboard, she found another change of bedclothes that looked equally familiar. She spotted a pair of Danny's shoes sticking out from under the bed, and she knelt down to look underneath the bed itself. Something had been shoved into a far corner, and she had to lie flat on the floor and stretch her arm in to reach it and pull it out. Ivy was disappointed to find herself looking at a rucksack. It had clearly been there for ages. Abandoning the rucksack, Ivy looked around her, puzzled. Surely the high-flying Rosa wouldn't live in such frugal conditions? And she'd hardly be willing to use bedclothes that came from Danny's marital home! This was no love nest. Clearly no one was living here, other than to spend an occasional night. But why would Danny keep a secret flat here when he appeared to make so little use of it?

A section of the room had been boarded off, and at first Ivy thought it was an ensuite bathroom. But when she opened the door, she found herself in darkness, and she pulled the cord light switch overhead. The light was a subdued red, and as Ivy gazed around her, her heart lifted. Danny had built himself a darkroom for developing his photographs! She spotted his old camcorder on one of the shelves along with several cameras, negatives, a sink with running water, tanks of developing solution and assorted dark-room equipment. Danny had always been interested in photography and filming, and clearly he was using the flat for his hobby. But Ivy's relief quickly turned to puzzlement. Why hadn't he told her? Besides, their own home was big enough to fit several darkrooms in it – why had he chosen to come here?

Leaving the darkroom, Ivy felt a sudden urge to look in the rucksack, and she crossed the room to examine it. It was packed to capacity, and she wondered momentarily if Danny intended leaving her, and was preparing a temporary base for himself. Then, as she opened it, women's clothing fell out, and Ivy stared at it in astonishment. So Danny was having an affair! But then she realised how ridiculous that idea was, since the rucksack was covered in dust and had clearly been under the bed for a long time.

With shaking fingers, Ivy pulled the rest of the clothes out. They were all very small, and had a girlish, dated look. What on earth was going on? Did the clothes belong to some other woman whom Danny was moving in? It made no sense – why would the mistress of such a wealthy man agree to live in a miserable flat like this? Surely Danny could afford to give her the best? A thousand confused thoughts were racing through Ivy's brain, but no answers came to mind.

Her hands were still shaking as she opened the side pocket of the rucksack. Inside, a bundle of documents were wedged tightly inside, and she snagged a fingernail trying to prise them out. Cursing, Ivy realised she had to hurry, since time was running out. If she delayed much longer, Mrs Brampton would be back from work, and her son Sean from school. Sticking her fingers down into the pocket, Ivy succeeded in getting another nail under the documents, and with a final heave, they spilled out onto the floor. Picking them up, she stared at them in astonishment. First was a passport, and when Ivy opened it, she found herself staring at a photograph of Rosa Dalton. The rest of the documents included Rosa's school reports, her birth certificate and a train ticket to London.

Ivy's heart plummeted. So Danny *was* having an affair with Rosa! Then she looked at the train ticket, and her blood ran cold. The date on the unused ticket was almost twenty years ago.

Ivy's mind was churning. Terrible thoughts were forcing themselves into her brain, thoughts she was afraid to entertain, even for a second. Because if she did, life as she knew it would be over. No, she was wrong, she had to be wrong . . .

Frantically, Ivy raced out onto the landing and headed towards the remaining room. She needed to see what it held, then get away quickly before Mrs Brampton and the boy returned. It was already getting dark, but she didn't dare to turn on any lights. By Ivy's reckoning, she had about twenty minutes before Mrs Brampton was due back from work and Sean from school. Why on earth hadn't she given herself more time?

Throwing open the door of the last room, Ivy saw a desk and chair, computer, notebook and pens, scissors, staplers and the usual office paraphernalia. There was also some electronic equipment on a shelf, but Ivy had no idea what it was for. She could also see several bundles of letters tied together with elastic bands.

With shaking hands, she turned on the computer, hoping desperately that she wouldn't need a password to get in. Her heart pumping, it seemed an eternity before the computer produced a list of icons. Clicking on Word, Ivy hoped this was the most likely place to get the kind of the information she was looking for.

As Ivy drummed her fingers nervously on the desk, she glanced at her watch again. Mrs Brampton was due back in fifteen minutes. There appeared to be only one file in Word, and luckily it opened without a password. Ivy scrolled down through the correspondence on the screen and felt her heart contract as she saw what was on the screen. The file was full of typed letters from Rosa to her mother. Ivy was instantly puzzled. So Rosa *had* been using this computer. The letters dated back years – in fact ever since Rosa had left Willow Haven.

Quickly, Ivy reached for one of the bundles of letters, and tore off the elastic band. They were all addressed to Rosa Dalton at 6 Cherrywood Road, Hampstead, and were written by Hannah. Still puzzled, she spotted the notebook on the desk. Opening it, she found herself staring at the words on the page. It was the same word over and over and over again. Rosa, Rosa, Rosa.

It was then that she suddenly put two and two together, and felt as though her heart was about to stop. It was Danny who'd been practising Rosa's signature! At last she knew the stark and painful truth. He was the one who'd been sending monthly letters to Hannah Dalton for years, typing them on the computer and signing them with his practised version of Rosa's signature. More recently, when he'd taught Hannah how to use a computer, he hadn't needed to use the signature or post letters and cards from far-off exotic places any more. No wonder Danny hadn't been on any business trips lately – he hadn't needed to go, since Hannah was now using email!

Overwhelmed by shock, Ivy felt an urge to vomit. Rosa had never made it to London. She was never coming home, because she was dead already. Had been dead for years. Ivy felt a lump in her throat. Poor Rosa, and poor Hannah, waiting and hoping for her daughter to visit. With a sick feeling in her stomach, Ivy realised that she'd finally found the answers she was looking for. The body in the car alongside Joe was Rosa's, and Danny knew all about it.

Chapter 57

Tears in her eyes, Rosa headed towards the village railway station, where she was due to take the next train to London. She didn't really want to go, and she'd almost changed her mind when she'd seen her mother's distraught face. But the shame and humiliation of facing her peers outweighed her concern for her mother. She'd go to London and make a success of her life. That would show them all that she wasn't fazed by Danny's rejection! She'd better things to do with her life than hang around a hick little village in the back of beyond.

Rosa's lip quivered. Who on earth did she think she was fooling? Truthfully, she was devastated by Danny's rejection. And if she left Willow Haven, she'd be leaving him to Ivy Morton. But she had one final string to her bow. Danny wasn't going to get off so easily, and she might still manage to destroy his relationship with Ivy Morton before it even got started.

As she reached the station, Rosa glanced over her shoulder. She could see her mother in the distance, still standing at her open front door and watching her daughter as she prepared to leave the village forever. She felt a momentary pang of guilt at the hurt she was causing her mother, but if her plan worked out, she mightn't be leaving at all. Since her mother was still watching, she went to the ticket-window and in full view of her mother, bought a one-way ticket to London, then slipped it into a pocket on her rucksack. She peered out the station entrance again, and was relieved to see that her mother had finally gone inside and closed her front door. Slipping out of the station, Rosa took a sharp turn down the side road that led to Heartley's Stores. She wasn't going to leave without a last shot at getting Danny back. If she was successful, she could get her ticket money refunded. If not . . . well, she'd still have time to catch the 6.15.

Danny was standing outside the store when Rosa arrived, and she felt that his presence there augured well for her future.

"Danny, I need to speak to you – in private," she told him quietly. "Meet me down by the lake in five minutes."

Without another word, Rosa turned and began walking towards the lake.

Surprised and slightly worried, Danny waited until she was out of sight before following her. He didn't want Ivy or anyone else to spot him with Rosa now that they were no longer a couple, but he was concerned by Rosa's air of calm superiority. The last time he'd seen her, she'd been hysterical, and he'd felt guilty. Now, she appeared like someone holding a trump card. But he'd no reason to be worried, had he?

Down by the lake, Rosa removed her rucksack and sat on it to wait for Danny. She felt surprisingly calm about what she was going to do. All was fair in love and war, and she was playing to win. She wanted Danny, and this was her last chance of getting him back. If not, she'd go to London as planned . . .

Danny made his way through the bushes and the reeds, standing in front of her, a concerned look on his face. "What do you want, Rosa? I really haven't time to play your little games. We're finished, and nothing's going to change that."

Rosa looked up, a smirk on her pretty face. "Oh, I think it might, Danny. Sit down and listen to what I have to say."

"I don't want to sit down. Say what you have to say, because I'm leaving."

"Well then, I'll stand up," said Rosa, getting to her feet. "I just thought you might want to sit down, since what I have to say might be a shock to you."

Danny looked defiant. "Go on – whatever you have to say, it won't make any difference to me."

"Oh yes, it will – I'm pregnant, Danny – I'm expecting your baby."

It was a lie, but Rosa was so desperate to get Danny back that she was prepared to do anything to make it happen. By her reasoning, he'd feel obliged to stay with her, and eventually he'd realise they were meant to be together. Then she'd conveniently have a 'miscarriage'. But by then, they'd hopefully be married . . .

Danny's face went white. "W-what? You're joking! You told me you were on the pill!"

"Well, I guess it didn't work," Rosa said smugly. *"I'll have to tell Mamma soon, and before long, everyone in the village will know. So we'd better start making plans for our future."*

Danny was speechless with rage.

Rosa smiled at him triumphantly. *"You'd better forget all about Ivy Morton now – I don't think she'd be happy to have a boyfriend who's got another girl pregnant!"*

Looking at Rosa's smug face, Danny finally found his voice. *"You little bitch!"* he screamed. *"You've done this to trap me. Well, you're not going to get away with it!"*

Rosa was still smirking when Danny grabbed her by the throat. As her expression changed from surprise to fear, she found herself struggling for breath, but she was incapable of making him let go. Suddenly, she was terrified. She'd never seen Danny so angry.

"You're nothing to me, Rosa!" he told her as he tightened his grip. *"Nothing! Do you hear me – nothing! You're not going to ruin my life – I'm not going to let you!"*

As though possessed, Danny dug his fingers deeper into her throat, and frantically, she tried to prise his fingers away, but it was impossible, and she realised she was fighting a losing battle. Why had she made up such a stupid lie? If only he'd give her a chance, she'd tell him the truth, but she was finding it impossible to breathe any longer . . . As he continued to crush her throat, Rosa slipped into unconsciousness, and was no longer able to hear what he was saying.

As Danny let go of her at last, she slid to the ground like a ragdoll. He'd broken her neck and she was now lying dead at his feet.

Danny's mouth was dry and his heart was thumping rapidly. What on earth had he done? He looked at Rosa's body slumped on the ground and felt an overwhelming urge to puke. She wasn't really dead, was she? It was just Rosa playing another of her stupid games . . . He knelt down and shook her body frantically. "Come on, Rosa – stop messing!" he croaked, his voice hoarse with fear and emotion. But as he looked at the deep red marks gouged into her neck, he had to accept the truth of what he'd done. Tears filled his eyes. How could it have come to this?

He licked his dry trembling lips. If she hadn't been so smug, he'd never have touched her. He hadn't meant to harm her, but she'd kept goading him . . . Oh God, what was he going to do? He looked down at Rosa's body once more. It was hard to believe she was gone. Everything had changed in an instant, and right now he didn't even know if he had a future himself.

Wildly, he looked around him, and was relieved to see that the lakeside was deserted. At this time of evening, most people were at home preparing dinner. Did anyone know that Rosa was planning to meet him? His goose was cooked if she'd told anyone. Of course, he'd claim he never saw her. Luckily, they'd each arrived at the lakeside separately, so no one could have seen them together, except outside Heartley's Stores.

Panicking, Danny wondered what he could do with the body. He couldn't risk leaving it here, even for a few minutes. Anyone walking by would see it, then he'd find himself serving a very long prison sentence. Calm down, he told himself. He needed to think clearly and rationally if he was to find a solution to his problem. Whatever decision he made now would decide the course of the rest of his life.

Danny was numb from shock and fear, but he needed to find a solution to his dilemma quickly. He knew that if he threw Rosa's body into the lake, it would surface before long, and the marks on her neck would confirm she'd been strangled. Soon the police would be crawling all over the village, and checking everyone's association with Rosa. He'd quickly become the prime suspect.

For Christ's sake, think of something, he told himself. His future was at stake here!

As he gazed at the lake, he suddenly thought of Joe and his father's car at the bottom of the lake. Eureka! If he could get Rosa's body into the car, no one would ever find her. Even if the car was eventually found, Rosa's body would hopefully be so decayed that no evidence of foul play would be visible any more.

Danny shuddered. The water would be freezing and he didn't fancy making the journey to the bottom of the lake with Rosa's body, but he'd no other choice. His brain was in shock and at this moment he couldn't think of any better option. Luckily he could swim well, and right now the stakes were too high for him to change his mind.

Quickly, he stripped off. He'd have to do it naked, since he couldn't go through the village afterwards wearing wet clothes. Dragging Rosa's body to the edge of the lake, Danny was astonished at how heavy she now was. He hoped that same weight would help him to get her to the bottom of the lake as quickly as possible. He was shivering from the cold, and terrified that someone would walk by and see him with Rosa's body, or spot her rucksack, which he'd hidden in the bushes.

Danny gasped as he jumped in, hauling Rosa's body in after him. The cold seared through him like a knife. Dragging the body down after him, he fought his way through the weeds and debris, hoping his sense of direction was correct. Relief flooded through him when he spotted the outline of the car ahead. As he reached it, he desperately needed more air, so he abandoned the body briefly and surfaced, hoping it wouldn't surface as well. Filling his lungs, he returned to the car below, relieved that Rosa's body hadn't moved very far and that the passenger window was open – presumably that had been Ivy's escape route.

Freezing and frightened, Danny pushed, dragged and manoeuvred, and eventually he got Rosa's body into the passenger seat. The weight of the water made it almost impossible, but he managed it at last.

As he tried to attach her seatbelt, he did his best not to look at his brother. But his eyes were inexorably drawn towards the driver's seat – oh no! He could see Joe, although he didn't look *anything like the brother he remembered. Tufts of his fair hair were weaving in the current, and his face seemed to be melting away. As he struggled to wind up the passenger window, so that Rosa's body would stay propped against it, Danny had to suppress the urge to scream.*

Looking into the back of the car, Danny spotted Ivy's weekend case and handbag. He pulled the case out but it broke apart, while the items of clothing inside fell out and floated to the bottom of the lake where he hoped they would rot away over time. He felt relief – no one would ever know they'd been Ivy's. He grabbed her handbag and carried it to the surface. Since Ivy was going to be his wife one day soon, he intended to protect her.

Danny left Joe and Rosa in their underwater tomb and swam to the surface. He was never going down there again! As he climbed out of the water, he vomited all over the ground. Then he looked back at the lake, but the water was calm, giving no indication of what lay beneath its smooth surface.

Using his underpants to dry himself, Danny did his best to get dressed. But his clothing kept sticking to his damp body, and he panicked as he struggled to get into it. At one point he felt close to breaking down, because his fingers were trembling so much that he couldn't even tie his shoelaces.

At last, he managed to get dressed. Stuffing his damp underpants into his pocket, he collected Rosa's rucksack and Ivy's handbag, and hid them in the drapes of his jacket, which he then carried in one hand, while doing his best to look as casual as possible.

Crossing the fields behind the village, Danny arrived back home without incident, and went straight to his room. Relief flooded through him as he dumped the rucksack and handbag on his bed. He'd made a drastic mistake, but he'd managed to extricate himself by staying cool and thinking things through.

Opening Rosa's rucksack, he found several hundred pounds in one of the pockets. He felt a pang of remorse – it was almost like being rewarded for what he'd done. He presumed Hannah had given the money to her daughter, but he could hardly return it, could he? And it would be useful when he and Ivy eventually left

Willow Haven to set up home in London. He placed the notes in a drawer beneath his clean socks. Eventually, he'd have to get rid of the rucksack, but for now he'd hide it beneath his bed.

In Ivy's handbag he found a plastic wallet containing her passport and the remains of her birth and exam certificates, but the print still clear enough to be identified as hers. He'd destroy them. Ivy could always apply for new documents.

Danny took a deep breath. What had initially been a disaster had actually turned into a golden opportunity, enabling him to protect Ivy from any connection to the bodies in the lake. Now all he had to do was make her fall in love with him.

* * *

At school the following day at lunchtime, news of Rosa's departure for London was the main topic of conversation. Rosa's mother had told Fred Heartley, who'd told his daughter Peggy, who told her friends . . . and before long, both the girls' and boys' schools knew all about it.

As Clara Bellingham passed Danny in the street later that afternoon, she made a snide remark about him dumping her. "She's only gone to London because of you!" Clara said venomously, and she was surprised when Danny apologised profusely.

"I never meant to upset her," he told Clara, looking sad. "But I want to be with Ivy. I really hope things work out for Rosa in London."

As he moved off, he couldn't resist a little smile, since he was suddenly filled with a tremendous sense of relief. The fates had conspired to save him! No one would miss Rosa because they thought she'd gone to London. It would be months, maybe years, before anyone –

Suddenly, his brief spell of euphoria was replaced by a sense of shock that almost winded him. What about Hannah? She'd be expecting a letter from Rosa before long. Oh God, what was he going to do? If Hannah didn't hear from her daughter in a few weeks, she'd report her missing, and an investigation would be launched. It was far too early for the body to be found – he needed it to decay sufficiently so there'd be no evidence of pressure on Rosa's neck. If the bodies remained undiscovered for several years, Rosa's injuries would probably be attributed to the car crash.

Danny chewed a fingernail while he racked his brains for an answer. At last he found it – he'd have to keep Rosa alive for the foreseeable future. She'd write glowing letters home to Hannah, who'd be delighted to know how well Rosa was doing. Then at some point in the future – well, he'd worry about that later.

Danny grimaced. It was obvious that things weren't going to be as straightforward as he'd hoped . . .

Chapter 58

Having escaped from the Hampstead house with only minutes to spare, Ivy drove back to Sussex, devastated by what she'd discovered about Danny. As she opened her front door and stepped into the hall, she could hear the landline ringing. She was tempted not to answer, but something made her pick up the receiver.

"Hello?"

Eleanor was on the other end of the line, with the news that Hannah Dalton had been rushed to the hospital in Allcott.

"She didn't want to go," Eleanor said sadly. "She's determined to die in that cold old house of hers. I blame Rosa – why on earth hasn't she taken her mother to live with her in that big mansion of hers in London? Lady Muck, that one – thinks she's too good to visit her mother or look after her properly."

Ivy gripped the phone so tightly that her knuckles turned white. "Poor Hannah," she whispered. "I wish I could have done more for her –"

"The one who should be doing it is Rosa," Eleanor said crossly. "I intend giving that daughter of hers a piece of my mind when she comes back to Willow Haven – *if* she comes, that is. Maybe she'll consider herself too grand to even come back for her own mother's funeral."

Ivy felt bowed down by all that had happened, as though a ton weight was resting on her chest. When would it all end?

"Is Hannah . . ."

"I don't think she'll be coming home again, if that's what you mean," Eleanor replied. "I doubt if they'll let her out of hospital. I mean, it's not as though she has anyone at home to look after her."

Ivy knew that this was another oblique reference to Rosa, but she was the only one who knew that Rosa wouldn't be coming back. Part of her was relieved to know that Hannah would pass away before Rosa's body was found, and she'd never need to know that her beloved daughter had predeceased her.

"I'll pay for a private room for Hannah," Ivy said firmly. "I'd like to make sure that her last days are spent in comfort."

"That's very good of you, Ivy," her mother said approvingly. "Of course, you shouldn't be the one who has to do it –"

Ivy didn't want to listen to a further diatribe about poor Rosa's shortcomings. She was already filled with guilt that she'd come to hate Rosa so much. How could she ever have believed that her old classmate had stolen her husband? Danny was the one who'd done the stealing – he'd robbed Rosa of her life.

"I'll ring the hospital straight away and get things sorted out," she said, quickly changing the subject. "And I'll come down to see Hannah at the weekend – give her my love when you visit her, won't you, Mum?"

"Of course," said Eleanor. "In the meantime, your father is ringing round all the airlines in the phone book. I was sure Hannah said Rosa worked for British Airways, but your father contacted them – and several other airlines – but no one there knew who Rosa was. We contacted her sister Joan, but she thought Rosa worked for Emirates or Cathay Pacific . . ."

"There are hundreds of airlines, Mum," Ivy said gently. "Rosa could be working for any of them. Anyway, I'm sure someone will find her soon enough."

"He also found Rosa's email address on Hannah's computer, so he sent off an email to her. But there's been no reply so far."

"Well, assuming she's busy, she probably hasn't had time to check her emails yet," Ivy said, thinking to herself that if Rosa was really alive, she'd undoubtedly have a modern phone that allowed her to pick up her emails instantly.

"Your father tried to decipher the plane's logo in that photo on Hannah's phone table," Eleanor added, "but he couldn't make it out. I wonder if one of her tenants would know what airline she works for? I think I'll write to that house of hers in Hampstead –"

"Don't bother writing, Mum – I'll call to Rosa's house myself," Ivy said hastily. "Please don't worry, you have enough to do – I know that you and Dad will be the ones taking care of Hannah's day-to-day needs."

Her mother grunted, pleased that her daughter acknowledged the supportive role they were playing in Hannah's life.

"Well, don't delay too long if you're coming to visit Hannah," Eleanor added, "I doubt if she'll be with us for very much longer."

Chapter 59

Later that evening, Ivy stood gazing out of the kitchen window across the pristine lawns of their estate. She knew what she was doing was simply a delaying tactic, something to occupy her mind while she tried to pluck up the courage to confront Danny. Because once she spoke to him about Rosa, their lives would be changed forever.

Ivy shivered. She'd no idea what the outcome of her confrontation would be, but she felt she owed it to Danny. She was still desperately hoping that he would deny everything, and could somehow prove to her that he hadn't been the one who'd harmed Rosa . . .

With a sigh, Ivy left the kitchen and headed for the drawing room, where she knew Danny was reading the daily newspapers. She couldn't put off this confrontation any longer.

Walking into the room, Ivy now wore a concerned expression.

"Oh, by the way, Danny – have you heard? Hannah's been taken to hospital. She's not expected to live much longer."

Danny looked up, a shocked expression on his face. "In hospital? Oh my God – I didn't think it would happen so soon –"

"You said you were going to let Rosa know about her mother – have you contacted her yet?"

"Er, no, I forgot, I mean –"

By now, Danny had jumped up from his chair and had started pacing the floor.

Ivy stared at him stonily. "I thought you'd also like to know that the Council are going to drain Harper's Lake."

Danny blanched. "Oh, my God – when?"

Ivy shrugged. "I suppose they'll start soon enough."

By now, Danny's face had gone totally white. Ivy's own heart was pounding so loud that she felt certain Danny must hear it. She knew he must be realising that his deception would soon be known to everyone. With Rosa in the lake for the previous twenty years, it wouldn't be long before all her letters to Hannah were queried. Even if Rosa's body was too decomposed to prove murder, the letters Danny had written would make the case against him.

Ivy took a deep breath. "I know what you did, Danny," she said softly.

"What do you mean?" her husband asked angrily. At first, it looked as though he was going to try and bluff it out, but eventually his shoulders drooped, and he almost seemed to shrink before her eyes.

"I'm sorry you had to find out, Ivy. I was hoping you hadn't seen Dad's car, and that the phone calls would keep you away from the lake –"

"So you were the voice on the phone that terrorised me?"

Danny nodded. "I found a piece of waterweed in the wash basket after you got back from Willow Haven, so I knew you'd been in the lake. I hoped I could prevent you from discovering Rosa's body."

Ivy smiled sadly. "I thought I was the actor in this family – but you played me like a fool, didn't you, Danny? All that concern about the mystery caller, and all those suggestions that I contact the police. You knew that I couldn't! And the letters, postcards and emails you wrote to Hannah – how could you be so cruel?"

Danny shrugged his shoulders. "But they made her happy. Besides, I know what *you* did! What I did wasn't any worse than what you did to my parents. We both simply tried to protect them from the truth."

Ivy was shocked – so Danny knew all about her own trail of deceit!

"Don't you dare try to put me in the same category as you!" she retorted. "I know what I did was wrong, but I didn't kill their child! You killed Rosa, and for years you cold-bloodedly kept up the pretence that she was alive!"

"For Christ's sake, Ivy, I was only seventeen!" Danny shouted. "It wasn't planned, and I'd no idea what to do when it happened. I lost my temper when Rosa told me she was pregnant – she'd sworn she was taking the pill. She threatened to tell everyone about the pregnancy, so what was I to do? My parents would have forced me to 'do the right thing' and marry her. But I only wanted you, Ivy – I always have."

Ivy's lower lip trembled. "How could you be so selfish?"

Danny shrugged his shoulders. "Whatever. I wasn't going to let her spoil my chances of winning you. You're a lucky woman, Ivy – you've never had to worry about me straying, because you're the only woman I've ever wanted."

They stared at each other in silence, and Ivy realised with a feeling of shock that there were tears running down Danny's face.

"I was in total panic – I didn't know what to do," he whimpered at last. "Then I remembered Dad's car in the lake, and it seemed the perfect place to hide Rosa's body. No one would find her for years, if ever, and even if they did, they'd assume she and Joe had been in the car together when it crashed."

Ivy found she could hardly breathe. "So you've known all along that Joe's body was in the lake."

Danny laughed bitterly. "Of course! I was the tiresome kid who used to spy on his older brother! You may have fooled other people, but I knew exactly where you and Joe used to go. I'd follow you and watch you screwing in the barn at Johnson's farm, or down by Harper's Lake in the long grass." He gave a faint smile as he looked at Ivy's incredulous expression. "Needless to say, I was riddled with jealousy. At that point I hated my brother so much that I wished he was dead. Then when it actually happened, it seemed like a wonderful opportunity to make you mine at last."

Ivy found herself trembling. "How did you know what happened that day?"

Danny grimaced. "I was up on the hill with my camcorder, when I heard a screech of brakes. In the distance I saw a red car plunge into the lake. I ran down the hill as fast as I could, not knowing if it was Dad's car or not. But by the time I got down there, I saw you climbing out of the lake and sitting on the bank, your hair and clothes soaking. I knew then that Joe must've been inside the car with you, and that it was too late to help him. So I hid and waited to see what you'd do – and when you went home and told no one what had happened, I knew I was being handed the perfect opportunity to step into his shoes. I hoped you'd feel so guilty that you'd need someone to lean on, and I intended being there to offer support." He smiled sadly through his tears. "Pathetic, wasn't it? But I wanted you so badly that I was prepared to keep quiet about what had happened. I let my parents and sister suffer so that I could have you. I let my obsession for you take over my life. I'd have done anything – and did – to make you mine."

Ivy shuddered, suddenly feeling unclean. Unwittingly, she'd enabled Danny to fulfil his sick fantasy.

"You'd never have married me if Joe hadn't died, would you?" Danny challenged her. "He was the one you really wanted to be with – I've always been second-best."

Ivy said nothing. What was the point in protesting that she loved him when she wasn't even sure any more?

In the silence that followed, Ivy's brain was trying to work out all the permutations of what she was hearing.

"But how did you expect to explain away Rosa's letters if her body was ever discovered?" she asked at last. "Because then people would know she'd never written them. And what about Hannah – didn't you think she'd wonder why her daughter never visited her in almost twenty years?"

Danny's face was now contorted with rage. "At seventeen, I couldn't think twenty years into the future – it seemed like a lifetime away. After Rosa died, I was in a total panic. And to prevent Hannah getting worried and contacting the police, I hit on the idea of the letters. I used to sneak into the school secretary's office during lunch hour and use the word processor there to type them. It was nerve-racking, I can tell you! Later on, when we were in London and I was earning a good salary, I was able to get my own computer, and eventually I kept it at the house in Hampstead. By then I was also able to include money each time I wrote to Hannah, to make her life a bit easier."

"And to ease your conscience," Ivy said sarcastically. "But you must have considered that Hannah might go looking for Rosa, or send someone to check up on her? You must have been thrilled when she started pretending she'd been to visit Rosa."

It had just dawned on Ivy that Hannah's pride had unwittingly aided and abetted Danny in successfully maintaining the deception. The poor woman had believed Rosa was alive – Danny's letters, postcards, phone calls and emails had assured her of that – and she'd accepted that Rosa was far too busy and successful to spare time for her mother. But Hannah hadn't wanted people in the village thinking Rosa was selfish and uncaring. So in order to hold her head high in her own community, Hannah had maintained the lie that she saw Rosa when she visited her in London and other locations, whereas she'd probably just gone to stay at a hotel or visited her sister Joan in Bicklebury.

Ivy grimaced. It must have been awful for Hannah, living near her own well-meaning but boastful parents. With an unmarried absentee daughter, it would have been like salt in her wounds.

Danny nodded. "Yes, Hannah's pride was a great help. But I knew that if the letters ever stopped, Hannah would definitely go looking for Rosa, or ask the police to search for her. I couldn't let that happen, so I had to keep on writing them, and have Rosa make the occasional brief phone call to Hannah."

"Oh God, I'd forgotten about the phone calls!" Ivy exclaimed, shocked. "How did you manage to do that?"

Danny smiled, a hint of pride in his voice. "When you thought I was working late, I was actually doing an evening course in sound editing for trainee radio producers and presenters – of course, I was never going to be using it for that. Afterwards, I bought my own editing equipment, and digitally edited fragments of Rosa's voice from the old recordings on my camcorder, making new words out of them. Once you get the hang of it, it's surprisingly easy to split or join words and syllables. For example, from words like "bad", and "Mamma's" I could make up the word "Bahamas". Then I'd dial Hannah's number and play Rosa's words back to her." Danny shrugged his shoulders. "Of course, the messages from Rosa had to be brief and the line quickly cut off, since there could never be any two-way conversations."

He clearly thought he'd been very clever, and Ivy had to agree. She'd been fooled by Rosa's voice herself.

"And the picture on Hannah's phone table – of Rosa in her flight attendant's uniform – I suppose that was your handiwork as well? And all the holiday photos Rosa sent her mother –"

Danny shrugged his shoulders. "They were just photos I borrowed from social networking sites, and in my darkroom I substituted Rosa's face."

Ivy found it difficult to breathe. "But at some point, Hannah was going to die – what did you plan to do then? At this very moment she's in hospital, and unlikely to ever come home again."

Danny lowered his head. "I couldn't even think that far ahead. You've no idea what all this has cost me, Ivy – not a day went by when I didn't worry myself sick about the situation. I even tried several times to buy the land that included the lake, but the Council wouldn't sell it."

"Aw, poor you!" said Ivy sarcastically. "What about poor Rosa? She's been denied all those years of life! She might have had a family by now, and Hannah might have been a grandmother."

Danny groaned. "I know, but I was desperate, so I didn't think beyond the immediate situation."

"But as the years went by, you must have realised you were getting yourself in deeper."

"Of course I did! I hadn't a clue how it would end – I even tried to get Hannah to leave Willow Haven – I made threatening phone calls, but she went to the police, so I had to stop."

He looked at Ivy. "Yes, I know it was despicable, but if I'd managed to get her away from the village, my troubles might have been over. If Hannah had severed ties with the residents of Willow Haven, when she eventually died, no one would realise that Rosa hadn't turned up for her funeral. But Hannah didn't want to move. Her network of friends and neighbours were in the village – so I had to think of something else . . ."

Ivy's lip curled. "And that something else was a computer. I thought you were helping Hannah because you were a nice person, but you were just making things easier for yourself. If Rosa could email her mother, you wouldn't have to post letters and cards from all over the world. All those trips you made – supposedly to retail conferences – they were just to ensure that Hannah got letters and cards from exotic locations, weren't they?"

Danny nodded, turning a sad face towards her. "I really *did* like Hannah – I couldn't do anything to harm her. I even thought of stealing the letters while she was alive, but I was afraid she might report them missing, or start asking neighbours about them. Then even more people would know about them. It was too risky, so I just had to keep on writing them."

Danny smiled tentatively at Ivy, as though looking for her approval.

"You're angry with me now, Ivy, but I wasn't a bad husband, was I? I did my best to make you happy. I bought you everything your heart desired – jewellery, cars, holidays – you and Joseph have always been the most important people in the world to me."

For an instant, Ivy felt a spiteful desire to wound him by telling him that Joseph wasn't really his son. But just as quickly she realised that by allowing herself a momentary pleasure, she might cause him to behave unpredictably. She was grateful that Joseph was away at university, and unaware that his parents' lives were unravelling by the minute.

As though reading her mind, Danny gave her a lop-sided smile.

"Oh, by the way, I know all about Joseph."

Ivy froze.

"I know he's not my son – but he's Joe's child, so he's family anyway, and since you were willing to pass him off as mine, that was fine by me."

At last, Ivy found her voice. "H-how did you find out?"

Danny gave her a sad smile. "Surprisingly, it never dawned on me, even when you gave birth 'early'. But when there was no sign of a second child, I went to a private clinic for a sperm test – and discovered I hadn't been responsible for the first child. The clinic told me I was sterile." He smiled sadly. "So I've been lucky, Ivy. You gave me a wonderful son, whom I'd never have had otherwise."

"So that's why we never had any children together," Ivy whispered. Then she gasped as another realisation struck home. "Which means that Rosa was lying – she must have been so desperate to keep you that she pretended to be pregnant!"

Danny nodded. "It was a silly thing for her to say – and it was all our undoing. If she hadn't tried so hard to hang on to me, she'd still be alive, and I'd have lived the life I was meant to."

In the silence that followed, they both looked at each other uncertainly.

Finally Danny spoke. "Oh, and by the way, you needn't worry about your possessions in the lake – when I put Rosa's body in Dad's car, I removed your handbag with your passport and certificates inside it, and burnt them. No one will ever know that you were there."

Ivy was relieved. No wonder she'd found nothing when she'd dived in herself.

"But I didn't do it for you, Ivy – I did it for me," said Danny, a hint of anger in his voice as he noted her relieved expression. "If anyone ever got round to finding the car, I didn't want them finding my wife's stuff in there, along with my dead brother."

Ivy stared at him. Danny had saved her for the sake of his personal pride. He couldn't bear for anyone to know that his brother had been her first preference.

But what might once have been flattering had become a deadly obsession.

Unable to look at Danny, Ivy looked down at her hands, watching as the little diamond in her engagement ring twinkled as it caught the light. Although Danny had wanted to buy her a bigger diamond, Ivy had always refused. She'd loved the ring he'd bought for their third month's anniversary – and he'd been so angry when she'd nearly discovered it under the bed . . .

Suddenly, Ivy felt as though an electric shock had run through her. She gasped, and Danny looked quizzically at her.

"Your bedroom, in your parents' house –" she whispered.

Danny nodded as he saw her touch the ring. "Yes, I had to keep you from finding Rosa's rucksack. I'd hidden it under the bed, meaning to get rid of it, but it wasn't easy to dispose of."

Ivy was now trembling. "So the ring was never there at all –"

Danny laughed now. "No, it wasn't. You really gave me a fright that day, Ivy! I had to think of some reason to stop you looking under the bed – that ring cost me an arm and a leg back then – well, actually, it was Rosa's money that bought it. I think Hannah must have given her the cash for her trip to London . . ."

Shuddering, Ivy peeled off the engagement ring and threw it on the floor. She felt unclean for unwittingly wearing it for the previous twenty years. She'd never, ever wear it again.

Danny shrugged his shoulders as though her gesture meant little to him now. Then he crossed the floor to the safe in the drawing room wall, unlocked it and extracted some papers. Placing them in the inside pocket of his jacket, he returned to stand before her, taking her hand in his.

"You probably hate me now, but all I ever wanted was for you to love me." He looked sad. "And since Hannah's about to die and the lake is being drained, I'm left with very little choice. I'm sorry to tell you, my love – there's going to be a tragic accident."

Alarmed, Ivy pulled her hand away and looked towards the door, suddenly fearful for her life. This man, to whom she'd been married for twenty years, was now a stranger, and suddenly she felt afraid of him. If he could kill Rosa, why not her, too?

Danny looked disappointed at her reaction. "Don't worry, Ivy – I'm not going to harm you. I love you, so I could never hurt you. I made one mistake all those years ago – and I suppose I should be grateful that I got away with it for so long."

He smiled whimsically as he moved towards the door.

"Danny –" Ivy could hardly speak, and his name came out as a croak, "– what do you mean, 'accident'? You're not going to do anything stupid, are you?"

Danny shook his head, but said nothing. He reached for the door handle, and as he turned back, Ivy could see that his eyes were glistening with tears again.

"Danny, where are you going? Is it to the police?" Ivy asked. "I'm sure they'll accept that it was an accident –"

Danny cocked an eyebrow. "It wasn't an accident, Ivy, and I've no intention of ending up in prison."

He opened the door.

"Besides, if I'm branded a murderer, your life and Joseph's would be ruined. Can't you see the headlines – '*Soap star's husband convicted of murder*'? No, my dear wife – Betterbuys must go on, for both your sakes. Joseph will be able to take over the reins as soon as he finishes university. It'll be a baptism of fire, but I have faith in his ability."

"Danny, you're scaring me – what are you talking about? Joseph's not nearly ready, and anyway, why would he –"

Looking at his wife's puzzled expression, Danny's face softened, and his eyes glittered through his tears. "I don't want you to have to scrimp like we did all those years ago when you were at RADA," he said gently. "We'd a tough time making ends meet, hadn't we?"

Ivy's heart filled with pain as she recalled those lean and difficult years, but Danny had worked hard to make her dream of becoming an actress possible. Yet even still, a retort was forming on her lips.

"Yet despite us being poor, you still managed to buy the Hampstead house behind my back!"

Danny grimaced. "I had to – I needed somewhere secure to write Rosa's letters, and to receive Hannah's. I was able to hide Rosa's rucksack there, and set up a darkroom so that I could work on the photographs and do the digital editing of Rosa's voice." He suddenly smiled. "You have no idea how difficult it was to convince the bank that I could service the loans for both the first small supermarket and the Hampstead house! I mortgaged us to the hilt back then, but I paid it all off as soon as Betterbuys started to do well."

Ivy looked at her husband and for an instant saw the man she'd grown to love, the dynamic man she'd married. Even when he'd been young, Danny had projected an aura of success. No one would have doubted that he was going to be a high achiever.

"Danny, let's think this through," she begged him. "We've always been able to sort out our problems before –"

Danny shook his head as he gripped the door handle, his knuckles white. "I'm sorry, Ivy – believe me, it's better this way."

"What way? For God's sake, Danny, what do you mean? And what did you mean about a tragic accident?"

Ivy longed to run to him, but she felt rooted to the spot by some strange inability to move. It was as though her limbs had turned to lead.

Ignoring her question, Danny still stood in the doorway. "Will you clear out my stuff from the Hampstead house?" he asked. "Then maybe you'd think of signing it over to Patty Brampton – she's a nice woman, and she and the boy deserve a break."

Ivy's mouth dropped open. "I don't understand – I mean, why can't you –" Then a sudden thought popped into her mind. "Did you ask her to pretend Rosa lived there?"

Danny nodded. "That's why I kept a tenant. I was always worried in case anyone – maybe even Hannah – turned up looking for Rosa. It was the only favour I ever asked of her."

Ivy bit her trembling lip. In a peculiar way, she was grateful to Danny for thinking of them all. And his concern for Patty Brampton almost caused her to break down. Her husband wasn't all bad – they'd had twenty good years together.

"Danny, you still haven't answered my question – please tell me you're not going to do anything stupid," Ivy begged him.

Danny smiled, his eyes glassy, and Ivy could tears running down his cheeks. "My beloved Ivy, just remember – this time, the situation will be reversed."

"What do you mean by 'reversed'? Please, Danny, wait –"

For a moment he seemed to hesitate, and Ivy took a step towards him. But then he was gone, and she stood paralysed at the drawing-room door, listening to his footsteps echoing down the marble steps outside. As she heard the front door slam, Ivy's knees buckled under her. She slipped to the floor and began to weep.

Chapter 60

That night, Ivy lay awake, alone and shivering in the big double bed that she and Danny had shared for so much of their married life. This was the bed in which they'd made love so many times. The bed had been their haven, the place where they'd snuggled up and held each other tight, to escape from the world outside. She longed for everything to be back the way it had been . . . but now that she knew the truth, nothing could ever be the same again.

Tears soaked her pillow and she wondered where Danny had gone. Perhaps he'd stayed at his London club, or in a hotel somewhere? Hopefully he'd walk in again the following morning. His words about Joseph taking over the running of Betterbuys had chilled her to the bone. He'd never try to – no, she wouldn't even give that idea space in her head. But what had he meant about an 'accident', and signing the Hampstead house over to Mrs Brampton? It all sounded so final. She could only hope that Danny had decided to go to the police himself, and he wanted her to take control of things in his absence . . . . She didn't dare think of any alternative.

Eventually she fell into a troubled sleep, filled with nightmares and vague shadows that were always just out of reach. She woke again as the first light of dawn began filtering through the curtains, and there was a moment before she remembered what had happened, and in that moment she'd been sleepily happy. But then her world came crashing down around her again. She felt consumed with guilt that she'd been able to sleep at all.

It was also dawning on her that if Danny didn't return soon, she'd need to get Rosa's letters, postcards and the laptop from Hannah's house. And she'd have to do it quickly, because once Hannah died the locals – maybe even her own parents – might decide to look through the letters for some way of contacting Rosa.

Ivy bit her lip. But she couldn't just turn up in Willow Haven out of the blue – where oh where was Danny? Although it was only first light, she reached for the phone on her bedside table and tried his mobile number. But there was no answer, and Ivy felt a deep sense of unease in the pit of her stomach.

Frantically, she leapt out of bed and hurried into the shower.

* * *

"We don't know exactly what happened, Mrs Heartley," one of the police officers told her apologetically. "But the boat was badly listing way out in the Channel, and there was no sign of your husband. The emergency services found a lifejacket in the water, so he may have been trying unsuccessfully to put it on." The officer looked at her closely. "Have you any idea why he'd have taken his boat out in such bad weather?"

Ivy shook her head, her eyes filled with tears. "Is there any hope –?"

The officers looked at each other, then down at their feet, clearly embarrassed and discomfited by her question.

"It would take a miracle, to be honest, ma'am," said one of the officers at last. "Without a life jacket, and in such rough seas –"

His voice trailed off as the other policeman took over.

"Obviously, we'll let you know when we find the – I mean, Mr Heartley."

After a shuffling of feet, the first police officer spoke again. "He wasn't depressed, was he?"

Ivy shook her head again, choosing to ignore the oblique reference to suicide. Her emotions were in turmoil. So Danny had chosen to end it in his own way. Now it was down to her to make certain that no one else came to that conclusion. She didn't want

Joseph suffering even greater stress by discovering that his father had taken his own life.

"Did your husband have any, er, financial problems?"

Ivy glared angrily at them through her tears. "Absolutely not. Betterbuys is doing brilliantly – he opened two new stores last month!"

The police officers gave her a sympathetic look, and Ivy suspected they were wondering how much she genuinely knew about her husband's business dealings. Perhaps they'd already assumed that Danny's behaviour was an indication that the company was in trouble. But they'd soon find out how well the company was doing. Ivy sighed. She'd gladly face bankruptcy if she could just have her old life back again.

"In the meantime, if you need any support, here are the phone numbers for the police liaison service, and several helpful organisations –"

With a nod of thanks, Ivy took the proffered cards. She'd no intention of contacting any organisation. She'd managed to keep her demons under control for half her lifetime, and she'd continue to do so in the future.

* * *

"Oh, Ivy – oh my God, I can't believe it!"

Ivy could hear her mother crying at the other end of the phone.

"Wait till I tell your father – Peter, you're not going to believe it, but Danny's dead – drowned off his boat. Poor Ivy, oh my God –"

Ivy's father took the phone. "Love, are you alright? I'm sure they'll find him. Look, he's probably made it to shore somewhere along the coast –"

"No, Dad, it looks like he wasn't wearing a life jacket – at this stage, there's no hope."

"Well, we can be on the next train –"

"Thanks, Dad – but there's no need, I'm okay. Joseph is due home later today. He'll have lots of questions, I suppose, and I need to spend time with him."

"Ivy, I insist! We can be on the train this evening – neither you nor Joseph should be on your own at a time like this."

"Actually, Dad – I was thinking of coming down to Willow Haven myself . . ."

"But don't you need to stay with Joseph?"

Ivy felt a fraud. But then, she'd been deceiving the people she loved all her life. Right now, she desperately needed to get into Hannah's cottage.

"Well, maybe I should go to see Peggy –"

"Nonsense – even though Danny was Peggy's brother, at a time like this she and Ned would expect to come to you! Anyway, your mother and I will go over there immediately to offer our condolences. Poor Peggy – she's only got Ned and the kids left now." Her father grunted. "Here's your mother again – she's bursting to tell you what's been happening here in Willow Haven."

Ivy heard her mother's voice. "Ivy, you're not going to believe this, but Hannah Dalton's house was burgled last night! The police think it must have been vandals, but they won't know until they've done those forensic tests – oh God, what am I wittering on about? You've just lost your husband, and I'm telling you about something totally trivial –"

Ivy felt a moment of relief. She no longer needed to go to Willow Haven. Danny had obviously been the perpetrator, making sure that all evidence of Rosa's letters and emails had been removed, ensuring that the link to him was broken forever. Ivy felt a surge of gratitude towards him for attending to this last part of the cover-up before he died.

"Needless to say, we're not going to tell Hannah what happened," Ivy's mother added. "The poor dear isn't expected to last much longer anyway, and it would break her heart to discover what those vandals have done to her home." Her mother sighed. "And there's still no sign of Rosa –"

Ivy stifled a sob as she thought of poor Hannah who would die without seeing her daughter.

"Love, are you okay?"

"Yes, Mum, I'm fine – well, not really, I mean, it's hard to take it all in . . . put Dad back on the phone, will you?"

When Ivy's father came on the line, Ivy was contrite.

"Dad, about you and Mum coming here – well yes, it makes sense, doesn't it? Sorry, I think I was a bit confused when you suggested it. So if you wouldn't mind taking the train this evening, I'd really appreciate the support."

"Of course, love. At times like these, you need your family around you."

"Yes, I'm so grateful to have you and Mum. But you don't need to stay long – I know that Hannah will be needing you, too."

Having arranged for her parents to let friends and neighbours in Willow Haven know about Danny's drowning, Ivy rang off feeling weepy and drained. She was deeply grateful for her parents' support – and she'd continue to need it while she played out the final act of the play that was now her life.

* * *

Ivy braced herself. Joseph was already on his way back from university, shocked and puzzled by his father's death. She'd explained it as a tragic accident, but her son knew what a skilled sailor Danny had been. She therefore had to hope he'd accept that the power of the sea had ultimately been greater than Danny's abilities. At least she could truthfully assure her son that there hadn't been any problems in his parents' marriage – until, that is, she uncovered the truth about Danny's other life.

Ivy wished more than anything that she could tell Joseph the truth. But that would mean telling him his father was a murderer. And she'd never blight his future by burdening him with that. Of course, truthfully, his father wasn't a murderer at all, since his real father was Joe Heartley . . .

Lifting up the receiver, she began to dial again. Firstly, she needed to speak to Peggy, then Owen, and of course, Brian . . .

* * *

Owen had been deeply shocked when she told him of Danny's death, and had offered to come to England right away to support her.

"Look, Brian and Charmaine can run the place while I'm gone –"

"No, honestly, everything's under control," Ivy explained gratefully.

"Mum and Dad are arriving here later this evening and Joseph's back from university. Needless to say, he's in bits, but I think he'll be okay."

"Losing your father at such a young age is bound to be a huge shock – and especially while he is still at university. Are you sure I can't be of some use? Obviously, I'll be over for the funeral – I mean, if there *is* a funeral . . ."

"I'll keep in touch and let you know if there are any developments," Ivy told her brother. "But the rescue people have said that because of the currents in the Channel, it's unlikely they'll recover his body at this stage."

"Will I get Brian on the line?" Owen asked astutely. "I'm sure he'll want to offer you his condolences."

"Yes, please," Ivy said, grateful that her brother couldn't see her blushes. Although she'd loved Danny very much, she was suddenly shivering at the bittersweet realisation that she was now free to begin a new life. As she waited on the telephone line, she envisioned being in Brian's comforting arms, then felt guilty for having such thoughts when her husband had only just died . . .

"Ivy?"

"Oh, Brian!"

Suddenly, they were both talking nineteen to the dozen, and Ivy told him everything that had happened.

Brian whistled. "So the mystery caller was your own husband!"

"Yes, and now we both know why," Ivy said dryly. "It's a relief that I no longer have to search in the lake – but I still need to make good the wrong I committed all those years ago."

"Would you like *me* to come to England? I'm sure Owen wouldn't mind – he and Charmaine can run Siyak'atala without me."

"No, Brian – thanks, but this is something I need to get through on my own. But I'll be thinking of you, and I'll take strength from knowing that I have your support."

Brian hesitated. "When it's all over – whatever that means – will you please come back to South Africa?"

"I will," Ivy said, and she was smiling through her tears.

* * *

In the days that followed, many things gradually fell into place, and Ivy found that incidents from the past assumed a clearer meaning. Obviously Danny had been the one who'd sent her the congratulations card from Rosa when she landed the starring role in *Bright Lights*. It shocked her to think he'd been so calculating. But clearly a successful murderer had to cover his or her tracks carefully in order to allay suspicion. It was hard to think of Danny as a murderer, but that was the reality she now had to face.

The presence of Ivy's parents at her home at Sussex had been a great comfort, especially for Joseph's sake. Peter and Eleanor had been able to give her son the support he needed, because every time she and Joseph were together in the same room, all they seemed to do was cry. But Ivy's feelings of loss were for the Danny she'd grown to love over time, not the murderer who'd managed to hide his crime for nearly twenty years.

Ivy was also acutely aware that her parents needed to get back to Willow Haven in order to support Hannah during her final days at the hospital in Allcott. As soon as Joseph felt well enough to return to university, she intended driving her parents back to the village. They would also be expecting her to keep up the search for Rosa – fortunately Danny's death had created an acceptable delay.

Alone in her bedroom, Ivy buried her face in her hands. I've covered up Rosa's murder, she thought, what sort of person does that make me? But then, I covered up Joe's death all those years ago, because I was afraid of getting into trouble. But now I'm not just covering up for my own sake – there's Joseph's future to think of. Nor could Peggy cope with knowing that her younger brother was a murderer, and that he had always known her older brother was dead at the bottom of Harper's Lake.

Ivy sighed. Anyway, Peggy would have enough to cope with when Joe's body was recovered. Because once Hannah died, it would be time for Joe and Rosa to be given a proper burial.

Chapter 61

As Ivy opened the boot of her car, she noticed that the boxes of assorted wigs and clothing were still there, waiting to be returned to the *Bright Lights* Props Department. She was about to take them out to make room for her parents' luggage, but decided against it. Once they were in the car, she was more likely to remember to return them. As she squeezed in the travel bags, she felt relieved that she wouldn't be needing all that paraphernalia any more – thankfully, her days of using disguises were over.

Joseph had left for the university earlier that morning, assuring Ivy that he was gradually coming to terms with his father's death and was more eager than ever to get started in Betterbuys. His resilience brought tears to Ivy's eyes as she waved goodbye to him at the train station.

That afternoon, as Ivy and her parents set out on the long drive from Sussex back to Lincolnshire, everyone was silent, each alone with their thoughts. Ivy felt exhausted and longed for the oblivion of sleep rather than having to concentrate on the road ahead. But she knew how much Hannah needed her parents' support. They had all agreed that there would be no mention of Danny's death in Hannah's presence. Even though she was now delirious much of the time, there was no point in risking any additional distress.

As she left the A1 and drove onto the A46, Ivy's thoughts turned to Danny. Only now was she beginning to understand how much he must have suffered over the years. It would have cost him dearly to appear the successful businessman and genial dinner-party host while secretly living each day in fear of discovery. Because he had wanted her so badly, Danny's life had been filled with subterfuge and stress. And despite eventually winning her love, both he and Rosa had both paid a terrible price for their obsessions.

Her eyes filled with tears and angrily she brushed them away. She needed to concentrate on the road ahead. Glancing in her rear-view mirror, she noticed that both parents had dozed off, her father's head resting on her mother's shoulder. They looked the picture of marital contentment, and Ivy was glad they each had a supportive and loving partner.

Then she thought of Brian, and a surge of joy supplanted her tears. He was the only person she'd ever been able to confide in, and it felt good having someone with whom she could share all the unsavoury details of her life, knowing he wasn't judging her. Tenderly, she recalled those piercing blue eyes in a tanned earnest face, remembering how good it felt to be held in his strong brown arms. And she remembered how desperately she'd longed to make love to him. Now, she was truly glad they hadn't, and not just out of respect for Danny, but because if it happened at some time in the future, it would be all the more special . . .

* * *

As Ivy and her mother walked into the private hospital room, Hannah's sister Joan was just leaving her bedside, her eyes red from crying.

"I'm sorry about your husband, Ivy," Joan said, gripping her in a tight embrace.

"Thanks, Joan," Ivy replied, feeling a fraud since she'd been daydreaming about another man on the drive to Lincolnshire.

"It's so good of you to come here, I mean, despite your own problems – and thank you for arranging the private room for Hannah –"

"How is she?"

"I've been holding her hand for hours, but the only person she wants is Rosa," Joan sobbed. "She keeps calling out her name, and I can't bear to see her so unhappy. Where on earth is Rosa? I'll never forgive her for putting her mother through all this suffering!"

Ivy bit her lip. She was the only one present who knew that Rosa wouldn't be turning up.

Eleanor sat down beside Hannah's bed, in the chair just vacated by Joan. "You look done in, Joan," she said. "Why don't you go back to your hotel and rest for a few hours? Ivy and I will sit with her until you get back."

Joan was staying at the Allcott Arms Hotel as she didn't feel comfortable staying in Hannah's house since the burglary

Joan wiped her tear-stained face. "Thanks, Eleanor – I really could do with a break. I'll be back after I've showered and changed."

Ivy and Eleanor both nodded as Joan kissed her sister and left the room.

Shortly afterwards, a nurse entered the room and checked Hannah's pulse.

"She's still very agitated," the nurse whispered. "She's calling all the time for her daughter Rosa –"

Eleanor grimaced. "Unfortunately, we don't know where Rosa is."

"Is Hannah aware of what's happening?" Ivy asked, but the nurse shook her head.

"She's hazy and confused, and slipping in and out of consciousness. She's not fully aware of what's going on around her, but she's very distressed, and the sedation doesn't seem to have helped. Her daughter would want to get here quickly – I don't think Hannah has long to live."

The nurse left, and Ivy and Eleanor surveyed Hannah as she dozed in her bed, her breathing laboured. She looked no bigger than a doll, her limbs shrunken and the bones clearly visible.

"Rosa!"

Ivy and Eleanor both jumped as Hannah let out a pitiful groan.

"Rosa, where are you? Please, Rosa, put your arms around me, I'm feeling so cold –" Hannah stared at them, but it wasn't clear if she recognised them. "Is Rosa here? I really need to see her –"

Ivy and her mother looked at each other, and Ivy could see the horror on her mother's face. She and Ivy's father had done all the practical things for Hannah, but the one thing they couldn't give her was her daughter. Yet that was the only thing she wanted.

Suddenly, Ivy had a daring idea. But could she pull it off? Or would she only make things worse? She beckoned to her mother and, outside the room, she outlined her idea.

"Oh God, Ivy – what if it went wrong? Hannah would be so upset, and Joan would be furious with us –"

"The nurse said she doesn't have long. Joan's back at the hotel, so no one will know but us. If she's about to die, we could help her to do it in peace."

"But shouldn't we call Joan if she's near the end? I don't know, Ivy –"

"Joan mightn't be able to get back in time. Mum, I'm an actor – let me do it."

Eleanor looked doubtful. "I suppose there's no harm in trying. I mean, if it helps –"

Even before her mother had finished her sentence, Ivy was running down the hospital corridor and out the main door, heading towards her car at breakneck speed.

* * *

Hannah's room was silent, except for the sound of her laboured breathing. Ivy and her mother watched, both apprehensive, as she drifted in and out of consciousness. Her pulse was faint by now, and Eleanor felt that Hannah was only hanging on by sheer will.

Suddenly Hannah's eyelids fluttered, then she opened her eyes and stared across the room to where Ivy standing by the door, wearing the fluffy blonde wig that had been in the boot of her car.

"Rosa, oh Rosa – you're here at last!" Hannah whispered. "Oh, I've missed you so much –"

As Hannah reached out her skinny arms, Ivy stepped forward and slipped into her embrace, allowing Hannah to hold her tight, saying nothing and keeping her face averted as she hunched over the bed.

Hannah was rambling now, her voice no more than a whisper. "It's been so long, Rosa, but you're here at last. Those photographs you sent me – are you going to marry that nice man in the photographs?"

"Yes, Mamma," Ivy whispered, knowing that this was what Hannah longed to hear. She could feel Hannah visibly relax in her arms, and as Eleanor watched, a beatific smile appeared on Hannah's face.

"Oh Rosa, I'm so happy for you," Hannah whispered. "I've put some money aside for a new outfit –"

Ivy stayed motionless in Hannah's arms, listening to her shallow breathing. Her back was hurting by now, but she didn't dare move. She was willing to suffer any discomfort so that Hannah could believe she was holding Rosa in her arms again.

Gradually, Ivy could feel Hannah's grip loosening, but still she stayed as she was, feeling Hannah's pulse gradually slowing down. Suddenly, Hannah gripped her tightly again.

"Rosa!" she whispered, straining as though to sit up. Then she fell back, and Ivy knew that Hannah had just taken her last breath.

The next few minutes seemed like an eternity as Ivy gradually extricated herself from Hannah's embrace. Leaning down, she kissed her old friend's cheek and gently closed her eyes.

"She's gone," she told her mother, taking off the wig and stuffing it into her handbag.

Eleanor burst into tears, and she and Ivy hugged each other tightly.

"At least she's at peace now," Eleanor sobbed, as they both turned to look at Hannah, who looked amazingly happy in repose.

For a long time, Ivy and her mother sat by Hannah's bedside, tears running down their faces. Eventually one of the nurses re-entered the room, and finding that Hannah no longer had a pulse, nodded sympathetically and whispered her condolences. Then she hurried off to inform one of the doctors.

A few minutes later Peter and Joan walked into the room, and Ivy embraced each of them in turn.

"She's just passed away – very peacefully," Ivy assured them, fresh tears running down her cheeks. "Hannah believed that Rosa was with her at the end, and she died with a smile on her face."

* * *

As Ivy left the hospital with her mother a little later, Eleanor looked at her astutely.

"Thank goodness you were able to help Hannah die happy, Ivy – it's almost as though you knew all along that Rosa wasn't coming back. Funny that, isn't it?"

Ivy nodded, afraid to look directly at her mother. "Yes, it is, isn't it?"

Eleanor then took her daughter's hand, a gesture that surprised Ivy. Her mother hadn't held her hand since she was a small child.

"I'm very proud of you," Eleanor whispered. "What you did for Hannah – well, I'll never forget it. I just wish Hannah had been as lucky as me – I've got the best daughter in the world."

Chapter 62

"Hello – Mrs Brampton?"

"Yes?"

Ivy extended her hand. "My name is Ivy Heartley – I'm Danny Heartley's wife."

She couldn't bring herself to say 'widow' yet.

"Oh! Well, come in, come in –" The woman looked closely at Ivy. "Don't I know you from somewhere – oh my word, you're Isabella in *Bright Lights*!"

Ivy stepped inside as Mrs Brampton continued to babble.

"Oh God, I never realised that Mr Heartley was married to someone as famous as you! He never said – oh, if only Sean was here, but he's playing soccer this afternoon –"

Mrs Brampton was in quite a state – she could hardly believe that the star of *Bright Lights* was standing in her own hall!

"I've come to clear out my husband's things from the flat upstairs – I don't know if you're aware, but my husband recently drowned at sea."

Mrs Brampton covered her mouth in shock. "Oh my God! I saw something on the News about a Mr Heartley of Betterbuys, but I didn't realise he was *our* Mr Heartley – oh, how awful! I was wondering why we hadn't seen him lately. Oh dear, let me get you a cup of tea –"

Ivy waved aside the offer of tea. "No thanks, Mrs Brampton, I'm just here to collect his computer and notes from his office upstairs."

"Of course!" said Mrs Brampton warmly. "Let me help you carry the stuff downstairs."

"No, thanks," Ivy assured her quickly, "I'll be able to manage them myself. On second thoughts, maybe I *will* have that cup of tea." She certainly didn't want Mrs Brampton having any opportunity to pry into Danny's clandestine activities.

While Mrs Brampton fussed around in her kitchen downstairs, Ivy made several trips to her car, bringing out the computer, Hannah's letters to Rosa, notebooks, camcorder, digital-sound-editing machine and Rosa's rucksack, and placing them in the boot of her car, which she'd parked directly outside Mrs Brampton's front door. It felt very odd being back in Cherrywood Road legitimately!

When she returned to the house after loading up everything she needed, Mrs Brampton was in her kitchen, pouring out the tea and looking decidedly uneasy. For a moment Ivy's heart did a somersault. Was something wrong? Had the woman somehow uncovered some aspect of Danny's sordid other life?

"I don't like to trouble you at a time like this," Mrs Brampton said falteringly, "but I suppose you'll be wanting Sean and me to move out soon. But if we could just have a few weeks' notice . . ."

Ivy smiled, relieved. "Mrs Brampton," she said, touching the other woman's sleeve, "my husband always intended the house to be signed over to you eventually. He said you were great tenants, and I agreed to transfer the house into your name if anything ever happened to him."

"What? Are you serious? Oh my God, I can't believe it!" Mrs Brampton looked shocked, incredulous and excited all at once.

"There's just one condition –"

"Anything!"

Mrs Brampton looked like an excited little dog about to be taken for a walk, and Ivy had to suppress the urge to laugh.

"You must never, ever tell anyone about Mr Heartley's generosity – my husband was a shy man, and he wouldn't have wanted any publicity. Nor would I." Ivy took a sip of her tea. "Since my husband's body hasn't been recovered yet, it may be some time before the house can be formally signed over to you. But until then, there's no need to pay rent, and my solicitors are already preparing the documentation that will ensure it's transferred to you in due course."

"Oh my goodness, I can't believe it! I'll never mention it to anyone – I swear!"

Ivy smiled, pleased at Mrs Brampton's obvious joy, and confident that she'd keep her word. Ivy needed to ensure that the paparazzi never learned about the transaction. If they ever started digging, they might find out about Danny's regular visits, and a whole can of worms might open up.

Ivy shook hands with Mrs Brampton, who was still shell-shocked and star-struck. It wasn't every day that a famous actress arrived on your doorstep and gave you a free house!

"My solicitor will be in touch with you soon," Ivy told her, "and you'll be asked to sign a confidentiality agreement."

Mrs Brampton nodded, looking as though she was about to cry. She grasped Ivy's hand, and the tears then began to spill down her cheeks. "Oh, I can't believe it – I must be dreaming! Poor Mr Heartley – I'm thrilled at his kindness to Sean and me, but it seems wrong to be profiting from his misfortune –"

Ivy patted Mrs Brampton's arm. "I hope you and your son will be very happy here."

"Oh we will be! God bless poor Mr Heartley – we'll never forget him. I still can't believe he's gone –"

Ivy pressed a finger to her lips, and Mrs Brampton immediately understood.

"I promise I won't say a word to anyone, and thank you both so much –"

Mrs Brampton followed her out to the gate.

"And any time you're passing, be sure to drop in for another cup of tea –"

Ivy was still smiling as she drove away. It felt good to make someone else happy. At least something good had come out of Danny's death.

Chapter 63

"I don't understand why Rosa didn't come home for her mother's funeral," Ivy's mother said plaintively as she filled the dishwasher in the kitchen. "It was bad enough that she missed saying goodbye to her mother, but to miss the funeral as well! Your father emailed her again, and we put notices in all the national newspapers, so I don't see how she could have missed it –" Eleanor looked sadly at her daughter. "Everyone in the village is talking about it. I mean, even if they'd fallen out over something, it would hardly be a reason not to turn up . . ."

"Rosa is probably abroad somewhere, and didn't read her emails or see the death notice," Ivy said.

"She should have been here, looking after her poor mother!" Eleanor said vehemently. "And I'll tell her that when I see her! I hope that if I'm ever dying of a terminal illness, you won't treat me like Rosa treated poor Hannah."

Her mother grabbed a cloth and began wiping down the kitchen worktops furiously.

"Poor girl – how awful to come home and discover that your mother had died and was buried while you were off globetrotting!"

Ivy smiled. "Only a minute ago, you were threatening to give Rosa a piece of your mind!"

"Well, I feel sorry for her at this stage. You have to admit, Ivy, it's all very mysterious. Why hasn't anyone been able to find her?"

Ivy shrugged her shoulders. She was grateful that Hannah had died without knowing what had happened to Rosa, and she was equally relieved that Hannah had been fooled by her own last-minute charade.

"Well, it was a lovely funeral," Ivy said firmly, trying the lift the sombre mood. "We gave Hannah a good send-off, and your roses were beautiful, Mum."

Eleanor was mopping the worktops, which were gleaming by now. "Well yes, I know Hannah would have liked them," she said gruffly, turning away, and Ivy knew she was devastated by the loss of her old friend and neighbour. "Hannah always admired my roses – I told her the secret was good compost, and I even offered her some for her own roses, so that she could dig it in around the roots, but –"

Suddenly, Eleanor was gulping great big sobs, and Ivy rushed to comfort her mother. Soon, they were both weeping.

Ivy's father padded into the kitchen in his slippers, silently filled the kettle and turned it on. He was equally mystified that Hannah's daughter couldn't be found, and he knew that this, more than anything else, was upsetting his wife. She was dreading having to face Rosa when she finally came looking for her mother and found nothing but a grave and a burgled house.

"You must be devastated about Danny too, Ivy," Eleanor whispered as she clung to her daughter. "I mean, so much has gone wrong lately, hasn't it? You've lost your husband, and Joseph is without a father. Fred and Julia are gone too, and neither Joe nor Rosa have ever come home . . ."

Suddenly, Eleanor looked up.

"Isn't it strange that in one small village, two of our young people could completely disappear?"

Chapter 64

"Are we ready? Episode 113, scene thirty, take one. *Action!*"

Ivy began walking down the road where her final scene in *Bright Lights* was taking place. Isabella was drunk and deeply distressed after discovering her husband's infidelity with her closest friend. Despite her own regular indiscretions, Isabella was appalled that he would stray so close to home, and for this reason, Ivy was now weaving from side to side as she stumbled along, oblivious to the car that was approaching and the accident that was designed to happen. The make-up department had streaked Ivy's face with tears, and indeed she felt very emotional herself. Having achieved her dream of starring in the country's top soap opera, she was now giving it all up.

Her agent, the show's producers and even her friends among the cast had all urged her not to make such a hasty decision. After all, they reasoned, it was only a few months since her husband had drowned. She was bound to feel traumatised, but that was no reason to give up a starring role and a job that paid her handsomely. They could write her out for several weeks, even months, if she needed time to mourn. But Ivy was adamant – her time in *Bright Lights* was over.

Somehow, the press had got wind of the story, and everywhere she went, reporters were lying in wait with questions about her proposed departure from *Bright Lights*. Was it true? If so, was she leaving to take up another role elsewhere? Still under contract, Ivy wasn't allowed to make press statements herself, so she simply referred the journalists to the *Bright Lights* publicity office – where she knew they'd learn absolutely nothing.

Several endings had already been filmed – in one, Isabella was seen falling from a horse, in another she was left hanging over a cliff. Luckily, Ivy hadn't needed to film either scene – a stuntwoman had been used in her place! The varied endings meant that even people working on the programme wouldn't know which scene would ultimately be screened.

Ivy's agent was adamant that Isabella shouldn't die. She'd insisted – and the producers had agreed – that off-screen Isabella would recover from her accident, but decide to leave the bright lights of the city and return to the countryside. That way, Ivy had options, and Isabella could return if Ivy or the producers wanted her back.

The scene now being filmed was the one being given most consideration by the series producers. By having Isabella hit by a car, they could keep her in a coma for weeks, and the audience on tenterhooks. Would she live or would she die? Would her errant husband be the one to turn off her life support?

The first camera unit was now focusing on Ivy as she stumbled along the road, and the second unit was taking close-ups of Isabella's tear-stained face as she made her way along.

On cue, Ivy turned her tear-stained face towards the nearest camera unit, giving them a final shot of her agony and confusion.

"Cut! That was really good, Ivy!" shouted the director. "Let's wrap for today, folks! Well done everyone! And all the best to you, Ivy, in your new venture."

Ivy smiled, pleased and relieved that all had gone well. The sounds of the car crash would be added at the post-production stage, and a series of already-taken close-ups of Ivy's distraught and bloodstained face would be used as a montage to complete the sequence ultimately selected.

There was a burst of loud applause for Ivy from the cast and crew.

"You were great, Ivy – we're all going to miss you," said Anton, slipping an arm around her. He hadn't been in the last scene, but like many other cast members, he'd come along to offer his support. Sarah, Emily and Dominic were also there, and there would be a special private party for Ivy later that evening in Soho. All the cast and crew would be present to say goodbye and wish her well for the future.

It was at moments like these, when surrounded by people she liked and respected, that Ivy wondered briefly if she was doing the right thing. But at heart, she knew it was time for a major change in her life. It was time to give something back.

"A penny for them," Anton said. "Thinking of your future?"

Ivy shook her head. She couldn't possibly tell dear Anton about her thoughts – he'd be shocked, as would everyone else in the cast, if they knew the secrets she'd been keeping for most of her life!

But now, she had one more job to do – one that couldn't be put off any longer. After the party tonight, she'd get a good night's sleep in the Soho hotel where she'd booked a room. And tomorrow, she'd go back to Willow Haven where it all started. And this time, the story would finally have an ending.

Chapter 65

It was a mild afternoon as Ivy drove to Willow Haven. The party the night before had been a wild, alcohol-fuelled event at a private London club, and she now had a substantial hangover. But she'd received a wonderful send-off from all her colleagues in *Bright Lights*, and she felt both weepy and nostalgic. Now, she was on her way, ostensibly to say goodbye to her parents before heading to South Africa. But only she knew she'd be staying in Willow Haven a little longer than expected.

I'm still deceiving people, Ivy thought sadly, but this will be the last time. After this is over, I'll finally be free of all the lies.

When she arrived in the village, her parents were waiting, overjoyed to see her but their pleasure was slightly tinged with sorrow. South Africa seemed so far away.

"Are you sure you're not being too hasty?" her mother asked. "I mean, throwing your career away just because Danny's gone . . . shouldn't you give it more time before making such big decisions? And what about Joseph – he's going to miss you terribly . . ."

Ivy's father cleared his throat. "Eleanor, please, it's Ivy's decision. Joseph will be fine – he'll be starting in Betterbuys when he's finished his degree, and he's clearly got Danny's flair for business . . ."

"Well, *we're* going to miss you!" Eleanor stated, refusing to be mollified, tears glistening in her eyes.

"Look, you're coming out to Owen's wedding, so it won't be very long before I see you again!" Ivy told them, tears in her own eyes. She couldn't have asked for better or more loving parents. They'd stood by her when she'd got pregnant as a teenager, baby-sat while she continued her schooling, and encouraged her to achieve her dreams.

"Did you pass Hannah's house?" asked her mother, wiping her eyes. "It's so sad to see it empty. The police still haven't found out who broke in." Eleanor sighed. "What do you make of it all, Ivy? Why on earth would a thief take Hannah's personal letters? We've looked up the phone directory and can't find any Rosa Dalton listed in Hampstead. I don't suppose you ever managed to contact any of her tenants?"

Ivy shook her head guiltily. "Sorry Mum, I meant to –"

"Oh well, I don't suppose it matters much now. I mean, nobody wants to interfere, but naturally, people are asking questions . . ."

Ivy's heart was beating uncomfortably. "I'm sure Rosa will turn up one day soon."

"And I'll give her a piece of my mind when she does!" Eleanor said angrily, stomping out of the room.

In his wife's absence, her father leaned forward conspiratorially. "By the way, Ivy – if you intend going for any of those power walks while you're here, tell you mother you'd prefer to be on your own – I'm sick of her attempts to get me fit!"

Smiling, Ivy nodded. That suited her plans perfectly, because what remained to be done needed to be done alone.

* * *

That night, Ivy sat at the dressing table in her old childhood bedroom, the room where nightmares had been her constant companion for so long. But tonight, she felt at peace, because tomorrow she would finally put an end to the mystery of Joe and Rosa's disappearances.

As she combed her hair, her thoughts reverted once again to Danny. Despite what he'd done, she wished he hadn't felt the need to end it all rather than work out a solution. Of course, there was no solution to murder. It was ironic that they'd both brought toxic secrets to their marriage, but despite all the deception, it had, in essence been a good relationship, and they had genuinely cared for each other.

Ivy abandoned her hairbrush and stared at her reflection in the mirror. Every moment of that last evening with Danny was still imprinted in her brain. Over and over it ran through her mind, like a demented newsreel, invading her dreams and demanding her attention during waking hours. It was as though she was meant to find some deeper meaning in it, but as yet she had no idea what.

Now she sat pondering on the last puzzling words Danny had spoken to her. As he'd stood at the drawing room door before he left, he'd said: "Just remember – this time the situation will be reversed." At the time she'd been too overwrought to consider what he'd meant. Now, she wondered if he'd been referring to something in their lives that he'd expected her to understand. Was she just being fanciful, or had it carried some kind of message meant for her alone? What was going to be "reversed"?

Suddenly Ivy gasped, feeling as though an electric shock had seared through her as the meaning of his words finally registered. People thought Joe and Rosa had been alive, whereas all the time they'd been dead – now people would think Danny was dead, but in reality, he'd still be . . . alive?

Ivy felt a bizarre and dizzying sense of relief. Danny had faked his own death! He'd taken the boat out into the Channel, knowing the tides would carry it out to sea. No doubt he'd made his escape in an inflatable dinghy and at that very moment he was probably in some far-off country, where Danny Heartley would disappear, later to emerge with a new identity. She knew that her husband had millions salted away in overseas accounts, where only numbers would be needed to gain access to his considerable funds. The night he'd left, she'd been too stressed to notice what he was doing at the safe. Now with hindsight, she realised he'd probably been taking the documents he needed to access his money. And when you had money, anything was possible. A few phone calls could always secure anything that Danny needed.

Ivy shivered, all kinds of emotions racing through her. Had he read about his own death online, or in some newspaper on the other side of the world? Danny would certainly have got a kick out of that! Was he, at that very moment, sipping cocktails on some beach in the tropics? Ivy knew he wouldn't be capable of idleness for very long. Perhaps he'd start a second retail empire on another continent . . . with all the money he had available to him, he could do anything he wanted.

Ivy wasn't sure whether to laugh or cry. She should have guessed that Danny wouldn't sacrifice himself! After all, he'd had years to plan his disappearance. He'd obviously worked out every detail in advance, knowing that if his crime was ever found out, his escape route had already been organised. He might even have bought a bolthole already, on one of his trips to post Rosa's cards and letters. Now she felt certain that Danny's body would never be found.

Suddenly she was angry. Her son was grieving for a father who probably wasn't dead at all! She was also furious with Danny for causing her parents and Peggy so much unnecessary grief, and for leaving Hannah to die without ever seeing her daughter again. But she was also aware that Danny had saved her and her son at great personal cost to himself, and preserved the Betterbuys chain that was his legacy to Joseph. So for all their sakes, she'd accept the eventual verdict of death by misadventure, based on the 'accident' she now suspected Danny had staged.

Ivy's feelings were veering from relief to hysteria and back again. She wondered if Danny was missing her and Joseph. She felt an irresistible urge to phone Brian, and she wondered what he'd make of Danny's faked death. But she wouldn't tell him yet – not until she'd done what she came to Willow Haven to do.

* * *

The following morning, Ivy was up bright and early. Luckily, it was a sunny morning, which suited her plans perfectly.

In the kitchen, her mother and father were eating breakfast.

"I think I'll go by the lake today – I might even take a swim," Ivy told them, buttering a piece of toast.

"I wouldn't, if I were you – you know how deep that water is!"

her mother warned her. Fortunately, Eleanor didn't suggest that her father accompany her, and Ivy and her father exchanged a conspiratorial wink before she left.

Her mind was still reeling from her discovery of the night before – yet the more Ivy thought about it, the more logical it seemed that Danny would have prepared in advance for his eventual disappearance.

Contrary to her previous trips to the lake, Ivy now made a special effort to meet local people as she walked along. And she told everyone she met that she was going for a swim in the lake as part of her daily health regimen.

Stripping down to her swimsuit, Ivy put a toe in the water and shivered. In fact, she didn't really need to dive in at all. She could simply pretend she'd been in the water, since Fred's car was unlikely to have moved since her last dive. Nevertheless, she wanted everything to be above board this time, and as close to the truth as possible. But first, Ivy went to her sports bag and took out a metal powder compact. She threw it into the water and watched as it sank to the bottom. Later, it would become part of her story.

Taking a deep breath, Ivy leapt off the bank and descended into the cold dark waters. She felt a brief moment of panic as the murkiness and debris seemed to claw at her, and she felt like surfacing immediately. Thank goodness she no longer needed to worry about her possessions being in the car!

It was difficult to see anything in the gloom, but as her eyes adjusted she spotted the outline of Fred Heartley's red car in the distance. She didn't need to go any nearer – all she needed to do now was surface, climb out, and tell the police what she'd seen.

Sitting on the edge of the bank, Ivy felt almost euphoric, although she knew her actions would bring sorrow to others, especially her dear friend Peggy. Her sister-in-law was only just coming to terms with Danny's drowning, and soon she'd have to cope with another death in the family.

Ivy quickly dried herself off, slipped on her tracksuit again and bundled her wet clothes into her sports bag. She decided to go home first, tell her parents what she'd seen, then ask her father to accompany her to the police station. That would make it all seem more natural. Everything in her rebelled against being so calculating, especially when it involved her own parents, but it was necessary for this last piece of the jigsaw to fit properly.

Back at the house, her mother received the news with equanimity.

"You know, I have a bad feeling about this, Ivy," Eleanor announced. "That car – were you able to see the colour?"

"No, Mum, it was too dark."

"Hmmm. You know, I wouldn't be surprised if it turned out to be Fred Heartley's red Ford. I've never subscribed to the notion that Joe went to Australia. He was too nice a boy to leave his parents worrying like that. Of course, I always encouraged Julia to believe he'd be back, but I've had my suspicions –"

Her father laughed. "Your mother's a great conspiracy theorist – I'm surprised she hasn't suggested that the Bermuda Triangle is down there too."

Ivy shrugged her shoulders. "Maybe it's just an old wreck that someone dumped there, but I need to let the police know anyway."

An hour later, having been driven by her father to the police station in Allcott, Ivy stepped up to the public window and tapped on the glass. She had her story well prepared, and up to a point, it was true. It was just twenty years out of date.

Fifteen minutes later, as she left the police station with her father, Ivy experienced a sense of peace she hadn't known for a long time. She'd done what she had to do, and she'd remain in the village until the car was recovered and the bodies identified.

"Let's go home, Dad," Ivy said, linking arms with her father as they walked to his car. "Right now, I could do with a strong cup of tea."

Her father grimaced. "Personally, I'd prefer a whiskey – I wonder if your mother could be right?"

Chapter 66

When the crane pulled Fred Heartley's red Ford out of the lake with the two bodies inside, which were identified as Joe and Rosa, Eleanor was so stunned that she forgot to claim credit for her earlier prescience.

"But all those photographs and letters that Hannah said were from Rosa – where did they come from?" Eleanor had whispered, her eyes like saucers.

"I suspect she wrote those letters herself," Ivy said softly. "She wouldn't have wanted people thinking that Rosa hadn't kept in touch with her – but of course, we now know where Rosa was all that time."

Ivy hated herself for implying that Hannah had deceived them. But she didn't feel she'd any choice since her own future and Joseph's were at stake. Only her mother, father and Joan actually knew about the letters and photos, and they'd all accept that Hannah had created them to bolster her own ego, and keep quiet out of respect for her memory.

Eleanor looked puzzled. "So all that malarkey about Rosa owning a house in Hampstead – that wasn't true, either?"

Ivy was unsure what to say. "No, I'm afraid not, Mum," she said at last.

Luckily, Eleanor had decided to return to the subject of the photos. "But your father and I actually *saw* pictures of Rosa, on those foreign trips of hers –"

"Hannah probably had them done professionally," Ivy lied. "Maybe she needed them for herself as much as anyone else. Anyway, since they've all been lost in the burglary, Mum, I think it's best if we forget we ever saw them. Otherwise, we'll look foolish if we keep harping on about something that no longer exists, won't we?"

"But how –"

Looking at her mother's tear-stained face, Ivy felt awful.

Ivy's father joined them in the kitchen. "Ivy's right, love. If Hannah felt the need to deceive us, it's not for us to tell anyone else."

"I'd never do that!" Eleanor said indignantly. "I'm just finding it hard to understand why she needed to deceive *us*. I mean, I thought we were her friends –"

"I'd say it was precisely *because* you were such good friends that she couldn't bear for you to pity her," Ivy said. "You've always had your daughter visiting regularly – Hannah didn't."

Eleanor nodded, managing a tearful smile. "Yes, it must be awful not to have regular contact with a child you love so much," she'd whispered. "If you didn't visit regularly, Ivy, and if Owen didn't phone at least once a month, I might find myself pretending to the neighbours, too . . ."

* * *

The funerals of Rosa Dalton and Joe Heartley took place together on a dull grey morning in Willow Haven. Everyone in the village attended the church service and followed the cortege to the cemetery, where both graves were festooned with wreaths, bouquets and cards bearing messages of condolence.

Rosa, who'd been identified by the gold pendant Hannah had given her, was interred in her mother's grave, while Joe Heartley joined his parents in theirs. There was a space in the Heartley grave for Danny too, if his body was ever found. Of course Ivy now felt certain that was never going to happen.

As she stood before the Heartley grave, she felt overwhelmed by emotion, remembering Fred's dying words when he'd still hoped that Joe was alive and would return home one day. She'd gone to the funeral parlour the night before, and asked to place Fred's letter in the coffin with his son. She'd also added a crayon drawing done by Joseph at the age of six. The page was a riot of colour, and Ivy felt that it was fitting that Joe should take something of his son with him on the road to eternity. Now, as Joe's coffin was lowered into the ground, Ivy's tears flowed freely. You're home at last, Joe, she whispered.

Joseph hadn't attended the funerals because he was under pressure to finish a paper for university. Anyway, Ivy felt there wasn't any need for him to be there – he was still coming to terms with his own grief and besides, he'd never met the man he believed to be his uncle.

Clara Bellingham and her new husband Bill were there, Clara's face wet with tears. "There's been so much sadness lately, hasn't there, Ivy?" she whispered. "I can't believe that Danny is gone – you must be devastated."

Ivy nodded, feeling a fraud.

Clara grasped her wrist. "You'll come to visit us before you leave Willow Haven, won't you?"

"How about tomorrow evening about eight?" Ivy suggested.

Clara turned to Bill and they both nodded.

"I can't believe Rosa's gone," Clara's voice caught in a sob, "and that she's been dead for years. And to think we assumed she was off living it up in exotic hot-spots, when all the time –" She turned to Ivy with a tearful expression. "She was so full of life, wasn't she?"

Ivy nodded, hoping that Clara wouldn't remember being told about the congratulations card she herself had received from Rosa. Perhaps, when she visited them tomorrow, she'd tell them the same lie she'd told her parents, about how Hannah had created a make-believe world to help her feel close to her absentee daughter. They'd understand and keep quiet – besides, nothing could hurt Hannah now.

"So how was your honeymoon?" she asked, trying to lighten the atmosphere a little.

"Wonderful!" said Clara, glancing shyly at Bill.

"Yes, we had a great time in the Canaries," Bill said, "but it was a shock to come back to such tragic news – first poor Danny, then Rosa and Joe."

As Ivy nodded sadly, preparing to move away, Clara tugged at her sleeve. "Ivy, you're not going to believe this – I'm pregnant already!"

Ivy scooped her old friend into her arms. "Congratulations, Clara – how wonderful! That's just what this area needs – the sound of children's laughter!"

As the graveside services ended, people began leaving the cemetery. Most of them were heading to the hotel where tea and sandwiches were being provided.

Eleanor appeared, linking arms with her daughter. "If you hadn't dived in to find your lost compact, Joe and Rosa might never have been found," she said.

"But the bodies would have been discovered when the Council started draining the lake," Ivy pointed out.

"Oh, didn't you hear?" Eleanor said, pleased to know something her daughter didn't. "The Council has finally voted against draining it – the project has proved far too expensive."

Arching her eyebrows, Ivy smiled to herself. Not so long ago, that news would have been music to her ears. Now it didn't matter any more.

As her parents fell into conversation with a group of neighbours, Ivy found herself embraced by her sister-in-law, Peggy. The two women hugged each other tightly, their tears flowing freely.

"First Danny, now Joe!" Peggy sobbed. "Oh Ivy, it's just all so horrible! Poor Joe – he never even left Willow Haven!"

"I'm so sorry!" said Ivy, now weeping too, but Peggy would never know that Ivy was also apologising for all the deception she'd practised in the past. If she'd been honest all those years ago, Peggy would have done her weeping for Joe long ago.

"Why on earth were Joe and Rosa together in Dad's car?" Peggy asked at last. "Joe didn't even like her. And he disappeared weeks before Rosa supposedly left for London –"

Peggy looked tearfully at her sister-in-law. "What do you think could have happened?"

Ivy's heart was thumping painfully. "Maybe he was bringing

your dad's car back to Willow Haven? He might have bumped into Rosa as she was leaving, and offered her a lift. I don't suppose we'll ever know what happened."

And I hope you never do, Ivy thought to herself. She longed to tell Peggy that she herself had been leaving Willow Haven with Joe. And she desperately wished her sister-in-law could know how much she'd loved Joe back then.

As Ned approached and slipped a protective arm around his wife, Ivy promised to follow him and Peggy to the hotel. But first, there was someone she needed to speak to.

Hannah's sister Joan now stood alone at the grave that held her sister and niece, and she cut a forlorn figure as Ivy approached her.

"I can't believe they're both gone," Joan whispered. "And I don't understand why Hannah lied to me all these years – she told me she met Rosa regularly in London!"

"I think she was afraid people would believe Rosa couldn't be bothered to visit her," Ivy said sadly. "Of course, we now know that was far from the truth."

"Hannah was always talking about some big house that Rosa had in Hampstead – I suppose that wasn't true, either?"

Shamefaced, Ivy lowered her head. "I'm afraid not, Joan," she replied. "I think it was just another story that helped Hannah to feel close to her daughter."

Looking at Joan's tear-stained face, Ivy felt a stab of guilt for the cover-up she was engaged in. But Joan would experience far greater grief if she knew her niece had been murdered. Better to let her think it was just a ghastly accident, as the police clearly did. Ivy was relieved that the police hadn't uncovered any evidence of foul play, and the injuries Rosa had sustained had been attributed to the impact of the crash.

Joan turned to Ivy, her eyes red-rimmed. "You've had your share of loss too, Ivy. It's never easy losing the people you love, is it? I still can't bear to look at Hannah's house. Since the burglary, it doesn't feel like a home any more. Now I understand how Rosa felt about this place – I doubt if I'll ever come back to Willow Haven again."

"Why don't you come to South Africa for a holiday?" Ivy said impulsively. It was the least she could do for this lonely woman who had no family left. It could never replace her loss, but a holiday in the sun might help to lift her spirits a little.

Joan looked at her uncertainly. "W-what do you mean?"

Ivy leaned forward confidentially. "I've left *Bright Lights* and I'm moving to South Africa," she whispered. "Please come out for Owen's wedding next spring – your fare will be my treat."

"You're leaving *Bright Lights*?" Initially Joan looked stunned, but then she recovered. "I suppose I'm not really surprised, Ivy. You've been through so much yourself."

Ivy hugged her. "Please come – I promise to make it the holiday of a lifetime!"

Joan nodded through her tears. "I can hardly turn down an offer like that, can I? Thanks, Ivy!"

"Come on, let's go for a drink at the hotel," Ivy said, hiding her own tears as she led Joan down the tree-lined avenue and out of the cemetery.

* * *

The newspapers attributed Ivy's departure from *Bright Lights* to the recent tragic death of her husband Danny Heartley, managing director of the Betterbuys supermarket chain, and Ivy saw no reason to enlighten them. Besides, it was important for Joseph to believe that she was mourning his father's death. In a way, she *was* in mourning for Danny – he'd been her husband for half of her life, and she'd grown to love the man she'd believed him to be. Since realising he'd probably faked his death, her confused feelings had vacillated between anger and grief, followed by guilt at allowing Rosa's murder to be covered up. But what use would the truth serve? It would ruin too many lives.

Gradually over time, her feelings for Danny had mellowed. She owed him a debt of gratitude for being her rock for twenty years, but most of all, for giving Joseph a father. In a way, she would always love him for that. And although he'd never again be part of her life, she was glad to think that he was out there, and she wished him well. They'd both made mistakes and, in forgiving Danny, she

326

would also be forgiving herself. Perhaps it was time to set aside the guilt they both shared, especially now that each of them was embracing a new and very different future. It was time to let go.

Ivy also made it clear to the press that she wouldn't be playing any active role in Betterbuys. "My son Joseph will eventually take over the day-to-day running of the company," she told reporters, "and Betterbuys will be maintaining the traditions that have made the company such a great success."

* * *

As she wheeled her suitcases into busy Port Elizabeth airport, Ivy looked anxiously at all the faces as people milled around her. Suddenly, she was filled with uncertainty and fear. Would he be there, or had she read too much into his offer of support?

For a moment, she felt scared. Had she travelled six thousand miles, only to be disappointed? What if he didn't really want her? Or if he only wanted a holiday romance, or maybe not even that? Had she somehow misread the signs?

Then suddenly, he was there, a big grin on his tanned handsome face.

"Ivy – oh Ivy, you're here!"

"Brian!"

Although they were surrounded by hundreds of people, it was as though there was no one else there except the two of them. As he rushed towards her, his broad smile held so much promise, and in his blue eyes she could already see her future. And this time, it would be a future without lies or subterfuge.

"At last!" she whispered fervently as she fell into his arms.

Interview with

LINDA KAVANAGH

It can be said that 'suspense' has always been women's favourite type of fiction but in recent years many fiction readers and authors have veered away from it in favour of 'contemporary romance'. Now it has swung back and Linda Kavanagh is ready to make up for lost time . . .

Why do you personally choose to write in the suspense genre?

Probably because they're the kind of novels I enjoy reading myself. I like a book that keeps me gripped – personally, I'll abandon any that fail to keep me interested. Therefore, I try to ensure that my readers are kept interested with a few twists and turns as each novel progresses!

Where do you find your inspiration? Purely from imagination or from real-life incidents you may experience or hear of?

It's probably a mixture of both – I'd say 90% imagination, but sometimes an idea is triggered by a news item or someone else's experience. Anyway, our imaginations are the accumulation of all the ideas, feelings and experiences we've stored over the course of our lives, and it's this shared humanity that gives a story its edge. Regardless of where we live or what language we speak, we all share the same feelings, worries, hopes and dreams. And sometimes we like them packaged into an entertaining read!

Do you find it disturbs you to write about very dark themes, such as those in Never Say Goodbye *and* Still Waters? *Or are you able to disassociate yourself from what you write?*

I have cried over the fate of some of my characters as I wrote particular scenes, and believe me, it's not easy to type when there are tears running down your face! It is actually quite difficult to write about bad things happening to good people. Some chapters have left me exhausted and emotionally drained, but I keep reminding myself that eventually I'll get to the happy ending (for some characters anyway!). After a difficult chapter, I give myself a few days off, and go out socialising to recuperate!

As a writer, do you need to have some degree of direct experience of the passions you write about? For example, are you drawing from your own experience (or that of those close to you) when you tackle such themes as bullying, revenge or being a victim?

Fortunately I've never experienced any of the above. I've had my fair share of ups and downs in life, but I don't believe you need to experience something firsthand to write well about it. Passions and feelings are universal, and my feelings are no different than anyone else's. So I just mentally put myself in my characters' shoes.

Your writing seems to have gradually become darker over the years. Is this anything to do with a change in your own world view?

Life is tough for most people, and few of us can avoid the pain of loss, illness and heartbreak. Of course, life is also tempered from time to time with joy and success. It's when the balance alters and one person's joy is achieved at the expense of another's – that is where the novelist steps in!

Regarding my worldview, it hasn't changed since my teens – I still hate how humans exploit each other, the creatures of the earth, and the planet itself for short-term personal gain. In my opinion, while most humans are kind and decent, sadly the baddies will always win because they are prepared to go further in pursuit of their aims.

Your books often include plots which have their roots in the childhoods of the characters or even more specifically in their schooldays. Why is that?

I believe that the legacy of our childhood, whether good or bad, shapes the rest of our lives. It is also a time when we are powerless and vulnerable, and some children may suffer at the hands of people meant to protect them. Schooldays can be fraught with fear, as children can become victims not only of cruel teachers, but also of their fellow pupils. In my novels, I have used some of my characters' childhoods to explain their subsequent behaviour in adulthood. As a story progresses, the reader gradually learns about the events of the past that have made the character who they have become in adulthood. Perhaps my own happy and uneventful childhood has led me to be fascinated and appalled in equal measure by those who haven't been so fortunate.

If you enjoyed
Still Waters by Linda Kavanagh
why not try
Never Say Goodbye also published by Poolbeg?
Here's a sneak preview of Chapters One and Two

CHAPTER 1

I feel sick with fear when the school bell rings at the end of the day. Why am I the one this is happening to? It's been going on for ages now, and I don't know how much more I can take.

"Oh my God – how could I not have known?"

Claire Ross bit her lip so hard that it bled, but she was oblivious to everything but the words she was reading. She'd just discovered her late sister's diary, and its revelations left her reeling. Suddenly, everything she'd believed about Zoe had been overturned in an instant.

As she began turning the pages, her eyes filled with tears. So Zoe's death hadn't been an accident. Her thirteen-year-old sister hadn't been snatched from the beach by a freak wave, as had been claimed at the time, because the proof was here, in Zoe's own handwriting.

Claire felt all the pain of loss well up inside her again. How could all this have happened to her sister without her knowing about it? Had their mother been aware of what was going on? And what about the school? Surely someone had been aware of the situation? Oh my God, Claire thought, it's like walking into a nightmare. Now I really know why Zoe died. And the world as I've known it has just been turned on its head.

As Claire read through the entries, anger rose in her throat and formed a lump that almost threatened to choke her. A month after her sister had written the final entry in her diary, her body had been found floating out at sea. Memories of that day came flooding back into Claire's mind. On that day she had, in effect, lost her mother too. Although her mother's drinking had been bad before her sister's death, the aftermath had been even more horrendous. From the day Zoe died, her mother was rarely sober again, and Claire had suddenly been thrown into a bewildering and frightening world of loss.

As a small child, alone and terrified, she'd crawled into Zoe's bed that first night without her sister, hoping to find comfort from contact with Zoe's possessions. She'd put on Zoe's pyjamas and pressed them tightly to her body, as though they might somehow connect her to her beloved sister again.

As the weeks went by and before social services waded in, her mother had consumed even greater amounts of whiskey to dull her own pain, and Claire watched broken-hearted as her mother retreated from her, sinking deeper into her own world of despondency and despair. Despite their shared sorrow, they hadn't been able to comfort each other, and Claire longed to scream at her mother: You had two daughters – one of them is still living – why can't you find some joy in me? Why do you miss the dead one more than you love the one who's alive?

Claire had been nine when her older sister died. Now, at thirty-eight, there hadn't been a day that passed when she hadn't thought of her sister.

Claire wiped her eyes. Was it only an hour ago she'd stepped into the gloomy interior of her mother's house? It felt like a century. Having recently inherited the house on her mother's death, she'd reluctantly made the journey back to the seaside village of Trentham-on-Sea where she'd grown up.

Opening the blinds, she'd glanced around the dusty, stuffy drawing room, feeling a pang of guilt that this house was now hers. It was years since she'd had any kind of relationship with her mother, but now that she was gone Claire felt her loss acutely. All those lost opportunities to say the things that mattered.

As she wandered around, picking up and touching things as she went, Claire had been filled with sadness and regret. Perhaps she should have made more of an effort to understand and support her mother. On the other hand, it had been difficult, if not impossible, to deal with a belligerent drunk who hadn't been sober in years.

Claire surveyed the old cooker, fridge and pantry with distaste. Nothing had changed since she'd left all those years ago. In fact, nothing had changed since her father left, a lifetime earlier. Her mother had made no attempt to modernise or replace anything. The same old pots filled the cupboards, and the ironing board wore the same piece of scorched gingham material that she remembered from her childhood.

Claire shuddered. They'd all have to go. In fact, the entire house would have to go. After today, she'd no intention of ever setting foot in it again. She intended getting a local estate agent to put it on the market immediately. Then, when the house was sold, she'd set a date to marry David. For the first time since she'd arrived, a fleeting smile crossed Claire's face. Her fiancé was the best thing that ever happened to her, and she knew that Zoe, wherever she was, would be happy for her.

Claire had then made her way into the room that housed the old-fashioned roll-top desk that had originally belonged to her father. It seemed like aeons since he'd been part of the family, and Claire wondered where he was now. He was probably dead himself. His departure had been the turning point in all their lives. Before that, their mother had been a happy woman. But after he left, she began drinking heavily, and her two daughters' young lives had been turned upside down. Not only had they to deal with the grief of losing their beloved father, they'd also had to contend with a mother who was becoming increasingly out of control. If he hadn't deserted them all, their mother wouldn't have started drinking, and maybe poor Zoe wouldn't have died.

Opening the roll-top desk, Claire gazed inside. There were bundles of bills accompanied by matching receipts, carefully rolled-up pieces of string, and out-of-date coupons cut from newspapers. Claire was suddenly overwhelmed with grief as she surveyed the trivia that represented her mother's life. In truth, the poor woman hadn't had much of a life. With the benefit of hindsight, Claire was seeing her mother as someone who once had hopes and dreams of her own.

The first two drawers were empty, but in the third drawer Claire discovered a pile of ancient newspapers, their pages yellowed and fragile. Gingerly opening the first of them, Claire found herself staring at the local newspaper's account of her sister's drowning. She shuddered. It was ghoulish of her mother to keep such mementoes, but as she smoothed out the papers' tattered edges, Claire realised these newspaper accounts had represented her mother's last link with her eldest daughter.

The first account detailed the discovery of the missing child's body. Claire remembered the hushed tones of Doctor Barker and the local policeman as they arrived at the cottage to give her mother the devastating news. Then, as nine-year-old Claire was taken away by a kindly neighbour, she heard her mother's screams and sobs behind the closed drawing-room door.

Another newspaper, dated a few days later, detailed Zoe's funeral, displaying a photograph of all the pupils from The Gables School for Girls lining the route from the church to the graveyard.

Claire's lip trembled. What hypocrites they'd all been! Once their moment in the limelight was over, they'd left Claire and her mother to their lonely and tragic existence, without a helping hand from that day onwards.

As the light began to fade, Claire had abandoned the newspapers and wandered into Zoe's bedroom. Everything was exactly as it had been the fateful evening she'd left, never to return. Idly, she touched Zoe's duvet, as though it could act as a conduit that would somehow link her to her sister.

Blinking back a tear, she wondered how different her life

might have been if Zoe had lived. With each other to lean on, they'd have struggled through, and eventually they might even have got their mother the help she needed. But it had been too great a task for one little girl to tackle, and now, many years later, Claire was left among the tragic remnants of three women's lives.

Claire lifted her sister's hairbrush and held it to her face. As she felt her sister's hairs against her skin, she remembered the times they'd sat together on Zoe's bed, whispering and laughing, making plans for the future – a future Zoe had cruelly been denied.

Looking around the room, Claire decided she'd just take a single memento of Zoe with her. She dismissed the bedclothes, the books and the hairbrush – she'd look for something more in keeping with the Zoe she'd known. Her sister had enjoyed art at school – if she could find one of Zoe's paintings, she could frame it and hang on her apartment wall. Then Zoe would always be with her.

Getting down on her knees, Claire looked inside Zoe's bedside locker, but it yielded nothing of interest. Bitterly disappointed, she leaned on it to steady herself as she got up. But it toppled over, and Claire ended up on the floor beside it.

Swearing, she hauled herself up onto the bed, angry and determined to leave the house as soon as possible. If ever she needed proof that this house was cursed, she'd confirmed it now!

As she reached out to put the locker back in its upright position, Claire noticed a book attached to the back, held in place with sticky tape. She tingled with excitement as she peeled it away from the locker. It was a diary, the kind companies gave away free to customers, and it advertised a well-known breakfast cereal on the front. Claire now remembered Zoe being thrilled when a local shop-owner, Mr Leonard, gave it to her. She hadn't even waited until January to begin writing in it – she'd filled the entire frontispiece and title page with her writings!

As she opened the diary and began reading Zoe's childish writing, Claire expected to discover details about Zoe's homework assignments, her favourite film stars and her dreams for the future. Instead, she found something very different and shocking. And as she read, a swell of anger rose up inside her, threatening to overwhelm her with its ferocity. Oh, Zoe, she whispered as the tears ran freely down her face, I'll avenge you, no matter what. I swear I'll make them pay for what they did to you.

CHAPTER 2

Anne Ellwood looked through the morning post. There were the usual begging letters, entreating her to intercede with her husband on the writer's behalf. As the wife of an MP, she was well used to people targeting her to find a route to her husband, The Right Honourable Clive Ellwood.

But this envelope was addressed in her elderly mother's handwriting. Then she remembered. Her mother had mentioned she was forwarding a letter that had arrived at the family home, addressed to Anne under her single name, Anne Morgan.

Tearing open the envelope, Anne was surprised to discover an invitation to attend a reunion of her school year. Her initial smile quickly changed to a frown, and her heart began to beat uncomfortably. She wouldn't go – she *couldn't* go.

Her bitterness was also tinged with anger – she'd actually like to go to the lunch and lord it over all those other girls who hadn't married as well as she had! But she wouldn't go. It would only bring back the past – that awful time from which she still tried so hard to distance herself.

Over the years, Anne and her three friends had tried desperately to forget about that tragic event that shaped their lives. It coloured everything they did, and it was always there between them. No matter how happy the moment, the spectre of Zoe Gray would suddenly creep out from the shadows and cast a pall of sadness over everything.

Anne looked at the invitation again. Presumably her friends Fiona, Jennifer and Emma wouldn't want to go either. Besides, she didn't need to lord it over anybody – her three friends gave her all the feedback she needed. None of them had married as well as she had – and Emma hadn't married at all – and over the years, she'd revelled in their envy. Clive had often expressed surprise that she still kept in touch with these friends from her school days. He thought her kind and loyal to maintain contact with people she'd left behind socially, but the truth wasn't quite so clear-cut.

Anne had made a career of being an MP's wife, and it was a career she took very seriously. She saw her job as ensuring that Clive's life ran smoothly, and his home was organised with the precision of a military campaign, so that his every comfort was taken care of when he was present. During the week, while he was away at the Commons and staying at his luxury Westminster flat, she'd plan menus, stock up on supplies, supervise the housekeeper and gardeners, all aimed at enabling them to spend quality time together at weekends. There were no children, so Anne devoted her entire life to Clive. He was her world, and before his arrival each Friday evening, she'd have her short dark hair trimmed, washed and blow-dried at her local salon, so that she always looked attractive and elegant for her adored husband.

Anne stared angrily at the invitation in her hand. Would she and her friends ever escape from that terrible tragedy that haunted their lives? It angered her that her emotions could so easily rise to the surface and threaten the composure she'd cultivated over a lifetime.

Angrily, Anne tore the handwritten invitation in two. Tonight, she'd phone each of her three friends, and confirm their collective decision not to attend. In the meantime, she needed to get on with planning the forthcoming garden party. Some South American diplomats would be attending, and she needed to theme the event in their honour. She'd get bunting in their national colours, and prime the musicians to learn some of their national songs.

Of course, she always invited, Fiona, Jennifer and Emma to these events, even though neither Fiona's nor Jennifer's husband would ever fit in with the calibre of people who'd be present. Fiona's weedy little solicitor husband Edwin became even more boring as any event wore on. As for Jennifer's uncouth and loutish husband, Benjamin Corcroft . . . Anne wrinkled her nose. She was well aware that Jennifer stayed with him only because he made obscene amounts of money. He built ghastly little boxes that masqueraded as houses, and they seemed to proliferate all over the country. Then there was Emma, who could always be depended upon to disgrace herself when she'd had too much to drink. Her career as a writer of children's books might add cachet to some events, but her ability to become a nuisance after her third glass of wine was guaranteed.

Still, they couldn't all be as fortunate as she was. She'd set out to marry a man of distinction and substance and, as soon as she'd met Clive Ellwood, she'd known he could be moulded into something worthwhile.

They'd met during their last year at university, and Anne, who'd been studying fine arts, immediately saw his potential. He'd already been approached by the various political parties and was leaning towards the Liberals, but Anne steered him towards the Conservatives, seeing little point in going into politics if you weren't ultimately aiming for the highest office. With equal determination and speed, she'd taken him up the aisle of her parish church in Trentham-on-Sea, before anyone else got the chance to snap him up.

And her hunch had paid off – Clive had become a very successful politician. In fact, the prime minister had recently assured Clive that in the next cabinet reshuffle, he'd definitely be in line for a ministerial post.

In the kitchen, Anne threw the fragments of the invitation into the bin, and made herself a cup of coffee in the state-of-the-art surroundings. She was relieved that today was Mrs Hill's afternoon off. In her present unsettled mood, she couldn't have endured her housekeeper's endless chatter. The woman was a great worker, but right now Anne just wanted to be alone. Tonight she'd talk to each of her friends, and they'd all take their lead from her, as they'd always done.

Looking out the window, Anne could see that the two gardeners were trimming the edges of the lawn. She nodded approvingly. All was looking good on the Ellwood estate. The lawn and the flowerbeds were looking marvellous, and everything would be perfect for the garden party at the end of the month. As always, everything would go like clockwork, since she demanded the highest standards of everyone who worked for her.

Turning away from the window, she bit her lip angrily. What a pity her private life wasn't as orderly and controlled as events at The Grange. No matter how often she tried to bury the past, it always returned to haunt her.

If you enjoyed this chapter from
Never Say Goodbye by Lynda Kavanagh
why not order the full book online
@ www.poolbeg.com